Vile

Book Two of Violet's Tales: A Duet and a Half

E. N. Chanting

Edited by Abby Woodland

Cover art by Ampersand Book Covers

ISBN: 979-8-9909556-1-5 paperback

ISBN: 979-8-9909556-2-2 eBook

Contents

Violet's Song List

Mayhem- Halestorm
Welcome to the Jungle- Guns-N-Roses
Freak Like Me- Halestorm
Dr. Feelgood- Motley Crue
Wild, Wild, West- Escape Club
The Violence- Asking Alexandria
Twilight Zone- Golden Earring
Lola Montez- Volbeat
Monster- Skillet
Sandman- Metallica
Strut- Bob Seger
Renegade- Styx
Thunder- Imagine Dragons
Monsters- Shinedown

Dedicated to all the real superheroes who don't believe they're brave.

Only a villain walks the night unafraid, only a villain believes they have nothing to fear.

When in doubt, ask yourself, what would Violet do?

WWVD?

Foreword

Dearest and most Enchanting Reader,

Just a quick note to let you know this duet and a half, Violet's Tales, needs to be read in order. The first volume is Origin of Violet Book .5, it's available for a free download when you subscribe to my newsletter at

Next is VioleNt Book 1, it's available for free on KU. Finally, the last volume is Vile, Book 2. All of these books deal with dark subjects and there are multiple trigger warnings so please be sure to look them over and trust me, if you have triggers, you'll want to observe the warnings.

Although these tales are dark, they're also about love. The love for your partner or in Violet's case, partners, and love for family even if you're not related by blood to a single one of them. The family we choose is sometimes the best family of all.

Violet holds a grudge, and she judges people for their actions, if you make your way onto her list, I'm sorry, there's no hope for you. You'll eventually be hunted down and gutted like a deer, she doesn't forget, and she doesn't know how to give up. I suggest you run and never stop because she won't ever stop hunting you.

If you really want to guarantee your safety don't be a monster. Don't hurt anyone, don't lie, and definitely never ever harm a child. Basically, just don't be an asshole. You can chat with Violet, she might answer your questions, she might not, but you can ask. Her personal email at the foundation she started with Colby is violent1robndahood@gmail.com who knows, you might even get through to Colby, just remember he has a sense of humor that's not for everyone.

Thanks for reading!

E.N. Chanting, Author

Chapter One

Violet

"Babe, are you sure you don't want to end this asshole?" Jackson asks.

"I'm good. You won, have fun."

I watch as Jackson and Austin hold down the disgusting pig who tried to harm Stephanie. She may not be my new mom yet, but I love her. The thought of this piece of shit laying a finger on her makes me want to slice into his fat gut and let his intestines splatter on the dirty floor.

I love playing games with my guys. We make them up as we go and the prizes vary, I won the game that brought us to Washington. I got to choose our vacation and as soon as Stephanie found out this scumbag was being released from prison, I knew we had to come here and *unalive* him. Poor Jackson didn't get his dream vacation to Disney World, but Austin was thrilled. We'll need to make a trip to Disney one weekend, maybe the next time Jackson wins a game he can choose a trip to see Mickey Mouse.

"Baby, can you hand me those pliers?" Austin points to his bag on the table, where the tool is sticking up, startling me out of my thoughts.

I hand them over and he pinches the monster's bottom lip in them. A scream gurgles from his mouth as he tries to pull away. Unfortunately for him, Austin lets the pig hurt himself while he just holds tight on the yellow grips of the industrial pliers. Eventually the monster shakes and gives up, tears streak his sweaty cheeks.

Jackson picks up the hammer, takes aim, and smashes into the teeth exposed by the tug of the makeshift vice grips. The yellowed stubs shatter on impact and pieces of his former evil grin scatter through the air in a shower of blood and neglected calcium. The desperate criminal screams, and faints, collapsing in his chair. The ropes hold him in place as he slumps there.

"Finally! His begging and squealing were enough to give me a migraine. I think you should smash his fingers and toes next. Do you want the smelling salts?" I ask Jackson.

"Not yet. He was giving me a headache too. I need a break."

Austin's phone rings and he looks surprised by whatever he sees on the screen. Without hesitation he answers, "Yo! What's up, brother?"

Jackson snaps his attention to Austin and watches him closely. My own curiosity peaked. I focus on Austin as well.

"Yeah? That's great. When?" Jackson and I exchange glances, his face is tight. I think he knows who's on the other end of Austin's phone call. Without a clue I can't be worried or elated.

"Yeah man, of course. We'll be back the day after tomorrow. Okay...great...yeah...see you then." He hangs up with a smile a mile wide.

"Well? I have to know!" I beg. Austin gives Jackson a look which eases the tension on his gorgeous face, then he turns to me with his bright smile.

"Our brother, Pierson, is coming home."

"Wow, really? I thought he had another year in the military," I query with a tilt of my head.

"He did. They discharged him early, for medical reasons. Says he'll explain when he gets here. Swears he's okay and he'll be home this weekend."

"Has he told mom and dad yet?" Jackson asks.

"He called us first. He's looking forward to seeing us and meeting Violet." They both look at me and I can't tell what they're thinking. They've told me all about their adoptive brother and their childhood. They were heart-broken when he suddenly decided to join the Navy. I'm not sure what to think about the mysterious brother or his impending arrival.

"Aaarrrrgh, nnnoooo!" Oops, forgot all about the creep who tried to hurt my pseudo mom. I wonder how soon Stephanie and Uncle Randy will get married. They haven't been dating all that long, but old people tend to move faster because they can see the end of days on the horizon. At least that's what Uncle Randy told me. I don't think he's that old, he's only forty-three. Lucky for him Stephanie is ten years his junior so if they want to give birth to kids it could happen. They already have Isabel and she's a handful. I wonder if they'll adopt more or decide to make more. I'd love a few more siblings.

"Aaaahh..."

Jackson uses the hammer still in his hand, making a huge arc through the air, he smashes the back of the monster's hand. More gurgling and squealing ensue, and Jackson makes an exasperated noise.

Austin holds a large blade out to his brother-cousin, Jackson smirks at him. With a smooth motion, Jackson slices across the scumbag's throat. A line appears before the deep red fluid begins to leak down his neck. His eyes bulge wide, and his mouth moves silently, unable to form sounds with his severed vocal cords. The flow of his life's blood increases, and a crimson waterfall tumbles down his front in a deluge. His body loses all of its tension, and he slumps for the last time as the gush of corpuscles slows, having pumped until there was nothing left to pump, his heart ceases to beat.

We carefully avoid the red puddle on the floor and pack up our instruments. Austin pours the flammable liquid onto the body and the sofa. We check that we've collected all of our belongings and exit. Jackson lights a rag once we're outside and tosses it back into the dilapidated house. He closes the door, and we casually make our way to the rental car parked around the corner from the property. Once we remove our outer layer of killing clothes and pack them into the trunk, we climb into the cabin ready to begin the rest of our night.

"Are you guys hungry?" Austin asks as he starts the Tahoe.

"Starved." I reply.

"I could eat." Jackson adds.

"Food it is. I'm going to that pizza place we passed, it smelled really good when we drove by."

Jackson teases, "You know the smell of garlic has no impact on whether they have good food, right?"

"I know, but it made me hungry for pizza. I checked Yelp, and it has good reviews. Quit being difficult."

Jackson glares at the back of Austin's head but doesn't escalate the argument. I keep checking behind us for any sign of flames. Finally, I see black smoke and smile. Jackson looks back over his shoulder and watches it with me until we turn a corner, and I can't see it behind the buildings. We park a few minutes later and make our way into the fabulously scented *Angelo's Pizzeria.*

After we receive our drinks I ask, "So, why do you think Pierson's coming home?"

"No idea," Austin answers.

"Do you think he's having PTSD trouble because of Megan?" Jackson asks. I watch their faces as they communicate in silence. I'm getting better at deciphering their brotherly language, but sometimes I still don't get what they're saying. I'll have to wait for them to elaborate.

"I think there's a good chance he's still struggling with what happened to her. He didn't talk it out like we did, he just took off the minute he was old enough. We dealt with our feelings, and he ran from his," Austin speculates.

"Is he staying with us?" Jackson asks.

"I don't know. He can if he wants, what do you think, baby?"

"Yeah of course. He's like a third brother, he should stay with us," I reply.

"We haven't seen him since that Christmas photo was taken. He hasn't called much either. I'm not sure he still considers us his brothers," Jackson states, noticeably forlorn.

"You'll have to straighten him out, you can't let him ruin your family. You have enough struggles without this piling on."

"You're right. I'm going to need to keep my temper in check with him until we know what's wrong. I can't start by kicking his ass," Jackson chuckles. Our food arrives and I agree with Austin, it smells heavenly and tastes even better.

After we're finished eating, we drive back to our hotel. It's a quaint historical building and I like it because it feels haunted. Ever since I saw *The Shining*, I've been hoping to stay in a haunted hotel. It even has long dim corridors, and I keep waiting for a little boy on a tricycle to come peddling around the corner or even better, some spooky twins who want to play with me. It creeps Jackson out, so I keep teasing him.

"When we get home, we should probably go see mom and dad before Pierson comes, make sure we're all on the same page," Jackson states as he reaches for the elevator button. I take a huge step back and Austin does the same.

Jackson side eyes us, "What am I missing?" he asks.

"Just getting out of the way in case a tsunami of blood pours out when the doors open," I answer innocently. Austin struggles to hold in his laughter.

Jackson looks at the elevator with trepidation and jumps away from the door when the green arrow lights up and the bell announcing its arrival dings. Austin loses the fight, and I burst out laughing too.

"You guys suck," Jackson says as he stomps into the elevator car with his arms crossed.

I lean up on tip toe and plant a kiss on his cheek. He grabs me and pulls me into an embrace, pushing his tongue into my mouth and kissing me breathlessly. A moan escapes my throat, and he moves his hands to my ass, lifting me closer. I wrap my legs around his waist and my arms around his neck kissing him with everything I have.

"This is our floor." Austin breaks into the fantasy in my head and disrupts the real one playing out in front of him. Without releasing me Jackson makes his way to our room, and Austin opens the door. He carries me right to the bed and turns as he falls on it so I'm on top of him when we hit the covers. Hands are in my shirt and unbuttoning my jeans, my shirt is removed and my bra unhooked, while my zipper slides down. I swear they only have four hands between them though sometimes it feels like eight.

Jackson rolls so Austin can remove my jeans and his hands are in my panties immediately. I can't stop kissing Jackson and rubbing myself against him. Austin's shirtless when I next open my eyes, and his pants are undone. I want him in my grasp, and I shove my fingers into his pants. While I grip his hard cock in my hand Jackson removes his own clothes and divests me of my panties with a quick yank, easily tearing the delicate lace.

Jackson's fingers work on my pussy rubbing just the way I like while I find his hardness with my free hand. With a slight shift my lips kiss him, and I circle my tongue around the edge of his pulsing manhood. He presses himself between my hungry lips and I suck as he reaches for the back of my throat.

"Mmmm..." I can't contain the sounds of pleasure forming in my mouth.

Austin twists himself around and kisses my belly, his tongue slips past my belly button and reaches my needy sweet spot. My hand strokes him, in a tight grip, using the moisture leaking from his tip as lube. I want him inside me, using my hand I guide him there and he doesn't need any more direction.

Jackson holds my cheeks as he thrusts into my throat while I suck and lick him. I love when he fucks my mouth, it makes me so hot. Austin swipes the tip of his cock through the arousal pooled at my center. He pushes himself inside me and the stretch of him sends pleasurable tingles spreading in every direction. His fingertip circles my clit, and I practically see stars.

Jackson begins thrusting faster and I can feel him swell as his balls tighten. He's close and I'm close. Austin is hitting all the right places. He thrusts faster and our skin slaps together as we all moan in mounting pleasure.

"Oooohh, yes, baby..."

"Mmmm..." I can't form words with my mouth full.

"Mmmm babe, yeah, I'm gonna come. I want you to swallow every drop."

"Mmmhmm!" I'm so ready when his release squirts into my throat, I continue to swallow until I've sucked every bit from him.

Austin reaches his climax with me only seconds later. He pumps with all he has, and his pelvic bone rubs perfectly on my clit bringing me to orgasm with a scream just when Jackson pulls his satisfied softening dick from my lips.

"Yes! Oh, my god! Mmm Austin!"

"Oh baby! Fuck yes!" When he finishes filling me with his release, he rolls next to me. Jackson is there cleaning me up, I smile appreciatively through my blissful haze. My eyes droop and my body hums with warm electricity buzzing from every nerve.

Once we're all wiped as good as a towel can get us, we lie next to each other in the afterglow of our love. I have no doubt I love them both with all my heart and they love me unconditionally with everything they have inside them. We're a throuple, I hate that word, but it makes me happy too, I'm a lucky woman.

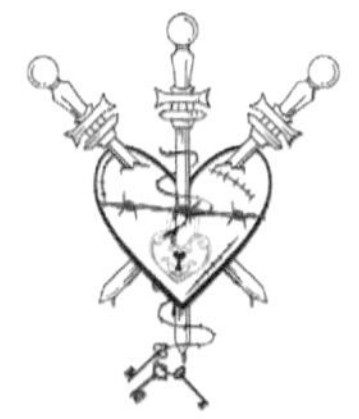

Chapter Two

Pierson

"Yes, sir!" I salute my commander for the final time. I'm glad I'm out of here and feeling lost at the same time.

What if Jackson and Austin have changed? What if we can't be brothers anymore the way we were? I don't regret joining the Navy, but it may have been a mistake. When Megan almost died, I went over a cliff and I couldn't get back to solid ground. I felt so guilty that she suffered abuse so horrific she wanted to take her life to end her pain. Why didn't I know? Why didn't I protect her? Even though she's technically Austin's biological sister, she was a big sister to all three of us.

I was there every day. I should've seen something was wrong, something happened that changed her. How did I miss the signs? We all did. We failed her. I failed her the most because I was closest to her. Sometimes she felt like the best big sister and sometimes I could imagine us growing old together. It was just a hope of having someone to love in my life forever. I didn't really have romantic feelings toward her, I just wanted her around all the time.

Even though they weren't my birth parents, Miguel and Angie, Austin's birth parents took in Jackson, his cousin, and me, just a friend. My birth father was a drunk who disappeared regularly until one day he didn't come back. My mom was also an alcoholic, and eventually a heroin addict. She never paid attention to my basic needs, like food and clothing. Austin's parents just gave me a room at their house one day and they became my mom and dad.

The three of us used to follow Megan around and try to be like her. She was older than us and she was mature, she was smart, and funny too. We wanted to be cool, the way we believed she was even though she was more of a nerd. Until she changed. We honestly believed she was just turning into a hormonal teenage girl, never considering something could be wrong.

Then I came home to find Jackson giving her CPR and Austin begging for fire rescue to hurry on his phone. Afterwards they took her away to the ER and eventually the mental facility, I couldn't focus any more, I couldn't function. All I wanted to do was hunt down the monster that harmed our sister. If I didn't leave, I was going to kill someone.

Now here I am, heading back home after almost getting court martialed. When my unit was assigned to retrieve the criminal kingpin, I thought we would be bringing justice for the people he harmed. When they ordered us to ignore the victims and only collect the bad guy, I lost it. I couldn't let those women suffer and possibly die. I could save them, and I did. Our mission commander was livid, I didn't follow orders. They brought me up on charges and if it weren't for the history of PTSD after my first foray into combat, I may have ended up in prison for a very long time. Thankfully, my lawyer was able to argue mental illness and inability to respond appropriately to commands in my defense.

My punishment is an honorable discharge if I seek mental health care.

I wonder if my adoptive brothers will be able to accept me as I am now. I'm angry, I want to hunt down all the bad guys in the world and tear them apart, make them suffer. Most of all, I wonder how they've changed because of Violet.

When they told me about her the first time, they sounded completely enthralled with her. Now, it's like she's a part of them. When they talk about themselves, they mean her too and I wonder how I'll fit in if they're brainwashed by some chick.

I don't want to stay with mom and dad. I think being in their house will bring up too many memories. Plus, it sounds like the girls are obnoxious teenagers and I can't stand arguing and doors slamming. I might need to rent a place; my savings are meager and won't last long, but will have to suffice until I get the money I'm due from my investment account. It doesn't seem like I'll fit in Austin's place with the three of them living there. I guess I'll have to see how it all works out once I'm home.

"Petty Officer Nash, your jeep is here," a young Seaman announces through the open door.

"Thanks," I answer and make my way to the waiting vehicle.

We drove the short distance to the waiting plane; I haven't left Africa in more than a year. I have a long trip on several planes to make it home to Florida. I watch the scenery fade as my first plane lifts into the sky, I don't really see it. My mind is firmly on my family back in the US. All the unanswered questions swirling in my head leave me to function robotically as I travel from city to city, base to base, and plane to plane.

When my Uber driver pulls in front of the modest house, I once called home, it looks exactly how I remember. It's still well-kept and inviting, though I'm not sure how welcome I feel.

"Pierson! I can't believe you're here!" Mom squeals in excitement.

She tackles me and I drop my bag just in time to catch her in my arms. She smells like coffee and chocolate chip cookies. I hug her close and let the warm memories from my childhood flood my mind.

“Let me look at you! You’re too skinny. Don’t they feed you in the Navy?” I chuckle, she always thinks I’m too skinny. I was as a child when she took me in, since then she can’t see me as the full grown, bulky man I am today.

“All right, what do you want to feed me?” I ask with a grin.

“Dinner’s almost ready. We’re having turkey and all the fixings. It's still your favorite, right?”

“Yeah, it sounds perfect. Where’s everyone else?”

“The girls are in their rooms, I'll call them. Dad's out back trying to fix the sprinkler. We expected you about a half hour from now. I spotted you through the window.” She wraps her arm through mine and pulls me inside. I need a moment, so I hug her again.

“I need the head. Where should I put my bag?” I ask.

“Just set it by the foyer table. You’re staying with the boys. Go ahead, I'll go tell dad you’re here.”

“Thanks mom.” Tears fill her eyes. She sniffs and walks towards the back door. I place my bag in the entry and use the facilities. Everything looks the same, only smaller and maybe more worn as well.

When I exit the head, I can hear angry music pounding the walls from my old room. That must be Tori’s room now, Kristin must still be in their old room. That means there’s at least one empty room. The memories blur my vision and begin to overwhelm me. I take a few deep breaths and close my eyes seeking calm. That seals whether they have room or not, I can’t stay here.

I make my way back towards the kitchen and I’m intercepted by dad, Miguel. The man who taught me to be respectful and considerate of others, the man I tried to emulate as a kid. Today I hope I can be half the man he is, he’s fair, loyal, and a good provider.

"Son! Good to see you," he shakes my hand and pulls me into a half hug.

"You too, sir."

"Come sit down, tell me how you're doing." He leads me to the living room sofa. I perch on one corner, and he sits in one of the armchairs across from me.

"It was a long trip, I'm a little tired, but happy to be home. How's everyone here?"

"Kristin is great. She's crushing her grades and she's on the honor roll. Tori is...well, Tori. She's an argument waiting to happen most of the time, but she's excited to see you. The boys are good. They're both living at Austin's now, with their girl, Violet, she's something special. Smart as a whip, and funny in a blunt way. The boys are head over heels. You'll understand when you meet her, they'll be here any minute."

A lot of things happen at once. Mom comes out from the kitchen with a platter of small hors d'oeuvres. She pushes it into my face and demands I eat. Kristin comes running from the hallway and dives into me for a hug. My mouth is full, and I try not to choke when her arm encircles my neck. She kisses my cheek, and I kiss her head hoping I didn't get crumbs in her hair. The front door opens and Austin walks into the room with a grin from ear to ear.

I place Kristin on the floor and step to Austin for a handshake. He laughs and grabs me in a bear hug. Jackson enters behind him holding hands with a woman. I can only see their silhouettes in the glare of the sun with the door open. When Austin releases me, he shakes my hand.

"Damn glad to have you home, brother!" he says.

"Happy to be home." I reply automatically.

Jackson comes forward and shakes my hand, then leans in and half hugs me the same way Miguel did.

"Good to see you," he offers.

“You too, man.” He closed the door and now that he’s moved, I can finally see the heralded Violet. She’s a little taller than I expected, with short blonde hair that’s streaked with blue. Her eyes are black as night and seem to hold all the secrets of the universe. The breath leaves my lungs as if I’ve been punched in the gut. I can’t inhale. I can’t swallow. I’m frozen in her gaze; she’s the most stunning creature I’ve ever seen. I instantly hate her. I know immediately she’s stolen my brothers and we'll never be the same.

Jackson proudly pulls her forward and introduces her, “This... is Violet, our girlfriend.” His face is covered in a very unJackson-like smile, full of pride and joy. It makes me feel ill.

“Pleased to meet you. I’ve heard so much about you,” she politely greets me. Her voice is melodious and husky, an angelic sex goddess wouldn’t sound so perfect.

“Hello,” I force through my frozen lips.

“Come in, sit! Dinner’s ready, everyone come to the table. Kristin, please give me a hand,” mom directs.

We move to the dining room and out of the corner of my eye I spot something purple. When I stop to see what it could be in my parent’s neutral toned home, I’m surprised to see our youngest sister. Tori. She’s added purple streaks to her dark hair and is dressed in black from head to toe. If it wasn’t for the purple, she would’ve been lost to the shadows.

“Hey. How’s it going Tori?” I ask, holding my distance. She’s not approachable despite the urge to hug my baby sister.

“It's s'okay.” Her eyes travel on my face and I see a flash of the little girl who used to beg me to play Barbies. I have to hug that little girl who always wanted our attention. Still trying to respect the teen before me in the present day, I hold my arms open and let her decide the next move. She glances past me at the backs of the others and steps into my arms. I squeeze her before she can get away.

"I missed you," she whispers and then she's gone. I watch her shuffle her army boots and ripped black jeans in the direction everyone else went. Wow, things have definitely changed. On my last trip home, she was in a Christmas dress for our family photo. It was bright green with little reindeer hopping along the hem. She had braids in her hair and red bows across her crown. That girl isn't here today.

When I enter the dining room the only empty seat is at the end of the table. Dad is at the other end and I'm between mom and Violet. I wonder if the guys placed her next to me on purpose. It won't make me like her.

"Pierson, do you want potatoes?" Dad asks.

"I want everything. I haven't had a good meal since I was on leave for a week, nine months ago. I'm on military food and airline food, everything looks amazing, mom."

"Thanks, sweetie. Okay, just pass everything."

All the food gets passed around clockwise which has Violet handing me everything. She holds dish after dish allowing me to take what I want. I don't meet her eyes, I can't.

"Careful, this one's hot," she says as she hands me the green bean casserole. My hand accidentally touches hers when the potholder slips. When her skin meets mine, sparks travel up my arm. It's like an electric shock, only not so unpleasant. I clear my throat and move away from her as quickly as possible.

"So, Pierson, you'll come home with us. We have a vehicle you can use and an empty room you can have until you decide what you want to do," Austin states.

"Yeah. I guess." Violet looks me over and I think she senses my tone. Nobody else seems to notice.

Jackson asks, "Do you have any plans? Do you know what you want to do?"

"Not exactly. I'm trained in IT and communications, but not in the real world, I need some experience outside a military installation. I'll look for work after the jet lag wears off. I don't have anything specific in mind."

"If you want, you can work with us while you figure it out. It's easy enough work if you're in physical shape. We always need guys to help with the digging and equipment," Jackson offers.

I consider his suggestion, "Yeah, that might work for a while so I can get my bearings. Thanks, bro."

"Of course. Whenever you're ready you can just come with us and they'll pay you by the day if you're temporary," Austin adds.

"Sounds good."

"Violet, sweetie, when do you go back to school?" Mom asks.

"Monday. I'm looking forward to it. I had fun on vacation, but I want to finish this year." Soon we'll be having a real Thanksgiving meal and celebrating Christmas. She must have a break between semesters.

"Tell us about your trip. How did you like Seattle?" Dad asks.

"It was beautiful there. We loved sightseeing and getting to meet some of the locals was interesting," Violet gives my brothers a smug smile. I wonder what that's about.

"Yeah. We had a wonderful time. We checked out some local establishments, off the beaten path. We met a few colorful Seattleites and hung out with them a little. The bay is beautiful there. It was a good trip," Jackson grins at Violet. They look like they're sharing an inside joke of some sort. I hate that I don't know anything about the inside jokes she has with my brothers. Austin is grinning too. I grit my teeth.

Our meal is filled with friendly chatter, only Tori and I are quiet unless spoken to. I'm hoping they think I'm just tired. Tori doesn't seem to give a shit what anyone thinks. She's grumpy and sullen. I think I need to keep an eye on her in case something's going on with the girl that we need to know about. Megan pops into my head, I refuse to let another sister fall victim to self-harm on my watch. I need to ask Dad how Megan's doing these days. She's been in the mental health facility for a few years, last time I asked, she wasn't doing well enough to leave.

When the dishes are done and all the food is packed away, including a care package for me, we all meander around the kitchen and family room. Finally, I yawn, loudly and get the point across that I'm tired and ready to go.

It's awkward in their car for me, at least Violet sat up front so I don't have to look at her. Austin sits next to me, and he rambles about the job so I'll have a clue what to do if I decide to work with them.

"We got the room ready for you, but we need to go to the grocery store. Help yourself to anything you want," Austin offers.

"How do you feel about cats, Pierson?" Violet asks.

"I don't."

"We have one, he's still technically a kitten. His name's Sawyer, if he bothers you just let us know and we'll try to keep him out of your way," Violet adds.

"Okay."

When we pull up at Austin's, Jackson pulls into the garage, and we enter the house through a mudroom. A kitty litter box with what looks like some type of automatic cleaning feature is in the corner. I'm surprised it doesn't stink.

Next, they show me the laundry room, and the kitchen, explaining where I can find things. Austin shows me to the room I'll be staying in and the bathroom that's closest. The linens are in a cabinet, and I don't need anything else. I beg off to take a quick shower and hit the hay citing exhaustion.

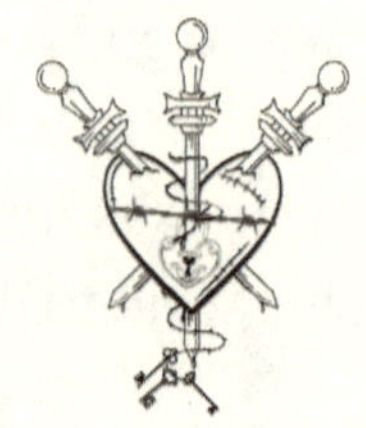

Chapter Three

Violet

I got the strongest feeling Pierson doesn't like me. I don't want to say anything to the guys until I know for sure. He was obviously tired after his long journey, but maybe he was just grumpy. I'm glad he went to bed. He was making me uncomfortable. I caught him staring daggers at me more than once.

Sawyer is stuck to me like glue, he doesn't seem happy to have a stranger in the house. The rest of us have been getting along well since we all moved in here. My warehouse and BASIL are still ours. We use the gym and the *facilities* for their intended purposes. I like living here. Austin's place is homey and comfortable. We fit better here. These two big guys in my tiny apartment above the warehouse wasn't cutting it.

I'm looking forward to working out tomorrow. We haven't been to the warehouse since we got back from Washington yesterday.

I wonder how long it'll take them to identify Dr. Dirtbag from his burned remains with Jackson's dental work, maybe they won't ever identify him. I don't think anyone will care enough to file a missing person's report and he'll probably end up in Potters Field as a John Doe. I won't lose any sleep over it. I'm going to tell Stephanie she's safe but I won't outright tell her any details. I'll just hint enough that she'll be able to relax so she'll know he won't be coming after her.

We fall asleep as soon as we lie down, it's been a long day for us too. Travel from the West Coast to the East Coast plays havoc with your internal clock. It's like it took an extra eight hours to get home with the time difference added into our itinerary.

I wake up to find Sawyer on my chest staring into my eyes and if I wasn't used to him doing this to me, it'd be unnerving. When I stretch and roll to my side, the furry munchkin doesn't even flinch and curls up against my chest on the bed.

"What's up buddy?"

Meow.

"Okay. Give me a minute." I can smell bacon and toast. My stomach growls in response to the tantalizing scent. I throw on clothes and make myself presentable since we have a guest. Hopefully, he'll hate me less today. Sawyer follows close behind me touching my calf with his cold nose on every step.

His dish has food when I pass it, and I'm not sure what's up with him. When I reach the kitchen, Austin's at the stove scrambling eggs. A big pan of bacon sits on paper towels next to him, and toast pops from the toaster as I approach the coffee pot. I grab it and jiggle it to avoid a burn and place it on the plate already filled with toast.

"Morning Baby," Austin kisses my cheek.

"Good morning. Thanks for cooking all of this, it looks yummy."

"My pleasure. Grab your coffee and sit, it's ready."

"Okay." I fill my cup and take a seat at the table. Jackson comes in from the laundry room, and Pierson follows him.

Jackson leans down and kisses my lips, "Good morning, gorgeous."

"Good morning, handsome. Good morning, Pierson. Did you sleep okay?"

Pierson doesn't look my way. "Yeah." He sits across from me.

Jackson brings over the plate of toast. The butter and jelly are already on the table and the places are set. Austin carries the bacon, now arranged on a plate, in one hand and the eggs in a bowl in the other. We load our plates and start eating. It's quiet except for chewing until Austin speaks up.

"Pierson, tell us about your discharge. How are you? You mentioned it was a medical discharge?"

Pierson instantly looks uncomfortable, clears his throat and says, "Yeah. I had some difficulty on a mission. I didn't follow orders and got into trouble. They concluded it was a mental health issue and decided to discharge me instead of sending me to jail."

"Jesus, what happened?" Jackson asks. Pierson looks at me and I can tell he doesn't want to talk with me here.

"Maybe you guys need to talk about this after breakfast. I was going to work out anyway. I'll go to the gym and you guys can have a family chat."

Austin examines Pierson and nods, "Yeah, okay." Jackson scrutinizes Pierson and isn't as understanding. His face softens when he meets my eyes. I silently communicate that I'm fine and he needs to spend some time with his brother. He gives in and agrees with Austin.

"Yeah, we can meet you at the gym later. Do you have any other plans today, Babe?"

"Just some schoolwork and I need to check in with everyone. Harmony's on my case to do some bridesmaid stuff."

"Cool. Did they pick a date yet?"

"Yeah, Valentine's Day is on a Saturday so they're planning a red wedding. She says Max is coming." My gaze falls at his name. I still feel bad about dumping him from my life when my parents died, but I just wasn't in any condition to resolve our relationship then. Harmony swears he forgives me, and he wants to see me and work things out. I don't know what he'll think about my two boyfriends. Both of them know everything about my past, including my relationship with Max and they're encouraging me to work things out with him and get my friend back. But It's not solely up to me.

When I raise my eyes again, Pierson is staring at me. He looks annoyed by my very existence. Taking the last bite of bacon, I've had enough. I stand abruptly and startle Sawyer, he recovers quickly when I offer him a bite of egg.

"I'm going to grab my stuff and head out. See you over there?"

"We'll call you if we can't make it, Baby." Austin takes my hand and pulls me in for a kiss, I don't fight it, if their brother wasn't here, I'd probably be in his lap. I give Jackson a kiss too when he lifts his lips towards me.

"See you later."

I collect my things and ride my bike over to the warehouse. When I pull inside it's too quiet and I immediately start my work-out playlist. I run up the steps and fill a bottle with water and I take a quick look at my computer. I have emails to answer. I'll do it after I burn off some of this anxiety. I don't know what I did to Pierson but I'm more convinced than ever that he hates me. Maybe he just has mental health issues and for some reason it causes an aversion to me, or maybe all women? Strangers? Who knows. I put him out of my mind and run through my usual workout routine.

After warming up and punching the bags I lift a few free weights and finish with some parkour moves and climb my homemade rock-climbing wall. The guys still have me beat with how fast they traverse rough and vertical terrain. I want to get faster so I have a chance at besting them.

When I'm covered in sweat and feeling much more grounded, I make my way back upstairs to contact all the people waiting to hear from me. Harmony fills my ear with her incessant chatter, she's wound extra tight about the wedding. It's not too far off, so I understand her excitement.

When I finish with her, I call Uncle Randy. "Hey Violet! How was your trip?"

"It was spectacular. We had a great time. How's everything with Stephanie and Isabel?"

"All good. Do you guys want to come over for dinner tonight?"

"I'll have to check with the guys, their brother is in town. I don't know if they made plans."

"That's fine, just text me when you figure it out. It's their brother who's in the military, right?"

"He's out now. He's staying with us while he figures out what he wants to do."

"How is he? Do you like him?"

"I don't know, I'm sure he doesn't like me. He's barely said two words to me, it's hard to gauge if I like him or not."

"People exiting the military can have some difficulty assimilating back into civilian life and their families. Give him a chance to decompress. Besides, how could anyone not like you?"

"You're biased. I'm sure plenty of people dislike me. Look at my grandmother, I never did anything to her either."

"Well, you can't go by Joyce, she's a hateful shrew who hates everyone," he chuckles.

"Isn't that the truth. She really hates me now that I won her lawsuit and got my parents' money. I'm sure I won't be having any holiday meals with her." I giggle at the thought.

"Definitely not, good riddance. Speaking of the holidays, we'll need to make plans, so all the parents get to see you. Have Miguel and Angie mentioned anything yet?"

"We ate there last night, and they didn't mention it, but with Pierson's arrival everyone was focused on him. I'll get the guys to speak to them."

"We're open to having a joint celebration, we enjoy their company. If she wants, you can have Angie call me and we can plan together,"

"Okay, I'll let her know. I'll text you later about tonight. Please hug your girls for me."

"Will do. Love you, Violet."

"Love you too."

Next, I call Colby. He's my best friend and he already knows all about our trip because I speak to him daily. I want to vent about Pierson, Colby's my conscience. He'll tell me if I'm imagining Pierson's dislike, or if I should do something to resolve it.

"What up, oh violent one?" He thinks he's funny.

I roll my eyes, "Not much oh ridiculous one. The guy's brother arrived yesterday. He's staying with us, and he hates me."

"How's that even possible? How can he hate you already? You didn't stab him, did you?"

"Of course not. You're a dickhead sometimes."

"You have to admit it's a valid question."

"I'll admit no such thing. He hated me at first sight. I don't think Austin's noticed, but Jackson might think something's up. Should I say something?"

"Not to them, to Pierson. If he gives you an attitude, ask him what the fuck?"

"I need to do something, it's awkward. Especially in our house, I felt unwelcome this morning."

"Yeah, that's not cool." We chatted for about a half an hour before I hung up to take a shower. I still keep some clothes here, and so do the guys so we can change if we need to while we're here to work out or *work* on other projects. I have a computer here for backup and to work on school or other *projects* when we're here, and I keep my weapons here in their special vault room. I only carry my regular everyday knives on me.

I collect some clean clothes and take a shower. When I'm ready to get dressed, I realize I grabbed the pants with a broken zipper. I need to remember to drop them off to have it replaced. They're a pair of pants my mom bought for me and I'm not willing to part with them. I towel dry my hair and then pad into the hallway in my underwear, towards the bedroom to get different jeans.

"Holy fuck!" A deep male voice startles me.

"Shit!" I try to cover myself with the clothes in my hand. Pierson is standing in the hall, staring at me with his mesmerizing eyes. He definitely saw every inch of skin on display. I thought I was still alone.

"Sorry, I didn't know you were here."

"I needed the bathroom. Jackson told me to come up here."

"No, it's fine."

"I didn't see anything."

"Yeah, you did. Excuse me."

"I didn't mean to see anything...I meant. I...shit."

"It's fine, I'm gonna get dressed."

I awkwardly exit the hall and close myself into the bedroom. Leaning my back against the door I'm flooded with embarrassment. Well, if he didn't hate me before, he's probably strongly debating it now. It's weird, but for a second it almost seemed like he was admiring the view. But I may have imagined it, because he definitely didn't look happy by the end of our encounter. Ugh! What the hell? I need to fix things with him not make them worse. I should've realized they might've been here by now. That was a stupid move!

Maybe I should ask Austin and Jackson what to do to get on his good side. I might never be able to meet his eyes after this. I get dressed quickly and try to compose myself before heading downstairs. They're in workout clothes, Austin and Pierson are at the weight bench. Pierson's on the bench lifting about two-hundred-twenty pounds while Austin spots him. Jackson's running on the treadmill. I hop onto the pommel horse and perch there watching them.

My mind swirls with thoughts about how to make things better with Pierson, but since I don't understand why he hates me, I'm at a loss. Giving up on what seems like a hopeless rabbit hole, I move on to my next order of business. We need a new game. I love it when we do hidden items or clues, especially when they involve specific tasks to complete. Austin is such a good sport it's fun to give him crazy things to do, like wear something ridiculous or collect weird items from strangers. Jackson isn't as willing to humiliate himself in public, he's really good at deciphering clues and hunting down items and information. They like to send me looking for treasure.

Maybe we need to try something new. We keep giving each other the things we enjoy, and I think it's time for something challenging for all of us. Maybe a race of some kind or a series of tasks we each have to complete that are the same. That way we all have to accomplish things we enjoy and things that push our limits. Hmmm...it could be like one of those racing shows on TV. We get a clue to begin and then we complete a task, the same task for all three of us, before we can have the next clue. First one to the finish line wins. In order for this to work, we can't be the ones who make the tasks, I wonder if Colby would be willing to set it up.

The weights clang as Pierson finishes his set and replaces the bar in the rack. I look over and see Austin swapping places with him. Pierson removes his shirt and wipes his face with it. It's difficult to swallow, holy shit, he's ripped, and he's got almost full sleeves of tattoos and they look incredible. My body heats and tingles at the sight of him. I look away quickly and meet Jackson's gaze. He's moving to the heavy bag now that he's warmed up. He winks at me, and it makes me smile.

My armpit burns at the thought of getting a tattoo. I haven't gotten the mangled mess of a tattoo there covered yet, I don't know what I want to cover it with. I should probably get *David Bowie*, my favorite blade. What I have is so dark and scarred from where I cut out the swastika that the bastard had inked on my skin, I need something to cover the rectangular shape and spread out into something I'll be happy to see in the mirror. When I was younger, I always wanted a purple Mustang with a winged horse airbrushed on the hood. Maybe I could figure out something with a car and a horse, I'll need to mull over my choices.

I need to speak to Nemo; the tattoo artist Colby knows. I wonder where Pierson got his done, maybe in Africa or Japan. I might try asking him about them to have a civil conversation and I'd love to get a closer view. Is it wrong that I like the way he looks? Except when he looks at me with hatred. I watch Jackson and forget about Pierson for the moment.

A sweaty Austin approaches and removes his shirt. *Mmmm, now that's my guy.* I give him a huge smile. My body reacts to him before he even touches me.

"Hi baby. What're you thinking about so hard?" His hands land on my thighs and he tilts his head as he leans in for a kiss.

"I was thinking how hot you are."

"Mmmm, good answer." He kisses me again and looks into my eyes as I stare back.

"I was also thinking we need a new game. What do you think about a race? We'd all have the same tasks to complete, and we can't get the details of the next task until that one's complete. Whoever finishes first, wins."

"I like it. What do I win?"

"Ha-ha. *Whoever* wins, would get something big. We'll have to think about it and come up with a great prize. Maybe control of another trip? A weekend getaway? I don't know, whatever they want?"

"Who's getting whatever they want?" Jackson asks, then gulps water from his bottle.

Austin smiles an evil grin at him, "Me. Violet says we should have a new game and when I win, I can have whatever I want."

"Fuck no. You're not winning anything, I'm going to kick your ass and we're going to Disney World."

Austin rolls his eyes, "Not this again. Dude, we're not going to Disney, get over it."

"We are if I win. Right, Babe?"

"Yeah. If you win." I'm not giving up. I won last time. I'll never go down without a fight.

"What are you winning?" Pierson asks. His shirt is thrown over his shoulder and his tattoos and carved muscles look even better this close up. My body heats, I'm surrounded by three gorgeous men and all my girl parts are primed with arousal. Is this what heaven's like? Ha, like I'll ever find out. I've no doubt I'll be resting much further south when my time comes.

"We're planning our next challenge," Austin answers as I watch his dimples play on his cheeks, and his eyes sparkle. My nipples feel tight.

"Challenge for what?" Pierson asks.

Jackson elaborates, "We like to play games, contests, like races or scavenger hunts. Violet and I started it when we first met. We would ask each other three questions and the other one had to answer."

"There were rules, like no sex questions, and we each got one pass where we could skip a question once," I add.

Pierson's face scrunches a little in thought. "Like a game show?"

"Yeah. Violet won our biggest game so far and she got to choose our vacation. The one we just got back from, in Seattle." Pierson examines me then he turns back to Jackson.

"What does a person need to do to join one of these challenges?" he asks.

"Normally it would only be for the three of us. But since you're staying with us, you could probably do it. What do you guys think?" Austin asks.

I shrug. That eliminates any sex prizes, but I don't mind if he plays. Jackson looks a little disappointed, I can tell he just came to the same conclusion as me. He nods like he just decided.

"You can play. But what're we playing for?"

"Oh! How about chores? Winner gets all of their chores done for a month. No cleaning the kitty litter, no scrubbing toilets, no laundry?" Austin suggests with a bright smile.

We haven't assigned Pierson any chores because he's a guest, but it looks like he just got drafted into the rotation. We decided when we moved in together the only fair way to take care of everything was to have a rotating weekly schedule. It works for us, no confusion about who's responsible for what. I hate laundry week, but I don't mind the rest. Laundry just never ends. I offered to hire someone to do all of it when I got my inheritance money, but they didn't want strangers in our space. It was a good point. Serial killers shouldn't let civilians into their home to clean the weapons and dust the skeletons in the closet.

"Yes. But we have to put Pierson into the chore rotation for it to work. Sorry bro, you just graduated from guest to roommate," Jackson announces.

"Lucky me. Yeah, I would've asked to be included anyway. Okay, I'm in. So, what's the challenge?" Three sets of eyes turn to me.

"I was thinking Colby could set it up, but I haven't asked him yet."

"Who's Colby?" Pierson questions, and he actually looks at me for an answer. Holy smokes! Is he engaging in conversation with me? His dark hazel eyes meet mine without malice for the first time.

"He's her best friend; you'll probably meet him at some point. He doesn't go out much, but he will for Violet," Austin answers for me. Pierson scrutinized my face again. Not sure how to respond, I meet his eyes with what might be a bit of defiance.

"That reminds me, Uncle Randy invited us to dinner. Are you guys free?" I ask Pierson specifically.

"Uncle Randy?" he asks.

"He's more like her dad. He's cool. Yeah Babe, tell him we'll be there. Are we done here?" Jackson responds.

"I'm finished. Do you want to go get a shower and then get some groceries?" Austin questions.

"Yeah. I showered but we need groceries."

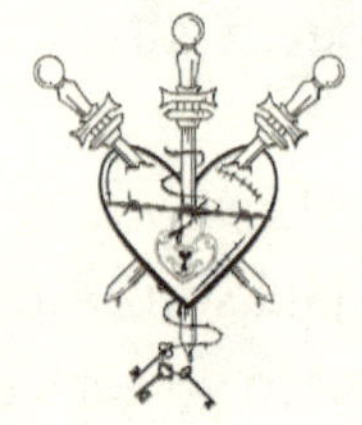

Chapter Four

Pierson

I can't stop seeing her gorgeous body on display. I almost swallowed my tongue when she burst out of the bathroom. She's perfection, which means dangerous. I wonder if I can get my brothers away from her. Probably not. They couldn't stop telling me how amazing she is when we had our chat this morning. They're not wrong, she's amazingly beautiful, no doubt.

I take my hard dick into my hand and stroke myself to completion with her imaginary lips wrapped around me and my cum squirting down her throat. I let out a growl when I finish. Part frustration that she's in my head and partly trying to keep her name from my tongue.

When I told the guys more details about my discharge they were surprisingly understanding, I thought they'd be freaked out or look at me differently. It was difficult to talk about what happened, especially with our history with Megan. But I couldn't do anything differently even though it meant I didn't follow orders.

I was on a mission to collect a wanted fugitive. We tracked him down to a well-known brothel in a town not far from base. When we got there it was obvious it was filled with criminals and under aged trafficking victims. The fugitive was in a room with an underaged girl, who had dark auburn hair and reminded me of Megan.

I lost it and beat the shit out of the guy until my team stopped me. Then I refused to leave the brothel until we rescued the under aged girls and the other women trapped there. In order to set them free we got into a shootout with the criminals in charge and killed seven men and one woman who ran the place and kept them prisoner.

The women and girls we released were rescued by a mission group from Alabama and Senegal. They agreed to care for their physical and mental health and help them return home or find suitable and safe living arrangements and to me it was a successful mission. Unfortunately, my commanding officers didn't agree.

Apparently, one of the men we killed was the brother of the mayor for the town. By killing him, we caused a political nightmare for the government officials who had to pay and work to resolve the situation I caused. My direct commander told me off the record he was proud of me, but the official government line was I needed to spend some time in a jail cell for what happened. The best I could do to avoid prison was a medical discharge. I had to go through several mental health evaluations, and they determined I was unfit for duty and authorized my medical discharge.

It was seriously fucked up in that brothel and I saw our sister in the faces of those girls. The vacant eyes, the loss of will to live, it was heartbreaking. Some of them were so damaged I don't know if there's any hope for them. I couldn't bear the thought of leaving them there, I didn't want to think of them on the floor, lifeless.

The problem now is I can't stop thinking about how good it felt to blow the brains out of the monsters who held those women there. I have this burning need to hunt down the asshole who hurt Megan, I want to see his brains splattered across the floor. Not just him but everyone like him. I'm supposed to continue seeing a shrink once I get settled, maybe that will help. I wanted to tell my brothers how I'm feeling but I couldn't find the words.

What if I tell them and they hate me? Or even worse, what if they're scared of me? How can I risk losing them? If only they weren't with Violet, I feel like we could get back to how close we were before I left. Then I could talk to them. But with her around they're focused on her all the time, always kissing and touching her, she's their everything, I don't even know where I fit anymore. Maybe I shouldn't stay with them.

Once I'm dry and dressed I join the others. They're talking to someone on speaker on Violet's phone. Since I was last to shower after we got back to Austin's I'm not in the loop and my mind keeps wandering to her. It's cool that Violet rides a bike, we followed her back. I tried not to look at her perfect ass and her legs straddled on the motorcycle, but how do you not think about her riding you when you see that?

I purposely sit so I'm not facing her. I can't look at her right now, not after what she did in my imagination in the shower. I don't want a boner in their family room.

"So, I get to choose all the tasks, right?" A male voice asks from the speaker.

"Yes, Colby, it's all you. We have to do whatever tasks you assign, and we can't know what's next until we complete the task at hand. What do you think?" Violet asks.

"You know I'm in. How could I pass up the opportunity to boss you guys around for once?"

"Don't let it go to your head dude. You're not bossing us around, just assigning the tasks and judging when they're completed," Jackson adds.

"Jax, man, that is bossing you around, at least in my mind. Let me have this, I never get to be in charge of anything."

"You're in charge, you're the boss. Just remember I support you. I'm also usually on your side, so you know, quid pro quo, bro," Austin eloquently campaigns. Violet smacks him and admonishes his crafty plot.

"Don't listen to him, no favoritism! Plus, their brother is joining the game, you can't cheat and mistreat him."

"When will I get to meet the infamous Pierson?" Colby asked. No time like the present.

"Hey, Colby. I'm Pierson, I guess I'm in the game and I'll meet you some time."

"Hi, Pierson. Nice to meet you. Yeah, if you stick around, you'll meet me eventually. Violet's been making me go out for a meal at least every two weeks and she's been out of town for a week, so a visit is about due."

"You said you didn't want to go to Uncle Randy's today, are you sure?" Violet asks.

"Yeah, I can't today. The parents are forcing me to join them. Maybe next weekend. I'll start working on the game and you'll get an email with instructions. Cool?" Colby asks.

"Yep. Take care Rob-N," Violet says.

"Later bro," Austin adds.

"See ya, man," Jackson chimes.

"Bye...Colby," I fumble.

"Bye guys," Colby ends the call.

"Do you think he's lying?" Jackson asks Violet.

"Maybe. It's possible his parents are making him eat with them though, I think they randomly decide to act like they care. We'll make him have a meal with us next weekend. He's right, it's time."

"What am I missing?" I ask, thoroughly confused.

Austin answers, "Colby has some quirks and mental illness. He has trouble leaving his house and some OCD tendencies. Violet helps him with his condition by taking him outside to places where he's comfortable and he does well in her company. He likes us too so we go when we can. He's a good guy and he's been a great friend to Violet. He's a computer genius and he does some cool shit with his skills."

"Yeah? Like what?" I ask.

"Violet called him RobN, it's short for RobNdaHood, his screen name. He hacks into criminal's accounts and returns their ill-gotten gains to their victims or donates it to charity. He's a virtual badass," Jackson explains.

That's interesting. I can't help noticing my brothers don't seem concerned in the least about the legal or illegal nature of his activities. I wonder why, maybe because they approve of his Robin Hood style justice. I watch as Violet smiles proudly at Jackson's explanation. What a unique set of people my brothers have become involved with while I've been away.

"Stellar." I'm not sure what else to say.

"What do you want to do until we need to leave for Randy's?" Austin asks, he raises his eyebrows suggestively and I don't want to think about it.

"Do you mind if I use a computer? I want to check out some things. Need to figure out my veteran's contact and medical benefits."

"Sure, Violet, will you show him where to sign on?" Jackson requests.

"Yeah. Come on." I follow her and keep my eyes off her pert little ass.

"I need to get a laptop. Are you happy with this one?" I ask her once I'm seated behind the desk.

"Yeah, it's pretty good. If you want, I'll help you pick one when you're ready." She leans over me to type on the keyboard and I get a whiff of the sweetest smell. It's like a flower but sweet and subtle, maybe jasmine. I take a deep breath trying to decipher the scent.

"I guess you have more experience with the actual hooking up the computer stuff than running the programs, huh?" she asks, meeting my eyes. Hers are black as night, but shine in an iridescent way like the glossy black scales of an indigo snake.

"Yeah," I keep my focus on the computer remembering I don't want to engage with her or encourage conversation. She gets the hint and leaves me to it. I spend the next hour checking emails, veteran's services, and looking at job opportunities.

Despite needing a job and a place of my own, I can't seem to concentrate on what I'm doing. Dark eyes and a perfect form keep invading my thoughts... I need to get laid. Maybe my brothers will take me out, maybe I can get them interested in some different girls, remind them they're young and shouldn't be tied down. They used to be all about body count but I guess things have changed since high school.

When you leave your hometown, somehow you think things will remain the same back there while you grow and change outside of your home base. But that never happens, everything changes, and it'll never be the same. I need my brothers to be the same, I need them to have the same relationship we had before I left. Right now, I need their support, so I don't do something stupid and go after the guy who hurt Megan or anyone else. Decision made, I seek out my brothers.

I find Austin in the kitchen emptying the dishwasher. It's funny to see him doing a chore that mom didn't assign. Are we really this grown up? Why don't I feel different?

"Hey. I wanted to ask you something."

"What's up?" Austin asks, serious for once.

"I want to go out, maybe find some company. Would you and Jackson go out with me tonight? We could talk some more, catch up," I ask tentatively.

His face twists in thought, "Sure, let me see if Violet and Jackson are up for a night out. We can go right after dinner at Randy's."

"Oh. Um, I meant just the guys." His face falls and I almost feel bad, but I remain steadfast.

"Oh, I guess I'll ask them. Are you all right?"

"Not really. I need to find my footing. I feel like everything's changed and I want to have fun like we used to. You know?"

"Dude, I want you to be happy, but you need to understand that things change. We're different, we don't do the shit we used to do. We still have fun, and we want you to have fun with us and I don't even mind going out, but I don't want to go out every night. I like spending time with Violet, I like hanging out at home with them. Jax and I haven't been out without Violet since we met her, it just doesn't appeal to us anymore."

It's worse than I thought. Even Austin who was always up for anything is wrapped tight in Violet's web. Damn, maybe I'll have more luck with Jackson.

"I get it. I was just hoping for a guys night to get us back to the closeness we used to have, I guess I feel disconnected. I know I've changed, and you guys have changed, it makes me think we lost our close bond. I miss it."

"Me too. I think we'll get back there with a little time, give yourself a chance to adjust to being on the outside. Besides, I'm still an instigator, Jax is still an asshole, and you're still an ugly dick with a stick up your ass, we're not that different." He gives me a shit eating grin.

I revert to our childhood and punch his bicep with my knuckle giving him a dead arm. He swings to get me back. I duck out of the way and we both bust out laughing. He aims for the back of my knee with his foot, and I step out of the way. He settles for mussing my hair and gives me his smug grin.

"You're definitely still a dickhead."

"I know," he agrees.

"Where's Jackson?"

"I think he's with Violet on the sofa," he directs.

I make my way to the family room and discover Jackson alone. The TV is on FailArmy, but he's doing something on his phone. That cat is curled on the chair in the corner, it raises its head and opens an eye to examine me, then dismisses me and goes back to sleep. I'm not a fan of cats but if it leaves me alone, I'll leave it alone.

"Hey man, what's up?" I ask.

"Not a damn thing. How'd you make out online?"

"Good. Got registered with the local V.A. unit, got an appointment this week. I wanted to ask you something."

He puts his phone down and gives me his full attention, "Shoot."

"I was wondering if we could have a guys night out tonight after the dinner thing. What do you think?" I ask.

"Uh, yeah, I guess. Is something up?" he queries.

"Just missing our brother bond. I was hoping to have a night out like we used to see if we can reconnect a little." I try to explain. His eyes narrow and he inspects my face while I hold my breath.

"Yeah. Okay. Where did you want to go?"

"Is Maybel's still a thing?"

"Been a minute since I've been there, but it's still open. I'm sure the food still sucks as bad as the music."

"Girls still slutty?"

"I wouldn't know, probably. All you need is one, right?" Jackson brings back my old motto. Maybe this'll work after all.

"You know it. Will Violet let you guys go?" I ask, hoping to make him think about how he's trapped in a relationship.

"She doesn't let us do anything. We do what we want, she's not like that. You should give her a chance, man. I don't think I've seen you say two words to her." Well, that backfired, Jackson always was the observant one.

"I'm just awkward. I'll work on it." I offer him a lame platitude.

"What are you guys talking about?" Violet asks as she enters and sits almost on Jackson. The cat jumps up next to her and lies down, he looks like a guard dog, er cat.

"Just catching up. Pierson wants to go out for a guy's night after dinner tonight."

"That's a great idea. You guys should have some brother time, and I can catch up on my homework." She smiles at both of us. I force a smile in return. Why does this girl make me so uncomfortable? It's like I need to escape my skin.

Jackson chuckles, "Violet's a genius, when she says catch up on schoolwork, she usually means get further ahead or finish the entire course that starts Monday." He smiles with pride.

"Don't exaggerate Jackson, I'm only a little ahead for this semester," she reassures me. It doesn't help Jackson's actions show exactly how much she has him in her clutches.

"What field of study does a genius go into?" I ask, pointedly saying more than two words to the temptress.

"I'm studying computer science. I learned some hacking skills when I was a kid and now, I want to be able to use it for legitimate purposes." She smiles like the Cheshire cat. I'm missing something.

"Violet and Colby have the most intense computer skills I've ever seen. The two of them could take over the world if they wanted," Jackson adds. There's that pride again.

"What do you plan to do when you're finished? How will you use your amazing skills?" I ask using more words. Yeah, I'm being a dickhead, Austin's right.

"I'm hoping to set up a charity for abused children. I want to make and maintain a database that matches kids in need with resources, grants, services, foster parents, everything an abused kid would need to get out and help them once they're free." I wasn't expecting that.

"Wow, that's a noble goal for someone so young." I sound like an old fart, why am I so damned awkward when she's around?

"It's important to me. So, where will you guys go tonight?" she asks.

"He wants to go to Maybel's," Jackson says with a roll of his eyes.

She looks at me and I try for an innocent expression, when her eyes squint, I don't think I was successful. She smiles at Jackson and I'm not sure, but I think I lost somehow.

"I'm going to finish up my laundry before we need to leave," I state and make a quick exit.

When we pull up at Uncle Randy's house I decide to make the best of it. My brothers have only good things to say about Violet's uncle and his family. Hopefully it will go by fast and we can get out to the bar as soon as possible.

When the door opens a little girl runs to Violet and hugs her. Then Austin grabs the girl and lifts her into the air before carrying her into the house.

"Isabel-jingle-bell!" He sings out as he carries her off. What the fuck just happened? Where did the kid come from? I might need to pay attention or ask some questions. I follow them inside and it's a nice house, warmly decorated, and I feel unusually comfortable being in a stranger's home. Violet hugs a man and Jackson shakes his hand.

He looks at me and smiles, holding out his hand to me he says, "Hey, you must be Pierson, I'm Randy. Thank you for your service."

I shake his hand and reply, "Nice to meet you, sir. Uh...you're welcome." I never know what to say when people thank me. It's unnecessary and with my discharge and everything that led to it, I feel like a fraud if I accept thanks for my service. He watches me and I swear he can read my thoughts, as he tilts his head like I spoke to them out loud.

The little girl runs to Randy and puts her hand on him while she looks me over. I smile and try to appear friendly since I haven't been around kids since I was one.

"Who's this?" she asks Randy.

"This is Austin and Jackson's brother, Pierson. Please introduce yourself."

She doesn't let go of him, "Hello, I'm Isabel. It's nice to neat you." When she finishes, she checks with him to see if she did okay.

"That was really close, but it's meet you. Want to try it?"

She looks at me again, "Nice to mmmeet you." He chuckles and I join him, she's pretty cute. She smiles at us proudly.

"Can we play race cars?" she asks.

"Yeah, if Austin wants to play with you, just remember you have to clean it up when you finish."

"Okay." She takes a step and shouts while she runs back to Austin, "He said yes! We can play race cars! I get to be purple!"

"I get to be green!" He claims his own choice. He's lying on the floor with a plastic bin in his hands and then proceeds to dump the contents onto the floor. Pieces of plastic track and small cars clatter as they fall into a colorful pile between them. He immediately begins snapping pieces together and now I can see it's indeed a racetrack.

"I see you've met our hurricane, Isabel. I'm Stephanie, it's nice to meet you. Violet and the guys told us you were in the military. Thank you for your service." She extends her hand and I shake it and awkwardly respond.

"Nice to meet you as well. You're welcome." Violet joins us and I'm not sure if I'm glad she came to the rescue or annoyed she's inserting herself.

"I was thinking it might help you if I explain who everyone is now that you can put faces to the names. This is Uncle Randy, he's also formerly my guardian. My adoptive parents passed away and he's the guardian they chose in case anything happened to them; he's a psychiatrist. Stephanie's also a doctor and his fiancé. Isabel's their foster child, but they're going to adopt her as soon as they complete all the steps. Any questions?"

"I think I got it. I'm sorry about your parents." As much as I don't want to interact with her, I can't help feeling sympathy for her situation. If I caught all that, it was her adoptive parents, who died. So, she was already without biological parents and lost her adoptive parents. She must consider Randy a parent figure at this point. I wonder if he's actually related to her by blood. I'll ask the guys later.

"No! I want that one!" Isabel shouts.

"Uh, oh. Please excuse us, we need to put a stop to that. She's been a little bossy lately." Stephanie and Randy march to Isabel and Austin. I don't see Jackson, but I can't avoid Violet, it's just me and her.

"So, what's for dinner?" I don't know what else to say.

"Randy usually barbecues. Do you want something to drink?" she offers.

"Sure, whatever's easy is fine."

"Root beer?"

"Fine."

I catch myself watching her move into the kitchen. Her movements are fluid, almost feline, her body seems strong, ready for a fight. I don't know why I think that, maybe because I feel like I need to fight her off to regain my brothers. She's armed, I can always tell, a habit from my military training. I wonder why she feels the need to be armed at a family dinner.

After she hands me a soda, I move into the family room and join Jackson on the sofa. He's watching Austin play with Isabel and critiquing his race car driving skills, he barely acknowledged my arrival. Austin is laughing and smiling with Isabel and for a moment it reminds me of when Tori was little. He was always the one who played with her, he was an expert at dressing Barbie and pouring invisible tea.

"Thanks for checking the kabobs, Jackson. It should be ready in about five minutes if you guys want to bring everything else to the table. Steph, will you get Isabel washed for dinner?" Randy announces and everyone moves at his words. Stephanie takes Isabel from the room and Austin breaks down the racetrack he just built. Jackson hops up and follows Violet to the kitchen. Not sure how to help, I go to the dining room and wait for someone to tell me where to sit.

Isabel is the first to join me, entering at full speed. She stops when she sees me.

She looks at my face and then asks, "Where do you wanna sit?"

"I was hoping someone would tell me where I should sit. Where do you sit?"

She looks at me like I'm not very bright and pulls out a chair with a cushion strapped to it.

"I sit here. Steff-nee sits right there," she points to the chair next to hers. "Violet sits next to me, she's my sister." She points at the chair on the other side of hers.

"What about Randy?" I ask.

"You're weird," she observes. Then answers, "He sits there." She points to the seat at the head of the table next to Stephanie's place. It leaves the chairs on the other side of the table and the far end open. I walk around to the other side and stop at the first chair, touching it.

I ask, "Can I sit here?" She shakes her head vehemently.

"No, Jackson sits there." I move to the next chair and touch it.

"What about this one, can I sit here?" She shakes her head and giggles.

"No! That's where Austin sits." I move to the final chair on this side.

"How about this one?"

"Nope!"

"Who sits here?" I ask, confused.

"Mr. Sunshine." She dead pans.

"Who's Mr. Sunshine?" I inquire, thoroughly lost.

"My horse, of course!" She bursts into hysterical laughter, and I can't keep from chuckling. She's obviously deranged.

"Horse? I don't see any horse."

She gives me a hard glance, like I must be the dumbest person she ever encountered. I'm feeling really dumb, how is a five-year-old capable of tearing down a grown man in mere minutes? She stomps to the large wood chair in question, pulls it away from the table, a monumental task for her little body, and lifts a sparkly purple stuffed horse showing me what an idiot I am.

"I stand corrected. Hello, Mr. Sunshine, I presume?"

She laughs again, "You could sit here now." She instructs like she's explaining it to a toddler.

"Thank you." I sit down and rethink my life choices. I've been bested by a little girl with a ribbon on her ponytail. She rolls her eyes at me and goes back to her own chair with Mr. Sunshine clutched to her chest.

"Isabel, are you behaving?" Stephanie calls from the kitchen.

"She's fine," I reply. Austin enters with two cups in his hands, Violet comes behind him and sets a bowl of rolls on the table. Austin puts a cup at her place and takes his seat, right where Isabel pointed out his chair. Stephanie places a cup with a lid and a straw in front of Isabel.

A flurry of activity fills the room as Jackson and Randy enter with their hands full and Stephanie leaves and returns with more bowls of something. Everyone sits and begins passing food around the table. It's a pleasant family scene. Conversation continues through the meal. The food is good, and the laughter is warm.

Randy pats his flat belly and proclaims, "Man, that was good, but I'm so full."

Everyone around the table concurs with Randy's status. We work together to clear everything, and Violet and Stephanie begin washing dishes and wiping down flat surfaces. The men and our boss, Isabel, recline to digest in the family room.

"So, Pierson, what are your plans for work now that you're out of the military?" Randy asks.

"For now, I'm going to work with Jackson and Austin at the boring company. I'm not in a rush to hunt for a job in my field. I need a break from it."

"That makes sense. It's good to decompress after an intense job like you had in the Navy. How are you doing staying with Violet and the guys?"

"Oh. It's fine. I don't think the cat likes me, but otherwise, yeah, it's fine."

Jackson looks up from his phone and examines my face, I pretend not to notice. Austin's engaged with Isabel who's still holding her noble steed.

"You gotta feed Sawyer a few times, then he'll like you," Austin interjects from across the room.

"I'll try that." Randy gets pulled into the board game Isabel is now playing with Austin and Jax is still on his phone. I decide to see if there's a beer in the fridge, a little pregaming for our night out.

Violet and Stephanie are locked in an intense conversation when I enter the kitchen. They're standing close and speaking softly, not sure if I should interrupt, I freeze.

"You're sure he's dead? Like gone forever?" Stephanie asks.

"Trust me, he won't be coming after you ever again. He's mostly ash," Violet replies.

Stephanie wraps Violet in a tight hug.

"How can I ever thank you?"

"I'd do anything for my family," Violet responds.

When I shift to move back to the family room and give them privacy my shoe makes a sound on the tile. Both women turn and look at me, Stephanie swipes at her eyes, while Violet's face tightens.

"Did you need something?" she asks.

I clear my throat, "Just wanted to see if there's a beer. Sorry, I didn't mean to interrupt."

Stephanie declares, "Don't be silly. You're not interrupting, there's beer in the fridge. Help yourself." I quickly grab a beer and exit the room. What did I hear? It sounded like, nah. That's ridiculous. I just walked into the middle of a conversation and misunderstood what they were saying, that's all.

When the ladies come back from clean up duty, we wrap up our visit. It was pleasant enough. Randy and Stephanie are cool and Isabel...well, she's something else. But the evening can't end fast enough for me, my dick's already at half-mast in anticipation. It's definitely not from watching Violet. I want to ditch her as fast as possible and get to Maybel's so my real night out can begin.

In the car I ask, "We're just dropping Violet off, right?"

Austin's face scrunched into a scowl, "What's with you dude? Why are you trying so hard to get rid of Violet?"

"I'm not. I just want to get to Maybel's."

His eyes narrow, "We'll get there when we get there. Chill out."

I decide the best thing to do is drop it which turns out to be a wise decision. Austin forgets about it, and we drop off Violet. They both kissed her for a little too long, while I tried not to imagine her lips on mine. Instead, I try to picture a hot girl at the bar who wants to suck my dick, like her life depends on it. Every time I picture her face it turns into Violet's dark eyes, high cheekbones, and sumptuous lips. I really need some female companionship.

When they finally manage to pry themselves away from their girlfriend, we point the car in the direction of slutty chicks and watery beer. It looks exactly like it did the last time I was here. I don't even remember when it was, I was on holiday leave, it must've been my second year. It seems so long ago.

"The bartender looks interested. Why don't you go talk to her some more?" Jackson suggests.

She's cute, really nice tits. Her straight blonde hair hangs to her jawbone, and I find myself wishing it was spiky with some blue streaks. I shake my head and approach her. She has multiple works of fine art on her chest and arms. She's thick and I like the meat on her bones.

"I like your dagger. It's well done, what's the symbol on it?" my deep voice asks.

"It's this thing with my sister, when we were kids, people always thought we were twins. It's a fancy Gemini sign to represent the two of us. You've got some nice ink yourself. I'd love to see the rest of it," she says and licks her lips following the move with a coy smile.

"Do you have more to show me?" I ask with intention, a smirk gracing my lips.

"Definitely. Give me ten minutes. Can I get you another drink while you're waiting?" she asks, looking at my empty glass.

"Sure." She pours me another beer with a perfect head, and I watch her round ass wiggle as she tops up the rest of the people at the bar. I spot my brothers engaged in a game of pool. The girls at the next table are desperately trying to get their attention and they don't even seem to notice no matter how hard the brunette tries to stick her ass in their paths. Shaking my head I wonder if it's too late to get them away from Violet.

When we were young, we used to talk about our ideal woman. She had to be beautiful, smart, blonde, with a perfect, strong body and she needed to be a badass. We were hooked on the reruns of Xena Warrior Princess. We wanted a girl who could fight like a goddess. We begged mom and dad for the Xena video game, you couldn't get us off the PlayStation once we finally did enough chores to earn it. I chuckle at the memory.

The biggest requirement for our dream girl was that she had to love all three of us. We wanted to stay together forever, and we figured if we all had the same girl, then girls would never drive us apart by taking one of us away. Our parental situations taught us that having separate relationships was a disaster that would ruin every other close relationship we had. My mom and her sister stopped speaking to each other. Austin's birth father and Jackson's mother would have huge fights and not speak for weeks before he died. We believed with all our hearts the only way for the three of us to stay together forever as the close brothers we were, was to share the perfect woman.

Now here we are, and they have a girl to share while I've got jack shit. It's my own fault I suppose, I'm the one who took off. But fuck, why did they have to find their girl before I could get back? What am I supposed to do? I need to move out of Austin's place, I'm intruding and they're obviously not going to ditch her, I think they're in love with her. Fuck. I don't even feel like playing with the bartender anymore.

When she comes back to talk to me, I break it to her, "Hey babe, sorry, I've gotta go. Have a good night." I lay out some bills and leave her a generous tip. She frowns at me.

"I thought you wanted to see my tattoos, and I have piercings you'd probably like. Do you really need to go?" She tilts her head and bites her bottom lip seductively. Normally I'd be all over that, but I feel nothing. My dick is soft.

"Yeah, I need to go. Maybe I'll catch you next time."

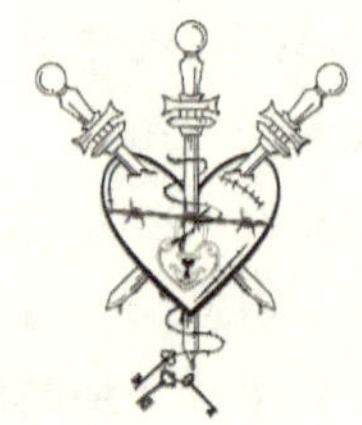

Chapter Five

Violet

It's well after midnight when my guys climb into bed. They both kiss me, and I kiss them back, I may have been asleep but I'm fully alert now. Austin's hands pull off my top and roam my chest as his lips make their way from my ear, along my jaw, and to my collar bone. He licks and nibbles there sending sparks to my nipples and parts lower.

Jackson kisses along my stomach just above my panties. His fingers tickle my clit through the fabric. He groans as he sucks on my skin. Those tantalizing fingers find their way beneath the cotton material and my body heats.

Austin's mouth surrounds a nipple as his tongue circles it. His teeth gently graze the delicate skin and I'm writhing with need. He sucks hard and twists the other peak just to the point of pain. He pushes the limits until I'm begging him to jump over the cliff. That little pinch of pain causes arousal to flow from my pussy soaking my boy shorts styled lingerie.

No matter, Jackson divests me from my remaining garment and presses his large body between my thighs. The air hits moisture as I spread my knees, and it crashes into the heat there causing a collision of sensations that make me shiver. He doesn't hesitate to lick my exposed pink skin. He sucks at my clit, and I can't contain myself.

"Oooh! Yes! Mmmm...oh...right there! Oh my god! Yes! Yes!"

Jackson inserts two fingers and moves them, so he touches that perfect spot. The stretch of his large digits and his mouth on me is making me move with him. Austin's kisses and sucking lips make my chest lift to meet him. I'm like a writhing cobra twisting and curling with each jolt of electricity that zips across my most sensitive nerves.

When I get too loud Austin covers my lips with his. My tongue swirls against his and he squeezes my breasts while Jackson sucks my clit into his mouth and my orgasm explodes like a cannon going off. Austin does a good job of keeping me from screaming too loud and as I come down a little from my climax, I realize he was probably trying to keep Pierson from hearing us. Embarrassment colors my cheeks at the thought.

"Mmm, baby, you're so beautiful when you come for us. Did that feel good?" I tremble, as tingles still travel across the nerves between my thighs. It makes me giggle which makes him laugh too.

"Um, yeah. It was amazing. You guys know how to wake up a girl." I reach for the tent in his boxer briefs, and he catches my hand.

"No baby, go back to sleep. We just wanted to make you feel good. You can return the favor in the morning if you want. Right now, we just want to cuddle with you."

"Listen to him, babe. You're gorgeous, but you're tired. Go back to sleep."

Jackson pulls me close to his chest. Austin squeezes in behind me. They nestle me between them, and I find myself completely relaxed. Austin's hand rests on my hip while Jackson holds my back. I'm curled into his neck and I breathe in the soft masculine scent of cologne and Jackson. Before I know it, I feel my mind wandering towards sleep.

When my eyes pop open, sunlight glows through the drapes. I feel warm and comfortable. But I quickly realize only one body is twisted with mine. Austin's one hand is under my breasts and the other rests on my pubic bone. His morning wood is pressed into my ass, and I wiggle my butt against him.

He presses his hard cock further into my cheeks. My nipples pebble and a warm current floods my lady parts making me grind into him. He pinches my chest and his other hand ventures between the outer lips of my pussy. I twist so I can face him, and he releases his grip enough to allow the move. Once I'm facing him, he pulls me close and rubs his dick on my clit which lights me up like the fourth of July. He rolls onto his back and lifts me on top of him. I sit up and he guides me onto his erect cock as he fills me to my limits.

With his hands on my hips, I begin to move up and down, grinding on him. He uses his grip to move me in a rhythm he likes. His face is taut with concentration, my eyes drift closed as I lose myself in the feel of him. Bright sparks shoot behind my lids as my brain interprets the signals from my sensitive skin. He moans with pleasure, and I mewl like a happy cat. As our movements speed up our skin slaps together and we maneuver against each other causing the most gratification we can manage.

Much too soon, a twinge alerts me to the rapidly approaching finish to our encounter. As I begin to explode, he sits up and grabs me tight. He moves my body so he can finish while making it perfect for me, he does it right because my orgasm lasts and lasts. Every time I think it's going to wither it surges back to life and my squeals of joy are loud. Austin shouts out as his climax hits, then we slow our movements grinding softly against one another to extend the bursts of pleasure.

When we finish, he helps me roll off of him without making a mess. He uses his underwear to wipe me clean, then he looks into my eyes, he kisses my lips and hugs me close. I could fall back asleep, I'm so cozy. But I know we have things to do, I'm starting back at school tomorrow for one thing.

When I begin to doze, he asks, "Are you hungry baby?"

"Yeah."

"Let's take a quick shower and then get some breakfast."

"Okay." I plant a kiss on the corner of his mouth, the closest place I could reach. We each grab some fresh clothes and make our way into the shower.

Once we're dressed, we join Jackson and Pierson in the kitchen. Sawyer is happily licking himself next to his empty bowl and I wonder if Pierson fed him. Austin told me about his suggestion for Pierson to win over our fuzzy beast. I hope he fed him, and he'll be on better terms with Sawyer now, maybe it'll help him hate me a little less if he doesn't hate my cat.

"Good morning, beautiful," Jackson greets me with a kiss.

"Good morning, handsome."

"Did you guys eat yet?" Austin asks.

"No. I thought we could go for a ride and eat while we're out." Jackson looks between me and Austin for an answer.

"What about Pierson? We don't have an extra bike," I question.

Pierson answers, "I'm going to look for a place, don't worry about me."

"Really? Why?" Austin voices my thoughts.

"I need my own space. Plus, I can't take advantage of your charity forever. I'm going to start working with you tomorrow. I've got enough for first and last, if I can use the car you offered for a couple months, I can swing it."

Jackson looks tense as he nods, "Sure, whatever you need. But it's not a problem having you here, you can stay while you get on your feet."

"I appreciate it, I just feel like I need my own place. You guys don't need to babysit me and feed me all the time. I appreciate it, but I feel like I'm in the middle of your relationship and you don't need that."

"Dude, you're being ridiculous. You're our brother, you're not in the middle of anything. Plus, if you leave, you won't be able to share the chores and play our game," Austin explains.

Pierson glances at me, "You really don't mind?" Then he looks at Jackson for a response.

"No, jackass, we wouldn't have invited you if it was a problem. If Violet doesn't mind, she can ride with one of us and you can ride one of our bikes. Come on, I'm hungry." Jackson questions me with a look and I silently agree.

I speak up, "Yeah, you can ride my Indian and I'll ride with Jackson."

"Hey! What about me, Baby?" Austin feigns jealousy.

"Fine. I'll ride home with you, happy?" I tease.

"Yep. Let's hit it, I'm hungry too. I worked up an appetite." Austin winks at me.

"We heard." Jackson states flatly. My eyes bulge in shock and I can feel my cheeks burn red with embarrassment. I can't look at Pierson. My eyes stay glued to the floor as we file into the garage. When I catch Austin's gaze as I pull on my helmet, he grins at me and raises his eyebrows a few times. Ugh! He's proud of it. I'm going to die of embarrassment and he's prancing around like a peacock, sometimes I don't get men.

Once I'm wrapped around Jackson with the vibration of his rattling engine between my legs, all of my emotions blow away with the breeze. Nothing soothes my soul like a ride, the asphalt speeding beneath the wheels and the wind on my face. Everything is right in my world when I'm in a leather seat rushing to my destination, or just rushing absolutely nowhere.

By the time we stop at the cute little diner off the causeway to the beach, my cheeks are sun kissed and no longer heated from within. We're able to park in front so I leave my helmet on the bike. I've only been here once before with my guys, but they have amazing French toast and my stomach growls at the thought of it.

When we're seated in a booth Pierson ends up across from me and Austin is next to me. After we order, I catch Pierson looking at me. He looks confused, like he's trying to figure me out. I want to ask him what he wants to know, but I don't think his brothers would like me calling him out.

"What did you think of Violet's bike?" Austin asks.

"It's nice. Never rode an Indian before. I might need to add them to my list when I'm ready to buy my own."

"It was my dad's. We used to work on it together." I told him.

"It's in great shape. I was surprised it had over fourteen-thousand miles. It looks new," Pierson adds.

"I keep up with the maintenance. It was important to him."

"I get that."

"Yeah, Violet rides all the time unless she needs the trunk space, or the weather prohibits it and she's a stickler for the maintenance. My bike has never been so well taken care of; she encourages us to do the same." Jackson smiles proudly at me.

The waitress brings coffee, and the food follows shortly after. We get wrapped up in a discussion about our plans for the rest of the day and then it moves on to our new game and Colby. We decide to check in with him and find out if he's made any progress with the details.

A chuckle greets us then Colby says, "I already know why you're calling. I'm done putting it together, do you want to come over?"

"Yeah!" Austin yells at the phone, his excitement overpowering his ability to be polite.

I chastise him with my eyes and answer in human volume, "Yes, we'd love to. Pierson is with us; will it be all right to bring him?"

"Yeah, it's cool. The parents left this morning for a cruise. I'm free all day and I'd love to have you guys over."

"Great! We'll take the long way and see you in about an hour."

"Sweet. I'll alert the guards. See ya."

"Thanks. Bye."

"What does he mean about guards?" Pierson asks, confused. I guess that is a weird phrase if you haven't been to Colby's before, it sounds a little foreboding.

"You'll see. It's kind of shocking the first time," Austin says mysteriously.

Pierson looks worried so I have mercy on him and explain, "Colby is super wealthy, maybe even a billionaire, I don't really know. But his house has a huge gate and a guardhouse with armed guards. It's a little overwhelming at first, but it's no big deal and Colby doesn't act like a snooty rich guy; he falls into the eccentric category."

"Wow, well this should be interesting."

"That's a good word for it, interesting," Jackson adds. Pierson looks at me again, but I don't offer further explanation.

We climb back onto the bikes and aim them to the beach. The waves are smooth, and the water is a beautiful blue. The snowbirds aren't here yet and the humidity isn't too high, traffic is light. It's a perfect Florida fall day to ride.

We meander along Bayshore Drive and enjoy the tropical scenery. The palm trees sway in a gentle breeze and the pastel island style buildings enhance the perfect view. As the homes transform from quaint wooden structures to plaster and barrel tiles, the size of the yards increase and more of them are contained behind ornate gates. The homes grow into mansions and the simple native landscapes become carefully designed award-winning works of art.

We make a turn away from the water into the richest neighborhood yet. It's not long before we turn uphill onto the fanciest street, it ends in a cul-de-sac right in front of a huge custom gate and guardhouse. Colby's home is finally before us, Jackson pulls to the gate first so I can speak to the guards because they know me.

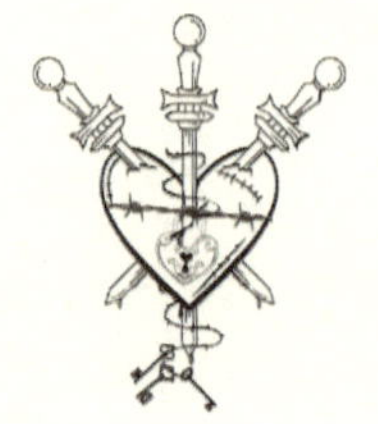

Chapter Six

Pierson

"Hi Julio, how are you?" Violet greets a huge guard with dark hair and a gun.

"Miss Henley! I didn't recognize you on the back of a bike. I'm good. Marguerite is doing well. We have high hopes for this treatment. How are you doing?"

"I'm great. You remember Jackson and Austin." She points to each of them with their names. Both guards are staring at me with hard looks on their faces. I didn't even see where the second guard came from.

Violet notices where their attention is focused and continues, "This is their brother, Pierson Nash, he's staying with us. How are you, Monty?"

The second guard, who's even bigger than the first, smiles warmly at Violet and responds with, "I'm doing just great, Miss

Henley. It's a pleasure to see you as always. You're looking very well."

"Thanks Monty. We're here to visit Master Colby. Is he ready for us?" she teases.

"He is, he asks that you drive through to his pool house," Julio answers.

"Thanks Julio, Monty, it's nice to see you both."

"Of course, Miss Henley. Mr. Hunter, Mr. Matthews, Mr. Nash, enjoy your visit." Julio nods at each of us. Jackson and Austin return a nod, so I follow suit. This is weird, I've never been admitted through a gate like this outside a military installation. Monty also nods at us as the gate opens and Jackson rides through. Monty never takes his eyes off me, even after I pass the gate, I can feel his eyes burning a hole in my back.

We slowly make our way around a massive structure. It looks expensive, with stone and wrought iron embellishments. The stone path continues through some trees which block the side view of the main home and as it curves, a smaller version of the main structure appears. By smaller, I mean probably four-thousand square feet of a beautiful two-story residence.

Once we're parked and our helmets are off, Austin asks, "What do you think?"

He's smirking at me, and I ask, "Only one guy lives here?"

"Fancy, huh? Wait until you meet Colby, he's hilarious."

Violet butts in, turning back to do so, "No he's not. He thinks he's funny, but he's definitely not."

Austin leans in when Jackson knocks on the door, "They fight like siblings, you'll see. He's an interesting character."

The door opens inward and a tall, thin guy with light hair leans down to hug Violet. Jackson shakes his hand and gives him a guy hug, followed by Austin. When I step inside all eyes fall upon me, I try to paste a grin on my face.

"Colby, this is Pierson, their brother." Violet introduces me.

"Hey," I say with a chin lift.

"Hello. Pierson Nash. Naval Petty Officer, medically discharged for PTSD and related symptoms, after mission Pixel Seven. Pleased to meet you." Colby doesn't offer his hand to me. My jaw is hanging open in surprise.

"How do you know that?" I can't keep from asking.

"Told you he's a computer genius, he knows everything. Don't worry, he's cool. He doesn't share with anyone." Austin smiles smugly at me.

I look at Violet and Jackson, neither of them is surprised or interested by what Colby revealed. I still want to know how he knows about my last mission. My head tilts and my eyes narrow as I wait for an answer.

"I check out everyone who's involved with Violet. I'm not going to let anyone near her unless I know they're safe. She's my best friend; we watch out for each other." He smiles warmly in her direction and my gut tightens.

"That's great. I'm more interested in how you know my confidential medical information, and a military operation's details," I responded with a hint of anger feeling violated.

"I can't tell you that. Austin's right, I don't share what I find with anyone, but I need to know," Colby defends.

Jackson, always acting as the referee, jumps in, "Look, he checks out everything about everyone. He always needs to know that Violet's safe, Austin and I appreciate how he always has her back. His illness makes him check everything. Since it's good for Violet and we trust Colby, we're cool with it. Does it really matter if he knows some information?"

"I...I just...I guess not. It's a surprise hearing a secret mission name coming from a stranger, that's all." I look between Colby and Violet, feeling once again like I'm missing something important.

Violet changes the subject. "So, tell us about our race, we're so excited." We followed them into a big open room attached to a huge modern kitchen. There are trays of sandwiches, salads, cut vegetables, and dips spread along the island. Austin stops and dunks a carrot in something white.

"Is this for us?" Austin asks while crunching like Bugs Bunny.

"Yeah, I had the kitchen bring them over, so we can celebrate my parent's departure. Bon voyage! I hope you hit an iceberg!" Everyone laughs at his remarks. I guess he doesn't get along with his parents. I begin a mental list of questions about the great and powerful Colby.

"Should we sit at the table?" Violet asks.

"Sit anywhere you want. I'm going to project my screen on the TV. You'll be able to follow along from any chair in the room," Colby explains as he sits in front of four computer screens in the fanciest looking office style chair I've ever seen, it must be a custom gamer chair.

Not sure what to do I sit on the corner of a leather sofa and observe. The massive flat screen on the wall across from me comes to life and looks like a computer screen and with some rapid flashes it becomes a list of rules for 'The Game.' Austin joins me on the sofa and puts a food laden plate on the coffee table in front of us. He continues to crunch on vegetables dripping with what might be ranch dressing.

I look over my shoulder and see Violet and Jackson seated at a table sharing a plate between them. I notice they have drinks too and I search the island for available beverages. When I spot some bottles and cups, I ask Austin, "I'm getting a drink, you want something?"

"Yeah, anything but ginger ale."

As I fill two cups with ice and root beer, I remember we all have an aversion to ginger ale. My brothers and I used to get ginger ale only when we were sick and once, we all got this awful stomach flu and ended up puking ginger ale all over Austin's room. None of us have been able to drink it since then. Even though it's a disguesting memory it makes me smile.

I rejoin Austin more relaxed. "Thanks man," Austin states as I hand him a cup.

Colby begins explaining, "The Game will start with the first task being emailed to each of you. Then when you complete each task, you'll receive the next one. Whoever finishes first wins."

Austin asks, "When does it start?"

"When you get the first task."

"When will that be?" Jackson queries.

"When I send it."

Jackson chuckles, "Okay. I get it, a surprise start. Awesome." He sounds less enthusiastic than his words suggest.

"Please don't start it when I'm in class," Violet pleads.

"Sorry no hints, and no special concessions, the guys have work too." She rolls her eyes and looks adorable. I check myself, WTF? She's not adorable, she's their girlfriend and my nemesis, my stupid grin morphs into a scowl with my inner dialogue.

Next, Colby pulls up a chart of chores. There's four weeks of chores and our four names in a rotation. Lucky me, I have bathroom duty first. Violet has laundry, I see her face fall as she sees her assignment. She must not like laundry, but it's better than scrubbing toilets.

"These are everyone's chores. The game will last approximately four weeks, or on rotation of assignments. When someone wins, the remaining chores will be divided like this, and the winner will be off the entire four-week rotation." Colby pulls up a new chore chart divided equally between only three participants.

"What if we finish faster than the four weeks?" Violet asks.

"The winning rotation won't start until the first round of chores is complete. The winner may have a few final chores to finish."

"What if we go over the four weeks?" Austin plays devil's advocate.

"I can't imagine Violet will need more than four weeks, but if that happens, we'll begin at the top of the next week after a winner is determined. Any other questions?" Colby looks at me.

I can't keep from saying, "It sounds like you're giving favoritism to Violet, how do we know you'll play fair?" Everyone turns at my words, and I stick my chin out defiantly. Violet narrows her eyes and examines me while I pretend not to notice.

"I realize you don't know me, so I forgive your accusation. The game will be fair and honestly judged. I don't cheat. Anyone else?"

Austin elbows me and whispers a chastising, "Dude." Under his breath making me jolt and feeling appropriately shamed, my eyes fall to the floor.

Austin continues much louder, "How will we prove we completed a task, to get the next clue?"

"When you finish a task, send me a photo or video proof, then you'll get your next task. Just remember, I'm a strict judge and I won't accept ridiculous substitutions. I'm also able to independently confirm certain things have occurred. I can access email accounts, text messages, cameras on buildings, you never know when I might be watching. One last thing, no discussing the clues between you, no teaming up, these are individual tasks."

"Let's watch a movie," Violet suggests.

Everyone jumps into debate about which movie and we decide on a new film by M. Night Shyamalan. I prefer action or superheroes, but Violet said she wanted horror, and they all caved to her preference. I filled a plate of my own with vegetables and crunched out my frustration.

They act like she's royalty and we should all bow at her feet. Other than her good looks and apparent skills in bed, (I'm assuming from the noises I've heard), I don't know what they see in her, she's nothing special. Her friend Colby seems pretentious and weird. But they warned me he was weird, so I'll give him a pass.

By the time the movie is over we're ready to head out. I exchanged contact info with Colby for the game, but I have no doubt he already had mine.

I have my first day at work tomorrow and Violet has her first day back at school. We opt for a quiet dinner at Austin's, and he offered to cook. I know I'm brooding over my frustration with my brothers and Violet, but I can't shake it off. When we get to Austin's, I jump in the shower and sit in my room until they call me for dinner. I spent my down time searching for a bike of my own, I really liked Violet's Indian.

I found an Indian two years newer than Violet's in my price range. One good thing I can say about her, she's got a nice ride. If I'm committed to staying here for at least a few months, I can use my rent money for a bike. Then by the time I'm ready for my own place, my investments should be free to remove without penalties and maybe I'll get my own house. The guy with the Indian agreed to meet me after work tomorrow. Maybe Jackson will let me use his truck in case I want to buy it.

"Did you get enough to eat, baby?" Austin asks Violet.

I can't resist the urge to tease him, "Yes, Sweetums, my tummy is full!" Jackson and Violet burst out laughing.

Austin gives me a dirty look that barely covers a grin, "Not cool brother!" He punches my bicep, and it hurts like a bitch.

"Dickhead!" I exclaim as I kick his shin.

"Ow, fuck! Bro that hurts!"

"Okay, kids, that's enough, let's get the kitchen cleaned up," Jackson scolds. Violet continues to giggle as she carries her dishes to the kitchen. Austin and I chuckle and collect our stuff too.

"Jax, I was wondering, can I use your truck tomorrow? I'm gonna check out a bike after work." He looks me over and nods.

"Yeah, sure. The ramp's in the garage want to load it up now?"

"Yeah. I'll meet you out there." I carry my dishes to the kitchen, where Austin and Violet are washing the dishes and loading the dishwasher. I drop off my stuff and wrap up some leftover food before I join Jackson, and we make quick work of the ramp. He gives me the truck keys and I'm ready for tomorrow. I rejoin the kitchen crew and they're almost done so I wipe off the counters to help. Jackson feeds the cat, and we all finish at the same time.

Austin speaks up, "We'll leave at 6, work starts between 6:30 and 7 depending on when the rest of the guys show. Dave will assign you wherever he needs help. We're planning to meet at the warehouse to work out after, you can meet us there if you want to work out. If you text us when you're outside, we'll open the big door so you can pull inside that way you won't have to worry about leaving your bike in the alley, if you buy it."

"Thanks man. See you guys in the morning." I wave at everyone including Violet, it's easier for me to include her in a group greeting.

I fade as fast as my head hits the pillow. The next sound I hear is my alarm. Thankfully, I feel well rested. Today is probably going to be physically strenuous, and though I work out, I haven't done any physical work in a while.

We grab a quick meal as we cross paths in the kitchen, Violet doesn't need to be up for an hour so it's a rare minute with my brothers without her and I make a point to enjoy it. We all head out together, them in Austin's truck and me in Jackson's.

At the jobsite, I'm immediately assigned to the far side of the property, away from everyone except Dave. He's an asshole who's high on imaginary power, I don't care, I focus on digging and ignore him.

"All right, Greenie, you did okay. You get thirty minutes for lunch. I suggest you hydrate and use the porta-potty while you can." Dave chuckles like he said something funny. I nod at him and start to walk towards the food truck that just pulled up.

He grabs my elbow and stops me, "Don't think you're anything special because of your brothers. They might be close with Ryder, but I'm the supervisor."

Not sure what that's about I nod at him, "Yes, sir." I had to listen to plenty of assholes who out-ranked me in the Navy, it's just another day at the office for me.

I walk off and order a burrito from the fancy food truck. They used to call them roach-coaches, but this one looks new and clean otherwise. I might not trust a burrito from a truck on a job site.

"Hey, how's it going?" Jackson asks before making his own burrito order.

I look around before I answer, "Dave's an asshole, but it's okay."

"Yeah, he's got a chip on his shoulder. Austin's friend, Ryder, is the nephew of the owner, he got us our jobs. Dave complains about favoritism and nepotism, and he's been passed over for promotion because of his attitude. He blames everyone but himself. Don't take it personally."

"I don't care, I've worked with plenty of assholes. I'm just looking forward to the end of the day."

"Yeah. Me too." His phone makes a noise, and he smiles at the screen as the server hands us each foil wrapped tortillas of what I hope is deliciousness. He takes off with his Mexican prize, no doubt to chat with his girlfriend. I find a shady bit of curb and sit to enjoy mine.

Okay, that might be the best burrito I ever had, and I spent some time in San Diego just above the border. I could see Mexican soil from there and many of their citizens made delicious food on our side of the wall.

My own phone chimes and I wipe my hands on my jeans before I snake my phone out of my pocket. I open the message and fireworks shoot off, confetti swirls, and a big banner pops up: Welcome to The Game! I guess Colby enjoys drama, clicking where it indicates causes a scroll to appear. The ribbon surrounding it unties, and the scroll unfurls.

It reads:

Hello Contestants,

Your first task is to visit these coordinates: 29.3977780, -83.2 017999.

You will meet a person there who requires assistance. If you can figure out how to help them, you'll receive your next task. You may need to search your sole for the right thing to do.

Good luck!

I read it over a few times. I copy the coordinates and paste them into a map app when it pops up, I can see it's basically the middle of nowhere. But it's not too far, it looks like a road to a nature path. I'll have to come prepared tomorrow and head there after work. I won't have time today.

After a grueling workday, I'm excited to check out the Indian. It looked great online and only has about four-thousand miles. The guy says he bought it to ride along the beach on the weekends and after two seasons, his wife decided it was too dangerous. He finally came to terms with it and agreed to sell.

It's perfect. There's a small scratch on the tank but the rest looks new. The tires still have great tread, and the maintenance was just completed with less than an hour on the new oil. After it starts right up with a purr and a short test drive, I decided not to barter much, it's almost a fair price. I offer two hundred below asking and he happily accepts. He helps me load it up and his neighbor notarized the title, and I'm back on the road in no time.

My brother's truck isn't outside the warehouse when I get there, I text and neither of them answer. I try banging on the door in case they're inside and can't hear their phones. The big overhead door lifts and I drive inside, parking next to Violet's bike. When I exit the truck, my ears are assaulted by heavy metal music. I bring my bag and head upstairs when I don't see her in the gym.

Having learned my lesson, I knock on the door to the apartment. Nobody answers so I open the door and call out.

"Hello! Violet? Are you in here?"

"No! I'm up here." Startled to hear her behind me I search the space and spot her on a beam high above the gym.

"What the fuck? What are you doing up there, trying to die?"

She laughs, “No. It’s part of my workout. Haven’t you ever heard of parkour?”

“Yeah. Of course. Me and my brothers used to try it all the time. I didn’t know you did anything with it.”

“They’ve been helping me improve. I have to come up here for a full workout of my skills. My rock-climbing wall wasn’t cutting it.”

“Okay. I’m gonna change. All right?”

“Yeah, go ahead. Help yourself any time you’re here.”

I enter the apartment and change quickly in the bathroom. It’s weird that she keeps this whole place just for the gym. It seems like it would be cheaper to join a commercial gym. I suppose she wouldn’t be able to climb in the rafters though.

When I get back to the gym area, she’s sitting on the bed of the truck checking out my new bike. The music is lower, and she hears me approaching.

“Wow, it’s nice, and much newer than mine. Did you get a good deal?”

“Yeah. The dude was asking a reasonable number, and I offered just under asking. I’m happy, but I’m just about broke for a few months.”

She stands and her long legs are encased in yoga pants and a sport’s bra which barely contains her breasts. I try to look anywhere but her chest.

“Sometimes it’s better to be cash poor and bike rich.” She smiles a bright smile that lights up her dark eyes.

“I can’t argue with that.” I smile in return. Then I remember I hate her and direct my attention to the gym equipment. “I’m gonna warm up.”

Her smile falls, but she recovers, “Yeah, go for it. I’m gonna make another round up top.”

She jumps from the bed onto the rock-climbing wall and scurried up to the beam above in no time. I step onto the treadmill and begin a slow run. I increase my speed until I’m at a full run.

Without my brothers to spot me I debate what to do next. When I scan the equipment, I spot Violet wearing purple gloves and punching and kicking the heavy bag.

Austin told me she does MMA, and they spar with her. Curious, I don some gloves of my own and begin hitting the speed bag. After a while I feel her eyes on me and I show off a little, maybe to intimidate her.

"Do you want to spar?" she asks.

"Sure. Should we put on headgear?"

"Definitely. There's some over there for you." She points to a cabinet. She opens another cabinet and pulls out matching purple headgear and a mouthpiece. I find a black set in the cabinet, there's also red and blue sets. I gear up, remove my shoes, and stretch out a little before joining her on the mat.

She holds up her fists and I hold up mine in response. I don't want to hurt her even though I don't like her. I wait for her to make a move. She sizes me up and steps to the side. I think she's going to just spin us in a circle for a minute, but she surprises me with a feint left to my chin and a kick to my unguarded side. My breath explodes out of me and before I can catch another, she hits my ear with a hook and then my chin with an uppercut, she finishes me off with a roundhouse kick that catches the back of my knee and when it gives, I fall.

She backs off and I feel like a frustrated chump. Holy fuck, the chick can fight, and she hits hard. When I catch my breath, I stand and look her over. She's difficult to read, her movements are quick and by the time I realized a hit was coming I was feeling it.

I remove my mouth guard, "I thought I needed to take it easy on you, being my brother's girlfriend and all. I had no idea they meant they actually spar with you."

She removes hers and says, "You thought that because I'm a girl, don't try to sugar coat your bias. Yeah, they actually spar with me, and I don't go easy on them." She smiles a twisted little grin at me and replaces her mouth guard.

"Okay. My mistake, it won't happen again." I replace my mouth guard and hold up my hands. Regardless of her strength or skill, she's smaller than me. I have a longer reach and more muscle mass. Her advantage is her speed. Trying to adjust to her swift moves I strike fast, a combination to her head then a kick. She avoids my hits, and I graze her with my foot, causing absolutely no damage. She assaults me quickly with three kicks, on the last I block her foot and knock her off balance. I take advantage of my lead and aim for her chin. I catch her jaw as she ducks my hit. She returns an uppercut and hits my chin. My mouth guard does its job and saves my teeth from crashing together painfully.

She goes all in and starts pounding on me with hit after hit and a few kicks while I try to fend her off and hit back. It's too bad nobody's here to witness this epic battle. I'm actually feeling winded and she's relentless. The gods finally smile upon me and somehow through my inept fighting against someone so much smaller, I finally catch her with a good kick, and she falls back. I thank my lucky stars and celebrate the break from her attack. She's like a pissed off badger.

I put my mouth guard in my headgear and rest my hands on my knees while I catch my breath. She removes hers and puts it on her stomach. She takes a few deep breaths and laughs. I watch her guard bounce on her toned abs.

"What's funny? I kicked your ass."

She laughs harder and catches her mouth guard before it can fall off her middle. She sits up and pops it into her head gear still chuckling. When she lifts her arm, I spot a weird black tattoo in her armpit with a gnarly looking scar in the middle.

"You did not kick my ass! You got lucky and made one good strike at the exact right moment. Don't let it go to your head. Want to go another round?"

"Fuck no."

"See, you can't even handle three rounds."

I rip off my shirt and wipe sweat from my face. She's not wrong, but I won't admit it out loud. It definitely felt good fighting with her, exercised some of my dislike for her. When I look at her again, she's staring at my chest, I look down to see what she's looking at. She startles and hops up, her cheeks pink. She holds her gloves up to me to bump with mine, and I catch sight of that black mark again. I bump her gloves and begin taking mine off.

She walks to her water bottle and takes off her gear. I get mine off and chug some water while contemplating what to say next. She begins wiping down her gear with sanitizer and I grab a couple of the wipes and do the same.

"Do you do anything special with the mouth guards?" I ask.

"Yeah, I run them through the dishwasher. The top shelf doesn't melt them."

"Can I ask you a personal question?"

She freezes, then says, "Sure. What's up?"

"You don't have to answer, I was just wondering what's with the black tattoo under your arm?"

She looks surprised, then troubled before she answers, "Oh, botched tattoo, from a guy in school."

"Ah, like a drunken dare gone wrong?"

"Something like that. I'm getting it covered up. I was wondering where you got yours done, they're really nice."

Oh, that's what she was looking at dumb ass. Like she would find anything about you attractive when she has two boyfriends. I want to punch myself. I feel so stupid.

"I got this arm done in Japan, and most of this arm in Kenya and South Africa. This one on my chest was Indonesia."

"What about this dragon? What does it say?" She points at the dark winged beast that goes from my chest over my shoulder.

"Okinawa, it says roughly: Only villains walk without fear."

"Cool. I like it." She smiles at me and she's way too close. I can smell her, maybe it's her shampoo, it's fruity like apples. I catch myself before I lean in and sniff her hair. Her eyes meet mine and her head tilts like she's thinking about me, trying to figure me out, then her eyes land on my lips and rest there for a minute. She shakes her head and steps back, but I'm not done.

"Can I take a closer look at your tattoo mistake?"

"Oh, um, yeah, I guess." She raises her arm by lifting her bent elbow. I step closer and examine the strange black rectangle with a bit of red surrounding the scar in the middle. It looks fairly fresh; it can't be more than a couple months old. What did she do? Why did she do it? It must've hurt like fuck under her arm like that. Maybe it was some kind of hazing. Was the scar there first and she wanted to cover it? I have so many questions.

"What happened in the middle of it?"

"It's a scar, I'm going to cover all of it. I'm looking for the right image to cover how dark it is."

"What do you like? What are you considering?"

"I love Pegasus, but he's a white horse and wouldn't cover anything, I haven't figured it out yet. I've been waiting for it to completely heal so I can get it done."

"I have a book of tattoo designs if you want to look at it for some ideas."

"Sure. Thanks." She smiles at me and my dick twitches. The door opens and bangs closed. My brothers come in and we step away from each other awkwardly.

"Did you guys finish?" Austin asks.

"Did you spar?" Jackson asks.

Not sure who to answer, I say, "Yeah."

Violet answers too, "Yeah." We exchange a grin and Jackson looks between us.

"Damn! Wish I could've seen her kick your ass!" Austin exclaims.

"Who says she kicked my ass?"

"Babe, did you kick his ass?" Jackson asks, looking at Violet.

"Not really, it was a good match."

“She’s being polite because she definitely kicked my ass, but I got a lucky shot at the end,” I admit.

Austin grabs her into a hug, “That’s our beautiful badass.” He kisses her lips and along her jaw, then pulls her close again. He finishes covering her in kisses with his arm wrapped around her and his hand resting on her firm, curved hip. Jackson leans in and kisses her lips, and I find myself imagining her in bed with the three of us. It’s intense and hot, making my dick grow hard.

I quickly take her mouth guard and turn away from them as I say, “I’m gonna grab a quick shower, I’ll put these in the dishwasher while I’m up there.” I take off as fast as I can and jog up the stairs. When Jackson calls out, I pretend not to hear.

“Wait a second bro, we want to check out your bike!” Jackson calls out.

I dodge into the apartment, place the guards in the dishwasher, and strip off while the shower heated. I try to think about anyone other than Violet. Sabrina Carpenter doesn’t work, Gwen Stefani can’t hold my interest, Kate Upton is a no go, the bartender from Maybel's morphs into Violet just like everyone else. I give up and take my thoughts in hand as I step into the stream of hot water.

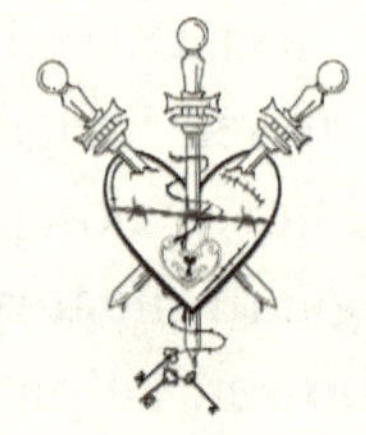

Chapter Seven

Violet

"What was that about?" Jackson asks.

I shrug and guess, "Maybe he was embarrassed I kinda did kick his ass."

"No doubt. Let's look at it without him," Austin suggested.

They open the truck bed and climb up to get a closer look. Austin sits on the leather seat and bounces a little. Jackson looks over the engine and nods to himself.

"He said he got a good deal, only has about four thousand miles," I offer.

"It looks great, I only see a small scratch on the tank. I love the midnight blue. I thought it was black."

"He seemed happy with his purchase, but he said he's broke now," I share.

"Yeah, he told me his money is locked into a high interest term account through the Navy National Credit Union, he's earning great interest, but he can't access his money until the rollover period without massive fines. He says the Navy encouraged the guys without families to invest their earnings and even offered a little bonus if they took the offer. Since he wasn't planning to leave the military yet, he thought it was a great way to add to his nest egg. Kind of like a 401k plan for corporations," Austin explains.

"That sounds like a smart investment unless your plans change. I still need to meet that investment manager that Krewe and Uncle Randy recommended. I don't care for money talk, but Uncle Randy wants me to do it. I know it's important, I just hate it."

"We'll go with you if you want. Austin's pretty good with all the money stuff, he pays attention. He could probably help you ask some good questions. I don't know much beyond how to balance my checkbook and pay my bills, but I'll go for moral support."

I lean in and kiss his temple. He's still looking at the engine and is seated inside the bed of the truck, for once I'm taller than him. He's so sweet, I admire him for a moment, his face is tense with concentration as he appreciates the bike.

"Are you guys going to work out?" I ask.

"It's getting a little late, aren't you hungry, Baby?" Austin questions.

"Yeah, do you want to go out or cook?"

"I can cook or whatever you want."

"I think we're gonna skip the workout today so we can get you fed. We burned up a ton of calories at work in the sun," Jackson adds to Austin's offer to cook. We put away the equipment and by the time Pierson returns fresh from his shower, we're ready to head out.

"We decided to go home and have dinner. Are you ready?" Austin asks Pierson.

"Yep."

"Nice bike by the way." Jackson smiles at him.

"I can't wait to take it on the road. Do you guys want to take a ride later?"

"Yes," I answer before anyone else can say anything. "Why don't you unload it and ride it home? Jackson can drive his truck."

"Yeah, come on, we'll get it down," Austin offers.

I hit the button for the overhead door. Jackson lowers the tailgate then he and Pierson get the ramp set up. Austin hops into the bed and straddles the bike.

"I get to drive it down!" He calls.

"Yeah, okay. But you better not fuck it up."

We all step back and watch as Austin starts the beautiful midnight blue machine. It comes to life with a smooth roar. Austin guides it carefully down the ramp and takes off up the alley. He makes a U-turn and comes right back.

"I just wanted to make sure she was facing the right direction," Austin explains with an innocent smile.

"Thanks. I couldn't have figured it out without you." Pierson gives him a smart-ass grin in return.

"You're welcome, bro, I'm happy to help. Okay, see you and Violet back at my place." Austin smirks. He gives me a kiss on the lips and pats Jackson's arm on his way out to his truck which I can see is parked on the street. Jackson kisses me and climbs into his cab.

Pierson waits for me to put on my helmet and jacket before I start my own bike. I type the code to close the overhead door into the keypad after Jackson pulls his truck out and we follow him to the street. He turns and we go after him, but once we're on the road we go faster. I keep pace with Pierson in case he has any trouble with the new bike.

When we stop at a red light I yell to him, "How's it going? Do you want to take the beach road to try her out on some curves?"

"Great! She's perfect. Yeah, let's take the long way," Pierson answers, nodding with a large smile across his face, it lights up his eyes with the most happiness I've seen from him.

When the light turns green, he makes his way into the left lane, and we turn towards the beach at the next intersection. I love driving on this road, especially this close to sunset, it's beautiful and peaceful. Pierson goes faster than I usually go on this route, but I have no trouble keeping up. When we pass the exit for a big mansion facing the water, a little red sports car speeds through the gate and comes within inches of hitting me. The guy honks at me and then blasts around Pierson by cutting over a double yellow line into oncoming traffic. A truck coming towards us slams on the brakes to keep from hitting the jerk head on. Then the jackass cuts back into our lane way too close to Pierson and floors his gas. Pierson waits for me to pull up next to him, and he slows below the speed limit.

"Are you all right?" he yells to be heard.

I nod, "Fine."

"Good, let's catch him." He doesn't wait for a reply and takes off. I have no issue with Pierson's speed, or his plan and I follow right behind him.

I can see the red car ahead weaving in and out of traffic. Pierson goes around a few cars at a safe distance. I continue to copy his moves. When we get behind the shiny little car, we stay with him, he eventually turns into a parking lot, and when he parks in a space Pierson blocks him in. I figure if the guy's crazy he might try plowing through Pierson's bike, so I park in a spot of my own to keep my beauty safe.

"What the fuck do you want?" The man is balding with a swoop-over, a fat gold chain, and a pinky ring. The little bit of hair he has is white while his skin is far too implausibly tanned and I'm guessing he visits a spray on tan shop a little too often.

"I'd like for you to apologize to my...friend. You almost hit her coming out of that gate!"

"I didn't see anyone. I'm not apologizing for shit. Move out of my way!"

Pierson doesn't move, crossing his arms he stares down at the guy with a fierce look. A seagull screeches above us and when I look up at the sound, I accidentally look at the sun. I don't have my sunglasses because the visor on my helmet is tinted. Before I can do anything to stop it, my nose twitches, my throat itches, and I sneeze.

"Achoo!"

Both men turn and look at me. The disgusting older guy leers as his eyes look me up and down until they come to rest on my chest.

"God bless you, beautiful," he simpers.

"Gross. You're old enough to be my grandfather, have some respect."

"My mistake, you're only beautiful with your mouth closed. Once you speak, you're an ugly bitch."

"Now you owe her two apologies." Pierson looks ready to kill.

"Look Clark Kent, I don't owe anyone shit. If you don't move out of my way, I'll phone the authorities." The man waves his phone in Pierson's face. Almost forcing him to knock it from the asshole's hand, Pierson wraps his fingers around the clown's neck and shoves him against his own car.

Then Pierson leans down into the lame guy's face and growls between gritted teeth, "I'm not going to tell you again. Apologize, now."

"What the fuck? Fine! Sorry! There..., are you happy?" He releases the guy's throat.

"Not particularly." Looking my way, Pierson asks, "You good, Violet?"

"Always."

"Let's go." What a weird interaction, I'm not sure what prompted Pierson to demand an apology, and I consider his actions the rest of the way home.

I'm hungry by the time we arrive, and I'm excited to smell something cooking when I enter through the garage. Austin's chopping vegetables for a salad and Jackson is at the island supervising. He spots me and holds out his hand for me, I embrace him, and he kisses my cheek.

"Did you have a fun ride, babe?"

I look at Pierson and his face is a blank mask.

"Yeah, we took the scenic route, it's always beautiful."

"Not as beautiful as you," Austin chirps from further in the kitchen. I make my way over to him and check out what's boiling on the stove.

"You're sweet, handsome," I say as I lean up to kiss him, before he can respond his phone rings.

His brow lowers in concern as he reads who's calling. Checking in with Jackson adds to the worry, he looks equally concerned. Pierson sits next to Jackson, and we all watch as Austin answers.

"Hello? This is Austin Matthews," he says with a serious tone.

He listens for a moment before saying, "Yes. I am...okay...I will. Yes, thank you. Yes. Thank you. I will. Bye."

After he hangs up, he stands with his back to us and his head bowed and I immediately think it must've been bad news. But he turns around with a huge smile on his face.

"What happened?"

"It's Megan. She's ready to be discharged!"

"Holy shit!"

"For real?"

"Wow! That's amazing!"

"I know, I can't believe it. They want me to go up there and stay a few days to go over the things she'll need and help her transition to the outside; she wants me to be the one to do it. I'm going to need some time off work. I need to leave the day after tomorrow." He and Jackson have one of their silent conversations. I'm getting much better at deciphering those. I think Austin asked if Jackson is okay with him leaving and Jackson said yes. Then Austin asked what to do about me and Jackson said he's got it.

In answer to their unspoken words, I hug Austin. "Go. Do whatever you need to do, Jackson and I will be fine. Plus, Pierson is here, we'll just split your chores and Jackson and Pierson can do the game. If you come back soon, you can catch up. If not, we'll let you skip some tasks. Megan is more important, right guys?"

He hugs me back. "I love you, Baby. Okay, I'm going to get my sister."

The three brothers spent the rest of our night reminiscing about when they were younger before Megan was attacked. We laughed hard and we got quiet a few times when the memories were more painful. The thing I learned during all their stories was how much all three of them love their sisters. They've missed Megan much more than they let on and I hope everything goes well with her release.

Colby has been in and out of the mental health facility so many times there must be a revolving door in his room. He usually doesn't do well for long on the outside, though he's been out since just before my parents passed away. It's one of his longer stays on this side of the locked doors since I've known him. I had my parents to help me adjust to my life outside. Megan's parents are wonderful, but I have to wonder why she wanted Austin to help her instead of her mother.

I lie between the two large bodies of my guys wondering about what she'll be like and what might prevent her from contacting her mom for help. Angie is the sweetest person, maybe Megan's just closer to Austin. I hug him tight, and he stirs, pulling me against his warm chest. I begin to fade as I listen to his heartbeat.

I jolt awake when an alarm goes off and Jackson silences the ship's horn blast then rolls me on top of him. He looks into my sleepy eyes, and I feel like he can read my brain right through their dark lenses like there's a marquee announcing my thoughts. He smiles with a slight lift of the corners of his lips and kisses me.

"No, I have morning breath," I plead.

"Babe, I would kiss you if you had a mouth full of garlic and I was a vampire."

"Gross. But I would kiss you if I was a vampire too. Where's Austin?"

"He's so excited about Megan he got up an hour ago and started packing for his trip. He's probably cooking us meals for while he's gone or something. I told him to get out of here before he woke you up."

I kiss him again. "Thank you. I love that you keep me from killing him when he goes all morning person crazy. I don't know how I fell for a freaking psycho like him." He chuckles.

"I told you he's a pain in the ass, but you didn't want to listen." He squeezes my ass against him in emphasis. I look at his phone and it's time for me to get ready for class and he needs to get to work. Too bad.

"You know I'm stubborn. It's late so I'm going to have to wait until later to do what I want to do to you right now."

"Aww, Babe, can't you just be a little late? Now I'm imagining what you're going to do, and I won't be able to concentrate at work." He gives me his cutest smile that always works better than begging, he knows I can't say no.

"Compromise...meet me in the shower in two minutes."

As soon as I step into the shower, I hear the door open. I smile as I stand under the hot water. A large hand grasps my hip and moves me out of the water while another starts massaging shampoo into my scalp. Then another hand rubs soap on my chest and I realize either Jackson has three hands, or both of my guys have joined me. I step back and rub against Jackson, then reach out with a hand and wrap my fingers around Austin's very erect cock in front of me.

"Mmmm, just what a girl needs for the perfect start to her day."

"Baby, seeing you when I wake up is always the perfect start to my day. Would you like to put my cock in your mouth?" Although it's not what I imagined originally, I'm nothing if not flexible. I bend over and suck his dick between my lips, and he lets out a satisfied groan. I use my ass to rub against Jackson's cock and encourage him to fuck me. He doesn't need much persuasion. He quickly gets the gist of my silent communication and plows into me. His dick is a solid rod as he presses into the slick arousal between my legs stretching me in the most pleasurable way. While he starts slowly moving in and out of me, the tip of his ample dick hits all the best places as he moves. My tongue encircles the head of Austin's cock as he pushes it into my throat with me pulling his hips to make it go deeper.

Jackson uses a soapy finger to explore my ass and at first, I freeze. But he's very gentle and just teases the rim. It actually feels nice when I relax. We haven't really talked about my ass, but we'll need to if he's interested. I know I can trust them with my sexual exploration, and I don't ever worry about something new. Because it's them, I'm willing to try anything.

"Oooh, Baby, I'm going to come!"

"Mmmm," I focus on getting his cock as far as possible down my throat. His movements become erratic, and I know he's about to fall over the cliff. My excitement makes Jackson's efforts all the more intense and I'm getting close. My pussy tightens and begins to throb while Jackson pounds into me in response.

"Babe, your pussy is perfection, it's squeezing me so good!"

"Yes! Baby!" Austin roars as his cum shoots down my throat. I climax because they're coming, and I can't scream out with my mouth full, so I make a strangled sound of pleasure.

Jackson growls out, "Yessss..." and his cum fills me causing my orgasm to spark harder. I feel it in my bones all the way to my toes and I make a squealing noise around Austin's softening flesh in my mouth. The three of us tremble and shudder as we come down from our group arrival.

"Baby, you're the best. I love you."

"I love you too. And you, Jackson, I love you."

"I love you too Babe. Let me wash you." Just like that, I'm off to a great start to my day.

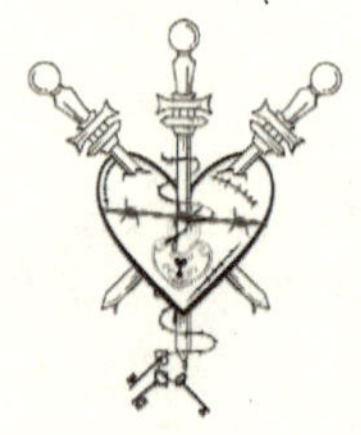

Chapter Eight

Pierson

They're at it again and I can't take it. Listening to them fucking is fucking with me and I need to leave. I toss the rest of my breakfast and grab my helmet. I'm so glad I bought my own ride so I can leave when I want. I rev my new bike making her roar like a lioness and head to the jobsite. I don't even notice the cars around me, I'm too busy fighting the images of her in my head and the tent in my pants.

Trying my best to think about anything else, Megan comes to mind. It's surreal that she's coming home. I've never been able to visit her. Mom has seen her the most, but even she hasn't made the trek more than half a dozen times. Megan just wasn't ready for visitors, at least that's how mom explained it. I wonder what she looks like now. She used to be beautiful, just a wholesome girl next door, with a fresh face and wild curls. Apparently, she takes after her father where Austin looks more like mom with lighter hair and eyes.

When I park at the jobsite my thoughts focus on my work, and I manage to put the females in my life aside for the rest of the day. At lunch Austin left, he said he had some errands to run before he leaves tomorrow but I suspect he's going to try to complete the first task in our game. Lucky for him, the boss was okay with him taking off for a family emergency. In his absence I'll be assigned to work with Jackson, learning some new tasks and I'm happy to get away from the grunt work I've been doing.

At the end of the day, I get a minute with Jax, "Hey, I'm going to make a stop on my way home. You guys don't need to wait for me to eat."

"Going to the game coordinates?"

"How'd you know?" I ask and don't include I'd be happy working late to keep from going home where she'll be.

"I'd be headed there myself if Austin wasn't leaving tomorrow. But I want to get home and make sure he's got everything he needs and check if there's anything I need to do with the house, that type of thing."

"And check on Violet?"

"Yeah, I guess." He tilts his head and examines my face.

"So, you'll let them know I'll be late?"

"Sure thing. See you." He walks towards his truck.

"Later," I call at his back, then putting on my helmet I climb onto my bike. I start her up and revel in the rumble of her engine. Next, I type the coordinates into my phone and click it into the holder in the middle of her handlebars.

It's a ways off the beaten path and I haven't passed another car in miles. When I pull up to the entrance of the dirt lot I look around. There's one car parked in the farthest space from the beach path. I park my bike and remove my helmet. Placing it on my seat I stretch and crane my neck to see down the path. Lo and behold, I can see a bare foot sticking out by what looks like a bench, but

I can't be certain from this angle. I pull up the clue on my phone and read it again.

You will meet a person there who requires assistance. If you can figure out how to help them, you'll receive your next task. You may need to search your sole for the right thing to do.

Good luck!

I shrug and walk the path towards the stranger on the bench. When I get closer, I can see a man who doesn't look dressed for the sunny weather. He appears to be wearing more than one shirt, covered by a hoodie. He's also wearing jeans that appear worn and dirty. His feet are bare and filthy, they look to be covered in calluses and dirt from a long walk without shoes. He's sitting upright on the bench under a large Oak tree. His face is tilted down, and he seems to be asleep. When I'm close enough to touch him if I wanted to, I stop and see a book in his lap. I think he's reading but his dark glasses don't reveal if I'm right. His bushy brown beard is storing some crumbs from his last meal. He doesn't acknowledge me.

"Ahem. Hey, are you the person who has the clue?"

He still doesn't look at me, I can see he's breathing so he's not dead.

I try again, "I'm Pierson. What's your name?" Nothing.

"Um, do you need my help?" He closed the book, removed his shades, and faced me.

"Yes." That's all. His cloudy eyes stare at me while his cracked and peeling lips remain sealed. It's creepy.

"How can I help you?" I try.

"I need to go to the bench at the end of the path, but I'm unable to walk there," he says expectantly.

"How can I help you get there?"

"That's the riddle of it now, isn't it?" A twinkle glows in mysterious faded eyes.

Play our game, they said, it'll be fun they said. I need to focus.

"Why can't you walk there?" I ask, hopeful I'll get a reasonable answer.

"My feet are sore, and the sand is too hot," the man explains.

"Do you know how far it is to the bench?" I question further.

His lips press together as he shakes his head from side to side. I think he feels sorry for me. I wonder if he feels bad that I'm dumb and can't figure out what to do or because I got roped into this stupid game. Not sure what else I should be asking, I decide to walk to the next bench and see how far it is. It's about a hundred and fifty yards away and it's also nestled under some trees. These might be sea grape trees with their large circular waxy leaves and deadly looking clusters of grapes. They're along a sand dune, and at the peak, I can see out across the white sugar of the beach sand to the Gulf waters lazily rolling on the shore. The water line is interspersed with some large rocks and clusters of mangrove trees.

I walk back to the man weighing my options on how to get him to the bench. When I stand in front of the man, I have an idea, and I hope it'll work.

"Am I allowed to get you there by any means or do I have to find a specific way to accomplish the task?" His head tilts again and I can only assume he's looking me over and deciding how to answer from behind his dark glasses once again perched on his face.

"You may. However, if you fail to help me get to the bench, you'll have to start over."

"Okay. I'll be right back." I cross the lot and climb onto my bike. I place my helmet between my thighs and ride over to the guy on the bench.

"Put on this helmet and get on. Be extra careful of the exhaust pipes, you could get a serious burn if you touch them with your foot," I say as I press my helmet into his hands. He pulls it onto his head and with a large smile, he mounts my new bike, carefully as instructed.

"Hold onto my shoulders so you don't fall."

I rev my engine and take off down the path to the other bench. When we reach the specified bench, I find a relatively solid piece of ground and when he dismounts, I engage the kickstand. Once I'm convinced it's solid enough to hold, I climb off. He takes a step and sits on the bench, then he opens his book.

"Dude, don't you have a clue for me now?" I question.

"Take my photo and email it to the Game Master, he'll send you the next clue."

"The Game Master? Did he tell you to call him that?"

"Yes," he answers matter of factly. I can't help rolling my eyes before I snap his photo with my phone.

I take a last look around and before I leave, I want to know, "What's your name?"

"Andrew, you can call me Andy."

"Nice to meet you, Andy. Thanks for your help."

"It's been fun."

"Do you need anything? A drink? Some money?"

"Nah, the Game Master is compensating me quite well but thank you for your kind offer."

"All right, take it easy."

"Yeah, you too."

I maneuver my bike around so I can go back the way I came. I give him a motorcycle salute as I pass his reading bench, carefully avoiding getting bogged down in any loose sand and I make it safely into the parking lot. As I breathe a sigh of relief hitting the hard packed lot, it's short lived. A siren chirps from the corner of the lot then red and blue lights flash. *Motherfucker!* When the bulky bodybuilder squeezed into a police uniform reaches me, he signals for me to shut down my bike.

When I remove my helmet, he finally says, "Did you miss the sign that says: *No motorized vehicles on the path*?"

"I guess I did. I'm sorry I didn't see it." I glance at the entry for the path and notice a rusted sign completely wrapped in vines that are turning brown. The words on the sign aren't visible, except for one in faded red, Vehicles, in the middle of the white rectangle.

"Looks like the sign could use some maintenance, it's not easy to spot."

"Ignorance of the law is no excuse. I'll need your license, insurance, and registration."

"I just bought it, I only have a temporary. I'm waiting for the official tag and registration in the mail."

"So, you don't have the registration?"

"No sir. I have the temporary paperwork and tag." I step off the bike, lift the seat and start rummaging around until I pull out what I have. "Here you go." I hand the papers to him.

"I'll be right back." He turns on his heel and climbs back into his truck in the air conditioning while I sit in the shade free parking lot with my black bike that's as hot as a skillet despite the calendar claiming it's fall.

After what feels like an eternity, he returns with my documents and hands them to me with a two hundred fifty-dollar ticket for, "Unauthorized use of a motorized vehicle on a pedestrian marked path." What a great fucking day. Shit! I don't have the funds for this. I thank him and ride towards home. No longer feeling the excitement of solving the riddle and completing the task successfully, I take the most direct route and feel a sense of relief when I pull into the garage. At least this day can't get any worse.

When I enter the kitchen, I don't see anyone even though there's steam rising from a pot on the stove at an alarming rate. Continuing on towards my room planning to change out of my sweaty work clothes, I almost get plowed over by Austin.

He hurls a, "Hey, man," at me on his way past.

"What's up?" I shout at his back before he disappears around the corner.

"Hang on-" fades as he vanishes. I continue on my way and make it to my room without any more close encounters. But as I pull my shirt over my head, something rubs against my leg. Actually someone, Violet's annoying cat, is in my room which means either I left the door open or someone else opened the door. I know I closed my door. It's a habit I've always had, I think it's from when I was a kid and my mom was always fighting with some guy she brought home. I was afraid my friends would hear her, and I always made sure the door was closed.

"Why are you in my room?" I ask the intruder.

He surprised me and made a sound like he wanted to answer. *Meow!*

"I don't care why you came in, but I need you to get out, I don't like cats. My mom told me cats steal baby's breath because they eat bad children's souls." You couldn't believe anything she said so I didn't, but years later, in the Navy, another soldier said the same thing. I mean, I don't believe it, but it freaked me out for a few days. The damn cat just sits there looking at me like I'm not doing what it wants. This is why I hate cats; a dog would just wag its tail and follow me to the door.

"Dude, move it. Please don't make me pick you up, it's bad enough you probably laid all over my shit. Ah man, you got your hair all over my pillow, didn't you?" His green eyes narrow and I'm pretty sure he's putting some type of hex on me. Fuck, I'm going to have to pick up his fuzzy ass.

"All right man, you chose to ignore me. Trust me when I say this won't be pleasant for either of us." I reach down and lift him trying not to touch his body to mine. Thankfully nobody is filming this because I'm pretty sure I look ridiculous holding him out as far as my arms will stretch. I open the door with my elbow and place him in the hallway.

"And don't come back," I warn him.

"What happened? Why was Sawyer in your room?" I startle at her voice. I was too focused on avoiding cat fur and didn't see her.

"Oh, uh, he was in here when I came in. I don't want him in my room, I don't like cat hair on my stuff. Can you keep him out of my space?" Now she looks startled.

"I'm sorry. Wait, let me rephrase that. I'm sorry?"

"I said keep your damn cat out of my room!" I snap. Anger is suddenly pounding in my veins. That fucking ticket!

"Look, Pierson, I'm trying my best to be nice to you despite how you're treating me. I'm trying because I love Austin and Jackson, and you're their brother but make no mistake, nobody mistreats Sawyer."

"I didn't, I wasn't...look, I don't like cats, but I'd never harm an innocent animal no matter how much they annoy me. I carefully carried him to the hallway and gently placed him on the floor."

"That's not how I heard it."

"I know. I mean, I told him not to come back in an unkind voice, but I was just hoping to make him understand I don't want him in my room. I did not harm your cat."

"I know you didn't, just now." She's looking at me with ice in her veins. Her dark eyes look sharp enough to nail me to a wall. I guess I found her soft spot. Good. Maybe she'll quit trying to chat with me.

I stand up a little straighter growing a little taller, I throw my shoulders back and stand my ground with almost a sneer on my face. Her eyes rapidly scan my demeanor, her own shoulders go back, and her chest puffs out. When her eyes stutter on my bare chest, I can only believe it was my imagination because when they meet mine, they're hard and cold.

"Be warned, if you hurt Sawyer I'll hurt you." She begins to turn away but I'm in a mood, damn that fucking ticket! I'm not thinking about my brothers at all. My frustration over the woman in front of me is at an all-time high. I mean it's her stupid friend who sent me there, his stupid impossible task. What the fuck was I supposed to do, carry the guy on my back? Fuck I'm fucking pissed about that two hundred and fifty bucks I don't have! Something is tingling in my brain, my brothers always said I had Spidey-sense. It's an uncomfortable itch I can't scratch, and I don't know why it's happening unless I'm subconsciously trying to prevent my next words from exiting my mouth.

"Who the fuck do you think you are? Don't fucking threaten me. You know just because you live here it doesn't make you the commanding officer of this house. This is my brother's house and if I have my way, you won't be here much longer." Wow, I shouldn't have said that, but I'm not one to back down especially when my temper has sparked.

She turns towards me again and her hands land on her curved hips, "You know what, Piers? You just stay away from me, and I'll stay away from you." Her lips purse and her eyes narrow in barely contained murder. "Unless you hurt Sawyer." With that she spins around and stomps off.

I feel sick. I'm furious, I'm guilty, and I'm ready to run to get away from her. I close myself back in my room and finish changing while I calm down. Once my anger is tolerable the guilt gets worse. Don't get me wrong, I don't feel guilty about what I said to Violet, she deserved it. Who the fuck is she to threaten me? Nope. I feel like shit because I'm actively trying to ruin their relationship. My brothers' relationship, where they say they love her, and share her, and fuck her every fucking day. Yep, I'm an asshole, but if I don't get her out of here, I'm going to do something even stupider and then their relationship will be fucked anyway.

When there's a knock on my door, I jump up expecting I'll need to apologize. But it's Austin, not Violet at my door.

"Dinner's going to be ready in like five minutes. Are you cool with me going to help Megan?" he blurts.

"Yeah, of course. She asked for you, you're the one who needs to go. I just want what's best for her and if I can help, I'm there. She's my sister too."

"Yeah, she is. I'll keep you guys posted and call me if you need anything, okay?"

"Yeah. Hey, do you ever think about what happened to Megan?"

"Of course. What's up?" he asks, concerned. His eyes bounce between mine searching for clarification I suppose.

"I just, sometimes I think about killing that asshole priest. He deserves to die for what he did, and you know she's not the only one, I just want to tear his guts out. I mean, like actually kill him dead. Do you ever feel that way?"

Austin looks a little pale as he clears his throat, "Ahem. No, I'm sure she's not the only one. I do think about his death and I'm not hating it. But the thing is, the guy's already dead."

I can feel my jaw fall open, "What? What happened? I mean how?" I can't believe it, on one hand it's great news. On the other hand I didn't get to inflict my own brand of torture on that piece of shit.

"The uh, police aren't sure because uh, he's just missing right now. But they uh, found a suicide note, so, um, he killed himself. Which sucks because yeah, he deserves the worst torture a guy could imagine. Hopefully, he suffered a lot." He grins as he says that last part. Something is definitely off, and my Spidey-sense is tingling again. He didn't really answer me when I asked if he would actually want to kill him. It's weird because we've been plotting his death since we found out, and he always gets graphic with what he would do if he had the chance. I try to ask him about it but Jax interrupted.

"Dinner's ready you guys!" he yells. I take a deep breath and follow Austin to the dining room.

"Is there anything you need before I go?" Austin asks me when we reach the table.

"Nah, I'm good, thanks. Just tell Megan I love her and I'm excited to see her soon."

"You got it." He pats my shoulder as we separate to reach our chairs.

Jackson is seated, we join him, and I look over the spread. I'm not sure who cooked, but it looks delicious and I'm starving. I love

Italian food and spaghetti is my favorite, especially with meatballs. I help myself to the salad and shove a forkful of green stuff in my mouth, it crunches loudly and I don't hear Violet approach. I look up and there she is and she's smiling pleasantly. Maybe she's back to treating me like one of three brothers and a guest. I try offering her a tentative smile and she completely ignores me. Her eyes sweep past me without any connection at all. It's as if she's erased me from her sight and I'm invisible to her. It makes a sharp pain lance through my chest which spreads down my arms and crushes my ribs as if my heart is being crushed inside by the angry fist of death.

I look down and stab my fork into another clump of green things, it drips some dressing back into the blue bowl, I bring it to my lips without lifting my eyes.

"Do you have everything you need before you go?" Jackson asks.

Austin answers, "Yeah, I don't need anything else. Is there anything I need to show you guys before I leave? I feel like there should be so many things to tell you, but I can't think of anything. I guess you should be able to reach me if anything comes up. I want to get to bed soon since I'm heading out early." He looks pointedly at Jackson whose eyes crinkle at the corners, and he grins like he knows a secret. I start on the spaghetti and it's the perfect temperature to shove too much in my mouth and finish as fast as possible.

"You got it. I'll take care of the dishes for you even though it's your turn and you're leaving us here to do all of your chores," Jackson teases him.

"Thanks man. I'll owe you."

"Don't worry about it. When I win the game, you'll be doing all of my chores anyways."

"Not so fast, I'm planning on winning, I'm already on the second clue," Violet interjects. My eyes snap to her face and she's looking at Jackson with mischief and something affectionate. He smiles at her and when he looks ready to retort, but Austin cuts in.

"Wow, Baby! That's impressive, I don't even know when you found the time. Congratulations." There's no mistaking the love on his face or the pride in his voice. I refrain from making any comment, it seems like a good time to slurp in another fork full of noodles and tomato sauce. I wonder if either of my brothers have been to see Andy yet. Then my gaze falls once again on the outwardly beautiful enigma that is Violet. How did she get him to the other bench? Knowing her, she probably wished it and the forces that be just moved him magically to the other bench. I can feel my anger flare the embers in my chest back to a smoldering glow at the thought. She gets whatever she wants, everyone loves her, and my brothers think she walks on water. She makes me crazy. One minute I want to put on my gloves and punch her in the nose and the next I'm trying to keep myself from touching her. I drop my fork, and it clatters on my plate.

"Piers, what's up?" Jackson asks. When I look his way, his face is pinched with concern. Shit, I didn't mean to get everyone's attention. But I don't have Violet's attention, she's smiling at Austin while she spins her fork in the noodles on her plate like I don't exist, and I never made a sound.

"Sorry. It slipped. I'll give you a hand with the dishes." I hop up and awkwardly collect my plate and a hot pot of red sauce. I can feel Jackson's eyes follow me to the kitchen. Not wanting to face her again I busy myself in the kitchen putting things away, wiping surfaces, rinsing dishes that were stacked in the sink.

Eventually, Jackson joins me and judging by the number of plates in his stack of dishes, Austin and Violet are finished eating. I confirm they've left the table when I check for more dishes. Maybe I can talk to Jax about how I'm feeling.

"Is that everything?" he asks when I step back into the kitchen.

"Yeah, this is the last of the dishes, but I didn't wipe down the table yet. Did you want me to save the leftover noodles?" I ask, indicating the platter I just brought in.

"Add it to the sauce and stir it up, it keeps the noodles from getting hard or sticking together. Spaghetti is the only thing Violet knows how to make, and she doesn't like to cook so we save it for leftovers. We can have it again this week or maybe make meatball sandwiches with a side of pasta." I inspect him. He looks like my brother but the words leaving his mouth sound nothing like him.

"What?" Jackson asks, rubbing his face like he thinks there must be some food on his cheek. "Why are you looking at me weird?"

"Do you hear yourself? You sound like a pussy-whipped loser. What the fuck happened to you? You're all domestic and shit," he chuckles, and it makes me more pissed off. That fucking bitch is destroying my family.

"You're ridiculous. I am domesticated, douchebag. I live in a house with a woman, and I don't want to live in a pig pen. What's the big deal with talking about leftovers?"

"It's just you sound like such a wimp; I'm not used to you like this. I remember the beer drinking, skirt chasing, fun asshole you used to be. Now you're about to sell me Tupperware or some shit, it's fucked up bro." He laughs and I don't think he's getting my point.

"I'm still your brother dick head, I'm just a little more mature than I used to be. It happens when people grow older, you know."

"But that's the point. You act like you're in your thirties and you're ready to get married and have kids. It's disturbing. I figured we'd be going out every night meeting girls, playing pool, having fun you know? Instead, we're doing dishes discussing leftovers. You're too young to be this domestic."

"I guess I've changed. I love Violet and I don't need to go out and party, I'm happy hanging out with her. You know you're welcome to hang out with us or go out and party if that's what you want to do," he offers, but he's not getting it.

"You don't understand. I was hoping to have lots of brother time like we used to. Remember Terry Parker's party? Or that time the carnival was in town over Halloween? Or what about the time we stayed out all night at the lake with the Fuller twins? You can't tell me that wasn't fun!"

"It was fun. But now I like to have fun that includes Violet. She's not opposed to going out and doing things you know. You're making it sound like we've joined the seminary to become priests or something. Violet took us to a college party with her school friends and we do other fun things, like going to the range, riding our bikes, and we practiced parkour in town at some abandoned buildings. We do lots of things that beats any of the stuff you just named."

A sigh forces its way out of me, he's never going to understand. I take a sponge and leave the kitchen to wipe down the table while he works on the leftovers. I can't watch him right now.

While I'm finishing up, I hear a distant shout of pleasure. I guess Violet and Austin are saying goodbye. Doesn't it bother Jackson? I decide I'm going to ask him, and I stomp back into the kitchen.

"Does it bother you when she's with him?" He turns and looks at me with his head tilted slightly, his eyes bore into mine and I feel like he's reading my mind.

"No. We're both in a relationship with her but it doesn't always need to be both of us. I love her but I love him like a brother too. I want them both to be happy and if they want to be intimate when I'm not there it's up to them. Plus, he asked me if it was cool if they said goodbye alone for a while. Which he never needs to ask, but since we're in this together with Violet, we respect each other."

"He told me the priest killed himself."

"Yeah, that's what they think happened. There was a scandal and some criminals were arrested, a trafficking ring was broken up, and they think he was involved somehow."

"I really wanted to kill him myself. You know how I explained what happened with my discharge, I've had this urge to hunt down the guy who hurt Megan since even before then."

"You're serious. You want to actually kill a child molester?"

"Yeah. I think I could do it without any remorse."

"You wouldn't feel bad taking a life? Have guilt?"

"No. I have some experience I'm not allowed to discuss but I wouldn't have any guilt if I ended a bad guy and saved some innocent victims from him."

"It would be different outside of a military sanctioned mission."

"Not really. I'd still be fine ending a sick fucker who was harming kids or women, actually anyone who didn't consent."

"Interesting." He doesn't elaborate and I'm ready to call it a night. I grab a beer and say goodnight, then head to my room.

Chapter Nine

Violet

I watch as Austin drives away and the twinge in my chest hurts at the thought of not seeing him for at least a few days. The door opens behind me and then a warm arm wraps around my shoulders. Jackson smells like masculine soap, a clean scent of leather, hay, and wood shavings. He leans his head on mine and his hand slides to my waist. The twinge eases and I feel safe and secure in his embrace.

"Come in and have some breakfast with me before we need to go."

As we make our way to the kitchen his phone chimes, a moment later mine chirps. We both check our phones, and I'm surprised to see a message from Jackson and Austin's youngest sister, Tori. She's never messaged me before.

"Shit." Jackson says ominously.

"Did she text you too?"

"I've got a phone message from mom. She called you too?"

"No. Tori texted; I didn't read it yet."

"Hang on, let's call mom first." He dials by putting her on speaker, and she answers out of breath.

"Oh, Jackson! I'm at my wits end with that girl. I think she's trying to give me a heart attack. You won't believe what she did! She snuck out of the house and went to a boy's house in the middle of the night!" In the background we can hear Tori yelling.

"I went with two other girls! I didn't do anything! I didn't drink or smoke, I just played video games! You're not being fair!" BAM! The door slams.

"Mom, why don't you calm down. Did she go with other kids?"

"Yes, I think so."

"Did she drink or smoke?"

"Well, no. She didn't smell like alcohol or smoke. But..."

"How long did you ground her?"

"A month! She's been so disrespectful and now this. I've had it with her, she doesn't seem to understand what happened to Megan could happen to her. She needs to be careful and definitely not be out at all hours, without us even knowing she's left. It's not safe. Couldn't you come over and talk to her?"

"I can, but I have plans after work that will keep me for at least an hour. With Austin gone, work might be later than usual too." While they try to work out a plan I check the message from Tori.

Tori: Hey Violet. My mom is crazy. She grounded me over nothing. I really need to go to the mall this weekend. Do you think you could take me? I'm pretty sure she'll say yes if I'm going with you. I'll owe you big. Thx

Me: I'll talk to your mom. I think we might be over later.

*Tori: TY! You're a lifesaver! *heart emoji**

*Me: Cool *sunglasses emoji**

Jackson asks, "Are you free tonight to go see my parents?"

"Sure."

"What did Tori say?"

"The other side of the story. She wants me to take her to the mall."

"She's crafty. She knows mom won't say no if you ask to take her to the mall."

"We'll find out tonight. We're going to be late if we don't hurry." We make quick work of breakfast and when I head to our room to take a shower, I pass Pierson in the hallway. I ignore him and he didn't even look up. He pissed me off so bad yesterday I might never speak to him again. Well, that's probably not true because I love his brothers but, man is he an asshole. I still don't know what I did to him. We were almost getting along and then out of nowhere he threatened my cat and then went off on me.

I put him out of my mind and focus on school for the next eight hours or so. My classes are getting boring, they aren't teaching me anything new. The only fun is in Professor Kunal's class because we have a mystery project to decipher, and I love my friends. We laugh so hard at lunch and when we're supposed to be studying. Wyatt and Aiden are still my closest friends at school, but I like Riley too. Bug and Durango are nice, but I don't see them as much this semester.

When I'm finally making my way to my ride at the end of the day I think about the first clue in our game. The game with my guys and Pierson, the jackass. The first clue was pretty simple, and I had a good time talking to Andy. He's a physics genius who has some mental health struggles. Colby met him in the facility he frequents. Of course I didn't know any of that until Andy told me.

When I spoke to Andy and found out I needed to get him to the other bench I thought about the clue and decided I needed to do something specific for Andy. I took him shopping and bought him some shoes and socks, a backpack, some water, snacks, and books. He tried to convince me it wasn't necessary, but his feet were in rough shape and I wanted to help him beyond taking him to the other bench. When we got back to the park, we walked to the far bench together with his aching feet safely encased in comfy shoes.

"I can't thank you enough for the items you bought for me. I've been waiting for the library to get this book and now I have my own copy. You'll need to snap a picture of me for the Game Master," he told me while holding onto his personal copy of Well of Souls: Uncovering the Banjo's Hidden History.

I got my next clue this morning and I'm still mulling it over. It's more riddle than clue and I need to figure out where I need to go and what I need to do when I get there. I think about it all the way to Angie and Miguel's where I'm meeting Jackson. When I pull into their driveway my phone chimes with Austin's tone.

Auz: Hi baby, how was your day?

Me: Ok. I'm at your parent's now, meeting Jackson here. How's Megan?

Auz: It was a very short visit just to start. She looks good, older. She's not the same bubbly girl she was before what happened and she's not the sullen detached teenager she was after that. She's quiet and mature, it's weird.

Me: I'm sure she'll open up once she gets used to you. You probably seem old and weird to her too.

Auz: Wow, way to wound a guy. How freaking old do I look?

Me: You don't! I mean since she saw you last, she probably pictures the kid in her memory and the grown up you is weird for her.

Auz: I guess. It was awkward. The doctor has us doing a session with him in the morning. Says we need to build trust.

Me: Makes sense. Are you going to tell her about Voldemort?

Auz: I'll ask the doc if I should tell her he's gone and she's safe. I miss you!

Me: I missed you the second you drove away. I love you.

Auz: I love you too. Maybe when you get back home, we can try out some video sex?

*Me: *eye-roll emoji* Now I know what you miss most.*

*Auz: Every inch of you baby! *heart emoji**
*Me: Right back at you! *Kiss emoji* *eggplant emoji**
*Auz: *tongue emoji**

Chuckling at his antics I pocket my phone and take a deep breath bracing for whatever family drama awaits in the cute house before me. I lock my SUV and knock on the door, which is yanked open by Angie. She embraces me by pulling me into a tight hug.

"Violet! Thank God! Maybe you can talk some sense into that girl. Did Jackson tell you what she did?" She takes me into the living room and hasn't let go of my waist. We stop in front of the sofa and she's closely inspecting my face, it's making me self-conscious.

"I'm sure Tori just had a momentary teenage slip; she'll probably try harder now." That she's caught. I don't add what I truly think out loud. She's fifteen, normal teens think they're invincible at that age and they do stupid shit. I can most likely scare her straight but I'm not sure that's the best course of action. Some teens would probably take it as a challenge to see how much they could escape.

"Sit down sweetheart, I'll get us some appetizers and a drink. Be right back." I know there's no sense declining her offer from experience. As soon as she leaves the room, I hear a door down the hallway close, followed by soft footsteps. A dark head of hair peeps around the corner.

I whisper, "The coast is clear."

"Thank God. She's driving me crazy. I knew she wouldn't let me hang out with my friends to play video games, so I just went. She knows all of them, even Kayden's mom, who was home while we were there. I don't deserve to be grounded a whole month for that. Kristin stayed out past curfew a few weeks ago and she didn't get in trouble at all. It's not fair."

"I don't know the details of what Kristin did, but you can't compare yourself to anyone else. Even your siblings. You're all different people who are different ages and need different things, including rules."

"But I'm almost an adult, I'm turning sixteen in a few months and then I'll have a driver's license. Don't you think I should have a little more freedom by now? She treats me like I'm twelve, it's so embarrassing. I have to be home before any of my friends and I have to do chores before I can go out. It's like I'm Cinderella and she's my wicked stepmother."

I can't keep the skepticism from my face, "Come on Tori, that's a little harsh don't you think? You're definitely not Cinderella and your mom is not wicked, not even a little bit. She loves you and she worries about your safety. She wants you to work for things so you're not an entitled jackass like so many young people today. But a month does sound like a long time for what you did."

"See! She's crazy, a month is nuts. Please talk to her, see if you can convince her to be reasonable."

"I'll talk to her, but I'm not solely on your side. You can't sneak out, it's too dangerous. But I think you can both compromise and we can make some progress if you're willing." I try to imitate Uncle Randy's serious look when he's trying to make me see reason.

She nods at me and her eyes snap towards the kitchen when we hear ice hitting glasses. She nods again and puts her finger to her lips before she quietly disappears down the hallway. I don't want to be in the middle of this, but I care about this family and I want to help. I hope I don't regret letting them pull me into their drama.

Angie returns, "Okay here we go. Have some cheese and crackers, it's cheddar and pepper jack... it's so good. Here's a glass of cold water for you."

"Thanks so much. Why don't you tell me everything that happened and let's see if we can come up with a plan to help Tori follow the rules and spend some quality time with her family members." I nibble on a hunk of cheese while I wait for her side of the story.

"Thank you, dear. You're so sweet to listen..." She spends the next forty-five minutes telling me every word Tori has said to her and every word she replied over the previous two weeks. Apparently, Kayden is a big part of the problem because it's obvious that Tori is smitten with him and he's not supervised well enough by his parents so he's a bad influence, according to Angie and her neighborhood spies.

I'm so relieved when Jackson shows up three chunks of cheese later. He comes inside and looks at me apologetically while I silently reassure him, I'm fine and it hasn't been all torture. None the less he joins me on the sofa and takes my hand into his large rough grip. He makes my heartbeat faster, the love he evokes isn't just emotional, I feel it in my bones.

He whispers into my hair, "I love you so fucking much. Thank you for doing this, I can tell whatever you said is helping. She's way calmer than she was earlier."

I give him a weak smile. I haven't gotten many words into the conversation, but I think she needed to vent, and I've been a great listener. He reads my thoughts; I'm getting better at the whole nonverbal communication thing he and Austin share. He usually understands what I'm trying to say but I don't always catch what he and Austin convey, especially between the two of them. They're like twins who develop their own language just for each other.

"Where's Tori now?" Jackson asks.

"In her room, she's supposed to be doing her homework. I didn't take her phone but if I catch her doing anything she's not allowed to be doing, it's gone," Angie explains. Jackson looks at me and he wants me to go talk to Tori. I understood his message and I feel so accomplished. I excuse myself and knock softly on Tori's door. Even through the angry music she heard me.

"It's open!" she calls and the volume lowers.

I enter her room, and I realize I haven't been in here before. It's a bit more girly than I imagined, with all the anger. I was picturing death metal posters, black drapes, and an alter for devil worship. In movies you always see the strangest things in angry teenage rooms. But Tori's room is pleasantly pale purple with lacy drapes in a crisp white color. Her bed has a fluffy looking blanket in rainbow colors and a large number of joyfully smiling stuffed animals piled on the corner. There's a desk where she's seated with a book and notebook open, and the rest of that wall is covered by a bookcase filled with books and knick knacks. My favorite thing about her room are the drawings that fill every empty space on her walls. Some of them are incredible, and she has quite the talent and imagination. I have a thing for winged horses and dragons, she's mastered both.

Although the girl herself is decked out in black clothing, her room hasn't been tinted as dark, yet. She smiles when she spots me.

"Hey. What's up? Did my mom send you in here?"

"Nah. Jackson asked me to come see you. I think he wants me to get more of your side of the story, I've heard everything from your mom's point of view."

"I don't really have anything to say. I just want to be treated like the mature person I am, like I'll be sixteen soon and driving. I should be able to hang out with my friends sometimes even if it's past when she wants to stay awake."

"What you're saying isn't unreasonable, but you need to act as mature as you want your parents to treat you. Breaking their rules when you don't agree with them isn't demonstrating how mature you are. If you have an issue with a rule, you need to talk to your parents in a calm and mature way and work out a compromise that works for both of you."

"But she's unreasonable! She won't compromise! It makes me so mad and then I say or do something that makes her mad and we don't get anywhere, so I have to sneak out if I want to do anything. It's not fair!"

"Okay, okay. What if you follow all of her rules to the letter for the rest of this week? Then I'll take you to the mall and we can talk to her after that about what might be a compromise she's willing to make. You have to be following the rules to ask for a concession."

"Yeah, you're right. Breaking the rules just gets me into trouble. Okay, I'll follow all of her rules this week. Can we go to the mall on Saturday?"

"Sure. I'm free, what time?"

"Do you want to eat lunch and shop?"

"Yeah, that sounds fun. I'll call your mom on Friday to ask her. You behave, and she won't have a reason to say no."

"Thanks Violet. I'm glad my brothers are dating you."

"Me too."

During dinner Tori is on her best behavior, she's polite and participates in the conversation. Miguel is happier than I've ever seen him. He's a stoic man most of the time, but tonight a smile graces his face and the resemblance to Tori and Kristin is much more pronounced, their lineage is unmistakable. Kristin is out at cheerleading practice, so we don't see her, but it's a good thing to allow the focus to be on Tori. She's more of a science nerd and a videogame connoisseur, where Kristin is athletic and popular. She's in clubs and on committees, she runs track and is on the cheerleading squad. She wants to be an elementary school teacher. With her good grades and sunshiny personality, I have no doubt she'll be a wonderful educator.

Tori is curious, she wants to know why and how everything is the way it is; she loves math and likes to draw. Thinking about her drawings reminds me Pierson said he had some tattoo books of drawings he could show me. I really need to get my underarm fixed and covered by something I actually want on my body. It dawns on me that Pierson and I aren't speaking, and I wonder why he didn't come to dinner with his family. Maybe he didn't want to see me. I'm sure Jackson told him we were coming here tonight. Fuck. I'm going to have to work out a compromise with him and see if we can get along well enough to avoid interference with his family relationships. I need to set a good example for Tori. Sometimes being mature sucks, I'd much rather stab him and forget about it. I wish I could explain to Tori that she should be enjoying this time in her life without the burden of adult responsibilities.

After making it through the pleasant meal, Tori says goodnight to us and her parents, she had homework to finish up. After she leaves the room Angie jumps from her seat and hugs me. I wish she'd quit doing that, it's hard to suppress my natural urge to punch people who touch me without warning.

"I don't know what you said to her, but it was like she's a whole new child! Even if it doesn't last, I'm just so happy to have a meal without any arguments. You're a miracle worker Violet! Jackson, I don't care what it takes, but you and Austin better give this girl anything she wants to keep her happy. You don't want to lose her." Angie points her finger at Jackson while she scolds him despite the fact that he hasn't done anything wrong.

"Damn straight, Ma. She can have anything she wants, she's one of a kind and we're never going to let her go." Jackson smirks at me. Lucky for him, I don't want anything but his and Austin's love and I'm going to stick around for it. He winks at me, and I know he's teasing, but he's serious too.

"Maybe it's me who isn't letting you get away. You're my prisoner forever." I'm a little serious too as I smirk back at him.

"Well, I guess we better get going. We'll come over again this weekend. Hopefully, Tori will do better the rest of this week." Jackson deftly changes the subject and gets us out of here before Angie can force feed us dessert. After a pleasant goodbye, we each leave in our own vehicles and make our way home.

When I get home Jackson pulls in behind me and we enter the house together. There's no sign of Pierson and I'm relieved. I know I need to try to make up with him, but I'm glad it doesn't need to happen right now. I want to snuggle with Jackson, maybe watch a movie. I change into something comfortable, and he takes a shower. While he's in the bathroom I stretch across our bed and think about the next clue.

A place where you can sit for hours in a comfortable seat or attend an event with people to meet. Rows organized by numbers and letters lead to enjoyment of the most entertaining kind, a place like this exists in most every town making it easy to find.

If you want to see something Built for Speed, this establishment has everything you'll need. Find the lexicon with the right title and then, turn to the inside designated with the number ten.

The name of something there which is shiny and red will be the code to let you get ahead. Enter that moniker correctly into the grid and suddenly you'll find yourself able to open the lid. But what exactly is the task? What to do, who to ask? The Game Master has the answers you seek, send him a photo or your outlook is bleak.

I think I might know where to go and if I'm right I think I know what to do. But if I'm wrong, I don't have any other ideas. I'll have to check it out tomorrow or maybe Friday and see if I figured it out correctly. While I was thinking about the game, I must've twisted myself over onto my side because Jackson joins me on the bed and spoons me. He's warm and his clean scent envelopes me.

He kisses along my neck and goosebumps raise across my skin. It tickles and feels amazing at the same time. Heat blooms in my chest, the warm glow fills my heart and gets pumped through my veins just like the red liquid which usually flows there. The feeling travels between my legs and I moan snuggling against him, so I'm pressed as close as possible to the man I love. His taut muscles are solid against my exposed skin. My shorts are small and don't cover much, my tank is bunched up revealing my middle, his hands explore my waist. When he squeezes my ass, I can't hold back anymore. I spin towards him and throw my thigh over his legs. I kiss the corner of his mouth and look into his beautiful golden eyes. He licks my lip, and I suck his tongue into my mouth. One of his hands finds the crotch of my shorts and moves them out of his way. His finger slips through my arousal, circles my clit, and playfully teases the entrance to my pussy causing my muscles to clench in reaction to his touch. The pleasurable sensations travel all of my nerve endings with a buzz, and I need more of him touching me.

I moan in pleasure again. He's on his side and I nudge him to roll onto his back. I climb to top of him and kiss him like he's going off to war. I rub myself on his very aroused cock and it twitches beneath me. His hands grasp my ass, and he helps me press my hot zone against him. When I wriggle my ass and take over the movements, he uses his hands to feel his way to my breasts. He plucks at my nipple and pinches the pink flesh as it peaks while he squeezes my other breast in his large, strong, hard-working hand.

I can't take it anymore and I lift off of him enough to pull down his boxer briefs. Then he helps me get my own bottoms off, then I rip my shirt over my head and launch it across the room. He holds his dick up for me to be skewered and I use his smooth tip to tickle my clit some more.

Jackson's phone rings out a strange tone. We both look at it vibrating on the nightstand.

"It's Austin," I tell him when I read his name.

"He must be video calling; that's a weird sound. Hand it to me please," he asks with a mischievous little grin.

He answers the phone, "What's up?"

"Nothing, I was trying to call Violet, but she didn't answer. Do you know if she's busy?" Austin's voice comes through the phone, and I press down onto Jackson. His eyes close and he groans.

"Jackson? What're you doing?" he asks.

"Me. Hi baby," I say and take the phone from Jackson.

Austin smiles, "Now we're talking. Show me everything, Baby." I pan the phone down my body and aim it longer on where Jackson and I connect. After a while I forget I'm even holding the phone, and the lens aims at the sheet.

"I can't see anything," Austin complains. Jackson takes the phone and pops the gizmo on the back, it lets him stand it up on the nightstand. I smile at shirtless Austin on the little screen, his pants are open, and my eyes follow the lines of his abs lower and lower.

"Look what you do to me, Baby."

Austin has his hard dick in his hand and he's stroking it in sync with how I'm fucking Jackson. For some reason it really turns me on, watching him while I'm fucking Jackson is extra hot.

"Mmm, Austin!" I pound onto Jackson and his pubic bone is hitting my clit just right, it sparks into an inferno of pleasure.

"Yes! Baby! Just like that! You're gorgeous! Your tits are bouncing so perfect... Fuck!"

"Ooh, babe, yeah fuck me harder!" Jackson adds right in the room with me.

We both thrust into each other faster and harder, I give him everything I've got, and my orgasm is building to epic proportions. Austin calls out his release with a jumble of curses, it launches my orgasm, and I fuck Jackson as hard as I can while he meets me thrust for thrust. We both climax and his cum fills me while his amazing cock hits the magical spot that makes my finale keep on going and going, like a pink bunny. When it finally begins to calm down, I open my eyes and see Jackson smiling at me, his face is pink with exertion and his eyes are glowing with satisfaction. My heart beats a happy rhythm, my man is content, and I'm delighted.

"Mmmm, that was amazing."

"You did most of the work, you're amazing, babe."

"Yeah! So, fucking amazing. My cum shot across the bed, I'm going to need fresh sheets already." Austin chuckles at his graphic description.

"On that note I'm hanging up on you before we end up with a sheet situation of our own. Bye, bro."

"I love you Violet, we'll talk tomorrow!" Austin calls out as Jackson disconnects him.

"I love you too!" I try to get in before Jackson presses the red button.

After I'm dressed, I leave Jackson to finish his cleanup efforts, I'm thirsty and I need something cold to drink. When I enter the kitchen, I'm startled to find Pierson sitting on the island, in the dark. Just sitting there. He's not looking at his phone or eating anything.

"Hey, you freaked me out for a second. Do you need something?"

"Oh, are you speaking to me now?" His eyes narrow and his lip curls into a sarcastic little grin.

"Fine, maybe I owe you an apology. But you were a serious asshole, and you really pissed me off. You can't say shit to Sawyer even if you don't mean it, because it sounded like you meant it and that sent me spinning."

"That's the worst apology I've ever gotten." His sarcastic grin gets bigger, he can be such a dick.

"I'm sorry you acted like a jackass, and we got into an argument," I say with my own hint of sarcasm, a smirk playing on my lips.

"That wasn't any better. Want to try again?" he questions.

"No. Why don't you apologize and then we'll see where I land."

"Fine. I'm sorry you misinterpreted what I said to Sawyer and then blew it all out of proportion causing us to exchange heated words. I wish...I wish it was easier to get along with you."

"Wow, your apology sucks worse than mine. What the fuck is so hard to get along with? I've been nothing but nice to you and most of the time you act like I pissed in your coffee. Like my presence is causing you physical pain. You've barely spoken to me, and when you threatened Sawyer you pushed too far. What the fuck do you want me to do to get along with you?" My heated voice is raised, and this isn't going well for an attempt to make up with him.

"I want my brothers back. You've changed them, they follow you around like lost dogs and it makes me sick. They aren't them anymore and you're the reason. I'm sure you're nice enough or whatever, and you obviously fulfill their sexual needs judging by the sounds every, single, fucking, day. But you're ruining my connection with them, and I want you to stop."

I'm stunned silent. I wasn't expecting him to be upset with me because he thinks I've come between him and his brothers, that never even crossed my mind. Shit. Am I ruining their relationship? Have I come between them? I never had a sibling until Isabel, she's a little kid and I'm not, so we don't have that type of relationship. But what he's saying is bullshit, I haven't kept them from doing anything together. I don't ever tell them what they can or can't do, they're adults they can figure that out for themselves. That's it! I don't give a fuck if he's family.

"You know what Pierson? I've tried very hard to be considerate and polite with you. I haven't prevented your brothers from doing anything with you, it's their choice. I don't know why you're so shocked that they changed while you were away for years, people change. They mature and grow, change is inevitable. You're acting like a toddler having a tantrum when we could all very easily be getting along fine and enjoying your stay. I won't make you leave because you're their brother, but I think you and I need to keep our distance from each other. You stay away from me and Sawyer, and we'll stay away from you."

"That doesn't really work for me Violet. Because you're still brainwashing my brothers into blindly doing anything you want." I don't know when he stood up, but he's looming over me in a menacing manner, and it has my hackles up. What the fuck is a hackle? I'll need to Google it. My heart is pounding, I'm on edge, my fight or flight reflex is fluttering trying to figure out if there's a threat to fight, I don't do flight. I feel hot and my skin is prickling with goosebumps, there's a weird twinge in my chest that almost feels like something Alien-esque is attempting to burst free. What's wrong with me? My emotions are bouncing off the walls like a little blue racquetball.

"We're obviously not going to see eye to eye on this. Like I said, I won't make you leave, but you need to stay out of my way." I know it's not nice but it's the best I can manage right now.

"I don't know how you think that's going to work, we live under the same roof, eat at the same time, and leave in the morning in the same direction. But I'll certainly try to avoid you, and I won't say anything to you when I see you, no problem," he grumbles.

"That'll have to be good enough. Just stay away from my cat."

"Why can't you let that go? I don't want your cat anywhere near me. I don't want it in my room, I don't want your stupid cat, but I won't hurt it either. Just keep it out of my stuff." He leaned even closer on his last word, making a whiff of something delicious reach out and tickle my nose, it throws me off because I wasn't expecting an enticing scent to overwhelm me in the midst of my anger. I take another sniff and warm sandalwood mixed with something irresistible like waffles with maple syrup, fills my lungs and suddenly I have the urge to lick him for a taste. Holy hell what's up with that?

I try to step back from him, but he steps closer, "I can't believe we're arguing over a damned cat. Do you realize how stupid that is? Why couldn't you have fucking dog?"

His face is inches from mine, and I can't shake the need to taste him, it fuels my anger into a new eruption and I react to his proximity without engaging my rational mind, my instincts take charge. My hands reach out and shove his chest, I need him to back off. It startles him when I knock him temporarily off balance for the briefest moment, but he quickly fortifies his stance and presses closer.

"Will you back the fuck up? You're crowding me!" I shout.

"Yeah? Well, you're the one who touched me, I would never touch you on purpose." A quick look of confusion crosses his face, and he looks surprised, like he just woke up and can't remember how he got here. He straightens up enough that he's not looming over me the way he was, but he's still uncomfortably close. His eyes scan my face and my insides twist with a strange feeling that's both pleasant and desperate. I don't understand the way he makes me feel. On the one hand I want to punch his lights out but a deeper animal part of me wants to caress his skin with my lips. My mouth tingles at the thought and my hand brings my fingertips to softly touch them keeping me from acting on the weird impulse.

His eyes are locked on the movement of my fingers against my lips. I don't know what's come over me, but I desperately need him away from me, right now.

"I need you to step back," I warn him.

"What, are you going to punch me?" he taunts.

"Yeah. Or worse, get out of my space." I stand tall and pull my shoulders back, defiantly standing my ground.

"Would it hurt you to ask politely?"

"Yes, back the fuck up," when he doesn't move my control snaps, and I shove him as hard as I can using my body weight to create enough force to physically move him. His hands shoot out and grasp my wrists either to stop me or to keep his balance, but his touch ignites my psycho side, and I'm no longer in charge of my actions. I throw my arms up breaking his hold, as I punch him with an uppercut and move my legs to place my foot behind him. At the same time, I use my body to continue the momentum and push against him. He's thrown completely off balance and while one hand reaches up to cradle his jaw where I hit him, his other hand flails around searching for purchase to avoid the inevitable fall. He stumbles back and lands on his ass, appearing truly stunned by this turn of events.

I'm a little surprised myself, regret instantly surges in my chest, "Fuck! I'm sorry. I didn't mean to do that. I get crazy when people touch me, and I just react sometimes. Are you okay?" I flounder trying to express remorse the same way he tried not to fall, flailing like an unsuccessful idiot.

A weird look of appreciation and attraction crosses his face before it settles into a mask of disappointment. He lifts himself from the ground staring at me all the while.

"Don't worry it won't happen again." With that he stomps out of the room. Now I'm disappointed and I can't seem to pinpoint why that is.

Chapter Ten

Pierson

What the fuck was that? I don't know what just happened. She's crazy, she punched me, and I was a total dick to her, I deserved it. What the fuck are we going to do now? Before I can make it into the sanctity of my bedroom, I walk into a brick wall. When I bounce off and look into my brother's eyes, I see a storm brewing like I've never seen before.

"Whoa, what's up?" I ask in my stupor.

"What's up with you? Would you like to explain what the fuck I just heard?" My eyes fall ashamed. Noticing the tile floor as I look down, I recall it's meant to be my turn to clean the bathrooms and mop the floors.

"Fuck. I don't know. We had a disagreement, we decided we'll stay out of each other's way. She punched me," I explain as I rub my jaw. When I brave a glance at his face again, he's grinning at me. "Why is that funny?"

"Because you deserved it asshole. What did you do to Sawyer? Did you touch her? You can't fucking touch her."

"I'm not, I didn't, I mean, I did. Look, she pushed me, I reached out to catch my balance and touched her. It was an accident, I didn't try to touch her, it wasn't like that, so put your jealousy away."

"No dumbass, I'm not jealous, I'm saying you can't touch her. She reacts violently when people touch her if she doesn't let you touch her. She has a rough history, so just don't touch her."

Surprised by his words I search his face, is he saying she's been hurt? Maybe like our sister? Who the fuck would lay a hand on her? I swear I saw murder in her eyes, she's not like other women, she's a little scary.

I need to know, so I ask, "Like Megan?"

Now his eyes fall. He takes a moment and seems to arrive at some decision. When he looks at me again, he's serious, the humor of my ass whooping from Violet forgotten.

"Let's take a walk." He passes me and heads towards the front door and calls out, "Babe, I'm going for a walk with Piers."

"Okay!" she calls back.

He steps into his shoes and pulls on a light jacket, he's only wearing sweats, I follow him through the door, across the porch, and down the driveway, when we get to the road he takes a right. We continue side by side in silence. I'm embarrassed by my behavior and I'm dreading what he wants to tell me.

After we've walked for a few minutes he clears his throat, "There are some things I should probably tell you. Remember how you felt when we found out what happened to Megan? Remember how you said you wanted to kill the monster who hurt her? You were just saying earlier you wish you could've killed that bastard yourself. You meant that didn't you?"

"Yeah. I really wanted to kill him."

"When Violet was twelve..." he went on to tell me a very disturbing story about Violet's childhood and I couldn't feel worse about the way I treated her and the things I said.

He continues, "Before we started dating Violet, she had hunted down two more of her attackers. Then she had an auction to lure in more abusers and caught a new one who turned out to be her friend's abusive father. By the time we got together she was already watching that evil priest, she named him Voldemort because she refused to say his name, like from those movies or books, I guess. She reads a lot. Anyway, she kept talking about tracking Voldemort and we were talking about this asshole who hurt our sister, we didn't know it was the same person."

I stop in my tracks. "Wait. What?"

"Yeah, that asshole priest hurt Violet too. So, we helped her hunt him down and we caught some other guys at the same time. Since then, we've been working together to hunt down her attackers, and a few other criminals. Colby helps too. He really is a genius hacker, and he's got all the gadgets anyone could possibly need to pull off that type of... expedition. I know I laid out a lot of information, so ask whatever you want." We begin walking again.

"I'm not sure where to start. Okay, you said she killed her stepfather, stabbed him to death, right?"

"Yeah, when she was freaking twelve. She took down a grown man." His smile is disturbingly proud.

"Then she hunted down two more guys who abused her as a kid. When you say hunted down, you mean, what exactly?"

"She stabbed them to death and burnt the house down," he says with a perfectly straight face.

"Then she caught a guy in an auction. What does that mean?" He explained in detail how she auctioned her skin for a tattoo and everything that went down after that. But my mind is stuck on the image of that scar and weird tattoo under her arm. I can't imagine how much that must have hurt and I want to imagine how she hurt him back. She has a thing for knives apparently, I didn't realize her affinity.

He continues his explanation and we're on our fourth lap around the block by the time he finishes. I'm in shock, I had no clue Violet was a killer, and my brothers are helping her. I have a whole new appreciation for the woman who makes me crazy, she's so much more than I thought she was, I mean my entire perspective has shifted more than a tectonic plate far below the ocean when a comet flies too close to Earth, of course that's just one hypothesis. I'm not even mad about her ending Voldemort instead of me. If anyone has the right to end their attacker, it's the attackee.

"Do you have more questions?"

"So many. But first, I want to tell you something. I told you about the guys I killed to make that rescue before my discharge, I didn't have to kill them to make the rescue or for my or anyone else's safety. I killed them because they were hurting women and children, and they wouldn't have stopped. I needed to stop them. I was completely serious that I wanted to kill Voldemort. I would have if he wasn't already dead. I'm not even a little mad that Violet killed him, I think justice was served."

"So, what are you saying?" he questioned.

"I want in." He stops. He looks me over with his head tilted.

"Want in on what?" he asks as his eyes narrowed to more closely scrutinize my face.

"The hunting, I guess. I want to help you guys get rid of the scum of the Earth abusers. It's what I've been trying to figure out, it's what I needed. When I made that rescue, something clicked. I wanted more, and I couldn't stay in the military and keep hunting the bad guys the way I wanted. In the Navy I had to do it their way, you know?"

"Well, yeah, it's how the military works. I'm going to have to talk to Violet, it's her operation, we just help out. Austin will need to agree too."

"Do you agree? Do I have your vote?" I ask with too much hope in my voice.

"It's not a democracy. It's more of a monarchy and Violet's the queen, what she says goes. Will you be cool about her decision? I don't want to hear any more arguments."

"I can't promise no more arguments, but I'll try not to piss her off. The problem is I'm really good at it, I'm pretty sure I could piss her off with a look. I'll be on my best behavior though."

"Your best behavior isn't so great, do better than that." He slaps me on the shoulder then pulls me into a brotherly hug.

"I've missed you bro," I tell him with a grin.

"Yeah, it's been good having you around." We aim for the house, our chat wrapped up, I'm still grinning.

"Oh. How am I going to get Violet to listen to me? I was such a dick she's never going to want to speak to me again. What should I do?" I plead.

"You should start by doing something nice for Sawyer. If you win him over, you're halfway there. Violet, she won't be so easy. Oh! I've got it, you guys got along best when you sparred, why don't you try to get her to spar with you?"

"Okay. I'll try it, thanks." Oh man, I don't know if she'll even be willing to punch me in the face let alone listen to anything I have to say. Jackson says goodnight and I'm left to ponder my options and everything Jackson told me.

I overheard Violet tell Jackson she's planning to hit the gym after school at breakfast this morning, so I'm going to work out after work. On my lunch break I went to the closest pet shop and bought a stuffed fish with catnip and some tuna treats cats love.

They look disgusting to me, but Mollie at the shop couldn't shut up about how much her cat goes crazy over them. The day flew by with my focus on Violet, which is weird because I swear just yesterday, I would've done anything not to have her cross my mind.

Even riding to the warehouse was a blur. My heart is pounding, and I've got butterflies flapping in my gut. I'm excited and I can't wait to win her over, so she'll let me join her band of retribution. I realized I have a problem, that there's something wrong with me which makes me want to kill this much. Maybe I'm a serial killer, maybe we all are, but I haven't felt this positive since I made my last kill and rescue. When I hop off my bike to open the overhead door so I can pull inside, I notice I'm wearing a big stupid grin on my face, and I probably need to tone down my joy while she's still mad.

I use the key that was given to me and open the door, once inside I don't need to mess with the alarm. Violet has it disengaged. I'm being blasted by extremely loud metal music; it's vibrating the building. The button for the door is a couple steps inside and I spot Violet as I press the red round control. She doesn't acknowledge the door opening. I don't know if she could hear it over the music but the shift in light couldn't possibly be missed. When I ride into the space, she's moved from the speed bag to the heavy bag and still has her back to me.

I close the big door and run upstairs to change, having come straight from work. I move quickly, the excitement making me rush, I can't wait to get down there and see what happens. When I step on the treadmill, she still hasn't outwardly acknowledged my presence, it's okay, I'll wait. I run on the machine for a while, then I move to the free weights. She's on the treadmill running right now, I'm pretty sure it's her second run. When I finish the weights, she cools down and by the time I glove up and start on the speed bag, she's removing her gloves and climbs up her climbing wall to the rafters.

I act like I'm focused on what I'm doing but I'm watching her hop and swing from beam-to-beam like a monkey. Eventually she bounces onto the roof of the storage rooms and jumps down from there. She disappears down that hall and I move to the heavy bag to wait for her to return. When she finally shows her face again, I stop what I'm doing and approach her.

"Hey. Look, I'm sorry about yesterday. I was a total dick. Can we start over?" She looks skeptical and I can't blame her.

"I don't know, can we?"

"I know I was such an asshole, and you have every right to never speak to me again, but I'm really sorry. I was not in a good mood, and it wasn't your fault. I just took it out on you, I'd like to try to get along. Do you want to spar?" Hope outlines my words.

"Yeah," she says, completely ignoring everything else I just said. But hey, it's something. I put on the rest of the gear and bite the mouth guard between my teeth before I turn back towards her. She's completely ready and stretching in the middle of the mat. How did she do that so quickly?

"Ready?" I ask around the plastic safety guard.

"Yep," she puts her mouth guard in correctly and I do the same.

She reaches her gloves out to tap against mine, her eyes are like ice, it's kind of terrifying. I think I know what her kills see as they take their last breath. She holds up her gloves and watches me with her cold stare. I'm more nervous than excited now and I have too much energy buzzing through my veins, I'm bouncing around on the balls of my feet while she watches me without moving, I don't even know if she's blinking.

When I settle down and face her, she still hasn't moved, and I drop my glove a little to see if she'll strike. She doesn't hesitate and hits me with a combination to my face and head. It rings my bell a little and I try to shake it off and take a few jabs at her. We have a few good exchanges and I'm feeling confident that we're fairly well aligned and maybe she'll give me a chance. Next thing I know I'm looking up at the ceiling and my head hurts.

"Are you okay?" she asks, resigned.

"Yeah. Just give me a minute." She backs off and stands towards the corner of the vinyl mat. She has her arms crossed in an unfriendly warning to stay back. Her face says it all, she's not panting or out of breath, I don't even see sweat, she's a statue of a serial killer. In this moment I can see the darkness she carries inside, she let it out like she wants me to see her dark parts, her dark soul. I wonder if she's imagining killing me, and where her blades would slice first. Maybe she's trying to scare me off to make me behave less like a dick, maybe she wants to get rid of me now. Or maybe she's testing me, checking to see if I'll hang around after I've seen the darkness that resides inside her. I'm so intrigued by the possibilities my senses have come back online and are focused to razor sharp. I tap her gloves and silently invite her to rejoin me in our makeshift ring.

Violet approaches me with an intensity that wasn't there before, she's all business and I'm here for it, I raise my gloves and try to defend her next assault. She jabs at me a little and I respond with a jab at her. She kicks out when I'm open and catches my side, while she's on one foot I twist and push my foot at her balancing leg. She wobbles and I pushed her back more with my fists. She does some crazy back rollover move and springs back up in front of me. Color me impressed!

I make a decision, and I hope it's the right one because if it's not, well I'd be fucked. I come at her with everything I've got. I'm punching at her gloves while she blocks her face, I kick and hit her hip. She counters with a left hook, I bob and when her glove drops ever so slightly, I throw an old school Haymaker which connects with her jaw, her head whips back and she collapses at my feet.

I spit out my guard and yell out, "Fuck!"

I fall to my knees and start ripping off my gloves, when my hands are free, using my finger I gently stroke her cheek.

"Hey, Violet? Can you hear me?" She stirs and a small sound that's half sigh and half moan leaves her lips. I watch her eyes carefully and they flutter before staying open with obsidian orbs evaluating me.

"You got me good. I don't think I remember what day it is."

"It's the same day as when we started. How do you feel?"

"I've been better." She shifts and I can tell the room spun for her.

"Why don't you stay there for a minute, Killer. I'll go get some ice for you." She watches while I remove her gloves and then put her gloves under her head to elevate it a little. Technically I should elevate her feet and not move her head, but if I was in her shoes I'd want my head up a little. I give her a stern look to make sure she doesn't move while I'm gone, and I run up the stairs to the kitchen. I quickly find a zip lock bag and fill it with ice, then wrap it in a fresh dish towel from the drawer, charging down the stairs I finish wrapping the ice bag. She's still lying where I left her, but her purple head protection is lying next to her and her feet are crossed like she's just sunbathing.

"How do you feel?" I ask handing her the cold towel wrapped bundle.

"A little better. Thanks for the ice."

"Shit, there's a bruise forming, here you need to put it this way, so it cools the whole area," I shift the bag from her hands and place it where the red mark is turning a suspicious purple-blue like a swirled-fruit Slurpee. Placing her hands back on the ice pack where they need to be to hold it in the right place, my hands are hot touching her. It's not even from the difference between my skin and the ice, it's something else, they're tingling and a weird feeling similar to an electric shock is zipping up and down my arm and detonating in my chest with sparks full of heat. Looking at my hand touching hers I try to decipher what's up with it. I can feel her eyes watching me. I feel her touch inside me as if she has a magical hand that can reach through the walls of my chest and clutch my heart in a tight grip. I shake it off and take a deep breath before I check her eyes for any signs of a concussion.

"Do you feel dizzy?"

"A little."

"How many fingers am I holding up?"

"One."

"What's your name?"

"Violet Henley."

"Will you forgive me and give me another chance? Please?"

"I don't think I'm doing very well." My heart stutters in my chest. "Some asshole just asked me to forgive him and give him another chance. I think you should call nine-one-one, I must be hallucinating." Her smartass grin is filled with sarcastic satisfaction, I've never seen anyone so pleased. Just like the mongoose who catches the cobra, who has every right to celebrate such a dangerous and hard-won victory, she's triumphant and she's beautiful. The strange energy in my chest returns.

"I notice you didn't answer my questions. I'm really sorry and I even plan to apologize to Sawyer and make up with him." My smile is earnest and overly dramatic, but desperate times.

"I'll make you a deal, if Sawyer forgives you and gives you a chance, I will too."

"Thank you. I'm sorry I hit you so hard."

"I'm not. It was good, the guys have gotten better but they never really give me their best effort even though they say they aren't going easy on me. I get it, you fight the urge to protect the girl, not punch her, but you fought hard, and I appreciate it."

A new respect begins in my heart for this beautiful woman, who's my brother's girlfriend. Do you ever hear that needle screech across the record noise like when a DJ scratches it across the record for an effect similar to slamming on the brakes? No? Just me? Fucking hell! What am I doing to myself?

Her voice finally cuts into my inner turmoil, "Will you freak out if I get up?" She proceeds to pull her feet underneath her and stand while using both hands on the makeshift ice pack. Without proper consideration I reach out to steady her, lacking an invitation.

Holding my breath, I wait for her to punch me, it's kind of her turn anyway.

When there's no death blow, I open one eye a crack and look around, she's looking at me confused so I ask, "Is the coast clear?"

Her laugh is a smooth chuckle that makes dragons take flight in my stomach, she's doing something to me, and it makes me ponder if she could be a witch with magical powers. It's like the wide range of feelings she's been making me feel have now come together on one path. Oh shit, it's just like the spaghetti models for a hurricane. At first, they're all over the place going around in loops sometimes, then as they get closer to hitting land more of the models begin to agree and the range of possible paths are still wide and far from complete agreement, but they all fit into a cone shape. When everything finally clicks and all the paths are completely aligned, the storm will finally make landfall, my feelings are coming together, all the crazy loops are smoothing out, it makes me wonder where I'll land.

"I'm not that bad."

"Well, I'm gonna need to argue against that statement. You freaking punched me because I touched you when I was trying not to fall over."

"That was only one time. Besides, you shouldn't touch a lady without permission."

"What lady? You kicked my fucking ass, twice!"

"Maybe we're even now."

"I guess I could agree to that. Where are we going?" She's led me down the hallway to the storage rooms. She stops in front of the second door on the left, places her hand on a metal plate which turns green, and then a lock clicks somewhere inside the door.

"Jackson told me that he shared my story with you, he said you're interested in what we do, are you?"

"Remind me to punch him when I see him. He made it seem like he wasn't going to say anything to you, and yes, I'm interested."

"Okay. Come on." She opens the unlocked door and disappears into darkness. Before I can cross the threshold, a smell hits me in the face. I've smelled it before and it instantly places me into the past. My head shakes like a horse with an itch and I force the images away. It was another time and place, and I can control when I want to visit the past according to my government shrink.

Taking a leap of faith right over a cliff, I search for a light switch and engage the lever illuminating the room. My first impression is that I'm in some type of morgue, but like a serial killer, the attacked corpse is on the metal table.

The corpse moves and I can't hold in my reaction, "Holy fuck! I thought that was a dead body."

"Just about. This is Andres Gomez aka The Cuban. He's the big dog in a trafficking ring over in Oakdale, well, not anymore. He seems to have disappeared."

"Hey Andres, I'm Pierson don't feel bad if you don't remember my name, since you're on your way out."

A terrible scratchy sound like the rasp of a dude who's been screaming for hours, moans across the room and the dead ringer for a corpse moves again.

"No. I told you I don't give breaks to child molesters; you'll suffer every minute of your death there's no get out of jail free cards for you."

"How did you get him here?"

"Last week I got an alert that he surfaced, and we knew where he would be, you know Colby is a hacker right? He can find information when we need it, any information. Anyways, I did some recon then I was able to drug him and when he went to the restroom the guys helped him into the van. I wanted to question and torture him, so he's been hanging out to suffer a little." She explains the same way someone would tell you about a play they saw in the theater.

"Then what?" I ask, mesmerized.

"First, we end him. Then his blood will drain from this table through here," she points out a circular opening. "Next, it goes through a drain in the floor the guys installed for me. I clean up sometimes depending on the circumstances, then Dozer usually handles the rest."

"What's dozer? Like a bulldozer?"

"Yes and no. He's a guy who's as big as a bulldozer. He works with a clean-up crew I use; they take care of everything." The corpse whimpers, if a dog made that sound, I'd put him out of his misery, but I don't feel an ounce of sympathy for this almost dead dude.

"Can you trust this Dozer guy?"

"Completely. He's proven himself ten times over plus you know Colby wouldn't work with anyone he hasn't completely checked out. Dozer's a good guy and he's part of our team. To put it in terms you'll understand, he outranks you."

A wounded look shrouds my face, and I pull an imaginary dagger out of my chest before I complain, "That's not fair! I'm family, I deserve to be higher ranked than some stranger."

"You don't deserve anything; you need to earn our trust and respect. Dozer has earned both and he outranks you. Everyone outranks you, except for me, I own you. Want to run yet?"

"Nope. I've got it." I don't know how to keep my eager excitement from her. It's oozing from my pores.

"How's your stomach? I'm assuming pretty good with your history."

Nodding, I agree, "Yeah, no issues."

"Great. I'm done with this fucker. Bye Andres, don't visit." She slices a large hunting knife across the corpse's throat, I don't know where she got the knife, it was just there in her hand suddenly. I need to pay better attention. Instantly blood falls from the huge gash in his neck like a tidal wave. His arms flail for a brief moment as he gags and chokes on the blood flowing down his esophagus, but he doesn't struggle for long, he goes still and never moves again.

"That was...unexpected."

"When I checked on him earlier, I decided I'm finished with him. He was gone anyway, and I was getting tired of dealing with him. Dozer's on his way; do you want to hang out and meet him or head home?"

"I'd like to meet him. How's my hair?" Her mouth opens in shock, "I wish you could see your face, gotcha!" She rolls her eyes, but I catch the hint of a grin on her lips.

"Do you want to see my weapons room?" She puts the bloody knife in the sink then I follow her back into the hallway. She goes to the door we passed earlier and uses a CIA spy lock again which unlocks the door with a click, she opens it and I'm surrounded by firearms, swords, and other weapons my imagination would never have conjured. There's a freaking ax on one weapon filled wall. She approached a large vault and used yet another fancy security lock. When the door swings open, I don't see anything but blackness inside her safe.

I realize she must've touched something because a light turns on and I can see black velvet from one side of the interior to the other. Her blades are swaddled in velvet beds, she uncovers one while I watch over her shoulder. A perfectly purple folding knife is tucked into the groove constituting its resting place.

"May I?" My eyebrows lift with my question.

Her hand acquiesces as she uses a spokesmodel move to illustrate her offer. I lift the grape and black metallic folding hunting knife and along the spine of the blade I read an inscription, you're always a winner in love.

I silently question her, using my animated brow.

"Oh, it was a prize in one of our games, I won."

"Can I ask you something?"

"Shoot." She's not much for embellishment, another point in her favor. I don't know why I'm keeping track.

"I was thinking you and I should play your three questions game. You said it helped you guys get to know each other, maybe it could help us get along, maybe you'll like me better if you get to know me. What do you think?"

Her head tilts and she gazes intently into my eyes. Her hand lifts to embrace my cheek as she steps close. My face heats and more electric zings bounce all over my skull and it's actually a pleasant sensation, though a bit disorienting.

"Maybe getting along isn't really the problem." The spark in her eyes makes my dick twitch and I'm overwhelmed by the need to kiss her. Without analyzing the consequences my hand cups her cheek and I move us to close the gap between our lips. The instant her soft mouth touches mine it's like the Fourth of July fireworks finale goes off in my head. I'm feral with the need to devour her. When her tongue moves against my lips begging for entry, I'm certain I've died and gone to heaven. Our tongues explore while our hands roam taking their own intimate journey, I feel her hands pulling against my back pressing our bodies closer together.

There's a loud knock on the door and we separate, she looks deeply into my eyes again and smiles before biting her lip. Damn.

"To be continued." Holy hell I'm so fucking turned on I need a cold shower and fast. I pop one last quick kiss on the corner of her mouth and take off running up the stairs while I call out to her.

"I'll be back in five minutes to meet Dozer, don't go anywhere."

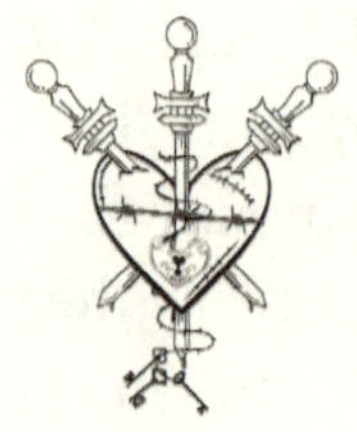

Chapter Eleven

Violet

Oh my God, he's so funny, I think as I watch him take off up the stairs to the apartment. I've been having a whirlwind of feelings about Pierson, and I couldn't figure it out, do I like him, or do I hate him? Last night Jackson and I had a long talk, and he said he thinks I'm attracted to Pierson. I laughed and told him how many times I've considered killing him, Jackson said it's definitely attraction because he's not dead. He also told me that I should go for it and see what happens, in his mind his brothers will get back to how they were if we're all together. He's actually rooting for us to get together because it's been his hope since Pierson said he was coming home. Worried I wouldn't go along with him fixing me up with his brother, he didn't want to tell me his hopes until I mentioned something that made him think I might like Pierson.

Despite Jackson's enthusiasm I worried about him and Austin feeling hurt or jealous if their girlfriend pursued a third boyfriend. After a lengthy chat with both of them I agreed I would see what happens but I won't put up with Pierson's asshole mood swings so they shouldn't get their hopes up. If they'd been in the same room instead of over the phone, I know they'd be high fiving each other. It's kind of adorable, I'm so lucky to have them. I love them so much. Pierson on the other hand is a complete unknown, when he kissed me, I felt it everywhere but when he makes me mad, I feel that all over as well and it makes me want to stab him a little.

Another knock sounds on the metal door and I'm thankful for the distraction, Dozer comes in with one other guy I've seen before. He's quiet, doesn't want to exchange pleasantries or names and I'm fine with it. Dozer sends Matt to my BASIL to get started, yeah Dozer told me his name, I've got to call him something other than the quiet guy.

"How's everything?"

"Pierson's here and he knows, he'll be down in three minutes to meet you."

"All right. Anything I should know?"

"He wants in."

"Jax told me. I meant with you, and Pierson." I examine my friend's face, and he lets me read loud and clear on his mischievous mug. My boyfriends recruited him to facilitate getting me and Pierson together. When I shake my head at him, he knows without a doubt I'm disappointed in his willingness to fall in with those troublemakers, my troublemakers.

"Really? You too? I'm not doing anything to make it happen. If fate takes a turn I'll go with it, but you tell your matchmaking partners to back off."

He chuckles, "They're your problem not mine, but I did enjoy their pitch. Plus, if it makes you happy, I'm cool with it."

"You know one of the things I like most about you is you're a man of few words, but now I've lost all respect for you. Gossiping with my troublemakers, tsk tsk. I'm so disappointed." I shake my head for emphasis.

"I'm going to get to work, your majesty." He waves his hand, bowing like he's addressing an actual queen and lumbers down the hallway where Matt disappeared a moment ago, still chuckling.

"You're not funny, chucklehead!" I call after him.

I chug some water and before I can finish swallowing, Pierson is making his way down the stairs. He's wet, like he was in the shower, but his teeth are chattering a little.

"Are you okay?"

"Y-yeah, just needed to rinse off." I'm so confused, it must be another guy thing I don't understand. He's wearing a tank top and basketball shorts, looking him over I'm surprised by his speed showering and changing, my eyes bounce between him and the apartment a few times. Deciding I'm not going to figure it out, I give up and move on.

"Come with me and I'll introduce you." Leading him to meet Dozer I debate what to do about Matt. "There's another guy helping him, just ignore him. Understand?"

He nods and responds, "Got it."

"They're in here. Hey, Dozer?" I call.

The door slightly ajar, opens wide to allow the massive man to darken its threshold. The Yeti sized behemoth surveys Pierson with extreme intensity. Pierson smiles a movie star worthy grin at us and holds out his hand to shake with Dozer.

"Hey, man. I'm Pierson, Jackson and Austin's brother. How's it going?" Dozer glances at me and reciprocated the greeting, pumping Pierson's hand.

"Nice to meet you, I'm Dozer, a friend of Colby and Violet's, I do whatever they need."

"Yeah, Violet was telling me you're on the team. So, how do you know Colby?" Pierson asks.

"Colby approached me and showed me some weak spots in my network, the kid is talented. I explained what I'm willing to do and he hooked me up with Violet. I worked for her on the first hunt but then I offered my assistance free of charge. Her cause is something I support."

"Do you have a sister?" Pierson questions.

"No."

"Nieces?"

"No." Something dawns on Pierson, and it shows across his face. "Daughter?"

Dozer's eyes flash to the floor before he answers, "Not anymore."

"I'm sorry man, that sucks. But I'm glad you're on the team; we need a wall of security."

Dozer's large, almost tree trunk-like arms cross over his chest, the corner of his lip's lifts in a barely perceptible grin, but just enough for me to catch it. I think he likes Pierson just barely the amount needed not to kill him, just like me.

"We're going to head out, we'll leave you to it," I tell Dozer.

"I'll text you later."

"Cool."

Pierson adds, "It was nice meeting you."

Dozer replies with just, "Yep." He turns back to the job at hand and closes the door.

Debating in my head what to do now, Pierson speaks up, "Will you go have a coffee with me?"

"I'm not interested in coffee, but we can stop at the café, and you can have some. I'm going to wash off really quick and change first." I start up the stairs.

"Okay."

I rush through a shower, and I'm done and dressed in about ten minutes, nowhere near Person's high-speed shower earlier. He's waiting in my desk chair when I come back to the living room. It doesn't look like he was messing with anything, my system is still asleep.

"Ready?"

"Yeah." He follows me out and we ride to the little café on Highway Twenty-one, it's on our way home. It's quiet when we shut down our bikes, I don't wait for him and he keeps up, we choose a booth when the waitress waves at us from behind a counter and tells us to sit anywhere.

"I wanted a chance to talk to you some more," he explains, but I don't need any explanations.

"Okay, talk."

"My first question is, how old are you?" He may as well know right away before anything else happens.

"Eighteen. Why have you been so angry with me?"

"Wow, you're cutthroat all the time, huh?"

"Yep." My eyes don't even blink as I stare him down.

"I told you why, but it's dumb. It seems especially dumb now." I keep staring, I'm not going to give him a break. "I just had this picture in my mind of me hanging out with them, going out looking for girls to hook-up with, going to the range, riding up the coast. I wasn't expecting them to be head over heels for a woman I've never even met. We had a plan, the three of us. We were going to have fun until we were all twenty-five, then we'd start searching for our dream girl, together. See, it sounds dumb. But I was away, and in my head those plans were still in effect, we were going to fall right back into place like I never left. Which I know is also dumb."

"Quit saying how dumb you are, it's not dumb. At least not until you got mad at me for ruining the plans in your head. Why did you leave if you had these plans?" He looks away and appears to be having an internal debate. When his eyes meet mine once again, he seems resolute.

"It's my fault Megan got assaulted. She didn't want anything to do with the priest, but I teased her. I called her demon baby because she never wanted to go to church. I told her the devil was going to get her and take her to Hell because she wasn't going to church and she never helped with any of the projects or classes. I was just being an ass; I didn't expect her to feel guilty and start going to church. It was just a childish taunt, but if I hadn't said those things to her, she wouldn't have been assaulted, and she wouldn't have almost died. I couldn't face her, or anyone, I thought my brothers blamed me and would tell mom and dad. After I was at boot camp, I found out they never said anything to our parents and didn't care what I said, it was nobody's fault but the asshole who attacked her. But by then, I was in the Navy, and I decided to punish myself for what I did. I worked harder than anyone because I needed to make up for what I did.

But when I made that rescue on my last mission, something ignited in my soul, I needed to kill the bad guys and save the innocent." His eyes plead with me to understand, I understand and I'm sad he went through all of those things.

I'm sad for all of them, especially Megan, it's terrible the way their family was completely derailed and ended up on a whole new path. If anyone can understand that it's me. My life is a long series of train wrecks between the briefest moments of joy. Of course, now most of my moments have some joy because of Austin and Jackson, could Pierson make me feel like that?

"I get it. I'm willing to let you join the team on a temporary basis, but remember, everyone outranks you. If anyone tells you to do something, you need to do it without question. Some pretty smart people help me out and if they make a request there's a good reason behind it. Are you going to be able to work with this rule?"

He looks like he just won a prize and he's bursting with excitement, "Yes! Thank you. I promise you won't be sorry if you gave me a chance. Can I ask my next question?"

"Go for it."

"Why do you hunt? I mean I know about your past and revenge or whatever, but why do you do this? Do you get some sort of pleasure from it? Or relief?"

"I never really thought about it. I killed my stepfather to get him and Voldemort to stop hurting me. After therapy and getting adopted, I worked through those feelings and decided to work on forgiveness, letting things go, and prosecuting the ever loving fuck out of them. But when my parents died...when they died, I felt a shift like my heart was suddenly frozen in a block of ice, I vowed never to love again because every time I love someone I get hurt."

"But you love my brothers."

"Obviously it didn't work. I already loved Uncle Randy and my friends, I was just distraught, like you were. Only I chose to kill child abusers, and you joined the Navy."

I feel like we've made progress when the waitress finally arrives, she brings water and breadsticks. After we order, our conversation continues with more questions.

"Were you mean to Sawyer?" I ask, knowing he wasn't, but I want to clear the air.

He looks surprised but answers, "No. I would never hurt an animal. I spoke to him in a stern voice just so he would know I was unhappy with him in my room. Seriously, I never hurt animals, they're innocent like kids." I can feel the grin on my face, and I strive to keep it from growing bigger.

"How did you get together with my brothers if you're only eighteen?"

I explained the story of how we met and how hard they tried to date me, I finally had to give in, it was embarrassing. We both laughed at my exaggeration.

"Yeah, but were there any complications because of your age difference?"

"Between the three of us, not really. But they wouldn't sleep with me until I turned eighteen. I wasn't happy about it, but I respected their wishes and the reasons behind them."

The waitress arrives with my pancakes and Pierson's burger with coffee. I enjoy my root beer and dig into the sugary goodness on my plate. I never knew I loved pancakes until I was adopted. Mom and dad used to make them every weekend, especially for me. I miss them.

"May I ask a more personal question?"

"You're out of questions, but I'll agree to a question for question chat this one time, go ahead and ask."

"Please let me finish before you answer, and I promise I'm not being a pig, it's a legitimate question." I can't control my eyeroll, and I know exactly what he's going to ask. He places his hand on mine as if he wants to keep me there to hear him out.

"How do the three of you... work out sex? Especially with your background. Isn't it weird for you?"

"No, it's not weird, it works great. They've been very sweet, and they've taught me things I never knew. We're really good at the logistics now." My eyes narrow at him, and I pull my hand away.

"Why do you want to know?" I ask him, he agreed to quid pro quo, right? His cheeks turn pink and it's adorable, he keeps being cute and it's breaking down my defenses.

"I was wondering for a few reasons. First of all, we always wanted the three of us to share a girlfriend, but that doesn't mean it works in real life. I see a lot of misunderstandings and jealousy when I picture it now."

"There's no jealousy between them over me, do they act like maniacs over someone else, maybe but usually there's a good reason, like when the guy ends up being a predator. What else?"

"I have to wonder, as a good brother, are my brothers happy? Does this sort of relationship satisfy them in all the ways they need? Does it live up to our expectations of how we imagined sharing a girlfriend would be?"

"Those sound-like questions for your brothers. They say they're happy all the time, they love me, and I love them. I don't know how they feel about our relationship, the way you're asking, but I'm happy with it. Anything else?"

A sparkle takes to his eye and a confident smile graces his unmistakably handsome face, "Yeah, one last thing. Would you have room for a fourth body in your bed?" I don't know if I should say what I'm thinking. Eh, what the hell?

"I'm not sure if you would fit, if that's what you're asking, but we can always get a bigger bed. I need to hear why you want to know and I need more words."

He pops up from his side of the booth and pushes his way into my side, he moves next to me, touching me.

"I like you, Violet. I know it's weird because I've been such an angry dick. But I think I was trying to squash my attraction, and I was jealous. Very envious of you three, I wanted to be included but I never thought for a moment you would agree to let me in. Will you go on a date with me? I want to get to know you better, if that's okay."

"Oh. I thought you were going to say something else," I say with exaggerated disappointment.

He leans closer scanning my eyes, his face looks like hope personified, "Like what?"

"Bzzzzt! You're out of time! Thank you for playing." I hold my head at an angle and wait for him to beg.

"Please, Violet, I have to know what you thought I was going to say," he pleads with sad puppy eyes, dammit it's my weakness.

"I thought you were going to say how much you want to fuck me," I deadpan.

"Ahem, are you finished with your plates? Would you like some dessert? Or anything else?" Bonnie, the waitress asks as she collects our empty dishes.

"Yes, thank you so much, nothing else for me," I reply to the frumpy, older gal, while I wait for him to collect his tongue from the floor where it landed when it fell right out of his mouth.

"Nothing else for me, just the check, please," he blurts with wide eyes. She nods and takes off. Pierson turns his attention back to me, he scans my face with his warm, chocolatey eyes, and locks onto my coal black orbs, he doesn't shy away, and I like it. He moves to an angle where his body is pressed against mine as much as possible in these close quarters. His hands land on my thighs and he squeezes hard but not too hard.

He touches my ear with his hot breath and in a voice as smooth and dark as maple syrup he says, "Make no mistake Violet, I'm definitely going to fuck you and you're going to want more. After you feel how many times I can make you come on my tongue, I'm going to rail you so hard you'll be begging me not to stop. My brothers are welcome to be there, if you want." I watch him intently and he seems sincere, his eyes remain locked on mine.

He finishes, "But I'd love the chance to get you alone first, I want our firsts to be ours."

Before I can get a word out, he pulls me onto his lap and kisses me like he'll die if he doesn't. I kiss him back with enthusiasm and I'm oblivious to our lack of privacy for a moment. But the illusion is shattered when an old lady with an oxygen mask with a big green tank starts coughing one of those loose rattling smoker's coughs that sound like a dying hellhound.

I kiss him a few more times across his mouth and remove myself from his tented jeans even though I want to take off my clothes and rub against him like a cat in heat. We quickly pay and hand in hand we rush out to our bikes, shortly taking off for home.

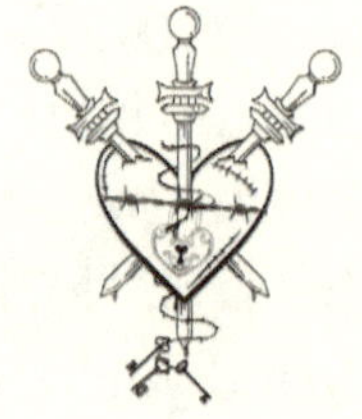

CHAPTER TWELVE

Pierson

I corner her just inside the door, "When can I take you on a date?"

"Does Friday work?" Her face is glowing, her skin is smooth and bright, she looks like one of those faeries, a pixie! She's got a beautiful glow about her and as soon as I think about it, my chest heats up and those winged beasts are back to fluttering in my stomach. When I lean into her a thrilling sensation travels from the ends of my entire body and blooms in my dick.

"Yeah. I'll pick you up at seven."

"Perfect." I kiss her cheek and go in search of Sawyer. I find him *lounging like a lazy lion in the library*, on his cat tree. He ignores me when I call him, but when he catches a whiff of the catnip toy, he's very interested.

When he's close enough I lift him up and hand him the spiced stuffed salmon. I carry him into my room and praise him while he rolls around on the fish shaped toy. I want him to be okay coming into my room, if I need to put up with a little cat hair to keep her happy, I can do it. Besides, I'm an outsider, Sawyer lives here all the time. Once I feel like I've apologized as well as possible to a cat, I enter the kitchen and find Jackson and Violet prepping vegetables for a meal.

"Can I do anything to help?" I ask eagerly.

"Yeah, chop that onion," Jackson orders.

"We ate before we came home, what are you making?"

"Violet told me, so now I'm making soup for tomorrow. Austin left me the recipe and instructions; I'm just going to make myself a sandwich for tonight since you guys ate. Austin says the soup's best if it sits overnight anyway."

"Great." I pick up the knife and start cutting the onion.

"Pierson, would you like to tell Jackson about our plans?" Violet asks in a voice full of innocence.

"What plans?" Jackson asks intently, staring at me.

"I asked Violet on a date for Friday, she said yes, but it occurs to me now maybe I should've discussed it with you and Austin first. Did I fuck up?" His gaze becomes more intense, and I can't tell what he's thinking, and I begin to have a minor panic attack but I also want to stand strong to stake my claim, it's a weird turmoil of jumbled up emotions.

"That's great dude! I'm so happy for you guys!" Jackson has a huge smile plastered on his face, he's completely serious and it's strange. What guy is happy that another dude is going on a date with his girlfriend? I feel like I've stepped into the twilight zone.

"It's not weird for you?" I question him.

"I didn't say that, but I think it's a good thing. I know it's unconventional, but I want Violet to be happy and if you can make her happy, I'm good. It's all I want. Plus, you're my brother and despite how much of an ass you can be, I love you. I love Violet too. If you guys like each other, I'll be cool with you dating her too." He looks lovingly at Violet and my eyes water. When I sniffle, they both look at me with sadness.

"It's the stupid onions. I'm not emotional," I argue.

Violet comes around the island and places her hand on my forearm in a comforting gesture, "It's okay if you're emotional, you can cry if you need to."

"It's the fucking onions!"

Jackson busts out laughing and Violet cracks up.

"You guys suck!" I admonish.

"Aww, are you sure you don't need a good cry? You seem upset, maybe hormonal, you know we're here for you," Violet teases barely suppressing more chuckles. I move my arm, so her hand falls away, then I huff an exasperated sound.

"You're not funny," I accuse and swipe at my runny eyes with my arm.

"Oh, come on, we're a little funny."

"Very little," I fake a pout. Violet kisses the corner of my mouth and goes back to peeling carrots into a large pot, almost a cauldron.

"I'm changing the subject," she announces and gains our attention, "Have you guys gotten to the second clue in our game?"

"I thought the Game Master said we couldn't discuss it between us," I muse.

"He did, but he said we couldn't collaborate, we're just comparing progress."

"By the way, what's wrong with him? Why do we have to call him *The Game Master?*"

"There's lots of stuff wrong with him, remember where I met him, but he didn't have anywhere near a normal childhood. When he does stuff like that, I think it's just him trying to make up for what he missed. If he gets out of control I wrangle him, but a silly name isn't anything to make a big deal over. Can you humor him?"

"Yeah, I can, I just feel ridiculous calling him that."

Jackson adds, "Around here we try to just go with the flow in regard to Colby's eccentricities. He's a good guy, he's just unusual."

"Okay. I'll call him *The Game Master* without complaint. To answer you, *Killer*, I'm on the second clue." I offer Violet a smartass grin.

"I'm on the second clue, and I think Austin is too. If we're all on the same clue maybe we could talk about it a little. What do you think, Babe?"

Violet looks between us before she smiles and shares her brilliant insight, "I don't want to cheat but I was thinking about visiting the library to work on the clue. You know, they organize books there using numbers and letters in the Dewey Decimal System. I think it's a good place to look for information about the clue. The books have titles that are capitalized and since they're in order I think it makes it easy to find a specific book, you know?" She watches us with that innocent look she's mastered. If she ever gets caught murdering people, she could probably get off with that sweet face.

"Yeah, we certainly wouldn't want to cheat. I might swing by the library to check things out myself. Maybe I'll see you guys there," I offer.

Jackson piles on with, "Well, if we're all going to the library, we shouldn't waste gas and take three different vehicles. That's not good for the environment. I'm sure the Game Master wouldn't want us to hurt our fragile planet."

"Yeah, Jackson's right we should probably ride together and save the Earth. Maybe tomorrow night, after dinner? If I'm not mistaken, they're open late tomorrow," Violet explains.

"That's a great idea. I was probably gunna go tomorrow anyway, it'd be great to save the planet while I figure out the clue," I agree.

"Okay, so tomorrow, after dinner. Cool." We all laugh. Jackson's right, being with them and getting along is nice, I'm excited for our date.

After we get the soup cooking, I say goodnight so I can take a real shower. Violet looks confused when I say I'm taking another shower, but she doesn't say anything, thankfully, because Jax would figure it out and I'd never hear the end of it.

This time I take a long hot shower and take care of the hard-on I've had all day with her name on it. She's so fucking sexy and she doesn't even realize it, she could have me wrapped around her finger if she figures out how to use that sexual power. I don't think I'd mind it either. I'm hoping things continue to go well between us because kissing her feels a lot better than arguing with her.

When I'm lying in bed, I keep imagining kissing her, and I struggle to fall asleep. I hit the kitchen for a glass of water and find Violet standing in the open refrigerator chugging orange juice out of the carton.

"That's not very ladylike, *Miss Never-Touch-a-Lady,*" I tease.

"Ahhh, yeah, sorry, I was too thirsty and didn't have time for a glass. I'm going to finish it and throw it away. I'm not a complete cave dweller." She grins at me, and it feels like she touched my chest with her hand, a physical touch against my skin.

"All right, I'll pretend I never saw you."

"Good. Thanks, Piers." Her smile broadens and her eyes twinkle, her hair is mussed and her cheeks are rosy, she's stunning in her long t-shirt.

I collect a glass and wait for her to move so I can get some ice from the door dispenser. She steps out of the way and leans her hip against the counter of the island. Her long legs look smooth and tempting, especially since her t-shirt accents them hanging to mid-thigh. Looking at her creamy skin, I ache, I want those thighs wrapped around my head so I can taste what's between them. My pajama bottoms tent when my dick gets thicker with my imagination going wild. I turn away to fill my glass, when I turn back, she's tracing my body with her eyes and her lip crushed between her teeth. She licks her lips when her eyes reach my tattooed chest. I hold still and watch her, when her eyes connect with mine, she's not embarrassed or shy about checking me out, she smiles boldly and holds my gaze, owning her interest. Damn this girl is killing me, at this rate I'm going to need another shower, I might need to kick in a little extra for the water bill.

When she speaks her voice is melodic and warm, "You said you had a book with some tattoo drawings I could look at, would you mind if I check it out?"

"Yeah, sure. It's in my room, come on." As I lead her out of the kitchen, she tosses the empty orange juice container and makes it into the trash bin. She surprises me and it's one of the things I find so attractive. Most of the women I date are worried about their make-up and how much money I'll make as a civilian, I've never met anyone like Violet before, I don't even think she wears make-up.

When we enter my room, Sawyer is curled at the foot of my bed and she looks between him and me but doesn't say anything. I dig through the stuff in my backpack until I feel the hardcover of the sketch book. I don't usually share this with anyone and it's a little difficult to get my hand to cooperate and give it to her. She takes it with two hands like it's a sacred heirloom and it warms my heart to see her care for one of my most precious belongings so gently. She sits on my bed and takes a deep breath before she opens the cover.

I watch her while I hold my own breath waiting to see what she'll think about my art. She looks at the first drawing for such a long time it causes a pain in my chest, and I unconsciously rub it with my thumb. Then she carefully turns the page, and I see the inspiration for my dragon tattoo colored there. Her finger traces the outline, and she looks at me, her eyes take in my tattoo no doubt comparing it to the drawing.

"When you said you had a book of drawings for tattoos, I thought you meant like a published book with tattoo art. I had no idea you were talking about your own artwork. These are amazing."

The breath I was holding comes out in a rush, "I'm glad you like them. I did one I thought might be good to cover up your problem tattoo."

"Yeah, about that..."

"Jackson told me. What a fucked-up situation to be stuck in, I'm sorry that asshole gave you that tattoo just to hurt you. I'm glad you ended him." I sit next to her and rub her leg in compassion.

"Yeah, I'm glad too. Show me what you drew for me." Taking the book from her hands I flip through quickly to the last few drawings I've done and stop on the one I did for her.

"I was thinking it would be on your shoulder blade and down your back with a little peeking around your side with the handlebar connecting under your arm to cover what's there but also use it's rectangle shape for the mirror," I say as I show her the drawing of her motorcycle.

She stays still and stares at the drawing, then she turns the page and looks at the same tattoo from another angle. Turning the page again, she sees a third angle of her body with a motorcycle tattoo that goes from her back and shoulder across her ribs. The motorcycle is exactly the one she rides, but it has purple wings attached. It's her iron Pegasus, like she's always wanted. The bike itself is a shiny, black beauty almost exactly like it is in real life, the wings are deep purple with an iridescent shimmer. Honestly, it's my best work but I don't think the motorcycle is why she's staring so intently.

"I'm not sure what to say. Pierson, these are gorgeous, you have so much talent you should be doing this, not IT work. I've never seen anything like this, it looks so real like it's going to fly right off the page. I'm surprised to see myself in your book, but it's incredible."

"Well, I uh, wanted to show how it would look and how I thought it should be positioned. Do you like it?"

"I love it, I just..." she looks at me with the same intensity as she used to inspect the drawings of herself with an amazing Pegasus motorcycle tattoo. The book is still in my hands, and she focuses on me instead. Her soft fingers trace my jaw and into my hair, her head tilts as she watches me. Then her hand moves back across my cheek and her thumb outlines my bottom lip. I carefully set the book on the nightstand and with my hands free I take her wrist and pull her into my lap. She straddles me and pushes me back onto the bed, I'm ready to explode, all of my nerve endings are singing out in need of her touch and when her hands caress my chest, I almost shoot off the bed.

"When did you draw those?"

"I did the first one the night after we sparred the first time. The others and more details came in the days after."

"So, you drew those even though you were mad at me?"

I swallow hard, uh-oh. "I wasn't really mad at you, it was more the situation. I took it out on you, but it wasn't really you making me mad and it was stupid. Aren't we past that?"

"Yeah, I'm just curious why you drew me looking so amazing if you hated me or you were mad. I would've expected me as a zombie or as the Wicked Witch of the West. Looking like a goddess was a surprise. I've never looked that good in my life."

"I draw what I see. That's exactly how you look to me."

She leans down on me and kisses me with wild abandon. I'm not sure where this is heading but I need to wait, we haven't even had a first date yet. *Sorry buddy you're not coming out anywhere but the shower until after we have at least one date.* I try talking to my dick so he'll calm down, but it doesn't work. So, I start thinking about the asshole priest who hurt Megan and Violet. It works and he deflates a little, now I'm able to focus on something else and I need to stop before I do something stupid.

Taking her face in my hands, I softly move her a little further away from my lips and stop kissing her. Beautiful dark eyes open in question.

"I'm stopping us until we have our date, I don't want to jump in too fast and fuck this up. I've been such a jackass, and I want you to trust me."

She grins and her lips are red from kissing me, her eyes are wild, and her hands hold my cheeks while she looks deep into my eyes, "Thanks Pierson, that's sweet. I guess I'll say goodnight." With that she kisses me one last time and extricates herself from my body and it's almost physically painful to lose the feel of her body on top of mine. My dick might not be speaking to me. Once she's standing next to my bed, she reaches over me and picks up the book.

"Do you mind if I borrow this so I can finish looking at it?"

"Sure, keep it as long as you want, I have others if I need someplace to draw."

"Thanks. Goodnight." She blows me a kiss and it's such a non-Violet thing to do I'm surprised once again. Apparently, there's no end to the surprises that await and I'm down for it, I want them all!

"Goodnight, beautiful."

Chapter Thirteen

Violet

Waking with a smile is a daily occurrence but since things changed with Pierson, my persistent smile is a little brighter. I hugged Jackson before getting up to start my morning routine. Looking forward to our trip to the library, and I wished for school to go by quickly. I might have magical powers, because all of my classes flew by, and it seems like my day was filled with lucky turns of fate.

When I pull into the garage, Jackson and Pierson aren't home yet so I call Austin on the speaker to check in, and start heating up dinner while I wait.

"Hey, Baby! How are you? I miss you so much," he blurts as his greeting.

"I miss you too! I feel like you've been gone forever. How's Megan doing?"

His joy deflates, "Not great. I took her out for lunch to a quiet restaurant as practice for when she'll be out and she had a meltdown with a full-blown panic attack. After she calmed down, she said the waiter reminded her of Voldemort. He didn't look anything like him, it was her imagination."

"Oh no! That's terrible, I'm sorry. Will you be able to try again?" I question.

"I don't know what's happening now. I have a meeting with her doctor tomorrow for a plan update, it could change everything. I have to wait and see."

"Wow, I hope it doesn't derail her release plans."

"Yeah, me too. It's definitely going to delay some things; she'd be getting out tomorrow if things had gone well. She has an intense plan when she does get out, daily therapy, practice in specific locations and situations with monitoring, and constant support. I think she can be successful with the plan they have in place, I'm just not sure she's ready."

"I'll keep my fingers crossed, not just because I want to meet her, but I also want you to come home. I miss you more than I thought I would."

"Baby, I miss you every minute, I'm so used to sleeping next to you it's hard to sleep here. Plus, Jax's nose whistle usually sings me to sleep." Laughter spills out of me and it's what I miss most of all, his injection of humor into every day of my life, I need it like an addict.

"It's louder when you're not here to poke him so he rolls over. When I do it, he wakes up. Other than the difficult outing, have you had any good moments with Megan?"

"Yeah, I guess, but she's so different it's mostly been like getting to know a new friend. She misses everyone and I think she'll be happy to be back home with Mom and Dad. I'm curious to see how she gets along with Kristin and Tori, they were so young when she left and now, they're practically grown. Oh! I just had an idea!"

"Spill! Don't leave me hanging." I can't contain my excitement.

"What do you think about introducing Megan and Colby? I was thinking how much she needs a friend on the outside. Originally, I thought maybe you would be a good friend for her, but just now Colby came to mind. Do you think he'd be willing to talk to her? I mean his experience inside and outside a facility would probably make her feel less awkward if nothing else."

"It's a great idea! I'll ask him when we hang up. I have something to tell you."

"Go on."

"Pierson asked me on a date for Friday night. What do you think?" I chew on my lip, nervous about his answer.

"Great, I think you guys will be good together, but I'll always be your favorite."

"You're free to have your opinion, but as I've explained, I love you both equally. There's no favorite."

"Come on baby, you can admit I'm your favorite over Piers at least."

"Well yeah, I don't know him yet and I'm in love with you, of course you're my favorite in that contest. We kissed though, and I'm feeling positive about our date."

"You kissed!?! Did he feel you up? Did you do anything else?"

"We kissed. It was nice."

"Did your pussy get wet?" My cheeks burn with his intimate question.

"Yes, just like when I kiss you. At this point just talking to you has me wet. I miss your body on mine, your tongue on me, and your big, hard, di--"

"Babe! We're home, are you ready to go to the library?" Jackson hollers when he comes through the door.

"I'm ready, and dinner should be ready soon, I'm talking to Austin, you're too loud."

"Sorry, I thought you'd be in the bedroom. Hey Auz, how's Megan?"

"Hey, Jackass, you just cock-blocked me, thanks for that."

"Ouch, sorry bro. Want me to give you a few minutes?"

"No, sounds like you guys have plans and I need a shower. We'll continue this conversation later, right, Baby?"

"I can't wait. Good luck and I'll let you know what Colby says."

"Sounds good, I love you."

"I love you too, bye."

"Remind me to grab a pen and some paper before I go. Pierson's outside on the phone; I think it's Tori."

"No need, I've got supplies," I say tapping the backpack flung over the back of the chair. "Do you think Tori and Angie are fighting again?"

"It didn't sound like anything serious, more like confusion because Tori's suddenly being wonderful and mom's worried she's up to something." He chuckles and I laugh with him.

"Sounds right. Will you please set out the bowls and cut the bread? I'm going to heat up some peas in the microwave, then everything should be ready for dinner." He kisses me and heads off to do what I asked. Pierson comes into the kitchen and looks around.

"Can I do anything?"

"Will you please get us something to drink with dinner?" I ask as I start the microwave.

"Sure. How was your day?"

"Good. I just spoke to Austin; I'll tell you both what he said over dinner. Jackson said he thought Tori called you. Is everything okay?"

"Yeah. She says it's been hard but she's doing great following the rules and being pleasant to Mom and Dad. I don't know how you did it, but you're amazing." My cheeks heat again.

"I just pointed out the most logical actions and invited her to the mall. I'm glad it's going well, it fits into my plan." My cheeks pull up in a wicked grin, I know it looks worse than wicked, more like positively terrifying. I can't help it, I'm new to dealing with kids and I've basically *collected* a few. Kristin and Tori at the teen end and my little sister, Isabel, fits the kid side of the scale, I'm enjoying the mental workout they give me. Tori is especially challenging and I'm excited to be making progress. She doesn't realize by following the rules successfully she's proven she's capable of following them. I'm looking forward to pointing it out to her at the mall and offering her a compromise. She's very intelligent. I believe she'll make the right decisions.

"Smells like dinner's ready. Babe, go sit, we'll bring everything out to the table."

We enjoy a delicious meal, and I update them on everything going on with Austin, they tell me about their day and before long we're walking through the library doors.

I love the smell of the library; it smells like paper and ink with a sprinkle of intelligence mixed with adventure. I haven't been to this library in a few months because I use the one on campus mostly. Jackson and Pierson follow quietly behind me as I make my way to the electronic card catalog. I type in what I believe is a book title from the clue I got for completing the first task. When it pulls up on my screen, I mark down the Dewey Decimal number of the book I feel is the most likely candidate, since more than one book has those words in the title. Using the category number, I lead us into the correct nonfiction section to find the book on the shelf.

"What am I looking for?" Jackson whispers.

Bending down I reach for the volume we need on the bottom shelf, "Got it!" I exclaim when I pull it free from the rest of the books about fancy cars.

"That was fast. Now what?" Pierson whispers.

"Come on, let's take it to a table in the young adult section."

"Why there?" Pierson asks as they follow me.

"Because nobody polices the noise level in the kids half of the building, but there won't be little kids making noise to bother us either."

We claim a round table in the young adult fantasy section, only one other person is anywhere near us, and she has headphones over her ears. Both guys move their chairs closer to me, I open the book and quickly find page ten.

Spread across pages nine and ten is a sexy, candy apple red, sports car, the clear coat is so perfect it looks like you could reach into the fender and pull out a gooey string of hot candy. The shine reflects the woods around the car and their bright fall leaves make for a stunning background. The McLaren P1 is a work of art and someday I hope to ride in one. I refuse to buy one because I can do so much good with that much money, but I would love to take one on a test drive, maybe I'll plan a day on a track for me and the guys.

"What are we supposed to do now?" Pierson asks.

"It says the name of the shiny red car is the code to open something, I don't know what."

Jackson reads from his phone, "The clue says the Game Master has the information and we should send him a photo."

"We can't let him know we did this together, I'll snap a picture here, then you guys take the book and take a picture somewhere else."

"You're so smart, I love you." Jackson kisses me and takes the book to another spot in the library for his photo. Pierson follows him to take his. I decide I'd rather see what's next sooner than later and I send my photo to Colby.

RobN: I knew you'd be first.

Me: I'm first? Cool. What's next?

RobN: Go back to where you found the book. Look closer at where it was and follow the directions I already gave you.

Me: Okay. I have a question for you that's not game related. Would you be willing to talk to the guy's sister, Megan? She's trying to leave the facility where she's been for a few years and she's struggling. I thought maybe you could be a friendly person for her to talk to who knows what it's like. What do you think?

RobN: Is she aware of me? My situation?

Me: No, Austin wanted me to ask you first. He'll handle it however you want if you're willing.

RobN: Yeah, I can talk to her. I'll tell Austin. He told me he was going out of town for his sister and needed to leave the game play for a little while.

Me: Great! Thanks, RobN, love you!

RobN: Yeah, I know, I'm your hero. Back at you!

*Me: *heart emoji**

*RobN: Later Vi. *Boat emoji**

Colby doesn't seem to have a grasp on the whole emoji thing, I never know what he's trying to say when he sends one. It never makes sense to me, but it probably makes sense in his head. I'll need to send him an emoji guide that says what each one means, maybe that will help him.

"When should we send him our photos of the book?" Pierson asks.

"I sent mine. He says the next part involves looking at the shelf where I found the book. So, let's do that and you guys can send yours later or tomorrow."

"That works. We'll follow you, beautiful," Jackson adds.

When we get to the spot where the book was shelved, I sit down on the ground and start pulling books off the shelf. I stack them next to me and Pierson moves them out of my way. I move them faster when I spot something black behind all the books, Jackson reaches in for it when he sees it. He pulls it out and turns it around in his hands checking each side.

Showing it to me and Pierson he says, "I think this might be where the keypad is."

"Yeah, there's a slight seam right there. Will you please, let me hold it for a second?"

When I have it in my hands, I'm surprised by its weight, it's a solid heavy item. I rub my finger across the side Jackson pointed out and when I touch it just right there's a green light glowing in a grid down the length of the box.

"Did you see that?" Pierson asks.

"Yeah. I'm going to try setting it down first." The three of us are huddled over the box and when I set it down a red-light glows across the side with the grid. I use one finger and slide it across the grid again and it lights up a steady green glowing grid. When I touch the first box the letter 'A' appears. I touch it again and it changes to a 'B'. T*his should be fun*, my inner sarcastic voice states. I keep clicking it until it has an 'M', thankfully, since that seems to be the correct letter, it locks in place. That's better, I was worried if I went past the correct letter I'd have to cycle through the entire alphabet and probably ten numbers as well.

"Hey! Great job, you got it." Pierson smiles at me as I continue to type in the letters. When I get to the last digit, I'm glad to see I was right, and the numbers come after the alphabet and '1' is the first number. When I lock in that last digit the box beeps and the lid opens with a click. Inside are four keys and a note.

Congratulations Player!

Take one key and go to this location: 355 E. Main Street, #401, Mystic Cross, FL. You'll see where your key belongs when you get there. Follow the instructions behind the lock, remember to send me a photo when your task is completed. The Game Master will send your next clue once the photo is received.

Return the box to where you found it, the lock will engage on its own.

Good job!

"Great work, Babe. Do you know what's at that address?"

"No idea but my map app will know," I giggle like a little girl as I type it into my phone. "Looks like a storage facility." I show both of them my phone. Pierson is about to close the box.

"Wait!"

He startles, "What?"

"Don't close the box until we all have a key." Jackson explains.

"Shit. Thanks man, it would've sucked to type all of that in again. Here," he takes two keys and hands one to Jackson. I take a picture of the note just in case and then I close the box, and we all work together to put everything back.

"What should we do now?" I ask, pondering visiting the next location.

"Come here, gorgeous." Jackson grabs me, pulls me close and I adjust myself until I'm straddling him, then he kisses me. When our kiss is finished, I look into his eyes and see horny mischief sparkling there. He looks over my shoulder and nods at Pierson, conducting their own silent chat. Jackson nudges me to turn a little towards Pierson who pulls on my waist to move me onto his lap, his lips meet mine and the heat awakened by Jackson turns into a flaming inferno as Pierson's tongue explores my mouth. My hands wrap around his neck, and I pull him closer, my center presses against the hardness in his pants.

Jackson takes my hips into his hands and squeezes in a way that feels like he's touching my clit and my nipples at the same time when a thrilling sensation shoots across the nerves in my most intimate places. As Pierson and I come up for air, Jackson pulls me onto his lap again with my back pressed against his firm chest. His hands squeeze my breasts next, and Pierson watches his hands with hungry eyes and a grin on his face.

"Bro, unhook her pants for me," Jackson requests.

Pierson searches my face, and I guess he didn't see any objection there, because he unbuttoned my jeans and then he lowered the zipper. He checks my face again and smiles at me, I return his smile and lick my lips. He takes it for the invitation I was offering and leans in to kiss me. While Pierson kisses me, Jackson pushes one hand into my panties and uses his fingers to find what he seeks. Two of his digits slide through my arousal, then he presses them in a circle around my clit.

Pierson keeps kissing me and one of his hands traces my ear while the other follows my neck to my shoulder then he finds my breast and uses his whole palm to feel the weight of it, squeezing it. I moan a soft sound and try to keep from doing it again. One of my hands reaches out for Pierson and I find his shoulder, I move it up to his neck and caress his ear. He moves both of his hands to my breasts and massages them in the most erotic way. My pussy is dripping from Jackson and Pierson's hands on me. Jackson pushes a finger inside my slick womanhood, and he stretches his finger to hit the spot that jolts me off his lap with another noise escaping in a muffled sound of pleasure.

"Mmm, Killer, you're so fucking hot, you make me want to lick you all over," Pierson whispers into my ear. I shudder in anticipation of him licking me, in this moment I want his tongue on my pussy more than I've ever wanted anything. Jackson presses a second finger into me, and he moves them both in the exact sequence and location to rub along that special place and make me fight against a squeal that wants to leave my lips and alert everyone within a mile to my building orgasm.

"Babe, I want your cum on my fingers, are you going to give me what I want?"

I nod and attack Pierson's mouth with my own to keep from screaming. I need Pierson to swallow the noise I'm going to make despite my best efforts. My hips wiggle in sync with Jackson's machinations in my panties and my hands pull on Pierson trying desperately to pull him closer. I want them both so much right now it's killing me not to rip off my clothes and press between them. "Yes, Babe, give me everything, you're so close, yes! That's it, beautiful!"

"Mmmm!!" My moan finishes in a squeal down Pierson's throat as I climax hard. The room spins and my whole body feels like electric eels are wrapped around me shocking from one nerve to the next with extra sparks hitting my nipples and my lady bits. Jackson holds me steady with his free hand and Pierson keeps the kiss going even though I'm practically screaming, he holds my face in his hands to keep me there. When I finally start to relax from the tension of the amazing release these gorgeous men gave me, Pierson leans back just enough to look into my eyes.

"You're fucking beautiful," he says in awe.

"Wait until you taste her, she's incredible," Jackson tells him, removing his fingers from my pants and putting them into his mouth with a slurp as he sucks my orgasm from them. He carefully helps me shift on his hard dick, so I don't hurt any of his sensitive man parts. I button my pants and pull up the zipper. Pierson offers me his hand to stand, once I'm somewhat composed, I look them over. They both have tents in their pants, and I want to take them home and continue this encounter naked.

"I need to visit the restroom; do you guys want to meet me outside?"

"Sure, do you need anything before we head out?" Pierson asks.

"Will you get me some water from the machine in the vestibule?"

"You got it, Killer. We'll meet you outside." He kisses the corner of my mouth.

"See you outside, Babe." Jackson kisses my lips, and I taste a hint of myself. They follow me to the restroom and then continue towards the door. I enter the large bathroom and choose the stall furthest from the occupied handicapped stall. After I finish my business and walk out to the sink, I see my hair sticking up at odd angles and my lips are red from kissing Pierson so hard. My cheeks are rosy, and my eyes are shining with satisfaction. I comb my fingers through my hair and try to make it look a little more presentable. The person in the end stall makes a pained noise and I'm thinking I need to get out of here before anything else reaches me.

Before I can get my hands dried, she hits the floor with a loud crash. She's an older woman but very small. I reach under the door and grasping her wrists I pull her out and thank God her clothes are in place. She's not breathing, I feel for a pulse and barely find the faintest beat of her malfunctioning heart. I begin CPR, and in between breaths I call out for help. When no one answers, I try a different idea.

"Hey Siri!"

"Uh, huh?"

"Call nine-one-one."

"Calling nine-one-one to your current location."

Once we get that call finished, I call out for her again, "Hey Siri!"

"Uh, huh?"

"Call Jackson."

"Calling Jackson, mobile."

"Babe? Is everything okay?"

"No. I called nine-one-one, I'm giving CPR to an unconscious and possibly dead woman in the restroom."

"Holy fuck! We're on our way!"

I keep counting and pumping, breathing into her mouth, and hoping she's going to live. After what is probably less than a minute but what feels like twenty, the door slams against the wall as Jackson and Pierson rush into the room followed by a scared woman.

"Oh my God! That's Mrs. Kennedy, she's our head librarian. Oh no! Please let her be okay, she wasn't feeling well earlier, I didn't know anything was really wrong. Oh my God!"

Pierson gently guides the hysterical woman to the door, "Okay, we've got this, why don't you wait for the paramedics and show them where we are when they get here? All right?" When she won't let go of his hand, they disappear into the library.

Jackson reads the directions on the AED machine he brought with him; it starts talking and tells him what to do. I keep up the CPR until he tells me to move back and shocks her.

Her heartbeat is much stronger, and the rhythm is steadier, the machine tells us to keep watching her until help arrives. It will alert us if we need to do anything.

"Are you okay, Babe?"

"I'm okay, I just want her to live."

"I think she will, because of you."

Pierson comes back with two uniformed men pushing a stretcher and the hysterical woman stands in the doorway watching everything with terrified wide eyes.

The paramedics quickly assess the librarian and question Jackson about what happened. He looks at me to fill in what happened before he arrived.

"She made a noise like she was in pain then collapsed, I dragged her out and started CPR and called for help. The door to her stall is still locked, that lady works with her, she might be able to give you more information." I point out the hysterical lady.

Pierson crawls under the stall door and opens it, the paramedic grabs her purse from inside and looks at a pill bottle he finds there. A female cop enters and starts asking the paramedics questions. They direct her to the hysterical woman and I'm ready to get out of here. When the cop looks my way, she holds up a finger at me which I take as a request to wait.

"Why don't you guys go back to the car, I'll be out as quick as possible. I don't think we should *all* chat with the police."

"We'll meet you outside. I love you," Jackson says as he heads to the door.

Pierson kisses my cheek, "See you in a few. You're incredible."

The unconscious woman has been rushed to the hospital and when the cop finishes with the no longer hysterical woman, she turns to me.

"Hi, I'm Officer Rosetti, I've got the whole story, but I just need your ID."

"Oh, I don't have anything with me," I hold up my empty hands.

"Okay, what's your name?"

"Violet. Henley. Is she going to be okay?" I figure there's no harm in giving my real name in this situation after considering a fake name.

"I think so, and if everyone's story is true, it'll be thanks to you." She looks me over and it makes me uncomfortable.

"Good. Can I go now?"

"I just need your date of birth and a phone number." I rattle off the information and she looks at me funny when I say my birthday. I'm not sure if I look much older or younger or what, but I don't care, I just want to go.

She hands me a card with her information and a case number, "All right, you can go. Thank you for what you did, you're a hero."

"No, anyone would've done the same. I'm glad I was there, thanks." I hold up the card in a goodbye wave. I can feel her eyes on me as I exit the building. Not wanting her to see the car or the guys, I turn and follow the wall of the building to the section without windows. Jackson must've spotted me because they pass me and wait for me to catch up.

"Let's go home," I state when I get my seatbelt hooked.

Chapter Fourteen

Pierson

Violet is quiet the whole way home, I imagine she's exhausted after giving CPR to Mrs. Kennedy, for who knows how long. What a weird night. Once we're in the house I don't want to leave her, there's a pain in my chest at the thought of it. I think she went to shower because I can hear water running somewhere. I perk up when their bedroom door opens, and I catch Jackson in the hallway.

"How is she?"

"Tired. Sad. I think maybe it brought up something about her parents, it's usually the only time she gets this quiet, she kind of shuts down when she's hurting about losing them."

"Would it be weird if I stayed with her? You? Both of you?"

"Nah, come on. She's missing Austin a lot too, maybe having both of us will help."

“I’m going to take a quick shower, then I’ll be there.”

“Yeah, okay.”

I take the fastest shower I can manage and I'm in their room before she comes out of their bathroom. I don’t see Sawyer at first, but then I spot him on the chair in the corner. Hopefully nobody minds that I’m in boxer briefs and a t-shirt; I need to do some laundry.

I’m sitting on the edge of the bed when she opens the bathroom door expelling a cloud of steam behind her. She walks past me and checks something on her phone, when she looks ready to climb into bed, afraid she’ll be startled by me, I clear my throat.

“Ahem. Is it alright if I stay with you tonight?” I can hear the plea in my voice.

“Yeah. Of course, I sleep in the middle so let me get in first.” She didn’t even flinch and I’m not sure if she’s too detached to realize I’ve never slept in her bed before or if she’s just perfectly fine having me lying next to her. This woman is such a uniquely enigmatic creature, it’s difficult to relax when I’m so keyed up wondering what she’s thinking.

I want her to talk to me if she wants to, so I lie on my side facing her. She reaches out and pulls on me until I’m pressed against her. She places an arm around my waist and throws her leg over both of mine, she’s completely wrapped around me. When Jax comes in he turns off the light and I can feel the bed shift as he settles in behind Violet. His hand pushes between me and Violet and comes to rest firmly grasping her breast. I can hear him mumble something to her and some kissing sounds. He must be kissing her because her face is pressed into my neck, I can feel her breath on my throat.

The next thing I know, it’s morning, my neck is hot from Violet lying on me, and someone’s alarm is going off like a ship's horn. I don’t want to move, but I’ve got work and so does Jackson. When my eyes open a fuzzy face is inches from my own. I look around and find Jackson on the edge of the bed having just turned off the alarm and Violet is nowhere to be found. I gently push Sawyer off of me, he doesn't care, he just falls back asleep where he landed like he's a stuffed cat instead of the real thing.

"Where's Violet?" I question with a sleep roughened voice.

"Bathroom. She climbed over me a couple minutes ago; she likes to be first."

"There's another bathroom," I point out, a little confused.

"Her stuff's in this one. She's quick." I can hear the faucet running.

"I'm gonna take my bike today, I have a few errands to run on my way home." He turns and looks at me over his shoulder with a smirking grin.

After I finish getting ready for work, I cross paths in the kitchen with both of my roommates who are currently at home.

"I'll be ready at seven tonight, I'm excited for our date." Violet has a brilliant smile that makes my day.

Even upon careful inspection I don't see any hint of the sadness that showed up last night. I'm relieved because I wouldn't have known what to do about our date if she was still upset.

"I can't wait. I'll pick you up at seven." Taking advantage of her happier mood, I lean in and kiss her while I squeeze her middle in a hug. She hugs and kisses me back and I float out the door for work on a cloud.

Work is work, I spend most of my day lost in thought about Violet, I can't get her out of my head, and I've pondered more than once over how quickly my feelings went from hate to not hating her. I've also spent a good deal of my time imagining what it will be like when I get to do everything I want with her. There's something so sexy about Violet and she doesn't realize it which makes it even sexier. She's got this ferocious quality that makes me want to tame her, but at the same time I want to let her wild nature run free just to see what happens.

At the end of the day, I'm first to my vehicle and I hit the gas hard so I can pick up all the things I have planned. It took my entire lunch hour to find a florist with violets in stock. I'm pleasantly surprised when I pick up the bouquet and it's bigger and more diverse than I expected. Then I swing by this little world-famous candy shop we have in town. They ship internationally and charge a lot of money for their artisan masterpiece chocolates. But they love to cater to the locals and offer us a huge discount when we shop in their store. I'm able to purchase a box of ten tiny works of art for less than twenty dollars, a fraction of their usual cost. Then, my last stop for her final surprise is a quick in and out, then I'm back on the road in no time.

When I pull up at home everyone else is already here. I rush inside and stash everything in my room before I take a shower and shave. Once I'm dressed, I pull on my good boots and check myself in the mirror, with a few adjustments to my hair I feel ready to go. Doing my best to wrap her special surprise I use the supplies I grabbed on the way home and it doesn't look bad. Trying to be cute, I pull the SUV they let me use out of the garage and knock on the front door at seven-oh-one. Violet answers and she's either a great actress or she's actually surprised I'm at the door.

"Hi. I thought you'd knock on my bedroom door when you were ready. Would you like to come inside?"

"Just for a minute because I got you these." I deftly pull the flowers and candy out from behind my back.

"Awww, thanks Pierson, how sweet of you. I recognize the violets and my favorite, a sunflower. They're really beautiful. Will you get a vase down for me?"

"Where are they?"

"There's two or three in the cabinet above the refrigerator. Oh, the blue one please. Thank you." I hand her the blue vase and she unwraps the flowers I brought, then fills the vase with water and arranges the bouquet in the vessel. It looks great, the shop did a good job with their choices to compliment the violets.

"They look good, but not as good as you." My eyes can't help roving her luscious form. She stands on her tip toes and kisses me.

"I love them, thank you. What's this?"

She turns the long thin box over in her hands, it looks like a jewelry box, and I hope she's not disappointed when she discovers the gems inside are edible.

"Just another little surprise for you. Have you ever tried the chocolates from Lola Montez Custom Chocolatier?"

"Yeah, but it's been a while, my parents used to have a client who would bring them a box for every holiday. I didn't always get some because people in their office would mob them, but they always tried to bring at least one home for me. I've never seen these before, they look like special editions. They're so pretty, I'd hate to eat them."

"We can have some later, you can admire them for a while before you eat any. There's no rush." I can't help chuckling at her excitement.

Her last surprise is for later and I don't want her to have any clues, so I hid it in the back seat of the car to be pulled out at the right moment. We drive to the restaurant chatting about our day and the game. We need to finish what got derailed last night with the almost death of, from all accounts, a lovely woman.

"Do you want to go by the address from the clue in the morning?"

"Yeah, but I need to be at your parent's house by eleven-thirty to pick up Tori. She was able to get permission to go to the mall because I'm the one taking her."

"It can wait until after the mall. You have a picture of the clue on your phone, right?"

"Yeah, want me to send it to you?"

"Sure, thanks." My phone chimes with her text sending me the photo of our clue.

“Did you remember to send the Game Master your photo from last night?” she asks.

“Yeah, and Jackson is sending his while we’re out.”

“I think he’s planning to play video games with Colby while we’re on our date, but he’s going to your parents to play. He said something about praising Tori while he’s there in hopes she’ll keep trying to get along with them.”

“Anything is better than the angry little witch, and I mean that literally, who greeted me on my first night back.”

“Yeah, she’s doing so much better, I’m proud of her.”

“Hopefully, she'll keep it up, it’s got to be a much better experience at our parent’s house if they aren’t fighting.”

Before I know it, we're at the restaurant, Mona Lisa's Trattoria, a family-owned restaurant with the best Italian food in town. I've only been a few times for special occasions, not that the prices are excessive, we just didn’t go out often when I was growing up.

“Oh! I’ve always wanted to eat here; we haven’t had the chance yet. Thank you for bringing me here.” A beautiful smile beams across her face and her eyes twinkle with excitement.

“Great. I’m happy to be with you for your first time. I hear they have award winning lasagna and cannoli.”

The hostess takes us to a small table in the back corner, it couldn’t be more perfect than if I arranged it this way. She leaves menus for us to read and comes right back with a pitcher of ice water which she pours into each of our goblets. There’s a scent of baking bread and a hint of garlic in the air. A waiter comes to our table with a wine bottle.

“Good evening, I’m Curtis, I'll be serving you. Would you like to try a complimentary glass of our new cabernet sauvignon?”

Violet doesn’t drink and I’m not much of a drinker either, if I imbibe it’s mostly with beer or whiskey. Curtis's face falls when I decline for both of us, nevertheless he vows to return for our order.

I watch her reading the menu and enjoy how she chews on her lip while she tries to decide. When she looks up and catches me watching her, she just grins, she's not the least self-conscious. She's so strong and she owns who she is without a care who might have a problem with it. Her bold attitude is such a turn on, well, everything about her turns me on. She's wearing hot pink lipstick, I've never seen her wear any before and it looks good, it makes me want to taste her lips. Her eyes narrow slightly as she scans my face and stops on my eyes, her head tilts a little like she's trying to solve a riddle.

"What are you going to order?" I ask.

"Why do you want to know?"

"Curiosity?"

"Why? Does it somehow impact what you're going to order?"

"Nope. I'm just nosy I guess, because I want to know."

"Gnocchi."

"Hmmm."

"What? What are *you* ordering?" she asks with attitude.

"Veal parmesan."

"Hmmm."

"What?" I question with attitude of my own.

"It's nothing. Enjoy your tortured baby cow."

"What the fuck is that supposed to mean?" I growl. I can't tell if we're pretending or serious with our anger.

"Well, if you must know, I'm anti veal."

"Why?"

"They're just so cruel to the baby cows. Did you know they're trapped in a cage their entire life?"

"So?"

"It's cruel. They're just poor innocent animals and they'll never have a life. The short life they do get is spent trapped in a cage, so they won't develop muscles, it's barbaric."

"I'm so confused. Please correct me if I'm wrong, *Killer*, but aren't you cruel?"

"Only to humans who've harmed an innocent person who was vulnerable and at their mercy."

"I don't see the distinction, isn't killing, killing?" I can feel my face twisting into a confused scowl. I'm pretty sure I'm not pretending anymore.

"No. There's justified vengeance and then there's a torturous murder of an innocent for one's own pleasure."

"Are you saying you'll be mad at me if I eat veal?"

She busts out laughing, "Dude! Come on, seriously? I'm a freaking murderess, which I like much better than murderer, I don't give a fuck if you eat veal, but they do treat them unnecessarily cruel, it's why I won't eat it."

My mouth is hanging open, "You were playing me? I'm going to get you back for that."

"Don't bet on it, *Hotshot*, I'm pretty quick." Her sarcastic smile is a little crooked and it's adorable. A warm sensation fills my chest, and I have this weird excited feeling in my stomach, my skin is pebbled in goosebumps, I've never felt like this before and it's all her. She does something to me, it's like when you're getting close to an orgasm, and it's right there, so close, you'd do just about anything to reach that pleasure, it's that level of excitement. It's the feeling of a coming climax, pun intended.

Curtis arrives and asks, "Madame, have you decided?"

"Yes, I'd like the gnocchi, with bolognese. Thank you."

"And for you sir?" He turns towards me.

"I'll have the lasagna, with Cesar salad, please." From the corner of my eye Violet's triumphant smile is unmistakable.

After Curtis leaves, I find myself admiring her again. She's wearing a dark burgundy shirt with a V-neck, it hints at her cleavage without actually putting it on display. She's also wearing skin tight shiny black pants, they look painted on and you can see every defined muscle in her legs and ass. Her feet are covered in black, heeled, boots that lace up but still look chunky and bleak. She's not short normally but with those boots and pants she looks long and lean, her eyes are up to my lips so she's about three inches taller than usual. She looks like a model ready for a photo shoot. She's edgy-gothic-dystopian-vampire-hunter-Barbie, in her dark clothes and riveting hair style.

"Do you have your sites on anyone, to hunt, for the near future?"

"Yeah, there's a few we're watching but I don't have anything planned in the next couple weeks."

"How's school going?"

"You know, I enjoy some of it, but they're really not teaching me anything. I already know how to do everything we've been learning. Honestly, it's boring. I think I'm going to drop out after this term is finished. I don't need a degree for anything I do, and I don't need to keep wasting my days learning stuff I already know, and paying for it. How's work going?"

"It's good. I'm starting to learn more while working with Jackson. The supervisor, Dave, said he didn't have time to teach me anything, but I think he doesn't want to, he's an asshole."

"Yeah, I met him the day I met Jackson."

"Jackson didn't tell me how he met you; I'd like to hear about it."

"I was at the twenty-four-hour market and when I came out of the store Jackson tried talking to me and I shut him down hard. He was persistent and when I still wouldn't give in, that Dave guy came out of the store, he grabbed me, and I decked him. Jackson and I had a moment after that, and I gave him my name. He showed up at my work and harassed me into friendship which turned into dating." She waves her hand between us like she means *we're* dating.

"Are we dating?" I blurt.

Our food arrives and it looks amazing. Violet doesn't wait, she starts eating her gnocchi and I dig into my salad. It's surprisingly good, even though it's salad. My lasagna is incredible when I finally get a bite.

She's still happily chewing, and she hasn't answered my question, "Well?" I prod.

She puts down her fork and analyzes me before answering, "You know about part of my life, but I don't think you know everything. Did Jackson tell you about the abuse in my childhood?"

Looking at the table I muster the courage to look her in the eye, "He did tell me you were abused and the connection to your current stabbing habits."

"Thing is, before I started dating Austin and Jackson, I never had any consensual...anything. So even though I wasn't physically a virgin, I'm very much a sexual relationship virgin. They've taught me a lot of things, but I don't have a lot of experience, I've only had one boyfriend before them, and it was only kissing and we're really more friends than anything. I've never felt like I feel about them, not for anyone else. I mean I love them, of course, but I was never sexually attracted to anyone before. I've never been attracted like that to anyone else, until you." She takes a sip of her water. I sense she's just taking a break, and she's got more story to tell.

My patience pays off and she continues, "I thought something was wrong with me when I had feelings for both Jackson and Austin, but it's been great. I knew they had another brother, but I had no idea you'd be here, or that I'd be interested in you. Nobody would ever believe me if I told them my boyfriends are encouraging me to date their other brother too. But here we are, and I like you, Pierson. I'm attracted to you in the same way as them. It worries me a little, what if I get attracted to someone else? Are we going to have ten people in our relationship? Where would everyone sleep?"

"Ten?" My voice goes up an octave as I finish the word.

"That's including you, Jackson, and Austin."

"Are you interested in seven other guys?"

"Not yet. But what if it happens? Are you going to be happy to let me see them too?"

"I don't know. I mean I feel weird now, I don't know how I'd feel about even one guy who's not already with us." She freaking starts giggling behind her hand.

"Awww, don't be mad Pierson. I'm not interested in anyone else, and I won't be. If you didn't exist there wouldn't be anyone else filling your shoes. Part of what I like about you is that you're their brother. I'm pretty sure they wouldn't be supportive of anyone else either. I'm trying to say I like you, I'm attracted to you, and I want to see if this will work, so yes, we're dating."

"I'm glad."

"There are also things I haven't tried yet, like I said I'm inexperienced and I'm still kind of waiting for the day I freak out during an intimate moment. You'll probably need to be patient with me."

"I can handle that. I have a feeling everything with you will be worth the wait." She smiles like she knows all the secrets in the Secret Garden.

We continued to chat through our meal and shared cannoli. She hears some of my military stories and I hear more about her first boyfriend and the friends she made in the psych-ward. Apparently, she's the maid of honor for her friend Harmony. I guess I'm going with her and my brothers to Tallahassee for a wedding in a few months. I'm excited to give her the surprise and I can't wait anymore, when we return to the car I reach into the back seat and hand her the wrapped box.

"What's this?"

"A surprise."

"I didn't get anything for you, and you already gave me flowers and chocolate."

"I know, but this is special."

She carefully unwraps the box, and she's able to completely remove the purple paper without tearing it. I'm impressed because I almost tore it when I was wrapping it. She looks at me before she opens the box, then she removes the tissue paper and freezes. She stares at the surprise so long I begin to worry I broke her.

Before I can do anything, she launches herself at me. Somehow without hurting either of us, she carefully puts the surprise on her seat and straddles me in the front seat of the car. Her lips pounce on mine and her tongue presses into my mouth. Her hands grasp my shoulders, and she pulls me close. I can't stop kissing her until she comes up for air and leans back a little looking deep into my eyes.

"Do you like it?" I ask with a chuckle.

"Yeah! Of course I do, it's perfect. Thank you!" She starts kissing me again and I don't want to do this in the car. I push her back a little to get her attention.

"Wait. I'm loving kissing you, but can we go home and continue this?"

"Yes of course. Thank you so much. As soon as I can get it done, I'm going to get it exactly how you drew it. I love the actual tattoo, it's perfect."

Sitting in the gift box is a full-size drawing of the exact Pegasus tattoo I drew in my drawings of her with the tattoo. Using this drawing, a tattoo artist can trace it and color it just like my drawing.

"I'm glad you like it." My own smile is large.

"Let's go home." Her eyes glitter with intent.

Chapter Fifteen

Violet

I love the drawing he made for me of the Pegasus motorcycle, it will cover my hideous armpit, and it makes me think of my dad. His motorcycle with wings like an angel, it's perfect. I can't believe how things have changed with Pierson. I want to kiss him some more. When we enter the living room he asks if I want to watch a movie, I don't.

"Come with me, please." I carefully place the box with the drawing on the dining table and make my way to Pierson's room with his hand in mine. I'm not even surprised to find Sawyer curled up on the jeans flung over the chair in the corner. I pull the door closed behind us and place his hand on my hip, my hands hold his shoulders, and I lean up to kiss him. As my tongue presses between his lips his other hand grasps my breast in a pleasant squeeze. We make out, swirling our tongues together while we feel each other. My hands roam his shoulders, biceps, chest, and back. His hold on my waist pulls me close, he alternates caressing my breasts and ass. I'm completely turned on and I want to rub my bare skin against his, I want his body to press on top of me while we pleasure one another.

I can feel arousal between my thighs as my pussy clenched in need and my clit pulses with desire. My nipples are so hard they might rip through my shirt. I can feel his hard cock pressing into my hip and it sends sparks of excitement to all my most intimate places. I grab onto his ass with both hands and rub his erection harder against my pelvis. His lips kiss along my cheek to my ear where he delivers a playful bite, then he continues along my neck, and I'm overwhelmed with need.

"Mmmm, I'm so fucking hot for you."

"I want you so fucking much right now, you're the most beautiful woman I've ever met. I don't think I've ever been this turned on and I've spent months at sea. You're so...intriguing, fascinating, I can't even think of enough words to describe you. I just know I want you."

I start unbuttoning his shirt and when I finish, he rips mine over my head. I kiss him while fumbling with the button and zipper on his dark jeans. His rock-hard dick springs from the confines of his pants and I feel it with only his boxers keeping me from his skin.

He has his hands halfway into the back of my pants when I stop and yank them down my thighs. Once they pass my knees they fall to the ground and I step out of them. We're both standing there in our underwear ready to pounce on each other, when Pierson stops kissing me, and he looks deep into my eyes while his lips curl into a cute grin I can feel to my soul.

"I want to make sure you're doing okay. I need to know you're thinking this through, and you really want to be with me," he says in a soft, sex roughened voice.

"I wouldn't be here if I didn't want to be with you. I'm good, but I think you should be quiet and fuck me." My own lips curve into a wicked grin.

Reaching for his boxers, I lean in for a kiss as well. He takes one last look into my eyes and devours me. Before long we're in his bed, naked, and rubbing against one another. He pulled me on top of him and his hands are busy with my nipples while I rub my pussy along his hard length. Then his fingers find my clit while my hands rub along his chest, playing with his nipples and feeling the muscles of his pecs. He's one fine tattooed man and I want him so much it hurts.

I lift my thighs off of his hips so I can maneuver him to my entrance, when the head of his cock touches my clit, I feel it all the way to my toes. I line us up and watch him as we join together, his eyes open and our gaze meets until I can see fire burning in his beautifully hazel eyes. He fills me with his hard dick and the stretch is delicious making me feel every inch of him until he hits my cervix sending waves of pleasure through me and lighting up my clit like an electric shock.

"Mmmm, you feel incredible, like you were made for me, Killer."

"I think I was." I tilt over and kiss him while I writhe on top of him grinding my most sensitive spot on his pubic bone igniting tingling vibrations through my body and making me moan out loud.

I can't slow down my orgasm and I detonate with a scream of pleasure. When my movements become erratic, he moves my hips to maintain our rhythm and I immediately feel the twinge of another climax building. He pumps up into me and I can't get enough of him, I want him to go deeper, harder, and I bounce on him to get us there.

"Oh, yes, Pierson! Yes!"

"I've got you; I want you to come all over my dick."

"I want your come to fill me up! Please, give it to me."

When I feel him tense, his thick cock becomes even larger as we work to reach our destination. His fingers pinch my nipples just enough to send a sting of painful pleasure through me. Our skin slaps together and it's a sweaty, slippery, sexy sound, his movements stutter, a growl starts in his throat, when I slam down on top of him, and he holds me there for a moment. I can feel him twitch inside me and as his hot cum begins to squirt against my walls a huge climax starts reigniting my first one, and it grows into a huge explosion of twinkling lights and rockets igniting behind my eyes. The Space-X launch comes to mind with the boosters exploding in flames with enough thrust to carry the tons of metal into space.

"Oh fuck! Killer!"

"Yes! Oh my God! So, fucking good!"

"Whoa! You're fucking amazing."

Our sounds quiet and we lay panting side by side in his bed, the covers having disappeared at some point without my notice. Finally, the ceiling fan working hard to keep us cool is successful at its job and my skin slowly dries giving me chills. Our hands are gripped together and I didn't even notice until now.

"Pierson, that was so good. Did you enjoy it too?" My vulnerability and inexperience are prominent in my question.

"That's an understatement, I'm not ashamed to admit that was the best sex of my life. You're really good at it for a person who has such little experience, and I'm glad because it was perfect."

"Good." My heart sings not only because of his praise, but something more, deeper in my heart and spirit, an emotional reaction that I recognize. My feelings for Pierson are growing in leaps and bounds and I search his face to decipher how he's feeling.

Before I can ask him what's going on in his head, we hear the front door slam closed and footsteps come down the hallway a moment later pausing in front of our door on their way. It has to be Jackson and I can't help but wonder what he's thinking. I catch myself chewing on my lip as emotions swirl through me. Will he be mad? Happy? Compelled to find out I offer Pierson what I hope is a reassuring smile before I hop out of bed and open the door.

Jackson is leaning against the door frame with a huge grin on his face looking like the cat who ate the canary, a look of satisfaction and excitement mixed with just a hint of concern at the forefront of his gaze. Seeing his smile, my own breaks across my face in what feels like that big smile monkeys make when their trainer tells them to mug for a picture, completely ridiculous and exaggerated. Thankfully, it must not look as ghastly as that because Jackson's eyes twinkle with joy.

"Hey, beautiful. How was your date?" His eyes scan my bare chest and his lip pulls between his teeth.

"I think it went well," I tease him, acting analytical in nothing but my skin.

"I ventured a guess that might be the case."

"I'm not sure what to do now. Should I stay here or go with you?" I ask.

He inspects my face and one side of his grin pulls in a little as he chews on the inside of his cheek in thought.

"Babe, do whatever feels right and makes you happy."

I take his hand and stand on tiptoe to kiss the corner of his mouth. It seems a little rude to kiss him with Pierson all over me when Jackson wasn't involved. I assess how I feel about the situation and come to a conclusion. Jackson knows me well enough to read my thoughts.

"Hey, Pierson?"

"Yeah?"

"Want to come to bed with me?" I invite.

I don't need to look at him to know Pierson's eyes are bouncing from me to his brother. Jackson gives him the barest nod and I know they had a silent communication. What am I getting myself into with *three* of them?

"Yeah." And with that one word, Pierson moves to our bed, permanently.

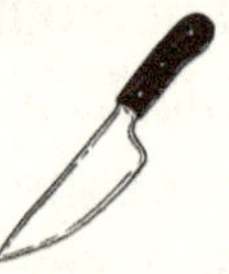

When I wake up, I can feel a sweet sting in my lady bits, we spent another hour in my bed with Jackson included, leaving me well fucked. Stretching I find I'm alone and I don't even see Sawyer staring at me or crying for his breakfast.

Checking the time I'm thankful I still have enough for a shower before I need to pick up Tori. I quickly collect clean clothes and hurriedly wash every dirty part of me, and I'm very dirty, in the most fun way. When I open the bathroom door a tantalizing scent reaches me and I recognize the delicious smell of crispy bacon.

Making my way to the kitchen with damp strands of blonde and blue hair, I'm surprised to hear Austin's voice.

"Yeah, of course, I'm sure. Me and Jax were hoping for this, I'm glad you're going to be with us now, it's how it should be." Austin sounds a little like he's in a tunnel.

"I'm glad you feel that way. I knew for sure Jax was on board but you're not here and I guess I needed to hear it directly from you."

"I get that, but I'm cool dude, I think it's excellent." I swear I can hear the sexy images going through his mind as he imagines the four of us together, Austin is a pig in the very best way.

"Whew! Thanks Auz. How's Megan doing?"

"Not great. She's back to not wanting to leave the facility. I'm going to stay a little longer so she can decide officially but she definitely won't change her mind. The panic attacks she has are so bad, I hate that I can't help her."

"Bro, you're doing everything she needs," Jackson adds.

"I'm trying. I think she's going to be more open to visitors now and that's a huge step. Maybe if we can spend more time with her, we can encourage her and help her take the chance and come home for a while at least. But I have to warn you she's nothing like the sister you remember."

"Mom said the same thing. When I visited, she didn't talk to me more than a few words, but it's been a long time since she let me visit," Pierson says sadly.

"She wants to see you. She wants to see everyone, and she's very excited to meet Violet. Wait until I tell her about you guys, she'll be happy, she was rooting for you."

I step into the room and make my presence known. I'm not a sneaky person and eavesdropping feels wrong, but I didn't want to interrupt. Jackson spots me first and holds out his hand to me, I take it and he pulls me under his arm. They're so sweet I can see that they made bacon and French toast, my favorite breakfast.

"Violet's here," Pierson tells Austin and then kisses me.

"Baby! Congratulations on landing my brother!"

"That sounds wrong, Auz."

"I don't care, I'm psyched," Austin announces.

"Thanks, I miss you."

"I miss you too. I might be coming home soon."

"I'm glad, but if what I was hearing is correct, Megan isn't doing as well as we hoped. I'm sorry."

"Yeah, she's not doing great, but she is better and I think with more time she'll be well enough to come home. She's looking forward to meeting you, and she said you must be crazy to date us so she's sure you'll get along well. She's not funny so I think she might've been serious." I can't help a laugh.

"She sounds perfect."

"I'll tell her you think so. I need to go, sorry, I have an appointment with her and the therapist. Call me tonight okay, Baby?"

"I will. I love you."

"I love you too! Guys, take good care of our girl. Later."

"We will. See ya."

"Later."

"Okay, I'm starving, let's eat." Both of them agree wholeheartedly and we dive into their thoughtful breakfast. While I enjoy a delicious meal, I can't help watching them and enjoying their gorgeous faces, strong bodies, and hearty appetites. I feel complete. My dark soul has a permanent core of light, it has three parts joined into one bright star, brighter than the sun. Even though the darkness of my soul still exists, it's relegated to the shadows in the corners where I can call it out at will, but it won't cloud my relationship, I won't let it. For the first time since my parent's death, I feel like I have a family, a home, and the safety and security that comes with it, nothing is missing. I have hope in my heart, something I'm not used to and as I get ready to pick up Tori, the feeling remains strong. I think today is going to be a great day, famous last words, right?

When I pull up at Tori's house, also the home of, for all intents and purposes, my in-laws, I feel excited and I'm hoping I can get through to Tori. Her family is wonderful, they love her, and she needs to realize how lucky she is before she makes a mistake and throws it away or loses it in some horrible tragedy. Reminding myself not to be cryptic, her parents aren't going anywhere, I knock on the door.

Footsteps stomp to the door and it opens, "Hello, Violet. How are you?"

"Hi, Miguel. I'm great."

"You know you don't need to knock, right?"

"Oh, um, sorry. Is Tori ready?" It's so weird how Miguel makes me nervous. Not in a bad way, just as someone I respect and want to oblige. I want to earn his respect in return and I don't feel that way about many people, usually I don't give a fuck.

"I think I heard her yell something when you knocked. Come in and say hello to Angie, Tori will find you."

"Thanks." I follow him to the kitchen and find Angie with her head in the refrigerator and all the contents of the fridge scattered across every surface around her.

"Hello dear. Please forgive the mess, I spilled juice on the top shelf and it dripped all the way down to the vegetable bin. It needed a good cleaning anyway but it wasn't my first priority this morning. I'm sorry, I'm rambling, how are you?"

"Good."

"Please drink something, the more you consume the less I need to put back. Go on, take something to drink, and have a snack."

"I just had breakfast I couldn't possibly eat now, but I will when I bring Tori home, all right?" The guys taught me to give in with Angie, she's relentless when it comes to feeding people.

"Okay. I can't thank you enough for spending time with Tori, your influence is so good for her, she's like a different person." Ha! If only she knew.

"Mom, quit bugging Violet, she's here for me. Hey, Violet, I'm ready to go," Tori says as she enters the kitchen. She takes a soda from the table and puts something in her pocket, it might have been string cheese. It makes me smile.

"Okay. Great, let's get going. Bye, Angie. Bye, Miguel. Thank you." I'm not sure why I thanked them, maybe for letting Tori go with me or for being great parents to all of my boyfriends, all *three* of them, holy fuck I can't believe I have three!

"Bye sweetie, bye dear, have fun."

"Tori, behave for Violet. Have a good time."

"Dad! Oh my God, let's go." Tori rolls her eyes so hard I'm surprised they didn't get lost in her skull.

I follow her and do my best to keep my giggles at bay. This is going to be fun. When we get in the car, I wait for her to buckle up before I take off for the mall. She sighs with exasperation and I grin, I can't help it. She's a nice enough kid, very smart and talented but she's a spoiled brat. I don't mean that with any dislike of her, it's just a fact. She has a wonderful family and a great life, she's never faced any adversity, she's just the baby of the bunch and they all doted on her when she was little. Now she expects to be given whatever she wants and when it doesn't happen, she throws a tantrum. I'm hoping to explain a few things to her today and see if I can make a difference in her outlook on her charmed life.

"Ugh, I'm sorry about them. I know they mean well but they just bug me so much it pisses me off, you know?"

"I think Miguel and Angie are lovely people who care about you more than anything in the world. They don't bug me at all. Well, that's not completely true, Angie is a little forceful with the food, but otherwise I love her. I wish my birth mother was like her."

Tori looks like she smelled something bad. I know she thought I was on her side or something, but I'm not on any side, I think they've all made mistakes and they're easily fixed with a little tough love and communication.

In an attempt to engage her I ask, "So, what's so important at the mall that I needed to bring you *today?*"

"Oh, um, please don't be mad."

"Why would I be mad?" I ask, assuming she's about to seriously piss me off.

"There's this guy, Kody, he's really sweet and smart, and so cute. He works at a store in the mall and I thought if I could accidentally bump into him, maybe he'll ask me out. But I heard that Kyrie likes him too and she's having a party next weekend, so if she talks to him first, he might ask her out instead of me, so I had to try before she has a chance, you know?"

"Sure. Okay." I'm not mad, but I'm not happy either and I can feel my brow crinkle with annoyance.

"Are you mad?"

"No. I need some new underwear, it's not a wasted trip or anything."

"Oh. Well, we can still shop around and have lunch, my treat." She babysits so I'm impressed she's willing to spend her hard-earned money on me, she may have just redeemed herself a bit. Plus, she's giving me such a pleading look it's hard to stay annoyed.

"Okay, I accept." She smiles and I can tell she understands I accept her offering as the apology she intended.

"So, where does Prince Charming work?" I question.

"It's this cool store, *Bluffs*. They sell all this trendy stuff, they have clothes and shoes, jewelry, they even have things to decorate your room. It's where everyone shops right now."

"Sounds amazing, I can't wait." I might have some sarcasm lacing my words.

I pull into the parking garage and drive up to the second level. There's nobody else up here because it's still early. I back into a space, a habit from hunting monsters, you always need to be prepared for anything. Tori chatters on about kids at school and I acknowledge her with the appropriate *uh-huh, wow, or cool,* as required. We make our way to *Bluffs* first for recon, when we spot the Incredible Kody, he's towards the back hanging up a rack of new jackets. She refuses to go inside until she has a minute to calm down. It's probably a good idea, she looks frantic.

"Why don't we go in and I'll pretend I'm shopping for a jacket, and you wait for him to notice you. Then it's just a coincidence that you bumped into him," I suggest.

"You're a genius. Okay, let's go."

We wander nonchalantly through the store, looking over the clothing and commenting about which items we like. When we're close to where Kody's working, I test out my acting skills.

"What I really need is a new jacket, maybe something leather. Oh, look there's some over there. Oh my God! That one has skulls, if they have my size, it's coming home with me."

"Yeah, it's totally cute, it'll look so hot on you." She keeps her back to him while I face him and pretend not to see him.

"Do you see my size?" I ask her. He looks at me and smiles then he looks at Tori and I see the recognition, his smile grows. Oh, he likes her, and he is cute. She wasn't wrong.

"I don't see one in your size."

"Can I help?" Kody asks Tori. She turns around to answer him and he smiles a brilliant model worthy grin. "Hey Tori."

"Hey, Kody. I didn't know you worked here."

"I've only been here a few weeks."

"Yeah? How do you like it?"

"It's okay. I see everyone I know in here, which is cool most of the time."

Tori laughs and he eats her up with his eyes. She's got this in the bag.

"I get that," Tori commiserates.

"Kody! Go get those two boxes by the back door!" Some asshole with slicked back hair and a bad mustache hollers at Kody. I'm not about to let this loser cock-block my girl.

"Excuse me, hi, what's your name?" I ask him, smiling brightly.

"Ramone, I'm the manager. May I help you?" He says his name with a bougie flair that makes him roll the *'R'.*

"Yes, I'm looking for a jacket and some boots, but I don't see my size in the jackets. Will you help me look for the boots?" He's not subtle about scanning my body, and I want to punch him, but I ignore it so I can help Tori get a minute with Kody.

"Absolutely, I'm sure we have something that will look fantastic on you. What size shoe do you wear?"

Tuning out the slimy salesman I keep an eye on Tori. I've sent him back for a different size and shoe three times, he's getting frustrated with me. Tori is laughing and smiling, having an animated conversation with Kody. He looks ready to follow her anywhere and it's adorable, I hope he has the nerve to ask her out.

"Yeah, this one is pretty good. Let me walk around in them for a minute."

"Okay, I'll be back to check on you." He rushes off and I imagine he wants a cigarette break, but who knows maybe he needs to place a bet or call his mother, sometimes stereotypes are spot on.

I continue to watch the happy couple and they both have their phones out, maybe a good sign. The boots actually do look cute and they're extremely comfortable, I might just buy them after all. They're a black, army boot style with skulls on the back of the leather right above the chunky two-inch heel. I'm all about comfort, style not so much, but black goes with everything.

"Hey Tori, I'm going to buy these boots, what do you think?"

"Yeah, you should definitely get them, they look perfect on you. Any luck with a jacket?"

"No. I couldn't find my size."

"What size do you need?"

"A medium or a nine, usually." Kody digs through the rack and pulls out a medium in the exact style I like with the skulls. It's fun to advertise my endeavors without anyone knowing it's one-hundred percent true.

"Wow! Thanks, let me try it on." It fits perfectly and it'll be great for my bike. Everyone thinks motorcycle riders wear leather because it's cool, but that's not why. Leather protects you from road burn if you dump the bike, nothing else works as well, except maybe Kevlar.

"Do you like it?" Tori asks.

"Yeah," I turn to Kody and ask, "Will you ring me up?" I'm assuming he'll get a commission; I figure it won't hurt Tori's chances any.

When we exit the store Tori is practically bursting with excited energy. I decide to wait for her to tell me what happened.

"Aaah! Oh my gosh, thank you so much Violet. He asked me out and took my number. He said he's been trying to get up the courage to ask me out and he wants me to go to Kyrie's party with him. He said he doesn't like her because she's stuck up. Ah!" Tori is walking at a fast pace so I guide us towards the underwear shop before we blow by it. She could probably win a marathon right now.

"I had no doubt he would ask you out if he had a brain in his head. Congratulations on a successful mission. Now let's find me some underwear that matches."

After twenty minutes, I have everything I need and then some. I'm ready to have lunch in the mall or head out to someplace else. Tori wants to eat in the mall in case Kody gets a lunch break. We decide on the Asian place in the food court, the sample of chicken they're handing out is delicious.

We sit at a table without anyone else around and I put my feet on another chair. Tori hashes over every word she and Kody said to each other. When she settles down, I decide it's as good a time as any to have my talk with her.

"What do you know about my past?" I ask.

"Austin told me you were abused by your birth family and then you were adopted but your adoptive parents died. I'm sorry by the way, what a shitty situation to go through."

"He didn't tell you the whole story..." I proceed to fill in some details about how the people I should've been able to count on most in the world hurt me, they broke all trust and harmed me in ways that left scars which will never heal. She listens with a sober look, she nods, and tears fall from her eyes at the appropriate places.

"...so, I'm not trying to give you a hard time. I know what a bad childhood looks like, I know what bad parents are like, my experience has taught me that if I find people I can trust and love who love and respect me, I hold them close and cherish their presence in my life. Your parents are wonderful, and I know you know that, you just need to work on letting them know how you really feel. Yelling at them, ignoring them, and criticizing them isn't a good look. You're old enough to acknowledge all the things your parents do for you and start treating them with the respect they deserve, they've earned it."

She jumps up from her chair and hugs me. Tears are falling freely from her eyes, and I think I got through at least a little bit, enough to have her thinking about her actions and that was my goal.

"Thank you, Violet. It's weird, I feel like you're not that much older than me, like we could be friends. But you're also like the wise elder who guides me with her ancient wisdom, kind of like Yoda." We both crack up at that.

"Then listen to me, you must. Be kinder to your parents while following their rules. Live long and prosper." I hold up my hand in the Vulcan accompaniment to the phrase. She looks horrified, and I crack up harder. A few families on the other side of a short wall are looking at us. No doubt trying to decipher what's wrong with the crazy girls laughing and crying while they hug.

"Sacrilege! Violet! I know you know better than that."

"Guilty. I just thought it was funny."

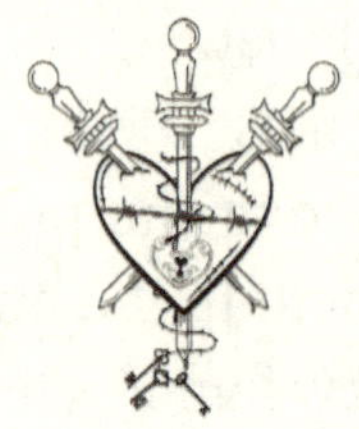

Chapter Sixteen

Pierson

I check my watch again, it's nearly four and we haven't heard from Violet. She should be at my parents by now to have dinner with them. She hasn't answered a text from either one of us. Jackson's trying to play it cool but I can tell he's worried.

"Has this ever happened before?" I ask, hopeful.

"Nope." My gut twinges at his response. I've been having very strong feelings for Violet, I've been afraid to admit how intense my feelings are even to myself. But the fear that something happened to her is brutal. I wouldn't even be worried because Violet can handle herself, I still have a couple bruises to prove it, but she's extremely reliable. She never disappears without telling at least Jackson and Austin where she'll be, and she always shows up on time. Not that she's late, but she knows we're expecting to meet her at our parents, she would've messaged us if she was wrapped up with Tori.

Jackson dials his phone, "I'm bringing in the big guns." I tilt my head in confusion.

"You've reached the Game Master, what have you found?" Colby answers in his GM voice. It's a bit like a game show host and definitely just as annoying.

"We can't reach Violet," Jackson blurts with worry heavy in his voice.

"She went to the mall with your sister, right?" He doesn't miss a beat, instantly serious.

"Yeah," Jackson answers in monotone.

"I'm assuming she took the SUV?"

"She did."

"Give me a second. Okay, got her car. She's parked in the parking garage, at the southeast entrance, it's between Macy's and Lord & Taylor. Hmmm, they got there at eleven-oh-seven, they walked into the mall entrance, and...there, they went to a shop called, *Bluffs* first."

I can't help but ask, "How do you know all this?"

"I can see anything if it's been in front of a camera. The mall has more cameras than customers, I can probably follow them every step through the mall by camera. Got them at the lingerie store, I'm guessing you'll be the beneficiary of that stop, Jackson."

"Not just me."

"Sorry, *and Austin,* but he's not there is he?"

"He's not, but I was referring to the development where Violet and Pierson are together now."

"Yeah? Nice. She wasn't sure if she liked you or hated you, Piers, but she finally decided she must like you since you're still breathing. I'm glad she made the move, congrats. I'm going to tell you what I told your brothers, *if you harm her in ANY way, even by mistake, I will destroy you.*"

"Uh, thanks, man. I would never harm her, I promise. Plus, she would kill me herself if I did anything to her."

"Yeah, she'd definitely end you, but while you're alive I'd make your life a living hell. I'll destroy your whole world, one click at a time."

"Okay. Gotcha. Anymore, info on Violet and Tori?"

"They ate chicken at the Chinese Gourmet in the food court. The same guy from that shop, *Bluffs*, joined them for seventeen minutes. Then they went to the restroom, and...huh."

"What?" Jackson demands.

"Give me a minute."

"Colby, what's going on?" I can't help questioning him myself.

"Hold your horses...I'm checking. Fuck me!"

Jackson and I both yell at Colby, "What!?!"

"Call your parents and cancel dinner, load up for bear, and come get me."

I take off to my room and pull on my army boots and a jacket. I remove the large case from my closet, strap on my shoulder holster, and then my leg holster. I check the ammunition in each firearm and secure them in their straps. After placing extra ammo in my jacket pockets, a knife is strapped to my belt. As I place a hat on my head, Jackson moves down the hall outside my room.

He yells out on his way by, "They disappeared from view after the bathroom. He's checking the entire mall and every camera, if he doesn't find anything he'll spread outward from there." I follow him and stand in his doorway.

"Why are we getting Colby? Shouldn't he stay at his terminal looking for them?" I ask.

"Nah, he has a laptop with satellite hookup or some shit for mobile operations. If he's with us he can observe things himself and maybe spot something we can't, like surveillance."

"Okay. Are you driving?"

"Yeah, we'll take my truck."

"I'm going to load it up." He hands me the keys and I grab some other things from my room. They have a closet in the garage with some of their gear, like Kevlar, surveillance equipment, and lots of weapons. Although, they keep the majority of their gear and weapons at the warehouse. I load what I think we'll need and some gear for Colby as well. Jackson joins me and grabs one more blade, he places it into the sheath on his hip.

We tear off out of the garage and make our way to Colby's at well past the speed limit. When we get to Colby's front gate, Colby is waiting for us at the guardhouse. The larger guard carries something in a case and loads it into the back seat, then Colby climbs in after it. The guard nods to us and steps back.

"Go! I'm in!" Colby shouts.

"Anything new?" Jackson asks before I can.

"Yeah, there's a suspicious van, but it leaves the area and I lost it when it got into the rural area north of here."

"Which way?" Jackson questions.

"We need to go to the mall, I need to see if I'm missing any cameras, we need to take the same route as the girls. The license plate on the van was obscured. I hate that Florida has no front plates; it helps so much when you're looking for someone." Jackson drives at breakneck speeds and we make it to the street the mall is on in no time and without a ticket, while Colby continues complaining.

"Dude, who gives a fuck? No whining! Keep looking!" I yell in exasperation.

"*Dude,* I can look and whine at the same time. Turn in here, it's the entrance for the parking garage."

We wind up to the second floor where we find Violet's SUV backed into a space. Colby wants to go to the food court and check out the hall to the restroom, there are no cameras there. We drive to the food court entrance where Colby and I get out, Jackson stays in the truck right outside the entrance.

"There!" Colby points out the hallway. We both practically run down the too bright corridor. We find the women's restroom and nothing is amiss, there's an exit leading to the outside next to the men's room, I open the door. No alarms sound, it's a commercial lot, probably for the employees. It's got five dumpsters and two beat up cars, no van. Colby walks out and looks at the buildings, he comes back inside and runs down the hall, I follow keeping pace.

We jump into the truck and Jackson speeds in the direction Colby tells him. Colby watches his screen while he calls out which way to go. The surroundings go from suburban to rural in no time. Town is mostly south of the mall, once you're past the mall there's nothing of note for fifteen miles, the more rural, the fewer cameras.

"That's it. I'm out of cameras, I'm checking this road in the next town, but I'm not seeing the van yet," Colby announces.

"Pull over, Jax, we don't want to be too far from his last sighting." Jackson pulls into a wide spot on the shoulder.

"What happened inside?" he asks. I tell him what we found, a whole lot of nothing. We fall quiet and focus on Colby. He's our only hope.

"I've got an image expert and AI working on trying to decipher the license plate based on what we can see. I'm scouring the area for any cameras and checking for a glimpse of the van. The satellites weren't in position at that time to be of any help. I'm trying to track down the pings on both of their phones to towers along this route. What else can I do?" I'm pretty sure his question was for himself. *Satellites?*

"I need to call Austin," Jackson says solemnly.

"Shit. Yeah, we have to call him." He clears his throat as it rings out loud on speaker phone.

"Yo!" Austin answers.

"Violet and Tori are missing. They disappeared at the mall, a van probably took them, Colby lost the van going north on sixty-eight. We're here now hoping he can find a trace or a new lead."

"Holy fuck! I'm on my way."

"Dude, please don't rush here like a beast, we'll keep you posted. You can finish with Megan, or at least let her know you have to go."

"I'm finished, I'm on my way. I left early and planned to surprise Violet. I'm forty-five minutes from home, where are you exactly?"

Jackson tells Austin how to find us and Colby continues his search while I sit helpless praying my girl and my sister will be okay. There's a terrible pinching feeling in my chest, it's painful and I rub my sternum trying to ease my discomfort.

After what feels like an incredibly long time, Colby says, "I've got the plate. Shit, it's a rental!" He rips off his shoe and chucks it at the door.

"What!?!" I yell at him.

"It was rented by a false identity. We're at a dead end for now."

"What if you check the rental company cameras and see who it was?"

"They rented it a month ago, they already recycled their digital files."

"So?" Jackson asks.

This time I answer, "They erase the footage from their cameras to make room for new footage. It saves space so they can have a cheaper digital plan."

"What he said," Colby agrees.

"Fuck! What're we supposed to do?"

"I'm checking everything I can think of, just be patient. Eventually, I'll find something."

"Patience isn't my thing," Jackson growls. Austin's truck pulls up behind us sending gravel flying, a cloud of dust shrouds him as he exits the still running truck.

"Any news?" Austin asks when Jackson rolls down the windows.

"Not yet," Colby answers.

"You guys doing all right?" Austin asks.

"Are you?" I question.

"Good point. We'll find her, remember who we're talking about. Our girl is one gorgeous badass, she'll probably kill them all and hang their severed heads on the front of the warehouse to warn others." I chuckle and release a bit of the tension holding me hostage.

"We need to consider telling mom and dad," I suggest with despair.

"Maybe we can delay that by asking if Tori can stay over?" Austin ponders.

"No, they'll kill us if we have to tell them later," Jackson says.

"What if...nah, that won't work. I'm out of ideas, we need to tell them," Austin determines.

Jackson agrees, "Yeah, we need to tell them. Maybe they'll trust us to find them."

"Good idea. I can guilt mom and she'll convince dad." Austin leans in the truck and dials his phone.

"Hey, son. How's your sister today?" He means Megan, Austin flinches.

"I'm back in town. She didn't change her mind; she's staying there for a while longer. I'm actually calling about Tori. Is mom around?"

"Yeah, hang on." We can hear shuffling, then muffled voices, finally he comes back.

"She's here."

"Hi Austin, what's wrong?"

"Hi Mom. Violet and Tori are missing. We're doing everything we can to find them, we have a computer expert checking every camera in town to try to spot them. We have the best resources working on it." Auz blurts everything in explosive word vomit.

She gasped, "What do the police say?" We all look at each other, we didn't discuss what to tell them about the police.

"We have connections in law enforcement, we'll call them if we need their help. I promise you mom, we have the best expert working on the tech stuff and we'll find them."

"Oh my God! I don't know what to do. I know you boys will bring them home. You call dad and let him know any updates. I'm going to have a drink."

He finishes with some stern and supportive words from dad. Our mom never drinks, she gets wasted from a few sips of champagne. I can't picture her having a drink of anything, she only ever has champagne if she's in a social situation where she's required to have a glass, like if there's a toast. If she's drinking something stronger, she's more upset than I've ever seen.

"That went well." I try to be positive.

"I guess, but it doesn't mean she's not going to call one of us every fifteen minutes," Jackson adds.

"Anything, Colby? What're you looking for now?" Auz asks.

"Trying to ping her and Tori. I think their phones are off."

"What does that mean?" Jax asks.

"We can't find them using their phones if they're off," I explain to him.

"How are we going to find them?" he asks.

"I'm looking into drones, if I can get some here, I can send them out looking for the van."

Austin gets a startled look on his face and I can tell by his expression something unpleasant has just occurred to him. His gaze falls to the ground and I wonder what could've come up that's this disturbing. I watch him closely as he seems to have a chat with himself, maybe a pep talk.

"We need to call Randy."

All three of us do a double take and I'm sure I look exactly like Jax and Colby, shocked. Why didn't we think about him sooner? I hope they volunteer, I just met Randy and Stephanie.

"I'll call." Austin might be my hero, without hesitation, he dials once again.

"Hey Austin, how's your sister?" Randy greets him.

"Hi Randy, she's okay but she's not ready to come home. I'm actually calling about Violet and Tori..." Austin explains everything we know and Violet's uncle agrees we shouldn't call the police unless it's a last resort. Randy makes a good suggestion, we need to alert Dozer, he has connections we don't.

The second Austin disconnected from Randy, Colby was calling Dozer. Before long he's in the loop and hitting the road in search of a black, Mercedes full-sized cargo van. If we forgot anyone else, I don't know who they would be. Everyone we know is informed and helping in one way or another.

"Guys, I have something. I'm analyzing the footage of the van compared to any other vehicles following exactly the same path based on camera appearances. There's a Ford Bronco that flags on the track, I'm getting the license plate info."

"Her phone is still off," I say as I try texting her again, I'm not sure what else to say, I want to punch someone but we don't know who and it's killing me.

"Yeah, straight to voicemail," Jackson adds, holding up his screen for us.

"Fucking hell. If anyone hurts them..." Austin growls.

"We're with you, man."

"I got the plate, it's registered to a company, which is part of another company, which is a front. Dammit! I have to dig further, as you were," Colby announces.

"I don't know about you guys, but I can't stand sitting here. I need to do something, who wants to go look for her?" Austin asks.

"I'll stay with Colby," Jackson volunteers.

"Oh, yeah, I was thinking we'd leave him locked in but if he finds anything someone needs to be here. Thanks. We'll keep you posted. Come on Piers."

I scramble out of the truck, happy to be moving and doing something, anything at all really, but going to look for one of those vehicles feels more productive. I jump into Austin's truck and buckle up; we hit pavement and take off back the way we came.

"I'm thinking we start where he last saw the van and take the first turn until we take them all. I'm going to drive until we find them, even if it takes a month to check every building off this road." Austin's completely serious, he's incredibly stubborn and he's always the last man standing in any stamina game, he never gives up, which I appreciate right now.

After three turn offs are fully checked, I message Jackson with an update. They don't have anything yet; I'm starting to think this may take a while. We're going to need gas eventually, and food, drinks, and supplies to keep going. Coffee! Lots of coffee. I don't want Austin to freak out if I suggest refueling and I keep my thoughts to myself for now. We've got almost half a tank, it's not urgent.

Colby sent us the address of the last camera sighting and we're heading back towards him and Jackson, taking every turn off we pass in search of those vehicles. So far, I haven't seen any place they could hide both of the large vehicles. It's a lot of empty space and the places that are inhabited are small without any buildings large enough to hold a vehicle. I wonder if Auz plans to check each building we find that is big enough. I'm not opposed to it, but we need to figure out what makes the most sense. I startle when my phone rings and for a split second I think it might be Violet. It's not, I answer Jackson's call.

"Hey, anything?" I say in greeting.

"Not yet. I'm thinking we need to have a meeting between all of us and Dozer. We need to coordinate a little better, maybe get the communication stuff from the warehouse. Get some long-term supplies, like if we actually planned instead of rushing out of the house without a plan."

I tell Austin what he said and he suggested we meet at the warehouse. Colby is comfortable in Violet's space and he can set up command there using all of Violet's stuff. Colby shares with Dozer and he agrees to meet us in thirty minutes. While we're driving and meeting, Colby's still got his robots looking for those vehicles, Violet and Tori's phones, and probably a million other things he hasn't bothered to tell us.

We arrive and the large overhead door is up with Jackson's truck backed in on one side and another truck backed into the other. I can see Dozer talking to Colby as we enter the building.

Jackson lifts his chin in greeting and follows them up the stairs. Dozer's carrying Colby's gear up the steps, and with the trucks clear I hit the button to close the garage style door. We don't need anyone stealing from us while we're inside the apartment.

Colby plugs in a few things and he's got Violet's system up and running. While he does his Colby thing we visit the facilities, get some water, and gather in the dining area. We sit at the table and someone, probably Austin, placed some snacks in the middle. I'm hungry, so I open a granola bar and it crunches when I take a bite.

Dozer speaks first, "We need a system. You guys," he points at me and Austin, "are driving up every side road checking for those vehicles but what about if you need to check a building? You need a way to mark buildings that need to be checked while you keep going. We should have a secondary team or two that checks those buildings. We need to be systematic so we don't miss anything."

Colby inserts his progress, "I got some drones, they'll be up in an hour."

Dozer continues, "That should help. We need comms, water, protein bars, and we need to calculate the fuel so we can refuel in shifts. I'm bringing in four more cars, with eight bodies, they owe me and two of them just want to help."

Jackson looks at Dozer for a minute before he asks, "Who just wants to help?" Dozer looks away before he answers and I'm thinking whatever he says will piss me off, I'm pleasantly surprised by his response.

"My brother and my cousin offered to help because they know Violet's a friend, they've only met her twice but she leaves an impression. They said they know she means something to me, like family, and they would do the same for anyone in the family. I'm just glad to have more eyes out there. I also have a reward out for the underside of our great state, they're spreading the word, and we should have more people looking for that reward."

"Great, thanks man. The comms are here, what about the food and water?" I ask.

"Yeah, we keep emergency supplies in storage. I'm not sure how many comms sets we have, might need to go one per car. Someone needs to go by home and check on Sawyer, he's going to be freaked out without any of us home at night."

"Dozer, I'm adding to your reward, I want everyone looking hard," Colby calls out.

"All right, let's split up and get what we need. I'll get the comms. I know where they are and how to work them. Austin, you get the food and water. Dozer and Pierson, you guys get whatever weapons we need for everyone. Make sure everyone has vests on hand too," Jackson delegates.

I don't wait for Dozer and head to the weapons vault. As I pass through the workout area, I can see Violet in her gear, punching the heavy bag, her twisted smile when she bests me on the mats, I want to kill whoever took her. I can't linger on the thought of anyone hurting her or I'll go nuts and I mean like shooting spree nuts.

Colby already sent me the code for the vault, and I have it punched in and the heavy door opened wide when Dozer gets there. I'm filling a bag with ammo and he's stacking some rifles near the door. Next, we work together filling the rifle cases so we can carry them where they need to go. It seems like we're finished quickly and back on the road in no time. Once again Jackson volunteered to go check on Sawyer and feed him. I hope Sawyer's okay, he's attached to Violet and he's never fully relaxed if she's not home. Jackson called and told us he brought Sawyer to Randy's because he was upset and Randy offered. Apparently, Sawyer jumped right in bed with Isabel and settled down.

Austin and I get back into the truck at our first stop, the gas station. I got two five-gallon cans while he filled up the truck.

We're full of gas now and even have some spares for emergencies. He speeds us back to where we left off in our search, it's eight-forty-five and I'm afraid we aren't going to find them tonight. My little sister is only fifteen, she's got no clue how to fight and I hate to think about it, but she's a bit of a spoiled brat. I don't want to imagine what being kidnapped will do to her, let alone if they hurt her.

"See anything?" Austin asks.

"Nothing."

"Fuck, this sucks. Where the fuck are they?"

"We're going to find them; we have to... there's no other option."

"You're right, I'm just freaking out, we've never been apart against our will and it hurts me, right in the middle of my chest. I have this terrible ache that stabs me when I think about her or picture her face. I love Tori too but it's different, it's nothing like what I feel for Violet."

"Speaking of loving Violet, how did you know you loved her?" I ask genuinely curious.

"I don't know, I just did. She's the first thing I think of when I wake up, she's the person I want to call when something important happens, and she makes me a better person, somehow, I think those things equal love. Why?"

"I'm having this pain in my chest, it hurts worse whenever I think of her. Before she disappeared, it was like a weird twinge in my chest and a warm feeling would spread out through my body, now that she's missing, it hurts. I think about her every waking minute and last night was probably the best night of my life. Does it mean I'm in love with her?"

"I'm no expert, but maybe. Hey, you see that barn?" My attention is drawn to a large brown, weathered building about fifty yards behind a small home. No lights glow in the windows of either building. I mark it on the map which marks it on a list, Colby worked out a formula to make it all automated. Now another crew will search the barn, they should already have our notification for a building that could hold a vehicle. It's a slick program and it should help us out if it works as advertised.

As we come out of a curve in the road I spot something, parked in a driveway in front of a rusted and battered mobile home, is a dark Ford Bronco. A thrill shoots through me filling my veins with adrenaline. Please let this be them, please!

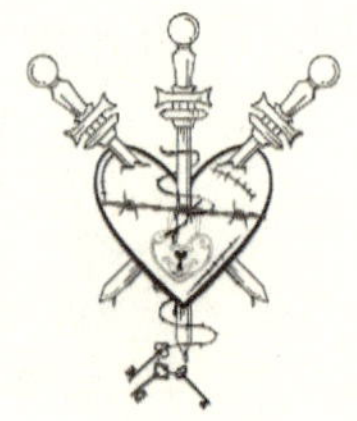

Chapter Seventeen

Violet

My eyes struggle to open until I can finally make my lids lift a crack, big enough to see I'm mostly in the dark in what looks like a house from the nineteen-fifties. Closing them I engage my other senses for more input. I can hear Tori breathing in a steady rhythm nearby, I know it's her by the scent of her perfume. There's a television playing in the distance, maybe two rooms away. I can't tell what our captors are watching, but occasionally I hear raised voices and it makes me think it must be some ridiculous reality show.

Assessing myself for injuries, my head seems to be the worst of it. There's a dull throb above my right ear and when I move my head or my eyes, it turns into a stabbing pain that pierces my skull horizontally from just above my ear and straight across to the other one. When that sharp pain gets really bad, a sword stabs the base of my skull and goes right down my spine expanding outward to all my nerves until it fades. They hit me and drugged me with an injection of something, I can feel the fog of foreign influence in my system, my head feels too heavy.

When I hear approaching footsteps, I hold still making my breathing smooth and even. My ears are attuned to the smallest sound, the person who has now entered this room is big and he has an uneven gait, maybe a limp. His steps are off, one is more of a shuffle and I can smell sweat, whiskey, and cigars. When he leans over me his putrid breath makes me want to vomit, but I hang tough and remain still.

A rough finger which smells strongly of cigar tobacco, touches my bottom lip and I want to bite it off and head butt this pig, but I don't know how many there are and I can't hazard it if he has help. There were at least two of them for sure when they grabbed us. I was ready to kill the guy who grabbed my arm, but the other one held a gun to Tori's head and I froze with my hands up. I couldn't risk anything happening to her.

"Don't touch the merchandise! Keep your grubby hands off, if the boss catches you touching them, you're toast." The smelly fingers retreat and I'm able to breathe more freely. The second guy is much lighter on his feet and I'm certain it's the thin guy who held the gun to Tori. But I didn't smell the stench of hop-along when I was grabbed so there must be at least one more guy. Chances are, the mysterious third dirtbag is the one who knocked me out.

"I wasn't doin' nothin'. They're pretty, much better than the ones we usually get. I just wanted to see what she feels like."

"Is it worth your life? Remember what happened to Mario."

"Yeah. Fuck that was bad, his brains splattered everywhere."

"So, don't touch."

"What're we supposed to do with 'em?"

"Nothing. The boss is coming to check them and tell us what to do, but for now the orders are *hands off*."

"When's the boss comin'?"

"In the morning. Go watch TV and stay away from them."

"Yeah, yeah." His shuffling walk fades, but the other one is still in the room. I need to know if any others are here but I don't want to let on that I'm awake. I don't move until I hear him leave the room.

I try opening my eyes again and it's not as bad as before. I let my eyes adjust and look over my circumstances. The room's empty except for the cots we're hooked to with flex cuffs. Tori looks okay, she's out, they must've drugged her too. I examine the cot and how I'm cuffed to it. Each hand is cuffed to the main bar on either side but my feet are free. I had a blade in my pocket and another on my ankle, they're both gone. I can't lift my arms to check for the small one in my bra. With a little wiggle I think I can still feel the weight of it in the special sheath of lace. It's in a secret little pocket under my left breast, so I can grab it with my right hand.

I try sitting up and it's not easy with the way they have me cuffed. I have to bend my knees and scoot my butt back to be able to bend my waist and keep my wrists next to the bars. It makes a metallic squeaking noise as the springs are stretched, and when I get into a seated position, I wait a minute hoping nobody heard the sounds. When I think it's safe to move again, I tug on my wrists and check how secure they are, and then I twist my arms to check the amount of give I have to slip my hands free. There isn't any space at all between the cuffs and my skin, but they aren't too tight either, just tight enough to keep me from pulling loose.

Before I can try to reach the blade in my bra, I hear footsteps approaching again and I have to move my ass enough to lie back down. It makes too much noise and I cringe waiting to see if they notice.

"I thought you might wake up. I tried to give you a light dose since you and your friend aren't very big. But I see it was too light.

Sorry, but I need you to sleep until morning." A man's voice says behind me.

When he approaches the cot, I'm ready to attack him with whatever I can, unfortunately he must have half a brain and he's cautious. He only comes close enough to reach my upper arm with a syringe. I'm able to see him before the drugs take effect and I don't recognize him, now I know for sure there's at least three of them here. It's my final thought before my vision begins to get blurry and everything starts to fade.

When I wake again, I listen carefully to my surroundings before attempting to open my eyes. I can tell I'm not alone. Tori is still breathing softly nearby, but someone else is also in the room. I can smell expensive perfume and I'm instantly alert for some sign of a woman, maybe there's another kidnapping victim. Someone moves to my left and I focus on the sound. Their clothing made a small swishing noise and a scrape of a shoe on the vinyl floor. Smooth but large fingers check my pulse and I know he's looking at me trying to see if I'm awake.

"Well?" Her voice comes from the far wall to my left and I recognize it instantly. It's none other than Joyce Morgan, my mother fucking grandmother. I'm so fucking pissed off I want to scratch her fucking eyes out. How dare she! If she hurt Tori, I'm going to fucking kill her. Scratch that, I'm going to fucking kill her either way.

"They're both fine. I don't want to give them any more, they might start to have side effects. Are we still sending that one with the politician?"

"Yes," her voice is like nails on a chalkboard to me.

"Where's the blonde going?" the man who drugged me asks.

"Nowhere."

"What a waste. Does she owe you money or something?"

"Yes. Lots of it."

"Damn, shame."

"You wouldn't want her, no one would, she's used up trash. I'm ready to go, take me home."

I'm boiling mad but I need fewer people here before I get free. When I hear their car start and drive away, I sit up again. I don't hear anyone else, no TV either. I have to move my ass as far back as possible so I can bend my chest down to my hand. When I get close enough, I can't quite reach the hidden pocket, my hand stops just out of reach. Twisting around, not caring about the squeaky springs, I'm finally able to get my hand into my bra, my little blade is still there. *Little Rudy, you might be my new favorite knife. You're saving my ass right now and I won't forget it.*

Ahh, relief. The flex cuff on my left-hand snaps and I'm free. I quickly cut through the other one and then I stretch and rub my wrists. They may not have been too tight, but they cut into my wrists while I slept, or was unconscious, which is actually more accurate. I hope they didn't give Tori too much so I can wake her. I quickly cut through her cuffs, but I leave her be while I check the house. I don't want Tori to get hurt in the fight, and there's going to be a fight because I'm seriously pissed off and ready to kill these assholes.

My legs need a good stretch too, I move into a dark corner, and quickly stretch my whole body so I'm ready for whatever I find. Before sticking my head out of the doorway, I listen and engage my sense of smell. It's clear. I check both directions and carefully move next to the left side of the wall in the hallway. Going in the direction of the sound from a TV last night, I don't check behind two closed doors along the way. I don't want to make noise opening doors until I check the rest of the house.

I spot the TV in a living room, there's no one here. Next, I sweep the dining room and nobody's there either. When I get closer to the kitchen I can hear voices, it's the stinky limper and the skinny asshole. I listen for a moment to confirm they're the only ones. They're sitting at a small round table having breakfast. I scan the table for weapons and spot a steak knife, hot coffee, and large ceramic plates.

Without hesitation I charge the skinny one, stab him in the neck making sure to puncture his jugular with my little blade. I know I've hit pay dirt when blood squirts across the floor and the color drains from his face while he struggles to form words. Nothing comes out of his mouth but a wet gurgling sound and its music to my ears. Now weaponless, I improvise, the smelly limper jumps up from his seat and fights indecision, he leans towards his partner in crime and back towards me, then him again. I'm not doing this dance; I collect the steak knife in my left hand and toss what I hope is very hot coffee into his face along with the mug. He screams and rubs at his eyes. I pick up a plate next and smash it over his head. When he bends over in response to my hit, I stab him at the base of his neck with the steak knife. It's not the right type of blade to sever bone and it goes in at a good spot but quickly gets hung up in his cervical vertebra. His screams are constant now and for some reason he's calling out for his Auntie Faye as his hands try to reach for the blade in his fat neck. The resulting visual is a twisted and spastic display of very poor coordination, like a dancing donkey with an itch he can't reach.

"Oh God! Auntie Faye, help me! Please make it stop, Auntie!"

I look for another weapon of opportunity and the table only holds one more plate which didn't do much the first time. Instead, I lift the wood chair the skinny gun holder fell out of and smash it over the limping dancer's head, silence at last. He's not dead, but now I can think.

I search the skinny one and find his H&K nine-millimeter in the back of his waistband. I check the clip and it's fully loaded with one in the chamber. Not wanting to waste time or bullets I shoot skinny bloodless guy in the forehead and the smelly hopper guy just above the ear. I would've loved to torture them, but we don't have time for games, we need to escape.

Though I'm sure we're alone, I quickly search the rest of the house. The good news is no one else is here, the bad news...

Chapter Eighteen

Pierson

After a sleepless night of driving from street to street, house to house, building to building, we're exhausted and we've found nothing. Colby is still trying to run down who owns the company that rented the van and he's got the name of a maintenance company, but no info on who owns it. Each crumb leads to a whole new trail without any rats to kill. He's frustrated too. Violet's uncle invited us to have breakfast and refresh a little so we can get a fresh start. Jackson didn't want to come, but we guilted him into it, explaining we'll never find her if we can't keep our eyes open.

My nerves got so raw with worry last night, and around three I noticed I was numb. I'm not hungry but I need to eat so I can keep going, we all have coffee in our hands and we're rehashing everything with Randy and Stephanie so they're up to speed. He wants to join Jackson when we head back out; his fresh eyes will do us good.

Isabel is attached to Sawyer and vice-versa. We're trying not to say anything to alert Isabel that her big sister is missing, but she's aware of the tension and knows all of her adults are upset. She's a smart kid and you can't just spell things to avoid her catching on. When the doorbell rings we all startle.

"I'm not expecting anyone," Randy announces as he walks towards the door, then waits for Stephanie and Austin to flank Isabel. He opens the door, and I can't see who's there from my spot in an armchair. Jackson has his Glock in his hand, held down next to his thigh.

"Oh! What are you doing here?" Randy asks with what can only be described as astonishment.

"It's nice to see you too. I'm trying to get a hold of Violet and she's not answering my calls, and she wasn't at her disgusting warehouse. I assume you know how to locate her," a woman's voice says, and I have no idea what she could possibly want with Violet. I shoot a questioning look at Jackson. He looks exasperated by whoever this person might be and I'm lost.

"Well Joyce, at the moment, I don't know where she might be, but I'll let her know you're looking for her," Randy answers in a stiff voice, he doesn't like her either.

Before anyone can stop her, Isabel steps forward and questions the older woman, "How do you know my sister? She's missing and we need to find her. Do you know where she is?" Sawyer darts out the door and Randy goes after him leaving the door wide open. Now I can see an elderly woman with perfectly coiffed white hair and bright red lipstick that would be too much for a hooker on a stage, in a musical. She's clutching a fancy leather bag close to her body and looking down at Isabel, I mean looking down her nose, behind designer sunglasses. This must be Violet's estranged grandmother, no wonder everyone is reacting like this.

"No. Why on earth would I know where your sister is? Who is this child? And what is she talking about, Randy?"

"This is my adopted daughter, Isabel. She's asking if you know where Violet is, she seems to be missing."

I watch as this bizarre woman almost smiles at Randy's explanation. I want to slap that twisted little grin right off her face, what the fuck is wrong with this bitch? Randy just told her Violet, her granddaughter, is missing for fuck's sake.

"You can't be serious. I'm going to contact my attorney. You know if she disappeared, I get everything my daughter left to that...*girl.* I want to be kept apprised of this situation. This is exactly what I needed to speak to her about, she owes me some of my daughter's property and if I don't get it, she'll be hearing from my attorney. Oh! Get this beast away from me!" Her tirade ends in a high pitched and fearful tone. I stand to get a better view of what she's talking about.

At her feet Sawyer has his claw snagged into her, probably extremely expensive boutique pants, it's as if he's trying to hold her in place with his teeth clamped onto the dark fabric just above his talons. Her face has drained of what little color it had by the feisty feline trapping her there.

"I mean it Randy! Get this animal off of me immediately! If it bites me, I'll sue you for every penny you have, move!" She pulls back her other foot as if to kick Sawyer and several things happen at once.

Isabel runs to save Sawyer and screams, "Noooo!" She tries to tackle him.

Randy also screams, "Isabel! Watch out!" He tries to catch her before she can get close to the wretched old woman. Austin and Stephanie also rush to get to Isabel. Jackson cocks his gun and looks determined to shoot the bitch. I decide to keep my brother from going to jail over her ratchet ass and I wrap my arms around him while shaking my head.

"Jax! Don't!"

When the dust settles, I'm holding Jackson back, Stephanie is holding onto Austin, Randy has scooped up Isabel who somehow managed to grasp onto Sawyer and pull him free.

Everyone freezes and checks who has who and if everyone is in one piece, Jackson disengages his trigger and holds his firearm safely at his side once again. Isabel's sweet face is scrunched up in anger, Violet's influence on the adorable and precocious girl is evident when she says, "I don't like that lady, daddy. She tried to hurt Sawyer, she's mean!"

Randy looks a little embarrassed by Isabel's lack of pretense, "Steph, can you take Izzy, please?" Austin collects Isabel and Sawyer and brings them both inside, Stephanie holds onto Isabel in Austin's arms and walks back inside with them.

I check on Jackson, "You good, man?"

"Yep." His answer is positive but he looks madder than a long-tailed cat in a room full of rocking chairs. I don't know why my granddad's saying pops into my head, but it fits. Austin carries Isabel and Sawyer down the hall with Stephanie in tow.

"I'm sorry about the cat, I don't know what got into him. I'll let Violet know you stopped by. *Ahem.* Have a nice day, Joyce." Randy sticks with diplomacy and I envy his ability to remain calm and respectful. I guess it's what helps him be a physician, nerves of steel.

"Well, if I become ill from those vermin touching me, you'll hear from my attorney. I'll also be sending you the bill for these pants and if my tailor can't fix the damage, you'll be getting a bill for their full cost. Honestly, I expect better from a respected physician. If you see that girl, you tell her she better call my attorney right away. If she doesn't return, I'll be expecting all of the property owed to me delivered immediately. I will give you ten days to make her appear, not a minute longer. Good day." She turns on her heel and stomps in a dainty old lady way to her chauffeur driven, holy fuck, Rolls Royce. She climbs in and her driver closes her door and drives her away.

Checking to make sure Isabel isn't within earshot I say, "What the fuck is her problem?"

"That was Violet's evil grandmother. She's never shown up here before, impeccable timing, huh?"

"Or not." We all turn and look at Stephanie.

"What do you mean?" Randy asks.

"Isabel says Sawyer smelled Violet on the grandmother from hell." She looks at Jackson.

"What did Austin say?" he asks.

"He said Sawyer's never acted like that before. He says he agrees with Isabel, that bitch knows where Violet and Tori are." Jackson puts his gun in its holster and pulls his phone from his pocket, he dials and puts it on speaker.

Colby answers, "What's up?"

"Check if Joyce Morgan has any connection to any of those dummy companies and phony IDs. Also, check if she owns any properties in our search area. We're going back on the road now, let us know the minute you find anything."

"On it," Colby responds and hangs up.

Jackson looks at Randy, "You coming?"

"Yeah, let me get my shoes on. You going to be okay Steph?"

"Yep, go find them." He kisses her on his way to the hall. Austin emerges a moment later, he starts putting our dishes in the kitchen and I help. By the time Randy is back with boots on his feet, we're all walking out the door. He kisses Stephanie again and we file out to our vehicles. Jackson and Randy lead the way, Austin and I follow in his truck.

"Is Isabel, okay? I thought we were careful so she wouldn't know Violet's missing."

"She's too smart for her own good sometimes. We can't keep much from her if she's within earshot. Remember that because she's asked me some uncomfortable questions when she overheard me talking to Violet." He gives me a goofy look and I can imagine what dirty things he said to Violet, he's always been a pig.

"So, you really think that old bitch knows where Violet and Tori are?"

"When Isabel said Sawyer could smell Violet, it clicked. I couldn't understand why he would act like that. He avoids strangers and he's never tried to hold anyone from leaving before. It makes sense if he could smell her."

"I think he doesn't realize he's a cat sometimes. That's dog behavior, isn't it?"

"I don't know, but he's definitely attached to Violet and the way he acted, I have to believe there was a reason."

My phone rings, "Yeah?"

"Let's split up like we planned and resume the search. Colby has Dozer's guys heading this way to follow us. You'll lead one group and we'll lead the other," Jackson says into Randy's phone.

"Did you get all that?" Randy asks.

"Yep, we're on it. We're turning off here, you guys go east and hopefully we'll get confirmation and an address from Colby."

"Ten-four, I'm out."

I relay what they said to Austin and we resume the hunt where we left off. After about fifteen minutes two cars come up behind us and pace our progress. When we pass a barn that could hold a large vehicle the last car pulls over and they get out. I watch in the side mirror as they walk up the short path in the weeds.

We're quiet, lost in our own thoughts I suppose. I'm rehashing everything that's happened in the last forty-eight hours, from my date with Violet and the amazing night that followed, to the absolute panic at the realization she and Tori are missing. I continue to rub my chest in that sore spot that must be rubbed raw by now. We have to find them, and soon. If that evil old lady had something to do with their disappearance, we're going to hunt her down and rip those red lips right off her plastic face.

"I'm so pissed off and scared, I'm not sure how to feel right now. How are you holding up?" I ask.

"I'm surviving on faith. Not in religious terms or anything, but faith in our girl. She's smart, strong, stubborn, she won't let anything happen to Tori. I know we're going to find them because Violet doesn't know how to give up."

"She *is* amazing isn't she. I'm pretty sure I'm in love with her." I jolt at what just came out of my mouth. I haven't come to that conclusion in my head, at least not consciously, but my mouth has other ideas. Well, there it is. I said it. Now we just need to find her so I can tell her.

Austin is chuckling under his breath and I narrow my eyes in question.

"Sorry man, but you should see your face. You looked like you stepped in something warm and wet in your socks. Jackson and I knew you loved her like a week ago. I'm glad you finally caught on."

"You're a dick."

"Yep."

"Do you think she loves me?"

He glances at me and gets more serious, "Yeah, I think she does. She's not always easy to read, but when she feels something, she doesn't hide it. When she didn't stab you, we figured she must be in love. Besides, how could she not love you? You're all cute and cuddly," he busts out laughing and I punch him.

"Asshole."

"Ow! No hitting the driver, man!"

"Yeah, yeah, whatever."

We passed another property with some larger buildings. They look like they hold livestock, but the remaining car behind us pulls off to check it out. After another fifteen minutes the first car that pulled off is back behind us again.

"Do you-" My phone rings again and I'm a little annoyed that the batteries died on our radios. It was easier to check in when it was just a click and everyone could hear the updates at once.

"What's up?" I answer.

Colby responds, "I've got something. It's an intricate web of false fronts and fake identities. But Joyce the Impaler's husband was a serious dirtbag. Turns out he was running a multitude of illegal enterprises including mafia style endeavors such as gambling, theft, fraud, and trafficking. Humans, drugs, and guns. I actually suspect he's a mob boss in the Greek Mafia, but I don't have confirmation. It looks like his real surname was Mouratidis... seems he changed it to evade interest from the authorities. I'm getting a list of properties owned by him and his businesses, fake or not. Three of the properties are in the area you guys are searching, I'm sending you two. The other one is closer to Jackson. Let me know if you find anything, and I'll keep digging." I was smart and put it on speaker, so I don't need to relay everything to Auz.

I click on the first address and the map expands, the voice in my phone calls out directions and we're only four minutes away. Before we get to that property, we pass one with a large barn and I don't tell them not to check it just in case, and we lose our tail.

When we reach the first address there's a concrete foundation with a brick fireplace and chimney jutting up into the sky, the rest of the building is a blackened shell of former walls. They aren't here, there's no place to hide anyone let alone a vehicle.

Austin lets out a low whistle at the devastation. We continue on to the next address. It's another ten minutes away and I have big hairy moths fluttering around in my gut with anticipation. I decided to make a silent plea to anyone with the power to help.

Dear God, or anyone who's listening, please let us find them safe. Please let them be at this next address without being harmed in any way. Amen, I guess. Thank you.

I always get awkward when I deal with religious stuff. We weren't super religious at mom and dad's house, but we weren't atheists either, we went to Catholic church sometimes for holidays, and of course we were involved enough for Megan to be exposed to *Voldemort.* My birth grandmother was extremely religious and she used to say my mother was going to hell and I was the spawn of Satan. It was a whole thing. I've always felt like I don't deserve a relationship with God and if I tried to become religious, I would burst into flames or something. If we find them unharmed, I might need to talk to mom and dad about what I should do with regard to religion. Of course, I'm not sure they accept murderers at church.

Before I can continue this doomed train of thought we turn onto the road for the second address. I'm carefully checking each mailbox for the numbers seven-eight-three-nine, when I see something out of the corner of my eye. It was a movement up ahead, like maybe someone or an animal maybe, dodged into some trees.

"Slow down."

"Why?" Austin asks, examining me.

"I saw something, a movement out of the corner of my eye. Up there by those trees. Go slow."

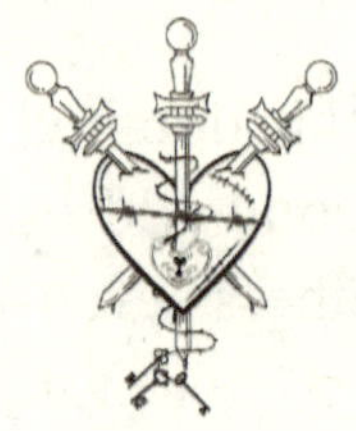

Chapter Nineteen

Violet

There aren't any vehicles here, we're going to need to escape on foot. I gently shake Tori and call her name a little louder with each shake. When her eyes flutter open, I smile down at her, she was *out* and that explains why she didn't hear the gunshots. I'm so glad.

"Violet? Where are we?"

"It's a long story, we need to go and I'll explain on the way. How do you feel?"

"Like I was run over by a bus. I have to pee. How long was I asleep?" Her voice is rough from too many hours not talking, she's hitting the ground running.

I lead her to the restroom and we both use it. I take a drink of water from the faucet and Tori does the same. When we walk out the side door into an open carport, my bags from the mall are there, sitting on a peeling and dusty black shelf. Our purses are in the bag with my underwear, well shit, can't beat that with a stick, or a chair. We each take a bag and make our way down the crumbling asphalt driveway that hasn't had any maintenance in decades. Large sections of it are just gravel and as we navigate the potholes, I'm really glad we're both wearing comfortable shoes.

When we reach the road, we need to choose right or left, for some reason the left is calling to me. Plus, something about the position of the rusty mailbox makes me think it's the right way to go. I take note of the numbers on the side of the ancient post box, seven-eight-three-nine, just in case I need to come back here to kill my fucking grandmother, the vilest monster of them all. I lead us left and I'm fairly certain we're heading East, and I hope it's towards a main road and salvation.

"So, your *grandmother* had us kidnapped? Why would she do that?"

"I'm not sure, but she's a vile, money grubbing, snobby bitch, she probably has her reasons. It doesn't matter now, we're free and as soon as we get to a main road we'll be headed home. I'm really sorry you got stuck in the middle of whatever this is."

"Don't apologize, it's not your fault your grandma is a vile bitch. I bet mom and dad are going crazy. Oh God, my brothers must be ready to kill someone. I would hate to be your grandmother, when they find out what she did it's going to be hard to hold them back."

"They can get in line behind me. I'm going to rip her a new one and maybe carve those ugly inflated red lips right off her face."

"Yikes! You sound serious, don't say that in front of the police."

"What police?" I ask looking around.

"I'm assuming mom and dad called the police as soon as they realized we were missing. My dad knows I would never stay out all night without telling them, even if I'm difficult sometimes, I'd never disappear on them. Plus, don't you think my brothers went nuts when they noticed we were gone? One or both of them might be in jail right now, thankfully Austin's with Megan so he won't be in jail. Oh no, do you think they called him home? I hope Megan's okay."

Wow, that spiraled quickly. Tori talked herself right into a freak-out.

"Don't worry, I'm sure nobody's in jail and Megan is fine. My friend Colby, you met him, is a computer genius. I'm sure they got him looking for us and they might not have even needed the police. Relax, okay?"

"This is one of those Yoda moments, you're so calm when we were freaking kidnapped! How do you do that?"

"Remember what I told you about my childhood?"

She sobers fast, "Yes."

"After years of abuse, you don't let stuff get to you like that anymore. I've learned how to be patient and calm no matter what's happening. It never helped me to get upset or freak out, it only made it worse. Now I can stay calm during extreme circumstances," I shrug. When we're a few houses away from where we started, I hear a car or maybe a truck coming. We can't risk it being one of our captors and I yank her into some trees just as I catch a flash of the sun reflecting off a large profile vehicle.

"Wha-!?!"

"Shhh, sorry, there's a car coming, we need to hide in case it's the kidnappers. Come on and don't talk." I whisper shout. She instantly complies, trusting me to keep her safe. I trek deep enough into the woods that we can't see the road and duck down. Tori copies me and we hold still and wait for the car to pass. I can hear the engine clearly and it's going slow.

"Do you think they saw us?" Tori whispers.

"I hope not. I can hear them. Shhh." I'm trying not to tell her to shut up, I think she figured it out, she's still and quiet.

When the sound of their engine continues past us, I signal to her to stay in the woods and we're going in the same direction as we were on the road. It's much slower going now that we're dodging trees, coral boulders, and sharp bushes. I'm ahead of Tori trying to find the best path to lead her through, it might not be my best idea.

"Ahhh! Ouch!" When I look back, Tori's shirt is torn and attached to the sharp thorns on a very prickly bush. I have to make her back up so I can unhook her formerly cute top from the foliage.

"Are you hurt?"

"Just a scratch." She lifts her shirt and shows me a thin line with a few drops of blood on her stomach.

"Okay, good. Why don't you go first and maybe I can keep you safer if I can watch you. We're heading that way," I speak softly and point in the direction I still think is East. She looks in the direction I'm pointing and then back at me, she doesn't seem confident in my new plan with her nose scrunched up and her eyes narrowed.

"All right." She takes a deep breath and starts trudging through the forest. The ground is uneven and littered with obstacles, Tori trips on a root but catches herself and continues onward. We've only made it about twenty feet further into the thick woods when I hear another car or maybe it's the same car and now, they might know I killed their buddies. I don't want to scare her so I quietly let her know we need to stop and listen. She looks nervous and I wish I could reassure her. It dawns on me there's a way to make her feel better and I pull her into a hug, it's not my usual M.O. but she's a kid and she's scared. Plus, I like her and she's almost like a little sister, my dark heart clenches and feels warm, it's like the moment when the Grinch's heart grows three sizes.

The truck, I'm fairly sure it's a truck, stops back where we first went into the woods. I can think of a million reasons why that's not good. Glancing around, there's no path and I don't see any way to get Tori out of here. We have to stay put and hide. Before I have a chance to break the news to Tori, I hear the most amazing thing I've ever heard.

"Violet! Tori!" A gorgeous masculine voice calls.

"Baby! Where are you?"

"We're over here! Walk east about thirty feet!" I shout back at them.

"Yes!" Tori fist pumps and I high five her.

"Let's go!"

I take the lead and barge through the forest in spite of the hazards and when I stumble onto the road, I fall right into Pierson's arms. I'm overwhelmed with joy, gratitude, and something more intense I don't want to name.

"Holy fuck, I missed you, Killer." Pierson kisses me and I attack him by jumping up into his arms and wrapping my legs around him. I kiss him like I've just returned from war. He holds me so tight, it feels amazing, safe, I'm so happy I can't keep from smiling and a giggle escapes me. His smile is brilliant and my love for him explodes right out of my mouth.

"I love you." He looks stunned for a beat, then his brilliant smile returns, and I swear there's a sweet twinkle in his eye.

"I love you too." He kisses me again.

"We're super happy for you both but I need to kiss my girlfriend I haven't seen in days. My turn, dude."

We switch and my gorgeous Austin is here! I haven't seen him in forever and I can't believe he's really here. He kisses me and I kiss him back, hard. He pulls me close and I squeeze his waist.

"Baby, I love you so much." He kisses me again and I'm lost in him. He feels amazing.

"I missed you. I love you too." I glance around and ask, "Where's Jackson?"

"He's on his way." No sooner did the words leave his lips than we hear a truck roaring up the road towards us and it skids to a stop right in front of Austin's truck slinging gravel. Jackson hops out of the cab and runs at me.

"You better go." Austin smacks my ass and I take off to intercept Jackson. For some reason I imagine this is happening in slow motion like those couples who see each other on a beach and run to embrace one another in the movies.

I launch myself at Jackson and he catches me with ease, he kisses me all over my face and neck.

"I missed you so fucking much, Babe. Don't ever do this again."

"You got it. I love you." My hands hold his cheeks while I look into his eyes.

"I love you too," he says as he presses his lips to mine. A throat clears and I can see my uncle over his shoulder. He opens his arms and I kiss Jackson one last time and wriggle free from his grasp. I rush to Uncle Randy and smack into him with a bear hug. He returns my affection and kisses my head. Then he holds me at arms-length and searches my face.

"What?"

"Are you hurt?" Before I catch myself, my eyes shift down as I debate what to say. He immediately locks onto my subtle tell and grills me.

"What did they do to you? Where are you hurt? Whose blood is that? Is it yours?"

Looking down, I shake my head, "It's not mine." The splatter on my arm is dried and a little sticky. I didn't even notice it before.

"But you're hurt, where?"

Reaching up to touch the knot on my head, I flinch when I reach the worst spot, "They hit me with something here and they drugged us. Tori was still out just a half hour ago. I had to wake her." He looks at my eyes, then glances at Tori who's happily chatting with her brothers.

Jackson takes my hand and turns it so he can look at the raw marks on the inside of my wrist. Then he holds my chin and looks into my eyes for a moment. His eyes shift to the lump above my ear and he seeks my permission with a sweet look, I grant it with a kiss. His fingers gently caress my scalp feeling for the lump. I don't flinch this time because I expected it to hurt.

"What do you say Doc?" he asks Randy.

"She's still under the influence of the drugs and she might have a mild concussion. She has a good knot and a nasty gash, but it's not bleeding so she can get by without stitches. I need to check Tori." With that he walks over to her and feels her forehead, I can't hear what they're saying.

"You need a hospital," Jackson says with a stern growl.

"I have a doctor, he's right there." I use my thumb to gesture over my shoulder.

"You might have a concussion, if something happens with that, you'll need more medical care than he can offer in his dining room."

"I might not have a concussion and the hospital will call the cops who will ask a lot of questions I don't want to answer if I want to be able to kill *Grandma Murder.*"

His bossy look fades and he grins. I smile back at him but I don't feel like I'm aware of why we're smiling.

"I'm happy to hear you say that. The bitch needs to die. Wait, how do you know it was her? You saw her?"

"Technically my eyes were closed, but I know it was her. I recognized her voice while she was telling her minions how she's going to kill me."

"She came to Randy's looking for you."

"Why?"

"She said some bullshit about property you owe her. She acted surprised that you were missing. But Sawyer could smell you, we think, and he wouldn't let her leave. He was a brute, grabbed her leg with his claws and teeth."

"Ahhh, he was at Randy's?"

"Yeah, we didn't want to leave him at home alone and Randy offered, is it okay?"

"Yeah, of course, Isabel loves him and he loves her attention. I guess we need to go there first so Tori and I can get treated. If your parents want to take her to the hospital, we'll need a story for them to cover our involvement."

"She can say she was at a party last night and someone spiked her drink. Hey, guys, I'm calling Mom," Jackson tells them.

"I called Dad, he said we should come over after we're done at Randy's," Austin says.

"What's going on Jackson?" Their mom answers his call loud enough for me to hear.

"We found them!"

"I know, but why aren't you bringing Tori straight home? Is she hurt? What did they do to her?" He takes a few steps away.

"Mom...Mom! She's okay, they both are but Tori was drugged so Randy will probably need to monitor her for a while. Violet's got a lump on her head, but she's good, nothing but empty space up there anyway." Glancing at me he chuckles at my pinched face.

"Yeah, Violet was drugged too, but they both seem fine, Violet's head is her main injury. She's alert, she knows who I am, she'll be fine. Okay. All right. I promise. Yes, bye."

Uncle Randy comes back to us and Jackson tells the others, "Let's go back to Randy's. You guys take Tori, we'll see you in a few minutes. A row of four cars shows up behind Jackson's truck with Dozer driving the first car and I think one of his brothers is with him. They're both smiling and raise a hand in greeting. I return it with a wave. Dozer holds his phone to his ear and nods a few times while he talks. Then he and his brother wave at me again so I wave back. This time it's a wave goodbye because he drives off and the other three cars follow. They must be part of his crew and I think I saw his other brother driving one of the cars. I guess Colby called in the big guns.

I doze in the truck, Uncle Randy keeps waking me, apparently, it's the custom when you think someone has a concussion, you royally piss them off by not letting them rest. By the time we get to Randy's house I'm ready to throttle him. Lucky for him my sweet little sister comes running out of the house before I can strangle him.

"Violet! Yay! I was scared you were lost. I thought maybe the Wicked Witch of the West got you just like Dorothy. Sawyer misses you and he needs a scratch from you."

"Thanks for taking good care of him for me and I promise I won't ever get lost. Did he sleep in your room?"

"Right on my neck!"

"Yeah, he does that. How's your mom?"

"She's great, she said if I have a good week at school, she'll take me to get a stellascope."

"Do you mean a telescope?"

"Yes! I learned in school we can see the moon with a stellascope. I want to go in space on a rocket and stop on the moon so I can jump really high. They have no grabity on the moon." She smiles at me with a bright and hopeful grin.

"That sounds amazing, can we go inside? I want to see Sawyer and get a shower."

When I exit the bathroom with my hair a little damp and wearing Stephanie's clothes, I signal to Tori that it's her turn. She smiles gratefully. I feel much better now and I notice my stomach is growling in hunger. The kitchen is empty when I open the fridge in search of a hearty snack. I chuckle when I find string cheese in the cold cut drawer, I'll have to tell Tori it's in there.

When I enter the Florida room, everyone except Isabel is in the comfortable space, including Sawyer. He's perched on the back of the couch and he looks like a wild cat, like a panther or maybe a jaguar. He's licking his paw and flicking his tail. Approaching him, I coo softly and thank him for being such a good boy for Isabel and for treating my grandmother the way she deserves.

Meow!

"I know cutie, I'm sorry I wasn't here." When I'm done consoling Sawyer, I sit on Austin's lap with one hand on Jackson and my foot pressed under Pierson's leg. Spending a few minutes listening to their conversation I'm able to piece together the series of events that took place while I was missing.

"Sweetie, why don't you tell us what happened to you and Tori." Stephanie hands me an ice pack for the lump on my head and I tell them how we were taken from the mall at gunpoint. Well, Tori had a gun to her head, I was forced to comply until they hit me and knocked me out. I tell them everything including how I killed those two assholes during our escape. Nobody bats an eyelash at my disclosure and I feel such strong love for everyone in the room.

When Tori comes in with her hair in a towel, we tone down the murder talk and let her tell us everything from her point of view. Thankfully she was out for most of our ordeal and she only remembered the guy pointing a gun at her as being a man with a gun. She didn't even see the guy who knocked me out, but she can describe the gun in perfect detail.

"When do we have to talk to the police?" she asks, and we were expecting the question.

Uncle Randy answers, "Because Violet's grandmother is involved, we were hoping to keep this as a family matter. Your brothers and Colby were able to find you with their resources and connections and they want to get evidence to prosecute Mrs. Morgan before they turn it over to the authorities. Right now, we have no proof she was involved other than Violet recognizing her voice. She can argue Violet was hearing things because she was drugged and has a head injury. Violet wants to get enough evidence to make sure that woman can't ever hurt anyone again. Plus, Colby knows some FBI guys, we're hoping to get her sentenced in federal court. Will you be supportive of this plan?"

Tori smiles at me nodding, "Yeah, of course. Violet saved my life, and I'll do whatever she wants."

"Thanks Tori. I appreciate the support and I'm going to make sure she pays for what she did."

"Great. Will Mom and Dad be okay without the police?" she asks.

Austin jumps in, "Mom took a little convincing, but she's okay now. I'm glad you're safe. Do you want to go home?"

"Yeah, my bed sounds amazing right now. I'm still tired even though all I've done is sleep," Tori replies.

Stephanie speaks up, "You've been through a trauma on top of the drugs, you may be tired for a few days. If you need someone to talk to, call Randy. He's got experience helping young people." She smiles sweetly at me and I return her affection. She's right, if Randy was able to deal with me, Tori's trauma will be a piece of cake. My affection spreads to him and when I glance his way he's watching me. He looks like a proud father who's relieved his child is safe. That's me, he's my dad now and I'm so lucky to have him and Stephanie. Actually, I'm completely blessed to have everyone in this room, and Isabel who's hopefully napping in her bed.

"I guess we need to take Tori home before mom explodes and let her see we're all safe. Do you want to bring Sawyer with us?" Austin asks.

Looking around I answer, "Let's leave him here for now, he can stay one more night with Isabel. We'll get him tomorrow. I don't want to keep him in a crate while we're at your parents. Is that all right?" I direct my question to Stephanie.

"Of course, Isabel will be thrilled. Why don't you come for dinner tomorrow?"

"Does that work guys?" I ask my boyfriends.

They all nod and Jackson answers, "Sure, we can come after work. Thanks, for all of your help. We'll see you tomorrow. We better get going." He directs most of his response to Stephanie and Uncle Randy. We all stand and hug each other, offer our gratitude, and I explain what we're doing to Sawyer who follows me into Isabel's room. When I kiss Isabel on her forehead, Sawyer curls up next to her and places his chin on her neck. I swear he knows I'm leaving him one more night and he's making it his responsibility to watch over Isabel. He's the coolest cat.

Chapter Twenty

Pierson

Mom won't stop hugging Tori, I keep waiting for her to have a fit and stomp off to her room but Tori's actually hugging her back. She's even smiling at Mom, she seems different. Maybe this experience has made her more mature. I hate that it happened, but if she's able to act her age and be appreciative of her awesome parents, it might be worth it. I probably shouldn't think that way, but I'm trying to make lemonade as the saying goes.

I'm impressed Tori isn't whining and trying to get sympathy so everyone will fall all over her. She's definitely different. I wonder if Violet had a chance to talk to her about what she wanted, maybe that's why she's behaving like a human instead of a brat. Either way, Violet saved our sister and if I didn't already love her, I would fall in love with her for that alone.

"Thanks so much Angie, I'm hungry, dinner sounds great," Violet tells Mom when she makes her usual request to feed everyone.

"I'm going to start getting everything ready for the table. Why don't you kids get something to drink and find your seats in the dining room?"

"Do you want something to drink?" I ask Violet.

"Yeah. Thanks. I'll take cranberry anything or water." She rubs her hand up my arm and I feel it in my dick. Hoping to slow the growing in my pants I rush to the kitchen and seek out something for Violet to drink.

When I meet her in the dining room, she thanks me for the cranberry and seltzer I hand to her. She's facing the window and I stand next to her. We're both admiring the sunset I guess, it's all pinks and purples on the horizon and it gives me a feeling of hope. I take her hand and she squeezes mine.

"What're you thinking about?" I ask.

"Just how much I'm looking forward to gutting that bitch."

"Wow, you're making me so hot. Do you always talk so sexy?"

"I knew I liked you." She giggles and it sends another twinge into my half stiff dick.

"I thought you loved me," I tease.

"I do. But I also like you, the two aren't always automatic. You're just fun enough and special enough for me to like you, not everyone likes killing enough to meet my criteria." She has an evil grin on her gorgeous face and my dick just went from half to full mast.

"Let's sit down," Dad says when he enters the room with Austin and Jackson right behind him. I let Violet lead me to the table, she sits next to Jackson and across from Austin. I sit on her other side without ever letting go of her hand.

When Mom comes in with her hands full, and Tori following her with food in her hands too, my jaw falls open. Tori is helping and smiling. I'm giving Violet the credit for this miracle, nobody else could've ever pulled it off.

"Tori, do you think you can avoid telling your sister what happened? With her at a cheer retreat, she's been unreachable, and we've decided it might be best if we just don't tell her," Dad asks once she's seated.

"Yeah, okay. No point in scaring her when everything's fine," Tori answers agreeably.

I catch Austin and Jackson exchanging a look of surprise. It's not just me who's amazed by Tori's easy-going attitude. I catch Austin's eye and give him my own look of shock. We get quiet as everyone digs into the delicious meal. Nobody makes a roast like our mom and it's always so freaking good. With all three of us here we devour every last piece of the food she served. I think I saw Austin licking the bowl the potatoes were in.

"Tori, is there anything you want to tell us about what happened? Today's a good time to talk about it before Kristin gets home," Mom asks.

Tori is staring at her plate and after a pause she looks at Violet while she says, "I don't remember very much because I was drugged, but what I do remember is Violet saving my life when they pointed a gun at me. Then I remember her saving me by getting me safely out of the house and back home. Violet's my hero, literally. Thank you, I don't think I thanked you. I wouldn't have survived if it wasn't for you." A tear falls from each of Tori's eyes and Mom sniffles.

"I'm so glad you're safe, but I think your brothers were responsible for saving both of us. Like I said before, I'm sorry my grandmother pulled you into her messed up agenda."

"Hogwash! Tori's right, you saved her and we can't ever thank you enough." With that, Mom leaps from her chair and rushes to Violet. Without asking first, which is normal for Mom she never asks, she pulls Violet up from her seat and into a hug. She's whispering something into Violet's ear but I can't hear what she's saying. Violet nods to whatever she says and Mom renews her hug and tears.

When I catch Violet's eye, she's taller than Mom, she smiles a sweet grin that makes me think despite Mom's annoying traits, Violet loves her and it does something to my heart. It stutters in my chest with a strong crushing sensation that turns into a thrilling excited tingle as it spreads through my veins like a roller coaster. I've never felt anything like it and I know it's because I've never been in love before.

After Mom finally releases her, Violet excuses herself to the restroom. Mom begins the animated chatter that takes over the table. While everyone's busy, I sneak off to follow Violet. I want to make sure she's okay. She's not one to easily share her feelings and she usually deals with emotions with a blade, I want to be there for her while that's not an option.

When the door clicks open and Violet tries to exit, I push my way inside with her and close the door behind me. Violet waits patiently for me to explain.

"I wanted to make sure you're alright."

She smirks, "I'm fine. How are you? Doing, okay? Feeling some emotions?" I don't know what she sees on my face or in my eyes.

"Are you?" I press into her and she's forced to rest her ass on the counter.

"I'm feeling something, but it's pressed into my thigh." Her little tilted grin returns.

My control snaps, something about her makes me crazy, I grab her arm and the back of her neck and pull her into me for a kiss. She instantly opens to me and I can't get enough of her. She smells incredible and I want to lick her. She's still in Stephanie's sweats, I tug on them and she moves to accommodate my removal of her pants.

I kiss her ear and her neck before saying, "Oh, Killer, I'm going to fuck you so hard you won't be able to walk for a week."

With a chuckle she responds, "I'd love that." She pulls my dick out of my pants after unhooking them. She squeezes my now fully erect and ready to burst, cock. I only let her stroke me for a moment before I move her hands, spread her legs, and plow into her. She's so wet my dick slides into her smoothly, her pussy is warm and squeezes me in a way that makes me want to press in further. I grab her ass and move her while I pump into her. My teeth chew on her ear, my lips kiss her neck, my mouth tells her how fucking gorgeous she is, and how good she feels. I'm in heaven and I want to stay buried inside her for the rest of my life.

"Mmmm, Piers, yeeeessss. Oh, yes! Harder!"

I slam into her and she purrs in my ear, pleading with me to go faster and harder. Letting her lead the speed and strength of our bodies coming together, I give her everything she asks. When my orgasm approaches, I begin to lose my coordination, she helps keep us in sync. Her pussy clenched hard and it sent me off the cliff. Bright lights flash behind my eyelids while every nerve in my body shoots my seed all over the tight pulsing walls of her beautiful pussy. My balls are so tight I can't stop squirting cum inside her. I have to lean my hands on the counter to keep from collapsing in pleasure.

Violet tried to be quiet but I don't think she was successful, and I feel like maybe I heard her yell out something. Her forehead is flopped onto my shoulder. Random leftover jolts of electric satisfaction travel my nerves again and again.

"That was amazing," she whispers and her eyes are glazed, her cheeks flush, she's stunning.

"Back at you, Killer. Wow, I need a drink."

"Me too. I'll be out in a minute. I just need to clean up."

"Here," I hand her a washcloth, then take one for myself. Once we're cleaned up the best we can manage without a shower, we attempt to sneak out.

Jackson and Austin are standing outside the door when it opens. Austin looks serious but Jackson has a knowing grin on his face and I can feel my cheeks burn.

"We had to tell mom about you two when we all heard Violet. Dude, you know she can't be quiet," Austin admonishes. I flinch and feel bad Violet might be embarrassed but when I look at her, she's calm and unaffected. She shrugs and leaves the bathroom, moving in her sure and strong way that mesmerizes me.

I follow her to the kitchen and she takes out the cranberry juice and gulps right from the bottle, finishes it, and tosses it into the trash like it's nothing. I grab a beer and continue in her wake to the dining room. The empty platters are gone and replaced with some fruit pie, I think it's apple and another is chocolate, a fancy looking pie with whipped cream and chocolate sandwich cookies decorating it. Violet sits in her seat and reaches for the chocolate.

Mom is having trouble looking me in the eye and her cheeks are pink, Dad has a crooked grin across his face, and Tori is solely focused on her apple pie. Maybe it's not so bad, I test the waters.

"Will you please hand me the apple?" Mom hands it to me, but her cheeks flame red again. I should've thought before I let my dick take charge. Oh well, they know I'm together with Violet, it's not a bad thing. God, why is Dad still grinning at me like a lunatic?

"Hand me the chocolate, bro," Austin orders and the air releases in the room. I hadn't noticed how the pressure was making the room feel stiff, but when it eases, it's like an audible pop even though I know it's not possible.

Violet's hand squeezes my knee and it makes me relax, "This pie is delicious, thanks Mom."

"Of course, Piers, make sure you have more if you want, I have another one in the kitchen."

By time we're ready to go I think my parents have stopped thinking about me and Violet fucking in their guest bathroom. Everyone hugs and thanks everyone else for everything. I'm so glad this day is over. I just want to be normal and go home to bed with my girlfriend. *And* her other two boyfriends, eh, whoever said normal was all that great?

When we get home Violet takes another shower and comes out in her pajamas. My own shower is as quick as possible so I can get back to her. When I enter the living room, I'm surprised to find everyone up in arms and I listen to figure out what's the problem.

"I don't care, I'm going, alone. You have work anyways."

"He's right, until you kill her, she's a threat," Austin says.

"She's no threat. She hires people to be a threat. Now that I know she's after me, I'll be on high alert. You can't go to school with me."

"If I can't go, you can't go. I'm not leaving you unprotected." Jackson stands with his sizable arms crossed over his wide chest and he's a formidable specimen.

"I don't need any protection. I'm less safe if you're there. If Tori hadn't been there, I wouldn't have been knocked out or kidnapped. If you're there they have a way to manipulate me. Just drop it, Jackson."

"No. I'm not taking a chance of something happening to you. Now that you know she's after you, maybe she'll just kill you. Not letting that happen."

Austin sticks up for her "Look who you're talking about Jax. Violet can handle herself."

"She's not bulletproof."

"Neither are you!" Violet points out.

"We can't lose you, I'm not taking the risk, period." He stands strong.

"I'm not agreeing to you coming to school with me. That's ridiculous. Besides, I can handle anything she tries, you know I can."

"Babe, I'm not trying to fight. I just think you need someone to watch your back."

"I'm not letting you miss work, and I don't want someone I care about with me for them to use again. Can't you get that through your thick head?"

"I'll show you thick," Austin grins. They both give him a dirty look.

"Why don't we ask one of Dozer's guys to watch her back? Nobody has to go to class with her, we can get one of his guys to watch her from nearby. Would that work for you, Killer?" I offer what I believe to be a good compromise.

"I guess, but whoever it is needs to blend in, so nobody notices them as a stranger following me."

"Let's call Dozer and set it up. Then you can make up with Jax," Austin suggests.

She gives Jackson side eye but she nods with acceptance.

After we get everything arranged for one of Dozer's guys to keep an eye on Violet, everyone acknowledges how tired we are and we head to bed. This will be different because Austin's home now and there's four of us in the bed, but I don't care, I'm staying with her. Last night was hell.

Violet lies in the middle and lets us figure out how it makes sense. We end up with Violet on top of Austin and me and Jackson each on one side of her. She has a leg wrapped over one of mine and a hand on my waist. I can't see which part of her is touching Jax. After a while she clutches my waist and starts making soft sounds. When I'm awake enough to focus on her I notice she's writhing in pleasure on top of Austin and his hands are in her pants, my dick instantly comes to life, ready for round two.

I decide to wait and watch instead of inserting myself into what they have going on. She's quickly out of her pajamas and on top of Austin. She straddles him while they kiss, her gorgeous breasts bounce as he pumps into her. My dick is pulsing with need and I want her so much it's not easy holding back. After a few minutes she turns around and faces Austin's feet, then she pulls Jackson to her and his dick ends up in her mouth. Holy fuck, it's like a live porno and I can actually have the girl. I'm not sure I've ever been this turned on, I feel like every time Violet does something to make my dick hard it's harder than ever before.

Jackson must've been turned on for a while too because his movements speed up and he calls out her name with his release.

She keeps sucking him and swallowing all of his cum until he can't take it anymore. She grabs him for stability as an orgasm hits her hard and Austin makes some loud groaning noises. When Jackson moves back from her, she reaches for me as her climax fades. This is even more like an orgy scene in a porno as everyone rubs against each other and it's all about the finish. It's not sweet and loving like I had with Violet the first night, but it's just as good because it's her and who doesn't like it down and dirty sometimes?

When I'm in front of her she kisses my mouth and then down my neck to my chest. She licks my nipple and my dick jumps. Her hands squeeze my dick and she strokes me from the base, her soft hands feel incredible, she's strong. I kiss her neck and my body sings out for her. She kisses down my abs and circles the head of my cock with her tongue. When she slides over the tip with her lips my balls tighten and goosebumps break out across my body. Holy fuck, my orgasm is racing to my dick. It's traveling all of the nerves in my spine and my balls ready to explode into her mouth. At the thought of my cum shooting down her throat, my dick twitches and I press it further into her hot mouth. My hands squeeze her breasts and I pinch her nipples just enough to send new sensations through her.

She's moaning wildly and the vibrations are adding to the pleasure she's delivering. She wiggles her ass as she moves up and down on Austin. He's getting louder and I can't keep quiet either.

"Yes! I'm going to come so hard down your throat. You're going to swallow every bit of my cum, aren't you, Killer?"

"Mmm, mmmhmmm..." She can't speak with her mouth full. That did it, my balls tighten hard and the pleasure travels from my spine through my nuts and comes out of my dick filling her throat with my cum.

"Fuck! Yes! Killer!" The moment my softening cock pulls from her lips she screams out her own release and I continue to play with her nipples.

"Yes! Oh my God!"

"Baby! Don't stop!" When Austin and Violet finish, I'm satisfied in more ways than I can describe. Watching her come with so much force has my chest humming with happiness. Jackson hands Violet and Austin moist washcloths to wash off. He hands me a glass of cold water and I chug it.

"Thanks man."

Jackson must've gone to get everything we would need as we finished because he has a drink for Austin and Violet too. Violet leaves to clean up better in the bathroom and we're left staring after her. I'm back in my pajama pants and Jax is in his boxers. Austin just has the washcloth covering him.

"She's fucking amazing, isn't she?" Austin asks.

"Yeah. We need to talk about her ass. With three of us it won't always work out the way it did tonight. I think we should start prepping her for anal," Jackson says.

"Has she said if she's okay with that?" I ask.

"She said she's willing to try anything with us because she trusts us. I think she'll be open to it. I really want to try it," Austin says with a smile.

"Me too," Jackson adds.

"I'm not against it. Have you guys ever done that with a girl together before?"

Austin grins a mischievous smile, "No. Not together. But I did it with Shari Sommers and Ryan Farro at that party for graduation, the one at West's house. It was weird, I heard she did it with everyone. I was drunk and seventeen, so I didn't think about it. But I wasn't close with Ryan and it was awkward. Have you done it on your world travels?"

"No. My one-night stands only involved me and one chick and lots of condoms," I chuckle. The Navy gave us condoms and *health training* so we didn't get any STDs. Some guys didn't follow the advice and crabs don't care about condoms. Thankfully, I avoided the prostitutes and never had any trouble. Before I can share anymore of my experiences Violet returns. She kisses Jackson then comes around the bed to me. I hug her close and kiss her, I don't want to let go but she releases me and chugs some of the water Jackson brought for her. Austin leaves for the restroom and returns a few moments later back in his pajama pants.

"All right, kiss me baby." Austin climbs into the middle of the bed and holds his arms open for her. She joins him and kisses him. Jackson and I lie back on the bed next to her. She reaches out to each of us and when I look at her, she's watching me, I smile. She kisses each of us and exchanges I love you's with us. Austin flips her over while skillfully avoiding a knee to the nuts.

"We wanted to talk to you about something, are you up for a chat?" Austin asks.

"Shoot."

"We were wondering if you're willing to try anal with us," he tells her.

She looks thoughtful before saying, "I'm willing to try it. But I also might freak out. Some of my worst physical abuse was related to anal and I'm going to be nervous even though I trust you completely."

"You don't have to try it if you're not comfortable," I add. She smiles at me.

"Thanks Piers, but I want to try everything with you guys. I want to at least try, if I can't do it, we'll talk some more. What do we need to do?"

Jackson speaks up next, "I ordered a set of training plugs. We work on stretching you so it won't hurt when we try. We also need to use plenty of lube. It can feel really good if you're properly prepped. We want you to feel good, we definitely never want to hurt you in any way... Unless it's something you like." He smiles at her, and I know he's talking about her nipples because she likes it when I tweak them.

"Okay, let's try it." Her eyes are drooping, and we need to let her sleep. Jackson sees it too. He presses a kiss to her head and lies next to her. She leans over and kisses me, then snuggles into Austin. I fall asleep with a warm glow from the sex and the love.

Chapter Twenty-One

Violet

When my phone rings I see Harmony's name and want to kick myself for being a bad maid of honor. I haven't talked to her in at least a week.

"Hey Harm, how are you?"

"I'm okay, but I have news. Are you sitting?"

"Yeah, go for it."

"We're getting married in three weeks."

"What? Why?"

"Mike got a job offer and we're moving to Austin."

"Texas?"

"Yeah."

"Why? I mean why there?"

"Mike got an offer he can't refuse. He's going to finish school virtually, take the bar on their dime, and I'm going to transfer to a nursing program there. They're paying for our move, renting us a place for a year, and giving us a company car."

"Holy shit! That's amazing, congratulations! But damn that's fast and far."

"I know, will you still be able to make it with the faster timetable?"

"I wouldn't miss it for anything. What's the date exactly and what are we doing and not doing now that it's so quick?"

By the time I hang up with her I have a plan forming and I hope the guys can get off of work for two days at least. I send them a group text so they can ask for time off right away.

Me: Hi gorgeous men! Harmony had to move up the wedding and it's in three weeks. Can you get off work for a trip to Tally?

Jax, Auz, Piers- I'll talk to Ryder and see what we can do. They owe us time off, but Piers probably only has a couple days.

Me- that's enough, I just want to take a long weekend.

Jax, Auz, Piers- We'll get it worked out, book us for a hotel and whatever else we need.

Me- Thank you! I love you!

Jax, Auz, Piers- I love you, Baby!

Jax, Auz, Piers- I love you too, Killer

Jax, Auz, Piers- Jax says he loves you. He can't stop what he's doing.

Me- okay. Ttyl

It's going to be weird seeing Max after so long. I've changed since I last saw him and he's been in Europe, lost his father, and inherited a fortune in the form of a family luxury hotel business. I wonder if we'll get along or if he hates me for breaking up with him. He told Mike he understands that I was right and we make more sense as friends, but that might be Harmony trying not to hurt my feelings. I'm nervous about seeing him. I don't usually get nervous about anything, but he's the only guy I ever broke up with and then I killed his father. I'm not going to tell him about that, I just hope he's doing well. I know he's better off without that sick, abusive asshole around.

When my phone rings I'm not surprised to see Colby's name on the screen.

"What up RobN?"

"Oh, VioleNt One, greetings and salutations. I'm assuming you've heard the news?"

"I have. Will you be joining us?"

"I think you'll be joining me. I'm taking the fast jet and I have room for your harem. I'm also booking a suite for all of us so don't make reservations either. My car will pick you up at six p.m. sharp, the Thursday before, any questions?"

"Are you going to wipe my ass too? Geez, dude, you're running my life and it's not cool."

"Aww, come on Vi, you know you're cool with everything I said, you just want me to waste time asking you. Here, are these arrangements acceptable to you, your majesty? Does that help?"

"No. You're still an ass, but I might be grumpy."

"Oh no, are you feeling hormonal, should I hide out?"

"No! I was just thinking about seeing Max. Should I feel bad about breaking up with him? Or what happened to his father?"

"Of course not, both of those events were necessary. You shouldn't feel bad about doing the right thing. Plus, Max is good and he's excited to see you, he wants to be friends, he misses you."

"I miss him too. Okay, I'm not going to stress over this anymore."

"Good. Mike says they don't have time for a bachelor party or whatever girls do, so I'm hosting a dinner party for them in the hotel the first night we're there. I thought you could be my co-host since you're the Maid of Honor. What do you think?"

"I like it. She said the wedding no longer has a theme, there's no time. Thankfully they're able to rush her gown so she doesn't have to go on the hunt for something that's ready to go. But my dress isn't even chosen yet. She just said 'get something red,' what if we do a *Red Party*?"

"Would you be cool with red and gold? I've got some ideas."

"Of course, you've got all the style in our partnership. I was hoping you might help me choose a dress for both events."

"Can you come over this weekend? I'll get my tailors and we can have a fitting for you and the guys can come and I'll get them tuxedos too."

"I don't know if they can afford custom tuxedos. They planned to rent them for the wedding."

"I mean I'll buy them tuxedos so they have them for the party and the wedding. It's my gift, like your dresses."

"Colby, you know I love you, and I know you can afford it, but I don't like you buying things for me and I don't think the guys will like it either. You can ask them, but chances are you're just going to piss them off."

"I know you don't like it and I usually avoid it because you're stubborn, but... this is a special occasion and I have some specific thoughts on how we should all look for the party and the wedding. What if it's an early Christmas gift?" he whines in a pleading voice. I don't want to hurt his feelings and apparently this wedding is important to him. Dammit.

"All right, I'll accept if you promise you won't get me anything else for Christmas."

"I promise. Do you think your harem will accept my gift if it's for Christmas?"

"I don't know. That's going to be between you and them. I wish you wouldn't call them my harem, it makes me sound like some evil bitch who owns them, like something my grandmother would do. How about we go with, *My Crew?*"

"That sounds too clerical, like they work in your office. What about *Vi's Vixens?*"

"Aren't vixens female?"

"Maybe. *Vi's Victors?*"

"No. How about, Squad? Vi's *Vicious Squad?*"

"Nope, it doesn't have a ring. I'll figure it out and let you know."

"Thank goodness! Now I can sleep tonight."

"Sarcasm isn't a good look for you."

"Sure, it is. I've got to get to my next class. We'll talk later about the party. Love you, Rob N."

"Love you, my Violent Queen."

Oh, I've got it. Not wanting to talk on the phone again I text him.

Me- Violet's Villains!!

RobN- Yes! Love it. Ttyl

*Me- *heart emoji**

*RobN- *umbrella emoji**

I smile through my last two classes. I'm so ready to drop out of school, it's boring. The only redemption is that I like my friends and one professor, but it's not enough to keep me coming to classes where I'm not learning anything. What's the point of that? I could be online with Colby hunting for the next target, after Grandmother, of course.

When I'm finished for the day, I discreetly wave at Dozer's guy who's been watching my back. He startles at my acknowledgement, but he's done a good job even though I spotted him right away. I don't think anyone else noticed him. He was great at blending in with the students right down to acting like he was glued to his phone screen. I don't know why he was surprised I spotted him; I knew he was going to be there. He follows me all the way home before turning off.

The guys aren't home yet so I work on my school assignments for an hour. I'm practically finished with everything due at the end of the semester. Then I focus on my grandmother, she needs to be dealt with sooner rather than later. I wonder what she thought about me killing her guys, I didn't do anything to dispose of their bodies. I left their gun, but I wiped off my fingerprints, no sense leaving incriminating evidence lying around that she could use to frame me later.

Wanting a full picture I decided to check in with my attorney, Krewe. He probably has a folder filled with things she's filed against me. I told him I didn't want to hear about it unless I needed to go to court. But I want to know now that she's trying to kill me to steal my inheritance.

"Violet, to what do I owe this pleasure? How are you?"

"Hey, Krewe. I'm good and you can thank my evil grandmother for my call."

"What's she done now?"

"She's trying to kill me."

"What the fuck!?! Sorry. I just...she pisses me off. Are you alright?"

"Yeah, I'm fine. She had me and the guy's little sister kidnapped by morons. We escaped, but I heard her plotting my murder, I just don't have proof. I'd like to know all the stuff I didn't want to hear about so I'll have an idea what I'm up against."

"What do the police say?"

"As you know, I don't have an affinity for them so I haven't involved them. I'm hoping to collect enough evidence to prosecute her, not some idiots she hired."

"As long as you're safe. I know you're quite skilled plus Jackson and Austin will never let anything happen to you."

"And Pierson."

"What?"

"I'm also together with Pierson, their other brother who was in the Navy."

"Oh. Yeah, Randy told me he was back, I didn't know you were dating him, too. Um, congratulations?"

"It's okay. I know it's not the average relationship, but when have I ever done anything average? I love him and he fits with us perfectly."

"I don't have anything against polyamory, if you're happy and safe, I'm good. I'm your biggest fan, and I look forward to meeting him."

"I'm sure he'd like to meet you too. How are you? How's Bethany? And little Penny?"

"She's getting so big. She said, '*Dada,*' the other day, my heart melted. Bethany's great, she's finally getting some rest now that Penny's sleeping through the night. We can catch up later, let's get you up to speed on the grandmother from hell."

"I'd much rather talk about Penny. But let's get it over with."

He spent the next hour filling me in on all of the documents her lawyer has filed, how he responded, and what the rulings have been for each lawsuit and requested court order. She lost every argument; she didn't have a leg to stand on and when the judge got a hold of her, he let her have it. He found it *reprehensible* the way she tarnished her daughter's memory by going after her granddaughter. She argued I was nothing to her and he enlightened her that as far as the law is concerned, I may as well be the biological child of my parents, they adopted me, that makes me their child. They also loved me, raised me, and left everything to me. She didn't have any rights to anything. Krewe has already drafted my will which leaves everything I own to Isabel with Uncle Randy as the trustee. It's ironclad, and there's nothing Joyce Morgan can do to collect anything her daughter left to me. If I die, Isabel gets everything but if she dies, Uncle Randy gets it, and on and on to everyone but her.

Her lawyer has been told she'll never get anything even if I die so I'm not sure why she thinks killing me will help her lost cause. It doesn't matter because I'm going to end her... soon. When Krewe sends me copies of everything, I create a file for the *Vile Beast.* Then I begin gathering information from the internet. I begin by finding all of her holdings. I'm especially interested in real estate, so I can start searching for the places where she stashed everything she trafficked.

I add everything Colby found while looking for us when we were kidnapped and it's a sizable amount of information. Her husband was definitely a mobster, all of his connections lead right to the Greeks. Apparently, when he died, she took over the operation, which is surprising to me. I always saw her as a snooty, plastic surgery addict who spent her days at the country club. I never would've guessed she's actually a ruthless mobster. I don't care, I'm going to kill her and destroy her illegal businesses.

I only went to her house once, when I met her, Milton Morgan was already dead and buried so I never met him. We went to her house for a Christmas party the first year I lived with my parents. Mom tried so hard to work things out with her mother so I could have a grandparent. Both of my dad's parents were already gone. But Joyce wasn't interested in a relationship with some *rejected child.* I didn't mind, she wasn't nice, I didn't want anything to do with her, she always upset my mom every single time they spoke. Who needs that?

Turns out Milos Mouratidis, became Milton Morgan after he came to America at the age of twenty-five, he was already working his way up in the Greek Mafia and needed to hide his heritage and his true identity from the authorities in Greece and in the U.S. He was only married to Joyce for nine years before he died of heart failure. Joyce's other husbands also died of heart failure, it's suspicious to me and I wonder if she killed any of them. Before she married a wealthy man and became the rich woman she is today, she was a nursing assistant. Is it too Lifetime Movie to think she may have just enough knowledge to have killed her husband's when she didn't want them anymore? Probably, but I'm open minded and if I see evidence of it, I'm going to use it against her.

Tired of reading about Grandma Murder, I decide to start cooking dinner when Sawyer distracts me. I'm trying to learn how to cook more things, Austin's been letting me help him in the kitchen, but I'm still best with simple recipes that use ground meat and don't take any skills beyond reading instructions. When Pierson comes home, I'm stirring a pot of marinara sauce and babysitting linguini in boiling water.

"Hello beautiful." He kisses me and I get lost in him for a minute.

"Hi handsome, how was your day?"

"Is something burning?"

"Oh shit!" I'm too late to save the rolls, I forgot to set the timer which should've gone off about four minutes ago saving them from a Viking funeral. Oh well, we didn't need the extra carbs with the pasta.

Before they stop smoking the smoke detectors go off, Sawyer jumps and runs to hide. I open the back door and throw the smoldering ashes outside. Pierson gets a broom and fans the screaming device.

"Hey, Baby! What happened?" Austin asks.

"I burned the rolls!"

Jackson comes in and starts opening windows. Austin gives me a hug and I think he says something encouraging, but I can't hear him over the alarm. Pierson keeps waving the broom in front of the detection device.

"Do you need help finishing dinner?"

"No!" The noise stops right as I yell at Austin. I finish my thought at a normal volume. "I already made a salad; without the rolls I'm about done. You can set the table if you want." He kisses me on the corner of my mouth and sets out to do what I asked. Jackson closes the windows and Pierson puts the broom away.

"Hello gorgeous. Thanks for making dinner." Jackson kisses me and gets the big bowl from the cupboard. Pierson comes over and puts some sauce from the stove into the bowl. Then he checks the noodles, he decides they're done and drains them. I collect the salad from the fridge and take it to the table. Jackson and Pierson follow me with the bowl filled with our entrée.

We had a nice meal and talked about what we did all day. Of course, they wanted to know how my day was with Dozer's guy watching my back. I fill them in on my evil grandmother research. Austin is fascinated with the idea she might've killed her husband's. I finally get around to the wedding and Colby's plans. Jackson and Austin surprise me when they agree to accept Colby's gifts as a Christmas present, but Pierson isn't so agreeable to the idea.

"I don't even know him, how can I let him buy me such an extravagant gift, even if it is for Christmas?"

Austin offers his opinion, "You should accept, he's going to argue until he wears you down. Violet has him pretty well trained not to spend money on any of us, but he's relentless when he wants to get his way. He's filthy rich and he has only a handful of friends, he likes to spend his money on the people he cares about. It really makes him happy to do it. I give in on the small stuff like a cup of coffee and I say no to the Lamborghini."

"He tried to buy you a car?" Pierson questions in disbelief.

"No, he tried to give me one in his garage. I just said it was nice and we argued for two days when he tried to give it to me. I finally let him buy me dinner to end the argument."

"Shit, Killer, what do I do here?"

"I know you don't have the budget to buy it yourself right now, and I think you should let him do it. Or you could let me do it. You and I are in a relationship so would you rather accept the gift from me?"

"No. I don't want to accept from anyone," Pierson says with a pout.

"Look at it this way, you weren't planning to attend a wedding and a fancy party in three weeks. You wouldn't be able to get a tux except a rental, but it won't be the same as Austin and Jackson's, and that won't work for Colby's plans. So, no matter what you need to accept it from one of us, and it's not fair to put you in the position to try to get it yourself on such short notice. I'd be willing to let you pay me back when you have the money if you insist, but it really would make Colby happy to do it. He has so few expenses and so much money, he could support all of his friends for the rest of our lives and never even scratch the surface of the amount of money he has. He literally has money to burn," I tell him with a shrug.

He looks between me and the guys and with a pained face he agrees, "All right, this one time. After this we're putting a limit on how much he can spend on gifts. A reasonable limit like a hundred bucks."

"Okay. He'll probably agree and make a game out of coming up with creative ways to bend your rules. It's what he tries with me, but I'm quick to shoot him down. Just be prepared for some push back."

"I can handle the game, now that I know this is a thing I can be prepared for in the future. What does his family do that they're so wealthy?"

"Tech stuff, but Colby's made millions himself with apps and video games, he doesn't even need his family's money."

"Wow, I feel like such a slacker. I haven't done anything but sail around the world."

"Well, correct me if I'm wrong but I think you served your country and protected us while you were busy being a *slacker*."

"There's that, but I haven't designed any games or apps with my lame IT skills."

"Bro, you're not lame, Colby is a genius freak of nature. I think he was born with a keyboard in his hands. Speaking of games, what's going on with ours? Did you guys ever go check out the next clue?"

"I was busy saving librarians and getting kidnapped. I haven't thought about it."

Jackson adds, "I didn't want to bring it up until Violet had a chance to get back to normal. There's no deadline, so we can finish whenever we want."

"Cool. So, I can get caught up with you guys."

"We'll have to give you what we have so you're on the same page as us," Pierson offers.

"Isn't that against the rules? Are you saying you're willing to cheat? I'm shocked." Austin acts like he's clutching imaginary pearls.

"We sort of worked on the last clue together. We were all going to the same place so it didn't make sense to take three separate vehicles to go to the same location, we were only thinking of the environment," I state with the righteous indignation of a vegan college girl sporting blue hair, the irony of my own student and blue streaked status doesn't escape my notice.

"Yeah, sure, you gotta save the environment. It would've been sacrilegious to drive three separate vehicles, of course you had to carpool. So, will we be carpooling to the next clue?"

"Babe, you should probably stop by the library and check on that librarian anyway. We could let Austin find the clue while we're there and then we could all ride together, for the environment, to the next clue. But dude, you can't tell Colby." He directed that last part at Austin.

Austin chuckles, "I think it's important to save the environment. I definitely think we should ride together. I won't say anything to the *Game Master.*"

"Do you wanna go tonight? It's still early."

They all agree and we make quick work of cleaning up the kitchen and feeding Sawyer. I grab my game backpack and we head out in the SUV. When I enter the library that old book smell hits me and I love it. The best parts of my early childhood took place at the library or because of it.

Pierson helps Austin with the clue and Jackson stays with me. He doesn't fool me; I know he doesn't want to leave me alone. I don't mind right now, if we're together he can watch and protect me all he wants, he's great at it.

When I spot a librarian, I wave him over. His name tag says, *Bill,* he looks exactly how I would imagine a librarian if someone told me to describe one. He's a graying, pear-shaped man, with very large, thick glasses, and a pocket protector. Is that even a thing these days? I've seen it in movies, otherwise, I wouldn't know what it was. Wearing polyester brown pants and a corresponding plaid button up shirt, I'm not surprised by his sensible brown loafers.

"Good evening, we're s-so happy you're here, may I help you?" Bill asks with a slight lisp.

"Hello, Bill. I'm Violet Henley, I was wondering if Ms. Kennedy is around?"

"*The* Miss Henley?"

"I suppose," I say giving Jackson a questioning look, asking silently if it's me or Bill who's crazy. Wisely he doesn't answer, choosing to shrug.

"Oh, Miss Henley! I can't thank you enough for saving our boss!" Bill is suddenly animated. Another librarian joins us and she's much younger than Bill, her tag says, *Candy.* Her mousy brown hair is pulled into a ponytail at the crown of her head, she's short and curvy.

With a quick smile she asks, "Did I hear correctly? Are you Violet Henley?"

"Yes, ma'am."

"You're a hero! The way you saved Ms. Kennedy was nothing short of a miracle. Thank you so much for helping her."

"I'd love to see her, is she available?"

"Yes, I'll get her," Bill states and leaves. I stand with Candy, and she awkwardly tries to initiate further conversation.

"So, have you saved anyone before?"

"Not with CPR, that was a first."

"Are you a lifeguard or something?"

"No." I can't explain that I'm a serial killer who only hunts bad people, it leaves me at a loss for her small talk topic.

"Miss Henley! I'm so happy to see you! I just can't thank you enough for saving me. I don't remember anything except not feeling well, next thing I knew, I woke up in the hospital. But everyone told me how you saved my life, the police, the doctors, everyone said if you hadn't given me CPR when you did, I wouldn't be here." She pulls me into a hug. I let her hug me because what else can you do when you save a person's life? You're almost required to let them say thank you with a hug. Besides she's a nice lady, I get really good vibes from her. She pulls back and holds me at arms-length, looking me over.

"How are you feeling? Shouldn't you be home resting?" I ask.

"Oh, no, I'm fine now. Apparently, my medication wasn't working properly. As soon as they adjusted it, my blood pressure and pulse went back to normal. They did a scan and said there wasn't any damage to my heart thanks to you. They released me the next morning and I'm on light duty until I'm cleared by my cardiologist in a couple weeks. I was hoping you would stop by. If you hadn't, I was going to hunt you down to thank you."

"I'm just so glad you're alright. You gave us quite a scare."

"I can't get over how young you are and how swiftly you jumped into action and knew what to do. You must have excellent parents, I'm sure they're very proud of you."

"They were the best."

"Oh, dear, I'm so sorry for your loss." She pats my hand. It's sweet, grandmotherly, and nothing like my actual grandmother.

"Thank you, ma'am."

"Please dear, call me Lily."

"Okay, Lily, please call me Violet."

"Certainly dear. I'd love it if you'd let me cook dinner for you some evening, as a thank you. Are you free on Friday?"

I look at Jackson who's been quietly guarding my back, in case the dangerous librarian's attack I suppose. He smiles with pride and nods. I shrug, I don't have an excuse ready to avoid it, I kindly accept. She gives me directions to her home and when Austin and Pierson join us, she invites all three of my *friends.* How do I explain three boyfriends to an older lady? I guess I'll find out, Friday.

For the first time in my life, I'm relieved when we exit the library. When we're all buckled in, we aim for the address on the clue. *355 E. Main Street, #401, Mystic Cross, FL.* None of us know what type of business resides at that location and I'm a little excited to check it out and use my key. Once we're parked in the lot behind the shops, we use the breezeway to cut through to the front of the buildings. Number three-fifty-five, is an antique mall. It's one of those places that have individual booths run by a variety of vendors all under one roof. It's a great tourist trap I'm sure. Mom used to love visiting shops like this when we traveled. She'd much rather collect an antique memento of our trip than some crap made in Asia. She had them all displayed on a beautiful antique piece of furniture. Some people would describe it as a China cabinet, but mom called it a *break front.* I don't know the difference and I'm not a collector of anything. That cabinet and all of its treasures remain right where mom left them. Mom could tell you where she got each item, what she paid, and her favorite memories from that trip. I loved hearing her describe them.

Walking through this shop brings back many memories of searching for the perfect item to bring home. She let me choose a few of them. I always made my choice based on if I thought it was pretty or not. Once I chose an amethyst crystal wine decanter and mom was a nervous wreck for the rest of our trip that it wouldn't make it home in one piece. I chose it because it was sparkling and purple, but also because I thought it was something she could use versus just collecting it to sit on a shelf.

When we reach the booth numbered four-oh-one, we enter and look at the items displayed for sale. It's a dainty vignette with lots of lace and small fancy glass items displayed in collections by color. The display furniture is mostly white or pale gray. It's a muted color palette except for one item pushed into the back corner. There's a black wooden set of drawers that only stands about eighteen inches high and has six tiny drawers, each with a handle and a keyhole. I take the key from my pocket and examine it; I think it will fit in one of the holes.

"Hey, guys look at this." They surround the little item and take out their keys coming to the same conclusion as me, they smile.

"Baby, I think you've found it. Let's try four drawers at once. We can pretend we're launching a missile at your grandmother. I always wanted to do that thing from the movies where they have to turn the keys simultaneously."

"Wow, Auz, I need to ask mom if she dropped you on your head when you were a baby," Jackson says with a chuckle.

"Hey! We used to play that exact scenario when we were kids. You used to think it was cool."

"As someone who's actually done that on a ship, it is cool. I always remembered playing that army game with you guys when we were kids. I knew you would appreciate it, Auz," Pierson defends Austin's childhood memory.

"Fine. Synchronize your keys," Jackson orders. I play along, I didn't have anyone to play this type of game with when I was a kid. By the time I was free, I was too old for imaginary games. But I always thought it looked fun in the movies. Who knows what we'll find inside this little black box. A twinge of excitement clenched my stomach.

"Turning in, three, two, one. Turn."

Of the six drawers only two click unlocked. Austin and Jackson move their keys to the last two drawers and try again. This time their keys work and their drawers unlock. It occurs to me it would have been an interesting twist trying my key in every drawer until one opened. We wait for Jackson to tell us when to open our drawers to check the contents and he rises to his role as our commander.

I pull my drawer all the way out so I can easily see what's inside. A large antique looking key about three inches long is tucked inside my drawer. I remove it and turn it over in my hand.

"A key. There's nothing else, how are we supposed to figure out where to go next?" Pierson asks.

"We can send a picture of it to the Game Master and see if we get another clue," our commander suggests.

"No, I know where these are from," I reveal.

"Don't tease us, Baby, spill," Austin cajoled.

"They're from the Cantina. We had them behind the bar to open bottles, this end is a bottle opener." I point out the lip that hooks under a bottle cap.

"Huh. But how would we know that if you didn't tell us? Do you think he knows we're working together?" Jackson queries.

"Yeah. I think he knows. Remember how he accessed all those cameras when you were looking for me and Tori? I think he's watching us and the clues. He probably saw us together and laughed when we staggered our clue submissions thinking we had him fooled."

"Well, he is the Game *Master.* I guess the title really fits. What do we do now?" Austin asks.

"No point in hiding that we're working together on this one. Let's visit the Cantina and see what clues we find."

Jackson finds a parking space right out front; I haven't been here since I picked up my final paycheck. I wonder who's working tonight. When we enter the bar is full and a few of the booths have couples and one has a family with teens. The acting hostess waves at us to sit anywhere and we choose a booth in the back corner away from any windows. Jackson and I sit with our backs to the wall.

Our waitress is Leila, the girl who replaced me. I trained her for two days and she recognized me immediately.

"Violet! Hey, it's nice to see you. How's it going?" She looks at my boyfriends and I swear her mouth waters, she swipes at the corner of her lips. Her chest is puffed out as she stands taller and she smiles at them.

"Hello, I'm Leila, do y'all know what you want?"

"It's nice to see you too. I'm great. How's everything here?" I respond.

"It's been really busy, but the tips are good when the seats are filled, right?" She giggles and plays with her hair. She's pouring it on thick. I'm finding it entertaining and I almost hate to break it to her that they're all mine.

Austin has no such qualms, "Hello, Leila, we're just here to speak with one of your co-workers. But I would like a root beer, and Violet is our girlfriend. Yes, all three of us, so you may want to back it down a notch. Thanks." He smiles his most brilliant smile and the poor girl swallows hard while her cheeks flame an angry red.

"Oh. I, I, I'm sorry. Violet, I didn't realize. I'm so sorry. Do you want anything?" She looks mortified and I feel bad for her.

"No worries, don't sweat it. I would like a glass of water with lemon. Do you want something?" I ask Jackson. He puts his arm around me on the booth clearly marking his territory, shouldn't I be the one doing that?

"Yeah. I'll have a coke. Piers?"

"A beer, do you have Stella?" He smiles politely.

"Yes, is tap okay?"

"Sure."

"Where are my manners? Leila, this is Jackson, Austin, and Pierson, my boyfriends, as Austin so kindly pointed out. Is Danielle here?"

She refuses to meet their eyes when I point to each one as I name them, and she focuses on me. I smile a gentle grin still throwing her a bone, she may be a thirsty bitch but my guys are gorgeous. She didn't know and I'm not upset. I trust them implicitly and I'm sure women throw themselves at them all the time, they handle it and I don't think about it. I'm not a jealous person.

"I'll be right back with your drinks and I'll tell Danielle you're here." She scampers off with her head down.

"You were a little rough on her Auz," Pierson points out.

"Well, she needed a strong metaphorical smack. She was coming on strong hoping one of us would bite. Are you jealous, Baby?" He strokes my hand.

"No. I don't get jealous about stuff like that. She didn't know and she was respectful when she found out. Plus, I trust you, I don't feel any need to be worried."

"You know I would never cheat on you. None of us would, you're perfect." He looks at me with a cheesy grin.

"Back at you handsome."

Danielle shows up with our drinks, "Hi Violet! How are you girl?"

"Great. How are you?"

"Don't even get me started. I kicked out Harry and kept his dog, he's been showing up at odd times trying to get him back. I changed the locks and he's seriously pissed off, but I caught the bastard in bed with my neighbor. What did he expect? Oh, I have something for you." She reaches into her pocket and hands me four sealed envelopes.

"I'm sorry about Harrison, but I think you're better off without him."

"Definitely. Who's this?" She smiles at Pierson.

"Well, you remember my boyfriends, Austin and Jackson. This is my other boyfriend, Pierson. This is my former co-worker, Danielle."

"Nice to meet you. Thanks," Pierson says when she hands him his beer.

"You need to teach me how you found three boyfriends. I can't even find one who's worth a crap. Oh, if the tall and handsome one who brought those envelopes is available, give him my number."

"I'm not sure who it was."

"Huge hunk of a man, bald, tatts, and hot. He looked like a cross between The Rock and Jason Momoa."

"Ah. That's Dozer. I'm not sure of his situation, but I'll offer him your number next time I see him." He's a widower and I don't ask for information he doesn't freely share, therefore, I have no idea if he dates. I'm not about to tell Danielle any of that but I will actually offer him her number.

"Thanks, girl. You need to come by and have lunch with me sometime. I miss you; nobody works as hard as you." She looks around and lowers her voice, "Leila is sweet, but she doesn't do anything without being told. I showed you a task once and I never had to think about it again. Javier won't even give her a key."

"Yeah, I'll do that. I miss you too." Surprising but true. After she leaves, we rip into our envelopes.

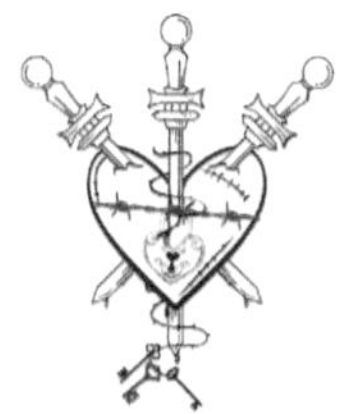

Chapter Twenty-Two

Pierson

I'm in bed holding onto my girl, I think over the clue. I wonder what's at the coordinates in the riddle and what task we'll need to complete. Remembering the events of the evening I smile when I think about what a strong impression Violet leaves behind. Everyone reacts so intensely to our girl. She makes friends fast and admirers even faster. She wasn't jealous of the girl in the restaurant, but how many guys throw themselves at her in a day? Am I jealous? What would I do if someone did it right in front of me like that girl did to her tonight?

Somehow, I doubt I'd handle it as calmly and expertly as she did, but I hope I don't ever need to find out. Falling asleep thinking about strange men trying to date our girlfriend led to some unpleasant dreams, it was frustrating. Violet kept falling for these dude's ridiculous fake lines and disappearing. I kept chasing her but she would vanish until I caught a glimpse of her and would run after her hoping to stop her from being tricked by the bad actors. When I jolted awake at six a.m. I called out for her. It didn't wake her, thankfully. Needing her touch, I press her palm to my chest and kiss her arm until I'm fully awake and over the disturbing dream.

"Morning. Are you alright?" Her voice is rough with sleep.

"Yeah, go back to sleep, you don't need to be up for another hour."

"Nope. I need to visit the facilities, are you getting up?"

"Yeah. I'll meet you in the kitchen for breakfast."

She smiles and leaves the room. I stretch before getting up and making my way to my old room. Once I'm ready for work I join everyone at the table. Austin cooked breakfast like he does most days.

"Where's Jackson?"

"He said he needed to take care of something and he'll see us at work," Austin answers.

"I might be late tonight, I want to work out," Violet says.

"Maybe we'll join you, we have a short day. There's a delay with one of the other contractors so we can only get about three quarters of the work for today finished."

"Did you hear from Dave?" I question.

"Nah, Ryder texted me. He said we can go over to the River Job if we need more hours but I told him I'm leaving after we finish at Hayez."

"That sounds good, I'll go with you."

I decided to carpool with Austin and leave my bike at home. Violet's meeting us at the warehouse for a workout after she's done at school. Jackson showed up on time for work and didn't share where he went. One of the things I like about this job is the physical challenge which is continuous through the day making it fly by. With such a short day, it passed like I just blinked my eyes and Austin was there telling me to meet him at the truck.

The warehouse is dark and empty when we arrive. Jackson pulled up behind us, and we parked in the spaces behind the building off the alley leaving room for Violet to pull her bike inside. We raise the overhead door for her. After we're in our work out gear, we begin warming up. Since there's only two treadmills, we alternate doing jumping jacks, burpees, and the jump rope. I climb the rock wall and search for purchase in the rafters when I reach the top. Violet makes this look easy but I struggle to shift from the wall to the beams in the ceiling.

As I lean out to a handhold, I feel the rumble of Violet's bike before she pulls inside the parking bay. I watch her from my perch and I can tell she's not happy. Searching for the fastest way down I try to listen to what she says.

"That fucking bitch filed a complaint against Krewe with the Florida Bar Association and she filed an anonymous tip with my school that I'm cheating. She said I used my computer skills to hack the school and alter my grades. Krewe is under investigation and so am I. Gah! I hate that woman. I don't give a fuck what she tries to do to me, but fucking with Krewe's career, that's low."

"Baby, I'm sorry. What can we do?" Austin attempts to console her.

"No, I'm sorry. I'm just so pissed off right now. I'm going to warm up and then I want to spar with you guys."

She starts ripping her clothes off and I'm frozen watching her. She strips down to a sports bra and yoga pants. She pulls off her shoes, those clunky old army boots she loves, and she laces up her equally beaten-up sneakers. Her eyes are narrow and her lips pursed, her jaw looks tightly set in her anger. She runs on the treadmill at breakneck speed then starts hitting the heavy bag. Her anger hasn't dissipated by the time she steps onto the mat. Jackson volunteered to go first and even though I know he's much bigger and stronger than her, I'm a little worried for him. Auz and I stand by to save him if he gets his ass kicked, plus if she wears him out, she'll need a new partner.

They go at it hard and she gives him a run for his money, despite his longer reach and considerable skills, she gets in some good jabs and rings his bell with a strong upper cut. Jackson taps out when his brow splits and starts bleeding, he would've kept going but he couldn't see.

"Quit touching it, jackass! It's fine, I don't need your help. Piers, hand me that gauze please. Thanks man." Austin pouts and joins Violet on the mat where she's stretching.

"You probably need a couple stitches, it's a good gash," I advise.

"Yeah maybe, I've got some butterfly bandages. I'll try that first. Will you look in the box I think they're in the compartment next to the Band-Aids? Good deal," he says when I hand them over.

"Do you need my help?"

"Yeah, can you hold this mirror so I can see what I'm doing?"

Holding the mirror, I shift my attention between Jackson's medical procedure to Violet and Austin's knock down drag out cage fight. They're going at it so hard and fast I'm impressed and concerned. I hear Jackson hiss and watch as he squeezes the slice together while pressing a tiny butterfly bandage into place. After a brief struggle to get it unstuck from his finger, he's got the adhesive in place and it's holding together.

When I turn back to Violet she's wailing on Austin in his mid-section. He's trying to block her but she won't relent. Finally, he hugs her close to him, trapping her arms in his hold so she has to stop striking him.

"Baby, Baby, you're going to kill me. My middle isn't protected and I think you're rupturing my spleen."

"I'm sorry. I'm just so mad." She hugs him back and their embrace turns from violent to loving. When she releases him, she throws her head gear in the general direction of the locker where she keeps it. Then she swipes at the damp hair pressed to her forehead, pulls off her gloves and throws them too.

"You know what? I've had it with her. I'm killing her this weekend. After we finish at Colby's I'm going to grab her. Are you in?" she says it to Austin but then she looks our way.

Jackson calls out while working on another strip of adhesive bandage, "I'm in. You know that, Babe, just tell me what you want me to do."

I shrug, "Same."

Austin hugs her and then looks into her dark eyes, "You know I'll do anything for you all you need to do is tell me what, when, and where."

"All right, come on, let's go upstairs and talk about it." She takes charge and doesn't look back because she knows we're following.

Once we're hydrating and seated, Austin asks, "How much of a plan do you have so far?"

"She goes to the club for dinner every Saturday, we nab her after that and bring her back here. Then I'll gather information from her about all of the businesses and connections she has and when it feels like I've gotten everything I can from her, the torture will begin."

"That sounds like a good plan. How many people does she normally have with her?"

"When I've seen her, she's only with her driver, even when she visited me at the kidnapping house."

"What else do we know?"

"I know the route she takes between home and the club," she answers.

Austin grows a dark smile across his face and I can feel my own lips pull into an evil grin. Eventually she pulls Colby into the meeting and before too long we have a working plan. Dozer asked to be included because, *'I hate that fucking bitch!'* was the nicest thing he said about the wicked witch.

Violet was tired once her anger faded and she calmed down. She looked like a kitten next to the wildcat from earlier. We didn't want to keep her up too late, so we agreed to make it a Violet night. Even though my dick is begging to be let out, the thought of taking care of her, of licking that pretty little pussy, is more appealing. When we get her home, we fill a bubble bath for her. Jackson rubs her feet, I rub her shoulders while staring at her soapy nipples, and Austin brings her a cocktail, some fruit, and chocolate. She's feeling better and more relaxed, a small smile teases her lips making me experiment to see which part of her neck makes it bigger or smaller.

When she's finished in the tub we give her some cold water with lemon, and then we rub moisturizer into her entire body. Jackson stands between her feet at the foot of the bed, leans over her smooth back, and whispers to her. She nods. He begins rubbing her beautiful, firm, ass and I find my gaze locked onto her skin while he squeezes her. A silver plug traces the valley between those perfect globes and he douses her with lube. Auz joins him on the outside of her legs and pressing his hand under her thigh he reaches for her delicate clit, stroking it gently.

She moans something incoherent and my dick is attempting a prison break. I think about my mother and all the shit she's done, then the mission that got me discharged. I finally stem the blood flow and regain some degree of my mental faculties. I lie down near her head in such a way that I'm able to kiss her. I start with her lips and work my way to her ear and neck. My eyes are still watching what I can see of Jackson working on her beautiful ass, eventually he's able to insert the whole thing and the end is finished with a purple jewel. It's weird and attractive in equal measure, it's absolutely mesmerizing. I'm so entranced I think I could have a root canal and not notice.

When she's comfortable Jackson encourages her to turn over onto her back. He kneels next to her hip while Austin remains at her other side.

"Does it feel good?" Jackson asks.

"Yes, but in a weird way."

He smiles at her, "Tell us if what we're doing is anything but pure pleasure."

Austin eyes me and moves his head to indicate I should join them at that end of the bed. My hand traces her curves along the way, only moving when I encounter Jackson in my path. When I'm between her feet I drag a finger from her feet up her calves, knees, and thighs tickling as I go. She jolts when my finger touches the sensitive little bump where her nerves meet and when I stroke those nerves, they sing.

Her sweet opening glistens with arousal and I'm unable to keep from lapping at her. I circle my tongue around her clit and softly suck on it, then flick it with the tip of my tongue until she shudders with pleasure. My finger presses into her and I quickly add a second, pumping them in and out while scissoring them a little so she can feel it. She moves and I can feel the smooth hardness of the plug through her vaginal wall and she purrs while goosebumps cover her body.

"Oooooh, yes! Mmmm, yes, oh yeah!"

Jackson taps her hip and moves her to turn over onto her knees. With her gorgeous, bejeweled ass in my face, I lick her clit from a new angle. Jackson turns the plug and moves it carefully, stretching her. Women's bodies are amazing, they stretch and squeeze, they're warm and slippery in the best way. It's very difficult to keep myself from stretching her with my hard cock. I want to rub my dick against that plug until she screams. While Jackson and I do our best to please her, Austin lies beneath her and sucks on her nipples alternating between them with nibbling bites.

She starts squealing and she moves her whole body to draw out the most pleasure she can find. We move with her and when she screams, I lick up the sweet gush of fluid that escapes her. She shudders again and then she collapses on top of Austin. Jackson and I continue with gentle touches and squeezes. She keeps moaning and when Jackson removes the plug she has another orgasm. Her walls flutter against my fingers and I tickle that spot that makes her climax last and last. When she stops writhing, I withdraw my fingers and lick them clean. She flops onto her back, and I see hickies left behind by Austin's efforts, it sends an electric charge right into my pants, and just like that my dick's rock hard all over again.

Violet kisses each of us and thanks us for a wonderful night. None of us ate, so when Jackson's stomach growls, we immediately order pizza so he doesn't turn into a hangry beast. Not wanting Violet to get up and create any tension in her relaxed body, we eat the pizza in bed. Violet falls asleep before we can even say *dessert.* It took me considerably longer, but she wasn't the only one snoring before midnight.

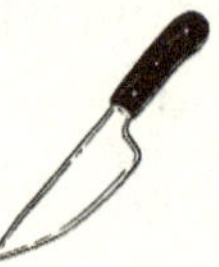

The weekend comes fast and before we know what hits us, we're in Librarian survivor Lily Kennedy's cottage for a home cooked meal. Austin entered with Violet and *Lily* as she asked us to call her, and was introduced to him first. When Violet went on to introduce me and Jax as her boyfriends as well, I was expecting shock or revulsion, a clutch of her pearls at the very least.

But Lily surprised us all, "How fun! You know, I've been reading romance books since I was in high school. Polyamory is one of my favorite tropes. I always find it fascinating that more than one man can be wrangled by one woman. I think it says a lot about you, Violet. If you weren't already a hero for saving my life, you'd be my hero for your unconventional relationship with three such handsome and kind men." She smiled at us in a way that made my cheeks heat, Lily the Librarian is full of surprises.

"Thank you. I love your house, it's like a fairytale library," Violet observes.

"I didn't plan it that way, it just happened over time. Being a librarian of course I have a love for books and I collect all of my favorites. People give me books for every holiday, or just if they come across something I might like. At first, I arranged them properly using the Dewey Decimal System, but I do that all day at work. One day it occurred to me I could try something more interesting at home. I saw a post on Pinterest and the books were arranged by color, it was beautiful. I spent two weeks moving all of my books to group them by color and it really made my bookcases stand out. I'm glad you like it. A few of my colleagues were offended." She chuckles at her joke, and I'm slow to catch on, but I get it eventually.

"I think it's amazing, I wish I had more books to arrange at home. I also love your décor. It's eclectic but it all goes together so well. I don't think I could ever accomplish such a cohesive look with so many different styles. It's beautiful."

"I'm so glad you like it. Please, have a seat at the table, dinner is ready. I was worried your guys would be hungry after a long day at work and I didn't want them to wait for food. I hope everyone likes ham." Violet cringes, she doesn't really eat ham except for well-done bacon. But she smiles politely and sits on the far side of the table where it comes close to a large piece of wood furniture with cabinets below and shelves above. She's the only one who could fit on that side besides our host.

"It smells great, I'm hungry so I appreciate your thoughtfulness," Jackson says with a rub of his stomach.

"Yeah, it smells terrific, do you need any help?" I offer.

"Actually, if you would be a dear and fill the water pitcher and everyone's glass, that would be perfect."

"Sure, just tell me where it is." I follow the petite woman into the kitchen and find her cabinets painted a pale blue with white knobs decorated by sunflowers. Everything in the room matches either the blue or the yellow of the petals. She points out a brightly colored ceramic pitcher and when I heft it, she points to the front of her oddly modern refrigerator.

"Just fill it with ice and water from the dispenser, it's filtered and tastes better than the tap. I grew up in the mountains and we had the best tap water, it was from the local stream. When I moved to Florida, I had no idea well water could be so bad. I lucked out that the previous owners installed top of the line filtration. I didn't want to ask Violet her age but she seems young, I have wine I just wasn't sure if it's appropriate."

"She doesn't drink, we're all fine with water." I fill the pitcher and make my way back to the table where Jackson is seated at the end of the table, and Austin is in one of the chairs across from Violet. I fill all the glasses and set the pitcher next to Austin before rejoining our host in the kitchen.

"Thank you. Would you please carry the potatoes? They're heavy, I've got the ham."

"Sure. Anything else?" I can carry the potatoes in one hand while she seems to struggle a little with the ham.

"If you can manage the beans as well, we're all set."

"No problem, I'm right behind you." I follow her back to the dining room and she gets a hand from Austin setting the ham in the center of the table. We have everything we need and I sit in the chair at the other end of the table after she sits next to Austin.

"I'm not formal, please dig in! Who's ready for ham?" She takes to the fork, ready to serve it up and Austin kindly offers to take over.

"I've got this, Lily. Please, let us take care of the passing." She giggles when he smiles at her, she's a little off but in a fun old lady way, nothing sinister.

"You are such gentlemen. Violet, I think they might be worthy of you. They're some good choices."

Violet smiles at each of us, "Yeah, I think I'll keep them."

"I knew you were smart." We dig into the food and it's very good. I cleaned my plate and Austin had seconds. Violet slipped me her ham when Lily wasn't looking, and Jackson looked put out she didn't share with him so Austin plopped another slab on Jax's plate when he shoveled seconds on his.

"I'm so full. Thank you so much for this, Lily. It was really kind of you to invite us," Violet pushes her chair back as much as the cupboards will allow, as if she can make more room for her full stomach.

"It's hardly anything in light of your saving my life, but I don't have any other talents. Books and cooking are it. I don't even know how to bake, so I bought a cake. It's chocolate with mousse filling, anyone save room for dessert?" Violet's ears perked up at the mention of chocolate and I think she decided she has room for dessert, chocolate is her one weakness.

Jackson stands and takes the ham platter and the empty potato bowl into the kitchen. Austin joins by collecting the other dishes.

When Lily looks like she might get up I reach out to stop her, "Please, let us take care of it. You made the meal, we can at least help clean up. Where can we find the plates for cake?"

"You boys are wonderful, thank you. The plates are above the toaster, the silverware is below the toaster, and the cake is in the fridge." Her smile beams.

When we return to the table with a fudgy, chocolate cake, and the plates and utensils to eat it, Lily and Violet are engaged in a deep conversation.

"The only time I was allowed out was one hour a week to go to the library. I would check out all the books I could carry. It was the best thing in my life, I still love the library and books."

"Me too, since I was a girl. I was an only child and my parents were both college professors, and scientists. We traveled for their work so I was able to see the world, but I spent most of my time alone. Books took me away, they were my friends, pets, adventures, and loving family, the things I never had in real life. When I got to college, I didn't hesitate to take Library Science and become a librarian. I've loved all of it. But as I get older and sicker, it's more difficult to lift the books."

"Do you mean your heart condition?"

"No. Actually, I have Rheumatoid Arthritis."

"That's an autoimmune condition, isn't it?" Violet asks, her attention focused on Lily.

"Yes. Your intelligence is quite impressive, I bet you're good at everything. Yes, it's an autoimmune disease that affects my joints, but also my organs and it's progressive so without medication my bones would deteriorate. Unfortunately, the medications damage my organs including my heart and now I need heart medicine too."

"I'm sorry, that's terrible. I've read it's incredibly painful as well."

"Yes, it can be. Sometimes my joints will swell and the pain is excruciating. It feels like someone is stabbing my knuckles with a hot poker. Lately I've been having pain in my hip as well. My rheumatologist is trying to get my insurance company to approve the new medicine I need, so I don't continue to lose bone in my hip. The arthritis just eats away at the bone and makes it sharp, then it severs my tendons. You see this scar?" She points to the back of her hand and there's a scar from the base of her middle finger halfway up her forearm.

I can't keep from saying, "Wow, that looks like a major surgery."

"Yes, it was scheduled for one hour with Twilight Anesthesia. When my surgeon got in there it was much worse than he expected. It took enough anesthesia to knock me all the way out, intubation, and three hours for him to repair two severed tendons, fuse my thumb, cut off the end of my ulnar bone, remove a wrist bone, and screw my wrist together, fusing it as well. I'll never be able to bend it more than this or turn my hand more than this." She holds up her scarred hand bending it just barely at the wrist and she can't turn her palm up. I feel bad for her, it's very limited mobility for someone who seems like she has a lot of life left.

"Lily, that's terrible. I'm sorry you have such a vicious illness. Will you need surgery for your hip soon?"

"I hope not. I'd love for them to fix these first." She extends her left hand and spreads her gnarled and twisted fingers. It looks like something from a horror movie, I can't imagine how much pain was involved with turning her bones and joints at such extreme angles.

"I'm even more impressed with dinner now. It seems you're able to accomplish quite a bit despite your disability," Austin offers her a small smile, conveying pride in her strength.

"I'm used to it. I adapt and forge ahead. I only notice it at work because I have difficulty holding onto the books. I can't tell you how many times I've scared everyone with the loud bang of a book hitting the floor in a quiet library." She laughs and we join her.

"I've started shouting, *fore!* To warn people, our regular patrons are used to me but when we get new people, they probably think I'm nuts."

"They can pound salt. I think you're amazing being able to do everything you do with such limited use of your hands. You're *my* hero." Violet smiles at Lily and she clutches her chest, I swear there's a tear in her eye. She must really be missing having a family.

"You're too kind. Violet, I think you might be my youngest friend."

"All right, Let's get this cake going before we all start singing Kumbaya." Austin wants cake, he's almost as bad as Violet with chocolate.

"Yes. Let's cut this delicious looking cake. I have a terrible weakness for all things chocolate," Lily adds.

"Me too!" Violet takes a huge bite of the multilayer confection. We all finished our dessert rather quickly and it was delicious, as advertised.

When we finish with what might be the best cake I've ever had, we talk some more and learn more about Lily. Violet shares a little more of her personal life, she talks about Randy, Stephanie, and Isabel. Lily looks a little sad when she has no family to discuss in her life. Both of her parents are gone and she never married.

She's the epitome of a cat lady, without the cats. Sadly, she's allergic because she always wanted a cat and happily looks at Violet's photos of Sawyer. When Violet starts yawning, Jackson intervenes.

"I think we need to get going. Violet's tired and we have a busy day tomorrow. Thank you, Lily this was very nice," Jackson makes it clear.

Austin comes in from the kitchen where he insisted on doing the dishes after learning about Lily's health conditions. I tried to help but he brushed me off. He approaches Lily and holds out his hand for hers, she lifts hers to him and he gently kisses the back of her hand without harming her twisted fingers.

"Oh my. Austin, you're making me blush!" Lily giggles and for just a flash she's a much younger girl, free from pain and the burdens brought on by adulting.

"You're a lovely lady, we appreciate your hospitality. Thank you so much for having us over, "Austin gives her his most brilliant smile and I watch her cheeks turn a darker pink.

"Yes, thank you so much. I'm so full I won't eat for a week. You're a great cook." Jackson adds his own friendly farewell.

I step up next, "Lily, I'm so glad Violet was there when you needed her. It's been nice getting to know you. Thanks for a delicious meal."

Lily sets her sights on Violet, she approaches her and looks into her eyes, "Violet. I don't even know what to say. I can never thank you enough for what you did, I appreciate it so much. I hope we can be friends and I'd love to do this again sometime. You'll always be welcome here. You're a very special person, there's something so special about you. I can't quite put my finger on what it is, but I can feel it in my sensitive bones. You boys be good to her!" She hugs Violet and my girl allows the intimate embrace from her newest friend.

"Yes, Ma'am!" The three of us respond in synch.

After we leave the funky little cottage, Violet is quiet and contemplative. We're not sure if she's figuring out something good or bad, past or present, we don't care. We hold her close in our bed and keep her safe. We swaddle her in love and let her know we're here when she's ready to share, or if she's not.

In a warm lump on the middle of the bed, the four of us fade out almost simultaneously. The last thing I know is when Sawyer jumps on the bed, he curls onto my pillow. I don't let the cat bother me anymore, he's going to do what he wants and I'd rather spend my time on things I can win.

In a whirlwind of activity in the morning we rush to get to Colby's pool house to have a crew of tailors fussing over our measurements and matching our eyes to fabric. I'm not up on styles so I let them figure it out. My input consists of how it feels, which isn't too bad for a fancy suit.

"Colby, come look at this, is it the way you pictured?" Violet questions, standing on an ottoman in a stunning red cocktail dress, or at least that's what Colby called it. I just think she looks like a sinful cross between Jessica Rabbit and a demon who has the power to seduce men, a succubus who is infinitely attractive and thrives on sex. She's fucking sexy as hell and doesn't have a clue.

"Wow, Vi, you look amazing. Are the pockets sufficient for your needs?" Colby asks her.

With her hands stuffed in them, Violet agrees, "Yeah, they're perfect, thanks for thinking of it." I wonder if he chose the dress with a small off the shoulder sleeves to hide her hideous armpit tattoo.

All three of us brothers are in varying degrees of completed tuxedos. We look sharp, I hope the finished product is even better. But Violet, she looks curvy and soft but firm at the same time and I can't stop watching her every move.

"Piers, you look so handsome. I kind of want to drag you into the nearest restroom," she speaks softly and winks at me.

"Not without me," Austin adds.

Jackson gives him a hard look before he asks, “What about me?”

“Of course I want all of you, I was just teasing Pierson because of the bathroom at your parents. You guys are so needy. I swear you probably time me on how long I spend with each of you.” She stares hard at Austin so he knows she mostly means him.

He flashes her a cheesy grin and she says, “Damn you're cute.” She returns his smile and he hugs her, causing the little foreign man working on his suit to meltdown into a fit involving what I'm certain are curse words in his native language.

“Sorry, Fernand, Ferdinand...what's his name again Colby?” Austin questions.

“These gentlemen are the Iannuzzi brothers who run a small family-owned tailor-made business, they're from Italy, and we fly them over when we need new tuxedos. The one with Jackson is Antonio, yours is *Federico,* and Pierson's is Lorenzo,” Colby explains.

When we're finished with our fittings and the Italian brothers have packed up their van, we all dress in black and put on our gear. Tonight, we're using comms and video. We each have night glasses with a bunch of special tech instruments woven into them including cameras. Colby quickly goes through the tests of our equipment, and we set off as soon as we're geared up. We had planning sessions multiple times this week. Dozer's meeting us at the site, he's been there for a couple hours surveilling our target.

We separate when we arrive at the club house. Jackson volunteered to be our bait, his hair and beard are different, so we're hoping she won't recognize him with the changes since she last saw him. He's in a black suit with a deep burgundy tie and a black shirt. It looks like a fashion statement but it's to hide things he's carrying and his trim fit Kevlar. He leaves the SUV with a valet and Violet steals the key as soon as he puts it in the box, she passes it off to Austin, he'll be our getaway driver. Dozer is inside at the bar watching Violet's evil grandmother.

Our recon of this location revealed an open window in the lady's restroom, or maybe Violet opened it. We left a step stool below the window for Violet to climb inside. If Dozer or Jackson alert her to an imminent bathroom visit from the Wicked Witch, Violet will inject her and lead her out the back exit, near the restrooms. If Violet doesn't see her, Jackson will drug her and join the witch in her car. We'll intercept the Bentley and disable the driver. Both of them will be loaded into the back of our extra-large SUV and we'll unload them into Violet's BASIL killing room.

When Grandma Grim started to look like she may leave, we sent Jackson over to sweet talk her into a drink which will be drugged with something to make her malleable and compliant. We follow when they leave together in her car with the driver looking angry and concerned until the Witch said something demanding, he caved like a wooden fence in a hurricane.

We can't hear what Jackson's saying, his mic goes right to Home Base, but Colby keeps us informed, "She's knocked out, Jax just whispered it into his mic. He's ready for our intervention, are you in place?"

"Go for One."

"Go for two."

Violet's with Austin and Dozer's with me, they're Team One. They're following in the SUV, staying out of the way while we get the car stopped in Dozer's truck. We want them to stay back in case there's a collision when we try to stop the target vehicle. It's not necessary, Jackson did something to get the driver to pull over. We watch as he pulls into a turn off for a long-closed gas station. The driver climbs from the car and leans into the open back door as we approach.

Jackson must have used his taser, the driver falls to the ground unconscious and Jackson steps out. He pulls on the motionless body of an angry old woman who made a big mistake the day she threatened Violet's life. Removing her from the seat he lifts her over his shoulder, he doesn't hesitate, she probably weighs a buck soaking wet. He quickly carries her to the back of the SUV. Violet climbs in with her and secures her wrists and ankles.

I join Dozer and approach the luxury vehicle double checking that there's no one else inside. Dozer and Austin carry the driver to the back of the SUV next. I call out to Colby on our comms and the bud in my ear crackles to life.

"Sit in the driver's seat. See the USB slot on your right? Plug the drive in there, start the car, and give me a minute."

"Okay."

"We're good. I'm in. I'll disable all of his cameras, GPS history, and the engine won't start when you're finished. Okay, go ahead and aim for the air strip. They'll pick you up."

"I'm gone." I've never driven a Bentley before but I've been in one twice as a passenger. Once for a funeral and once in the military, it was the preferred vehicle for a taxi company in Dubai. It's a smooth ride and I wish I could afford a car this nice, it feels well crafted.

When I get to the air strip, I'm careful to follow all the regulations and Colby's directions. Like he promised, the overhead bay door is open on the second hangar building. I pull the car all the way to the back wall and cover it. I close the overhead door and exit through the front door. When I step out, I press the lock on the handle and make sure the door is secure before racing around the side of the massive metal building. I make my way through a small, wooded area and when I step out to the road, my ride is waiting for me.

When I climb inside, Violet squeezes my shoulder with affection.

"Good job, any trouble?" Austin asks.

"Nah, everything was exactly how it should be, any issues for you guys?"

"All good. Dozer's behind making sure we're not followed or pulled over." I remember this part of the plan; he'll do something reckless in front of the cop if one tries to pull us over, so they'll forget the SUV. I wouldn't have thought about that, but Violet's mind works in mysterious ways. She's intuitive in a manner that seems like it can only be some sort of mystical powers but I suspect she's just that smart, so much so it seems magical to regular people. She catches me looking at her and her lips tilt into a grin.

I mouth, "I love you." Her smile grows and she blows me a kiss.

When we have our quarry unloaded and strapped down inside the warehouse, we all change out of our heavy clothes. The driver is strapped to a metal chair that's bolted to the ground, he's still unconscious and his head is flopped onto his shoulder. The Witch is tied to a metal table, it's meant to drain into a floor drain and it gives you a cold feeling in your stomach.

"She even looks like a bitch when she's out, talk about resting bitch face, look at that frown."

"I think she's had so much plastic surgery she can't make a smiley face anymore or her skin will crack," Austin offers his opinion.

"What did you say to her to get her to have a drink with you?" Violet asks Jackson. He cringes and she waits patiently for an answer.

"I just imagined she was a kind human, and I pleasantly offered to buy her a drink. It wasn't easy, but I kept my eyes focused over her shoulder and she thought I was looking at her."

Caught up in the story I ask, "What was over her shoulder?"

"The ladies room door, I knew Violet was in there, so I thought about her."

"Nice work, you were definitely the one for the job, my acting skills suck and I would've said something to blow it," Austin adds his two cents.

"I can imagine, *pardon me madame, may I buy you a drink so we can end you?*" Violet teases and Austin tickles her in response, she runs to escape him. They throw open the door and disappear into the warehouse. Jackson and I look over our prisoners. I want to slice this bitch open, and Jackson looks like he's debating the same thoughts.

I'm not sure how long the drugs will last for either of our *guests*, I'm thinking it's going to be a while because neither of them has moved, not even an eyeball under a lid, nothing.

"Do you think she'll start tonight?"

Jackson considers my question before he answers, "No. I think she wants them awake to get information and they're completely out. We can probably go home and come back in the morning."

Chapter Twenty-Three

Violet

Catching my breath from racing around the warehouse with Austin, I invite the guys upstairs to watch a movie. I don't want to leave. I feel like I need to be here.

"I'm tired, don't you want to go home and sleep, we can come back at first light," Austin explains his feelings.

"We can stay, there's a couch and a bed, we can take turns," Jackson suggests.

"I'm up for a movie," Pierson states.

"Let's watch one of the romantic ones you like and then we'll check on them. If they still haven't moved in a couple hours we can go home and sleep."

"Which one do you want to see?" Austin asks.

"What's the one with that blonde chick I like?" I ask.

Jackson answers, "You mean Kate Hudson, she's in *How to Lose a Guy in 10 Days*, or *Fool's Gold*."

"It's disturbing that you know that," Austin observed.

"Shut up!"

"Let's watch the *Ten Days* one," I announce putting an end to the brewing argument.

It's a cute movie but I'm having trouble staying focused on it. I can't stop thinking about the evil woman in my BASIL and I want to carve into her so much it hurts. My fingers itch to hold a blade to her throat. I keep thinking about the businesses she's into, when you're in bed with the mafia you always need to watch your back, or they'll watch it for you. They protect their assets.

"What did you guys do with their phones?"

"Turned them off and collected them for Colby, just like we planned. Why?" Jackson asks.

"It's nothing. Let's get back to the movie. The guy she likes is blowing it by plotting with that model loser." When I look around, Pierson is looking at me, I tilt my head in question.

"Are you alright? You're on edge," he asks.

"I know, I'm not sure why but something's bothering me. Do you ever feel like you left the oven on but you weren't cooking? I feel like something isn't right but I don't know what or why."

"Maybe it'll come to you if you make some more popcorn," Austin says with the pleading look of a lazy man.

"Yeah? Why didn't I think of that?" I tickle him and run to the kitchen.

By the time the popcorn quit popping enough to remove it from the microwave I've decided I'm on edge because I must be hormonal. I dump the fluffy kernels into a big bowl and rejoin our movie in progress.

When the credits roll, I feel better about whatever was bugging me before and I agree to head home for a good night's sleep. But once we're in bed I can't relax, my foot won't stop tapping, my heart pounds in my chest, and my palms are itchy. Unable to settle down and sleep, I move to the kitchen and drink some juice. Sawyer follows me and when I sit at the breakfast table, he hops up onto it and rubs my hand with his cheek.

Raow! His distressed cry makes me focus on him.

"Hey buddy, what's up?" I scratch his head and neck.

Meooow!

"Yeah, I couldn't sleep either. What am I missing? What's wrong?"

Maohowow!

"You feel it too don't you. Maybe I should go check on the BASIL, see if I can figure it out. What do you think?"

Rahow!

"You stay here and watch over my guys, okay?"

Meow.

"Thanks handsome, I love your furry face." He licks my arm, I'll take it as a return of affection.

As quietly as I'm capable of, I grab some clothes and get dressed in Pierson's old room. I load up my blades and a three-eighty pistol, just in case. When I have my shoes laced up, I pull on my new leather jacket and cover my hair with a skull cap. Dressed in black I hold my breath while the garage door lifts. Since Jackson oiled it, the tracks are silent and I'm especially thankful right now. I push my bike to the road before climbing on to start it. As I'm about to kick it over, a hand grabs my arm and scares the shit out of me.

"Where do you think you're going?"

"The warehouse, I couldn't sleep."

"Babe! We talked about this. It's not safe for you to take off alone especially when we have no clue you even left. If it wasn't for Sawyer climbing on my face, I wouldn't have known you were gone!"

"Little traitor."

"What?"

"Nothing. What do you want from me Jackson? What will get you off my ass about this?"

"Stop doing stupid shit when someone's trying to kill you. Don't go out in the middle of the night, alone. Telling us where you're going would be a good start."

"Fine. I'm going to the warehouse. Are you coming?"

He scowls but says, "Yeah. Give me two minutes."

I sigh, a big annoyed sound that moves my whole body. Then I remind myself, *I love him. I love them. They love me. They're trying to keep me safe. I love them...*

My frustration eases after I repeat it a dozen times. When Jackson pushes his bike next to mine, I look him over. He's dressed in black leather too and armed to the teeth. I start my bike as he starts his, we take off and stay together the entire trip to my former home. When we pull up, I can feel it in my gut, something's wrong. I don't want to drive inside, my skin is covered in goosebumps and the back of my neck tingles with anxiety. Having been around Jackson and Austin long enough I've learned their silent language, and with just a tilt of my head and a look in his eye we're on the same page. I unlock the door as quietly as possible, it's old metal so it's not silent. I pause before entering and communicate further to Jackson without a word.

He insists on entering first and draws his nine-millimeter. I draw my Sig and we enter like the FBI raiding a building, checking every corner before moving a step. I hear a soft scrape, maybe a shoe, from the workout area. I put my hand on Jackson's arm to stop him. He freezes and we both hear a small click because we both react the same way.

"Down!" We dive for the ground and crawl behind the stairs to my old apartment just as bullets fly over our heads, pinging the wall exactly where our heads were just a moment ago. We return fire and I catch a glimpse of a large figure as they dodge behind the heavy bag.

"Stay down, I'm going to crawl that way and see if I can get behind them. Watch for my signal to cover me," Jackson whispers then he fist bumps me and takes off. I focus on the sounds, I have exceptional hearing, I don't know if it's a natural gift or something I developed for survival in the Beast's house.

I hear heavy breathing coming from the general area where I last spotted our foe. Maybe we hit him when we fired back. When Jackson is where he wants to be he signals and I aim for the breathing. The large figure moves low from behind the bag and goes for the van in the parking bay. But when he moved, there was Jackson, able to get behind him and he quickly dispatched him with a head shot.

Not knowing if there's anyone else, I keep low and join Jackson. He's checking the guy's pockets. He's a big guy with tan skin and dark hair. His face isn't all there so I'm not sure if I've seen him before. Jackson finds a small bag of white powder, a money clip with about two-thousand dollars in hundreds, a phone, a strip of condoms, and the firearm in his hand. No ID of any kind, nothing to tell us who he is.

We leave the corpse and carefully make our way to my BASIL room, the place we left my wicked grandmother just a few hours ago. When I try the door, it's open, it's been pried by the latch. I'm surprised when I turn on the light, the chauffeur is still unconscious strapped to his chair. But the metal table is empty. That bitch is gone!

"Mother fucker! Where the hell is she?"

"I don't know, but we need to search every inch of this place." The door on the front of the building, facing the main street, slams closed, and we take off after whoever it was. When I make it through the door I see a dark SUV across the street. It starts up and peels off, they probably have Grandma Grim, and we'll never catch them now.

"Shit!"

"Let's make sure there's nobody else inside."

"Yeah. Okay. Dammit! You're bleeding."

"I am? Where?" Examining my arms, I spot the blood on my hand. I holster my Sig and take off my jacket. There's a minor gash in my upper arm, the blood dripped to my hand. He pulls a bandana from his pocket and presses it to my wound. It's not a bullet hole, it must've grazed me. He ties it over the injury and we regroup to search the building. Nobody got into the weapons room, and it wasn't tampered with, there's nobody else in the warehouse. It's time to call for reinforcements.

"What's up, oh VioleNt One's Villain?" Colby answers on the first ring, I don't think he sleeps. Jackson has him on speaker so we can both talk to him.

"Hey, we need the clean-up crew at the warehouse," Jackson barks into the phone.

"I thought you were waiting until tomorrow. Couldn't keep from stabbing her, huh?"

"No. She's gone. We have one of her rescue party."

"What the fuck!?! How?"

"We're hoping you can tell us," I explain.

"We showed up before they could take the driver. They had a dark SUV across the street," Jackson adds.

"I'm checking your cameras, son of a...they disabled the alarm it's why I didn't know anything happened. They didn't get the cameras to shut off, I've got them on here. Yep, they took her. A huge guy with dark hair carried her out. He went back in when you guys got there. You prevented him from getting the driver. His partner came out and took off with the Witch. I don't see anyone else in the car but they could be crouched down. Dozer and the crew will be there in thirty minutes."

My phone rings, "Hello?"

"You made a mistake. You won't get her again so don't even try or I'll stop you permanently. I'd rather not do that, so don't make me." A deep voice delivers the cryptic message and hangs up.

"Who was that?"

"I don't know but he threatened me if I go for her again."

My phone rings again, "What?"

"Damn, Baby, what's wrong? Where are you? Why didn't you tell us you were leaving? Please say you're with Jax."

"It's difficult to tell you anything if you keep asking questions and don't let me talk, Austin."

"Sorry. What's wrong?"

"The Witch is gone, we killed one of her rescuers but one got away and someone just called and threatened me if I try again."

"Are you at the warehouse?"

"Yeah, *with* Jackson."

"We're on our way. I love you. Pierson loves you too. I told her, shut up! Bye, Baby."

"I love you too. They're on their way," I say the last part to Jackson and Colby.

"Good. I have the dead guy's phone but nothing else, no ID," Jackson resumes the conversation with Colby.

I check on our remaining prisoner when we finish going over everything with Colby. One of Dozer's guys will run the dead man's phone to Colby along with Grandma Grim's, so he can try to get more information about the rescue team and her connections. I still have a bad feeling. Plus, I'm seriously pissed there's a hole in my new skull jacket!

The driver remains asleep, so Jackson and I move him to the table while he can't fight us. Once we have him strapped down, Jackson checks his pockets. I guess we were so focused on Grandma Murder, we forgot to check him after we got his phone. He has a wallet and a chauffeur's license is prominently displayed in the plastic window.

His name is David Grianaros. Another Greek name, maybe he's the mob's guy and somehow, they tracked him here? He's wearing a thick gold bracelet and he has a wad of cash filling his cowhide billfold. There's a receipt in one pocket for a coffee shop, and I place it next to his other belongings.

After we have everything laid out on the counter, I look at each item carefully. The receipt is from this morning for three pricey coffees. His bracelet has diamond initials *DGM*, and it's gaudy and over the top. When examining it closer it feels off, the weight doesn't match the sheer size of it. I pull out my phone and use the camera to zoom in on the back of the nameplate. There's a little notch in the flat rectangle of gold. I use my small blade to pry into the notch and the back of the plate pops off making a clatter of metal against the granite countertop. Inside the compartment is an electronic device. Out of an abundance of caution I wrap it in foil and put it in a metal lidded pot. Jackson looks at me funny when I conceal the device into what I hope will keep it from sending a signal anywhere.

"It might work. In theory the metal barrier will keep a signal from making it to a satellite."

"That seems far-fetched. Aren't phone or GPS signals able to reach a satellite even if they're inside?"

"Yes and no. It connects with a tower which boosts the signal to the satellite, but with a barrier of certain materials you can prevent it from making the connection. I'm using aluminum and diamond coated steel with the pot. I'm not sure if it'll work but I may as well try it. Plus, whatever this device is, it may not work as well as a phone," I shrug. Dozer comes in and looks over the items I have laid out and he looks at the driver.

"What do you need taken to Colby?" As we load up Dozer's guy with the phones and tracker for Colby, we get Dozer filled in on what was in the pot and the disturbing phone call.

"Who do you think it was?"

"No clue, but based on his voice I'd say he was older than any of us but younger than Grandmother. It was weird, he acted like he didn't want to kill us, but his guy, the dead one, was showering us with bullets so obviously he didn't get that message."

"What do you want to do now?" Dozer asks.

We're watching the crew load up the dead body into some tarps and scrub the floor with an enzyme wash that removes all traces of the blood. If the police ever came here with their forensics team and their little blue-green lights, nothing will be left to make the blue glow. I'm ready to get some answers from the sleeping man.

"Let's go wake our guest, he's had enough rest." Austin and Pierson arrive and after we get them up to speed four large men follow me into my BASIL.

Pierson waves the smelling salts under his nose and he jolts awake with a yell. He instantly goes into a frenzy trying to free himself from the restraints. It's no use, all he accomplishes is to rub his wrists and ankles raw. His eyes are narrowed and squinting like that makes him look like a terrified old man. He's not ancient, probably in his late forties, but his circumstances have aged him.

"Who are you?" he shouted at me.

"I'm pretty sure you know exactly who I am."

"What do you want?"

"Information. How long have you worked for my grandmother?"

The driver looks to the right before he answers, it's where Dozer's standing. He's an intimidating figure, unless you're Danielle.

Which reminds me, "I forgot, my waitress friend, you gave her the envelope? She's interested in you and asked me to give you her number. I didn't make any promises other than offering her number."

He looks at the chauffeur thoughtful, before he answers, "Sure."

The driver looks offended that my full attention isn't on him.

"Well?" Jackson prods our guest.

"Seven years."

"Did you ever work for her husband?"

"A short while, he hired me originally. I don't think I'm going to say anything more."

"Perhaps I should clarify some things for you. My grandmother is trying to kill me, as you know, I'm not in the mood to be defied by you. If you tell me what I want to know I won't hurt you. If you piss me off, you'll regret it." I smile my maddest grin and hope to scare him by showing him my inner demons.

"Who runs things?" I ask, expecting an answer.

"What do you mean? Runs what?"

"There's no need to act innocent, I know she's involved with the Greek Mafia and you were there when she threatened to kill me. I'm not a cop, I just want some straight answers."

"I can't say, but she's very close to the top because Milos was running things before he died." He speaks with a slight accent and pronounces Milos, Mee-lōs.

"Again, I knew that. I want the name of the top man."

"No."

"Are you sure that's how you want to play?"

He presses his lips together as if the words will escape if he relaxes. Looking away from me he inspects all three of my boyfriends and Dozer. He swallows hard looking at the largest man. Little does he know I'm the real danger.

"Name?"

"I can't," he whines.

Without a plan I plunge my small blade into his left hand, the short but incredibly sharp implement cuts right through to make a metallic clang against the table. His scream is a wail of shock and terror, it's a sound I enjoy. Maybe I should record it the next time I use this room.

"Have you reconsidered your answer?"

"No! Please! Don't make me, I'm a dead man if I talk."

"I don't think you're in a great position here Mr. Grianaros. I'm willing to stab through multiple extremities, I'm not one to discriminate."

"Pleeease! Have mercy! He'll kill me!"

"Do you think I won't? Let me take a poll...Austin?"

"Dude, she'll cut your fucking heart out and go have lunch. Make a smart choice."

"Jackson?"

"My girlfriend loves to cut into strangers until their blood stops flowing."

"Pierson?"

"I'm fairly new here but not long ago I watched her end a guy on this very table. I think she'll gut you like a fish if you don't tell her what she wants to know."

"Dozer?"

"You might think I look big and scary, but this young woman is the scariest thing I've ever seen. She doesn't flinch, or stop."

"I, I uh, w-what else do you want to know?"

"I already asked my question." I wave *David Bowie* in front of him so he has an up-close view of my favorite partner in crime.

"His name is Kristos Chitto." The name means nothing to me, I press on.

"Who is he in the community? What's his position?"

A tear escapes his eye, trembling as he speaks softly, "He runs the operations formerly run by Milos, he was under Milos, an enforcer so to speak. When he died Ms. Morgan wanted to take over, but the *organization* doesn't allow women at the top. The family assigned the second in command to take over but because of all her money he still lets her be involved, she likes to have some say in what happens."

"Where does this Kristos hang out?"

He shudders and his lip trembles still as he says, "He has an office, it's downtown, in the bank building. His company is on the top floors, his office is in the penthouse and it faces the water." I know the building, it's the tallest in our small downtown area and the rents are extremely pricey. I'm not surprised in the least to discover the Greek mob has an office in our sleepy little city. I already encountered Russian mobsters here, why not some Mediterranean's as well?

"Where does he live?" Dozer asks, and I smile at him.

"H-he has a c-condo, it's on the water. The Coves, h-he has the t-top floor, one unit is his and w-one is for employees or w-women."

"See, these aren't difficult questions. How many bodyguards does he have?"

His eyes rapidly shift between me and Dozer, "He always has Nicholas with him, b-but sometimes he has two others, I don't remember their names. You know your g-grandmother is an evil woman, she hates you, and blames you for losing her daughter. She won't s-stop until you're dead."

"Lucky for me I'm going to kill her first."

"You won't be able to g-get to her if Kristos has her, if he's protecting her, you'll never get close enough. He p-promised Milos he would take care of her, plus he likes her money, he won't let you k-kill her."

"I'm not going to argue with you. Who put a tracker in your bracelet?"

"It has a tracker? Your g-grandmother gave it to me." He looks disappointed with the news.

"What does my grandmother do for the *organization?*"

"She spends a lot of her t-time with other wealthy women, they have lunches and charity events. She meets with Kristos at least once a week, I'm not p-privy to her meetings or events."

"I understand you're her chauffeur, but I'm also sure you overhear many conversations. I want to know which pots her dirty fingers are in, does she work with guns? Drugs? Human trafficking? What?"

"I'm not sure, but we visit a club, *Thrall*, it's like a s-sex club, but I think most of the female participants aren't there voluntarily. I don't agree with the m-mistreatment of young people, I have a d-daughter, but th-they threatened to k-kidnap her and p-put her in the club if I don't k-keep my mouth shut and d-do what they s-say. She lives with her m-mother, but they know everything about her, w-where she goes to s-school, everything. I don't have a ch-choice."

"You know, I've heard that before. We all have a choice, you're here because of your choices. Now it's my choice to kill you...or not. We're going to give you a break, I suggest you rest."

"I need the bathroom, p-please."

"Dozer, would you mind?"

"No problem. I'll meet you upstairs."

"Thank you. If he gives you any trouble you can do whatever's necessary to deal with it." I give the nervous little man a pointed look and he flinches. I'm surprised he hasn't peed himself if he has to go.

Austin leads the way up to the apartment. Pierson holds my hand and squeezes my fingers in a sweet supportive way. He's such a considerate person, it's still surprising after the way he acted when we first met. I'm glad we're past all that, I really love him.

"We need to call Colby and let him know what the driver said. We need more information about this Kristos," Jackson suggests.

"Let's hold off on Colby, I want him to focus on the electronics for now. I can do a search on Kristos. His first name sounds Greek, but his last name is something else. It might be native American, I think I've read something with that word before. Chitto." I pronounce it the way it was phonetically written in the book I read, CheeT-Tow, it almost sounds like a snack, but there's a hard stop on the first 'T'.

I notice Austin staring at me with a look of awe on his face, "What?"

He chuckles, "Sorry, Baby, was I staring?"

"Yes. What's up?"

"Sometimes you blow me away. You're so fucking smart I get caught up in the things you say and I can't get enough. I love your brain."

"My brain loves you too." He gives me a kiss on my lips and I take a minute to kiss him deeper. He holds me close and it's a nice reprieve from the tasks at hand. With a few little kisses across my lips he steps back and lets me fire up my computer.

"Here, drink this." Jackson hands me a glass of ice water.

"Thanks," I say with a smile. The cool drink feels good on my dry throat.

"Is that the dark web?" Pierson asks over my shoulder.

"Yeah. I have some programs running all the time collecting data about the guys we hunt. I wrote this one, *Comet*, to seek out the users who visit certain sites and click on certain images. Colby uses a modified version to send a bot back to them which collects their banking and personal information. It's how he steals their money for our *foundation*."

"It's impressive. What are you doing to find Kristos?"

"Just a comprehensive search for any government files, arrest records, history like birth, marriages, divorces, anything that would be filed with a clerk of court. Colby goes a step further with all of the financial stuff."

"What's that?" Austin asks, pointing.

"It's a native American tribe, a lot of the Seminole Indians were absorbed into other tribes but the ones that remain are still in Florida and they're an umbrella for tribes like this, the *Ishkohatchee*. They're divided into clans like a family tree and each one is associated with an animal. *Chit-to* means snake. His last name is a Loxakoosa Indian word, it's the Clan of the Snake. Their clan is nearby, on the edge of the river and they're part of the Ishkohatchee."

"By the casino? Is it theirs?" Pierson asks.

"Yeah."

"Are they rich from the casino?" Austin questions.

"The tribe does okay, but that money has to support everyone and all of their infrastructure. It's not enough to make anyone rich in the way Hollywood makes movie stars rich. It's more like how taxes support a whole city, all the roads, schools, beaches, it's never enough to take care of everything they need. Especially after Hurricane Isaac last year, I don't know how much damage they suffered but I'm sure it cost millions to repair everything."

"Yeah, that storm was rough." Jackson looks lost in thought like he's reliving the effects.

The program begins to pile up the documents it's finding. I open the first one and find his arrest record, and it's long. He has charges that go back to his childhood including a record with the department of family services. They don't have a birth certificate on file, his date of birth is a guess based on tribal records. He was born in the tribe, his father was an Ishkohatchee Indian. His mother was Greek, and they were never married but the tribe allowed his mother to stay in the tribe while she was pregnant, but after he was born, she left with him. His interactions with DFS were after he started elementary school because his mother neglected him and he was often hungry and dirty. Eventually he was taken in by his mother's brother and his wife, the uncle was in the mafia.

It reads like a sad story not too far off from my own. He suffered abuse and neglect from his immediate family who was supposed to love and care for him. He tried to live in the tribe with his father when he was thirteen. When he was fourteen, he got in trouble stealing a car, it seems after that he devoted himself to the mafia and never looked back at his Native American side. Although he must receive some compensation from the tribe, they have a system in place for any blood members of the tribe to share in the profits of the casino and any other tribal businesses.

He has multiple drug possession charges, robbery, auto theft, assault, and domestic violence. I freeze when I see the domestic assault filing. The name of his victim in the assault glares off the page like an evil beacon, it's Vanessa Paredes, who eventually became Vanessa Raider, who is none other than my fucking birth mother! What the fuck?

"Babe, what's wrong? You look like you just saw a ghost." Jackson is looking at me with concern, with his words two more sets of eyes scan my face.

I can't make my mouth work. This can't be. I checked the dates, the domestic violence charge was about six months before I was born. She was pregnant with me when this guy was in her life, she always refused to tell me his name. She said I ruined her life and she wasn't sure who my father was, but she was wasted once and told me he was tall with thick dark hair and beautiful dark eyes. She hated my dark eyes, I guess they reminded her of my father.

Now all three of them are surrounding me and watching me with worry etched on their faces. My lips refuse to cooperate, my vocal cords won't make a sound. I clear my throat and try to shake it off.

"I... Uh... I think he might be my father." My voice is a strangled rasp and my eyes fill with water, I blink trying to stop them, but the tears overflow and travel down my cheeks.

"What? How?" Austin blurts.

"Why?" Pierson mumbles.

"What makes you think that?" Jackson asks.

"Look." I show them what I found and they come to the same conclusion, there's a good chance he's my father. I search for a photo of the man and when his driver's license begins to come through appearing line by line I see a strong chin first, full lips much like my own, a straight, strong nose, high cheek bones just like mine, and dark intelligent eyes exactly as dark as the ones I see in the mirror every day. I feel like someone punched me in the stomach, the air leaves my lungs and doesn't want to return. The room grows fuzzy around the edges and the guys seem far away. Their voices are becoming more and more urgent but I hear them less and less, my chest aches with the lack of oxygen. I fall into a dark tunnel and the faces of my loves twist in anguish and disappear into the darkness enveloping me.

My eyes flutter and light meets them through the tiny crack they open, a gush of air fills my lungs as I gasp for breath, sound rushes back, and the men leaning over me watch closely as I begin to come back to reality. They're not crowding me, only Austin is touching me, my hand is in his.

"Baby, are you okay?" I nod.

They all look relieved, even Dozer was looking worried. I take a few deep breaths and repeat my safety mantra in my head. It's been a long time since I needed to say those words. Jackson knows what I'm doing.

"You're strong, you're safe, you're a badass, you've got this, Babe." I grin.

"I love you," I say to all four of them. They smile, each knowing how I love them. Dozer has become a good friend and he knows I care about him but I've never said I love him until now. He looks pleased and it makes me feel better.

Pierson asks, "Was that a panic attack?"

"Yeah." I haven't had one since I found out Voldemort was the same person who hurt Megan.

"Do you want to call Randy?" Austin offers.

"Yeah. I should." He hands me my phone from the desk. Pierson helps me sit up where I collapsed on the floor, then he guides me to the sofa. Jackson gives me a new glass of ice water, I take a few sips and begin to feel more like myself. Dozer hangs by the desk and watches me. Feeling a little self-conscious I decided to move into the bedroom to make the call.

"Violet? What's wrong?" Uncle Randy answers with a sleepy voice and I remember it's the middle or the night, or too early in the morning.

"Hi. I'm okay. I'm sorry to wake you but something happened and I needed to talk to you."

"Are you hurt?"

"Not physically, I'm not sure what I am beyond shocked."

"What happened?"

I told him about what I found. He agrees it's likely Kristos is my father. I was hoping he would poke holes in my theory. I don't want another vile relative, haven't I had enough of those?

"I think you should take a DNA test and find out for sure. I know you don't want to be connected to an evil guy but maybe someone on that side of your family is wonderful and you'll be happy to meet them. It's not necessarily all bad."

"I knew you would find a silver lining. You're my dad now, even though you're my uncle. I don't want anyone else to be my father, but I especially don't want some vile monster who traffics women and children. I can't let him live. I don't care if he's my biological father."

"Let's find out if he is before you plot his demise."

"It doesn't matter. He's a monster whether he's related to me or not. I need to end him and stop what he's doing."

"I love you no matter what and I'm here for whatever you need. Are you feeling any better?"

"Yes. Now I'm just mad, which I can handle. Thanks, *Dad*."

"I love you, Violet. Please call me later for an update. If you need anything at all, you call me. And Violet, I'm proud to have you as a daughter."

"Thank you. I love you, too. I'll call you later. Go back to sleep and apologize to Stephanie."

"You got it. Bye, Sweetie."

"Bye."

Chapter Twenty-Four

Pierson

Violet scared the crap out of me when she had a panic attack. She looks good now, but her face was so pale, ashen, and her eyes were vacant before she passed out. I don't ever want to see her like that again. I was impressed how Austin handled it though, he surprised me with how well he was able to cope with the emergency. He's always such a joker. You don't expect him to act responsibly and be mature in such a situation. It's good to know he has the capability.

We're all watching her closely and I'm trying not to make it obvious but I'm sure she knows. Her senses are stronger than most, she seems to have at least six maybe seven, where the rest of us mortals only have five senses. She's preparing a plan to get a DNA sample from Kristos, finish grilling the driver, and hunt down the Wicked Witch. Seeing how her mind works is fascinating, she really is brilliant. I have to agree with Austin, her mind is hot as fuck.

"The coffee shop on the driver's receipt is right next to Kristos's office, I'm going to assume he visits it regularly. We're going to stake it out and collect his DNA without him knowing, then we're going to follow him until we catch sight of the Wicked Witch. I want her back on my table right away."

Dozer speaks up, "I've got some guys who can handle the DNA collection. They've done it before, and they can help with surveillance too."

"Great. All right, let's crash for a bit and then we'll talk to the driver again. Who wants to get Colby filled in?"

"I'll call him, I have a question for him anyway," Jackson offers.

"Perfect, thank you. I'm going to bed, I probably won't sleep but I'm going to try. Dozer are you good with the couch?" she asks.

"Yeah. I'm going to get the DNA team assigned first."

"Thanks guys, I know I said it earlier, but I love all of you."

I responded first, "We love you too. Don't worry, we'll get her back and we'll stop them."

She kisses my cheek, then Jackson's, and Austin. Dozer gives her a one-armed hug when she passes him and she looks content and sleepy. Maybe she'll be able to catch a few Z's after all. I follow her to the bedroom watching as she strips off her clothes and crawls into the middle of the bed. I remove my pants then climb next to her on the far side and Austin strips down and moves behind her. She snuggles into me and flings her leg over mine, her preferred position. It makes me feel like I can keep her safe and happy, I hope it's true.

Her breathing evens out quickly against my neck and my mind slows its rapid thinking about every possible thing that could go wrong to a few things that are right. Her face appears in my thoughts with that smartass little grin she gets when she proves me wrong, and I fall asleep with a smile on my face.

Everyone gathers for breakfast, and we quickly wolf down some toast and scrambled eggs whipped up by Austin. Violet is chomping at the bit to question the driver further. Jackson finishes first and they take off, I swallow one huge final bite and follow them leaving Dozer and Austin to clean up. Violet stops before entering the locked room. She looks at us and chews on her cheek in thought.

"Will you be okay if I start off quick?" She directs her question at me.

"Yeah, if you need my help just ask. I'm good with anything you need to do to stop these pricks."

"I'm glad you feel that way. I might try something different."

I nod my agreement and Jackson does the same. With both of us at her back she enters her BASIL and turns on the light. The chauffeur blinks and presses his eyes closed at the intrusion of light. Violet goes to the sink and I'm expecting her to pick up something sharp and stab the guy, as is her usual way, but she surprises me and fills a cup with water. She adds a bendy straw from the drawer and holds it carefully for Mr. Grianaros to sip.

Jackson is stoic, but his eyes watch her every move. I have to close my mouth after it fell open with her actions. She lets him drink as much as he wants.

"Do you need the restroom, Mr. Grianaros?"

He eyes her wearily before answering, "Yes. Please."

"I'm going to turn away and they're going to help you. Don't do anything to cause injury to yourself, understand?"

"Y-yes miss. Thank you." She turns away and busies herself with a couple blades on a rack, they're clean and shiny. She puts them into their sheaths. Jackson unhooks the driver's restraints and helps him from the table. I position myself in front of the door so I can stop him if he makes a break for it. He shuffles his feet as he walks into the small restroom. It smells strongly of cleaner and all of the obviously new surface's sparkle when Jackson turns on the light.

I step closer to the bathroom and wait to help if Jackson needs a hand with the thin man. He uses the toilet and washes his hands, behaving like a model prisoner. I'm a little surprised when he voluntarily hops back up on the table holding out his arms for the wrist restraints. I fasten his ankles while Jackson gets the rest.

"Are you hungry?"

"Yes." Violet hands him a protein bar and his wrist restraints are connected so if he lets one hand stay on the table his other hand can reach his mouth. He takes a large bite out of the oat and grain bar with his eyes carefully following her every move.

"I want to know more about the women Grandmother spends time with the most. You said she sees them at the club, is there a schedule for these get-togethers?"

"Yes. She has dinner every Saturday at the country c-club and she has lunches with some of them on Tuesdays and Thursdays. Charity events usually happen on Friday evenings and they're often at the club, but sometimes another location. She went to one two weeks ago at the big resort on the beach, the Mystic Palms Resort. The event was in the ballroom there and the husbands of the country club wives usually join them, but that night they were at the sex club while the wives had a ladies only affair. I saw male d-dancers enter the resort in costumes, I think they were strippers."

"I'm going to need names of these women and their husbands. I want physical descriptions and anything else you've heard about them. I have a feeling my grandmother knows all the gossip and you've overheard it all."

The driver looks away, a show of guilt in my eyes. I think Violet nailed it and this guy knows all kinds of dirt. We need Colby to talk to him and find all of the money and debauchery these creeps are dishing out.

"All right. I'll tell you everything I know."

"Hang on," Violet aims her phone at the chauffeur and begins recording or maybe she's streaming directly to Colby. "Okay, start with the women she usually meets for lunch..."

Violet spends over an hour grilling the guy and to his credit he answers every question and she was spot on, he's a wealth of information. Rich people are so stupid, they don't see *the help* and they say too much because they're invisible. Lucky for us, but not so much for most of the upper crust in this county and a few neighboring counties. By the time she's finished, Violet has a list of the most influential people around, along with a majority of their indiscretions.

I feel bad for the driver spilling his guts, he seems to deflate as he tells his tales and he looks like a flat tire by the time she deems him finished. Then she surprises me again.

"I like you, Mr. Grianaros and I want you to be able to provide for your daughter. Normally, I would kill someone in your position, but I think you're telling the truth. I believe they threatened you. Here's what I'm going to do, you're going to hop on a plane to the Pacific Northwest, with just the clothes on your back. You're going to move your ex-wife and daughter out there. You're going to have new names and you're going to keep them safe. I'm putting you in my own witness protection program. Do you understand? You can't ever come back here, you can't speak to anyone here. Got all that?"

He nods but looks perplexed, "I don't have money for a plane or a way to m-move them."

"I'm going to take care of it. They're going to be mad when I collect them without being able to pack, and they'll be safe and eventually, they'll forgive you. But you need to keep them from breaking the rules. Understand?"

"Y-yes. Thank you." He looks at his captor with awe.

"Show me your appreciation by doing what I say. Someone will come for you later today. I suggest you try to rest until then."

"Yes, miss. I w-will."

She leaves the room and I follow her, Jackson doesn't exit right away. When the door closes, she speaks to Colby, I guess he was watching live.

"You heard everything, any questions?"

"Yes, my Violent Queen, I'm on it, but I do have a couple questions. How much do you want to give him? Should the kid's *chaperone* collect anything from the house? Any preference on where to send them?"

"Olympia and Seattle were nice, plenty of jobs for both parents. Let's do fifty but monitor in case they need more. They'll need everything when they get there. Maybe find furnished homes for them to see? The *chaperone* can grab jewelry, a favorite toy, and a photo album or two, they don't need anything else. Thanks RobN, I'll check in with you in a few hours."

"You got it boss. I'm making good progress on the names he shared, our program is hard at work and delivering terabytes of data already. Stay stabby!"

She laughs, "Stay weird." She continues to chuckle after she disconnected the call. Jackson joins us and we all head upstairs where we left Dozer and Austin.

Dozer isn't in the apartment when we enter and Austin's lounging on the sofa watching something on the TV, his hair still damp from a shower.

"How'd it go?" Austin asks.

"Good, got lots of info. I'm putting the chauffeur in my new witness protection program, and Colby's collecting data on the degenerates my evil grandmother hangs with. Are you guys ready to go home? Sawyer's going to be furious, he's probably pooping in my sneakers right now."

I speak up, "I fed him and left extra food for him before we left. He might not be too mad."

"Thanks." She kisses me and I want to hold onto her but she's right, we need to get home. Lots of things need to be accomplished and we're not getting anything else done here.

She and Jax rode their bikes so they pull on their leather and leave first. Having come in Austin's truck, we lock up and follow them. When we walk into the house Violet is on the kitchen floor with Sawyer trying to get him to eat a square of cheese, it must be her peace offering. He ignores her until the smell of the cheese makes his mouth water and he gives in. I've never seen a cat drool before. He grabs it from her fingers with an angry growl, I swear he's angry with himself for giving in. He's a weird little creature.

"Hey, Killer, I'm going to grab a shower, do you need anything before I get in there?"

"Want company? I need one too." She smiles seductively as if I need convincing.

"Mi shower es su shower, Gorgeous."

"Thanks, I'll meet you in there."

I whistle as I find some clean clothes. I get a towel for each of us and start the shower so it'll be hot by the time we step in. When the door opens, I expect my beautiful girlfriend, but it's Jackson.

"Do you mind if I join?"

"Sure." Everything becomes a community activity around here and I don't mind it, I've wanted this relationship since I was a kid. Growing up like I did, having more people to love now is perfect. For whatever reason it's not weird to share her with my brothers. There's something magical about seeing her happy and my brothers make her happy. I continue to whistle while I shave, Jackson leaves and returns with another towel.

The door opens again and the violent beauty I love finally joins us. She tears off her clothes and steps into the shower.

"Oh! This feels amazing. I didn't realize how much I needed this," she exclaims from beneath the steaming water.

When I join her, she's in front of me shampooing her hair and that perfect ass draws my attention until I spot the bloody bandage on her arm.

"Let me see how this looks." She nods and watches me remove it. The gash isn't as bad as I imagined. She's been shot twice now and she'll have another scar. Maybe she'll let me draw more tattoos to cover them.

"Well? Am I going to live?"

Jackson comes in and he looks over her wound, "You'll live. It actually looks pretty good."

He consults me, "What do you think Dr. Pierson?"

"I concur with my colleague, you're going to make it." She giggles and it sends sparks through my heart and right into my dick. "But you should definitely let me wash it so it doesn't get infected."

"I have to agree with Dr. Pierson, we need to scrub you from head to toe, for your safety of course." Jackson gives her a cheeky grin before he fills his hands with body wash.

"Well I certainly can't argue with medical professionals," she agrees with a mischievous smile and a sexy glint in her eyes.

She accepts a handful of body wash from Jackson and I take some as well. She rubs her hands on my pecs and my dick stands at attention. Jackson washes her chest from behind, filling his hands with her perky full breasts. I start on her taut stomach and quickly slide my way to her thighs. When I look up at her I find her eyes closed and her head leaned back on Jackson's shoulder. After I've washed her legs, squatting down, I work my way to the inside of her thighs, and encourage her to lift her knee over my shoulder.

When she opens her legs for me, her pink pussy glimmers with arousal and I wash her gently, paying particular attention to her sweet little clit. She moans and I know I'm doing it right. My cock twitches in response to her vocalized pleasure. I let the water rinse the soap from her pussy and I use my tongue to see if I can make her squeal.

"Oh! Yes! Fuck!"

Using a finger to press inside her warmth, she gives the hot shower a run for its money, and I want to thrust into her. Inserting another digit I twist my fingers to feel her muscles and when she makes the noise I was hoping for, I double down and lick her trigger faster while I tickle that special place inside. Her cries get louder and her tight tunnel locks down on my hand, then she shudders and her insides flutter as she screams out her release. I continue my efforts until she stops trembling.

When she settles, she grabs a handful of my hair and pulls me up to put her insistent lips on mine. She bites my lip and tries to force her tongue down my throat sending goosebumps across my skin. I grab hold of her curvy ass and press my hard cock into her stomach. Jackson is kissing her neck and he pinches her nipples, she breaks our kiss and looks into my eyes. I see nothing but hunger in those dark orbs. She pushes me back and bends over taking the tip of my dick into her mouth. Before I can adjust to the overwhelming stimulation, she pushes her lips to my pubic bone and my cock is down her gullet. I can't keep a groan from leaving my body and my eyes fall closed as I enjoy her tongue swirling around the head of my dick while she sucks on it. I gently thrust into her mouth and she clutches my ass pulling me further into her hungry throat.

"Fuck, Killer..."

"Mmmm!"

Jackson begins fucking her from behind and his thrusts drive my dick further past her gag reflex. She chokes a little but continues to pull me closer. I'm feeling an orgasm building quickly and I don't want to finish too soon but I can't stop the runaway train of rapture coming around the bend hard and fast.

"Babe, your pussy is fucking perfect!" Jackson calls out.

My spine tingles and a new crop of goosebumps sprouts across my flesh as I shudder with impending blissful, orgasmic release. The sensations put me at the top of the highest peak of the rollercoaster I'm on, to the point just before I'm about to fall over the edge into unknowable thrills. The cars keep going click, click, click, as my nuts pull up tighter and tighter, and just when I'm sure I can't take another second, holy fuck! I plunge over the cliff exploding into her mouth, my hot cum shoots down her throat, she purrs while she sucks harder, collecting every drop in her greedy mouth and swallowing it down.

"Mmmmm!"

"Mother fucker!"

"Fucking hell!"

We all moan and curse while we convulse with collective gratification. My own body continues to vibrate with satisfaction even after she releases me from her talented lips. When Jackson is finished filling her with his release, he kisses her softly and begins washing her.

She leans into me kissing my chest right over my pounding heart and it's as if she carved me open and stabbed the multi chambered organ there, directly with her love. I kiss her temple and whisper to her.

"I love you, Killer. There's no one else like you."

"Back at you Pierson, I love you too."

"Spin," Jackson commands and he begins washing the rest of her before himself.

"I love you, Jackson." I can see the pleased little smile on her face in her profile.

He looks into her eyes and says, "1 love you too, Babe. Piers is right, there's nobody else like you."

"You both make me so happy. I love you so much, and Austin. You're everything to me."

She looks at me over her shoulder emphasizing that she means me too and a warm burst of light sizzles in my already cleaved chest making my heart beat with happiness. I smile at her and kiss her cheek before exiting to dry off.

After we're dressed, we join Austin in the kitchen where he has coffee and some cinnamon rolls waiting. He kisses Violet and then holds her for a long moment.

"I just hung up with Colby. He's got everything arranged for the chauffeur, his child, and his ex, they'll be on a plane by early afternoon. Dozer's guys are watching Kristos, and they're collecting anything they see him touching. Dozer says they should have a good sample before the day is over. They haven't seen any sign of the wicked Grandmother of the West. They're watching her place and Colby has cameras in her neighborhood on it as well."

"Great."

"Oh, and he said to tell you one of Dozer's guys will be stopping by to collect your DNA for comparison. He has a lab setup with RapidDNA technology, so they'll have results in a few hours," Austin adds.

"That's faster than I expected. I'm not sure how to feel about it."

I place my hand on her forearm, "It's not going to change how we handle things so let's just move forward with our plans and whatever the results, it doesn't really matter."

"Yeah. Okay. I want to break into Grandmother's house and see if I can find anything incriminating. I have a key and her alarm code, my parents had them, I never thought I'd have a reason to use them."

"Okay! We have a plan, let's get ready, to Grandmother's house we go! We already know she's the wolf, so load up on the clips and blades." Austin claps like he's a social director getting guests excited about pickleball in some overpriced resort. I shake my head at his antics before heading off to load up some gear.

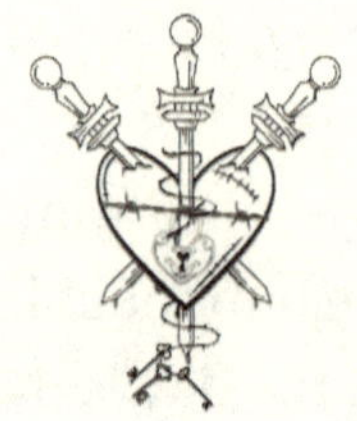

Chapter Twenty-Five

Violet

We decided to dress in regular clothing to avoid drawing attention to ourselves, which would have been an issue if we appeared in tactical gear. I have blades stashed everywhere and the Sig in the holster at the back of my waist. All three guys have firearms and blades as well, but they each carry a backup gun. When we pull up to her gate, I press the intercom and wonder if anyone will answer.

"May I help you?" a male voice crackles out of the speaker. It must be her butler, Roman, he lives on the property in servant's quarters beyond her pool house. I was hoping he'd be out since she's not here.

"Hi. Um, I don't know if you remember me, it's Violet Henley. Mrs. Morgan is my grandmother, I was wondering if I could come in and speak with you?"

"Oh. Yes, Miss Henley, I do remember you. I was so sorry to hear about your parents, your mother was a lovely woman. Yes. Of course, please come up." The gate swings open and I smile at Jackson who's next to me in the front seat.

"Thank you." After we pull away from the gate I add, "Give me two minutes. If I'm not back by then you can come find me."

Austin questions, "What if it's a trap?"

"Colby's been watching, and he hasn't seen any activity here. And I said you can bust in after two minutes if I'm not out."

"I don't like it, a lot can happen in two minutes," Jackson argues.

"Fine, who wants to go with me?"

"I'll go," Pierson offers first. Jackson turns and gives him a stern look.

"Don't let her out of your sight, shoot first and ask questions later, okay?" Jackson orders.

"Yep. I got it."

"All right, you two give us five minutes since I'm not alone. Don't argue Jackson, we've got this." I preempted his argument, he's not happy but he doesn't say anything else. Pierson and I walk to the door and before I can ring the bell the large elaborate door opens and the older gentleman from the intercom shows us inside.

"This is my boyfriend, Pierson. Thank you for letting us in."

"Of course, miss, and I'm pleased to meet you sir, please call me Roman." He actually bows at Pierson. "Your grandmother isn't at home. She decided to take a last-minute trip up the coast and she hasn't been home since yesterday."

"That's fine, I just wanted to collect some of my mother's things Grandmother saved for me. She said they're in her office. Would it be okay if I get them?"

"Oh. I'm sorry she didn't tell me about any items for you. Do you know where in her office?"

"She said she had a few small boxes in a cabinet. I would normally wait for her to be home, but my mother's birthday is coming up and I wanted the pictures Grandmother put aside for me." I sniffle to really sell it.

"Certainly, miss, I'll show you to her office and you can collect whatever you need. Would you like something to drink? A snack?"

"No, thank you. I'll be quick. I don't want to be any trouble."

"Please, take your time. Since Mrs. Morgan isn't here there's no need to rush. I know she hasn't always been kind to you and I'm sorry about that. She can be a difficult woman."

"That's for sure." I chuckle to put him at ease. I bet he's dying to tell me what a horrible woman that witch really is behind closed doors.

Pierson and I follow him past a lavish sitting room down a long hallway. Our steps echo along the marble tiled corridor until we stop in front of a large carved door.

Pointing to a device on the wall the gray-haired gentleman explains, "Here you are, I'll be in the kitchen if you need anything you can call me on the intercom. Take your time, there may be other items of your mothers inside, it may do you good to see them all and choose whatever you like." Oh, he's bad. He's offering to let me ransack her office, I bet he hates that evil witch.

"Thank you so much Roman, you're very kind."

"My pleasure." He bows and turns like he's marching in the military before walking off and leaving us to plunder her office. I send a quick text to Jackson and Austin, so they don't storm the castle. Then I look around and try to determine the best place to start.

A large painting behind the desk catches my eye first. Pierson begins opening cupboards while I check out the painting. It doesn't look familiar but I have no doubt it's an expensive piece of art.

"If Roman is in the kitchen, do you think we should get them to come in and help us?" Pierson asks.

"Yeah, it'd probably go faster with more help. Will you go let them in? I'll text them again." I quickly shoot off another text and tell them to meet Pierson at the door.

He hurries off and I examine the painting. When I try to look behind it the frame pulls away from the wall on hinges and as I suspected there's a wall safe behind it. *Wow Joyce, could you be any more cliché?*

It's a digital keypad locking mechanism and I try my mother's birthday. When that doesn't work, I enter my grandmother's birthday, her anniversary, and it's none of those combinations. Then when I decide to think like an evil witch, I get an idea and I type the date her husband died.

Beep! Click!

I can't believe it worked, I pull on the handle and the heavy door swings open. Holy shit! There's a stash of USB drives, some ten by thirteen envelopes, a check ledger, stacks of cash, and a black case. Curious, I reached for the black case, it's incredibly heavy for its size and I think it must contain lead to weigh so much.

Placing it on the desk I open the clasp and inside I find rows of small gold bars. They each say *one ounce.* Still curious, I quickly searched the going rate for an ounce of gold on my phone, it's over twenty-seven-hundred dollars an ounce. There must be at least a hundred bars in the case, that's a lot of gold. I put it back in the safe and removed the drives and envelopes.

"Whoa, how did you open the safe, Baby?"

"I just tried a few dates until I found the one that worked. Take off your backpack. I want to take these with us. You guys go through all the cabinets and drawers while I try her computer."

He packs everything for me and then starts opening drawers with Pierson and Jackson. I open her laptop and check if it needs a password, it does. I open the drawers closest to me searching for anything with passwords on it. All I find are office supplies, for some reason she has dozens of Sharpies in every color. I check under the laptop and a sticky note there says *Godiva$48* written in blue ink, not marker, oddly.

I type it into the password queue and her laptop starts loading the welcome screen. I quickly search her files and I find several listed as *MM Holdings*, they must be *business* files. Taking an empty drive from my pocket I copy all of those files and when I continue going through the list, I find a file named *Violet.* That might be interesting, so I copy it too.

"Hey, Killer, do you want these?" Pierson holds up a group of folders.

"What are they?"

"They look like ledger entries, but they have codes instead of names. It looks suspicious."

"Yeah, anything suspicious or out of the ordinary, grab it."

After I copy all the files I want, I remove the drive and swap it for another. This one uploads Colby's modified version of my *Comet* program. It will send him all of her financial transactions and let him into her computer for anything he wants. Jackson puts some items into his backpack, and I put everything back where I found it in the safe, minus the files.

While they finish up in her office I sneak further down the hall to her bedroom behind the double doors at the end. Pierson followed me. I don't want to waste time arguing so I let him stay. I check her night stand and find lots of pills and wrinkle creams, nothing important. Her dresser has some jewelry boxes with fancy costume jewelry, but again, nothing important hidden in her panty drawer. Her walk-in closet is enormous, as big as some people's entire house. There are endless rows of expensive shoes and handbags all neatly lined up. An island in the center of the room has three drawers of designer sunglasses alone. I own one pair I picked up at the market where I met Jackson, for nine bucks. I can't physically roll my eyes any harder.

One of the hat boxes captures my attention, it's not in line with the others and I pull it down from the shelf. Inside it's filled with photos of my mom. My eyes water and I replace the lid.

"What's wrong?"

"Nothing, let's go." I take the hat box with me. Pierson examines my face and his is pinched with concern. I don't want to talk about it here so I leave and return to the office.

"Did you find anything?" Jackson asks.

"Just some photos. I'm ready to head out. You guys good?"

Austin answers, "Yeah, we searched everything in here. We're done."

"All right, you guys go out to the car. I'm going to say bye to Roman."

"Piers, you stay with her." Jackson directs and I'm too weary to argue about his overly protective streak. But he catches me pursing my lips in annoyance, he tilts his head at me as if to say, *you heard me.* An exasperated sigh escapes me but I don't say anything I just want to go home.

After they're gone, I make my way to the kitchen, "Thanks so much Roman."

"Did you find what you wanted?"

Holding up the hat box I answer, "Yeah, I've got the photos. We'll show ourselves out. Thanks again."

"My pleasure Miss. Please take care."

"Thank you. You as well. Goodbye."

"Goodbye, Miss. And Mister."

"Bye," Pierson responds.

I'm quiet in the car and the guys keep giving me sideways glances. I hate feeling like a lab specimen.

"I'm fine. I just found some pictures of my mom. It's no big deal."

"We're here for you, beautiful, if you want to talk. I'd also love to look at the photos with you if you want," Austin offers, always so sweet. Jackson reaches out a hand and squeezes my knee in a comforting gesture. I smile at him appreciatively.

Once we're home, I divide up the stuff we collected to look at in order of importance. Jackson unloads the things he took and organizes them into the piles I made. When we're finished, I'm left staring at the hat box. Thankfully one of Dozer's guys shows up and swabs my mouth. I'm happy for the distraction but he leaves to deliver it to the lab in under five minutes.

"Okay, we can look at the pictures. Just, it's not that I'm having a meltdown or anything... I'm just a little emotional between Kristos, my grandmother escaping, and seeing new photos of my mom. It's a lot of stuff at once. But you don't have to treat me like I'm going to break, I'm fine."

"We know, we just want to help. Whatever you need, we'll do it," Pierson explains.

I smile at them, I don't need to say anything, they know what I'm thinking.

We sat at the table with the box. Sawyer sniffs it and I know he's dying to climb inside. I open it and dump out the photos then place the empty box in front of the fluffy feline offering it to him. He doesn't hesitate, he steps right in and begins sniffing every inch of it.

The photos are all mixed up and some are face down but they're still looking at me waiting for me to acknowledge them. With a small hitch in my chest I picked up a photo of my mother and father. They're standing in front of a beautiful ocean view where the sun has just begun its descent, their faces stretched with huge smiles. They look so happy, so alive.

"This was your mom and dad?" Jackson asks as he looks over my shoulder.

"Yeah. I think this was before they got me. But not too much before because they looked almost the same when I met them. I think this was their trip to Hawaii right before I met them, mom was tan and had some lighter streaks in her hair from the sun then. She was beautiful."

"She was. Both of your parents were nice looking and very happy by the looks of it."

"I would agree if you only look at their smiles, but their eyes show a void. They told me they always felt like they were missing a part of them without children. Like their children were supposed to be there, but they got lost and it left a void behind. They said meeting me and adopting me filled that empty space and a bunch of other cracks and gaps they didn't even know they had. They said I was like the spackle that finally made them complete. Well, that was Dad. He always had a ridiculous dad joke way of saying things."

"He sounds fun," Pierson said and squeezed my hand.

"He was, they both were. We tried to spend lots of time together and they wanted me to be safe so they worked hard to teach me self-defense, weapons, wilderness survival, and some other life skills." I say thinking about the prepper training, the human anatomy lessons to kill or maim more successfully, the knife throwing practices, yeah, they wanted me safe and strong. They just didn't prepare me for losing them, the most painful thing ever to happen to me.

"How long did you live with them?" Pierson asks.

"I just turned thirteen when I met them and they died right before I turned eighteen. I had about five years with them, it seemed like a lifetime but also like a flash gone too fast to see clearly."

"It's not long, but it was during the longest and most educational time of your life. Remember how in high school a week seemed to last forever, you couldn't wait for the weekend and it always took so long for those five days to pass. Now, the weekend comes much quicker. It's also the time in your life where you soak in and remember the most information. With your brain, Baby, you probably learned a hundred times what regular people do." Austin smiles at me and it makes me smile too.

"Now that's more like it!" He kisses my cheek.

I pick up another photo and it's just mom, she looks young, maybe not even eighteen. I turn it over and the date confirms my guess, she was seventeen. She was so pretty her smile makes her look like a movie star, no wonder dad fell for her.

I handed it to Pierson, "Mom was seventeen here." We continue going through the photos and some have dates to give me a clue when they were taken and some don't. In the middle of the pile I find a letter addressed to Grandmother from my mom. I look it over and figure out it's from when she was away at college, she was about to graduate and tells Grandmother about her new job at the investment firm where she eventually met dad.

It's an oddly formal letter, as if mom was writing a government official not her own mother. Grandmother must have been on her second or third husband by then, my mom doesn't mention a stepfather. She was probably glad she didn't have to live with her mother and her myriad of spouses. Even though mom tried to keep her tone conservative and appropriate I can picture her jumping up and down with excitement about her new job.

At the bottom of the letter in different handwriting and ink is a name, phone number, and a note that says: *recommended by Milton.* The name is what snags my attention, it says, *Kristos*.

"Do you see this? How old do you think this is?" I ask the table.

Jackson takes it and scans the details, "Hmm, there's no way to tell but some people keep their numbers for a long time. Our mom has had her number since college. This looks like it was before she was married to *Milton,* so that's what ten, fifteen years at least? When was your mom in college?"

"A long time ago, before Milton was married to the witch. I don't care about the number, I can find his online in two seconds. I wonder what she would've hired him for if he was recommended by the mob boss. If he was second in command eventually, it seems like he wouldn't have been hired for something small. Let's finish looking at these later. I need to start uploading the files so I can start analyzing the information."

When I'm finishing uploading all the files into my programs my phone rings.

"Hello?"

"Hello, I'm calling from Synergistic Solutions for Violet Henley." I put in on speaker and the guys stop what they're doing and listen.

"I'm Violet." After I satisfy him with my personal details to prove I'm me, he continues.

"I have the DNA results for you."

"Okay, go on." That was so fast.

"The two samples were a match, 99.86902% chance *Sample A* is the child of *Sample B*. If you're interested both samples contain a majority of Native American, Mediterranean, and lesser European percentages of heritage genes. *Sample A* also contains South and Central American heritage. You'll get all the details in the mail, we're required to phone in the results when it's a RapidDNA test. If you'd like to give your opinion about our service today you can remain on the line for a brief survey. Have I answered all of your questions, and have we met your expectations today?" I didn't think he was ever going to stop.

"Yes. Thank you, Good-bye." I hang up before he can speak again. Thankfully I'm already sitting because the floor falls away beneath my feet and my insides race as if a runaway train is careening around my chest.

Pierson rushes to me, "What can I do?" I'm gasping for breath.

Jackson and Austin close in and all three of them rub my skin in a soothing way while they pepper me with soft kisses. I focus on my mantra and repeat it a few times before I'm able to take in a breath that doesn't scorch my lungs.

"I'm okay. Thank you." I touch each of them and they give me a little space. After a few deep breaths I begin to feel better.

"Do you need anything?" Jackson asks.

"I'm good. I've finished uploading everything, so the program is working. I was waiting for that call and hoping I was wrong, but I wasn't blindsided by the news. Yeah, it sucks but it is what it is, let's get ready to do some surveillance after dark. I want to find her and I want him. We're going to need a bigger team to get him though, unless we can catch him alone somehow. Austin, will you check in with Colby while I change?"

"Of course. Yo! What up boss?" he speaks into his phone and walks out the back door. Jackson and Pierson give me one last touch before I head into the bedroom to get ready.

We all move quickly and efficiently, having us loaded and ready to go in about thirty-seven minutes. When we get to the park across the road from Kristos's building, we watch the entrance in silence. We don't have any way to know where the visitors are going once inside the twelve-story mixed use complex, and I want a closer look. I grab my hoodie and cover up what I'm wearing as much as possible. Jackson chooses not to protest when I give him a look showing my emotional state.

There's an upscale fast-food place inside the building lobby, a few luxury stores, and a fancy spa that takes up most of the commerce on this floor. I purchase an apple caramel crunch muffin and a coffee before I enter the first elevator in the bank of four cars and check out how it works. There's a residential lobby on the second floor, so I hit the number two button. If you have a residential keycard, you can bypass the lobby and enter your floor directly, if not, the default takes you to the second floor.

When the doors slide open, I plaster a bored look on my face and hold out the bag while walking towards the elevators in the hallway behind the desk.

"I'm going to the penthouse," I call out.

"Sorry, miss, you'll need to sign in first," the balding but sturdy looking guard insists.

"Aw, come on man I've got two more deliveries dying downstairs," I pout.

"Sorry, I can't let you up until I check you in. Which penthouse is it?"

"Oh shit. They didn't tell me there was more than one, they just said penthouse. I thought this would be quick, can you call them?"

"Yes, sign in here. I'll need to see your ID." This is going from bad to worse.

"It's for that rich lady," I go on to describe my grandmother. He nods and I think maybe this isn't a total bust as I cross my fingers.

"She's staying in Penthouse One, perhaps I can ask her to send someone down for it so you can go," he helpfully suggests. Score!

"That would be ideal." I offer him a smile, set the food on the granite, and lean on the counter making my cleavage more prominent. He takes the bait and his eyes migrate to my chest every time he thinks he can get away with it.

He dials, "Yes, this is Odin at the front desk. I have a delivery for Miss Morgan. Can you send someone down to get it? All right. Thanks."

My smile is genuine now, "Dude, thanks so much. You saved me. I'm new, but I hope I'll see you again." I flutter my lashes and act a little shy as I enter the elevator back to the first floor.

"Hey, what's your name?"

"Lizzie. Bye, Odin." The doors close and I whisper *Borden.* He probably wouldn't get the reference but why push it on just a recon mission?

When I climb back into our SUV Jackson isn't there. He shows up as I buckle my seatbelt.

He yanks open the door, "What the fuck Violet?"

"What?"

He lets me have it once he's seated, "You know what you did. Didn't we just have a talk about being careful because she's trying to kill you? Why did you go upstairs alone?"

"I just wanted to recon the residential lobby in case we need to go upstairs at some point. I wanted to know how many people were in there, check out security, the usual."

"Bullshit! If that guy had let you upstairs, you would've gone without even telling us. What would you do then? You would've been outnumbered, trapped up there, alone with the enemy. You promised to be more careful. Fuck!"

"Jackson, I can take care of myself, you know this, why are you giving me such a hard time?"

"You've been shot *twice*."

"One was barely a graze."

"Really?" I swear steam is coming from his ears, "Look, I know you're highly capable, but you're not bulletproof, Babe. You've got to be more careful. How would you feel if one of us got shot?"

My eyes snapped to his. "I would die if something happened to you."

"How do you think we feel? If something happens to you, *we'll die.* Please, I'm begging you, stop taking unnecessary risks." I climb into his lap.

Straddling him I place my hands on his cheeks and look into his eyes, "You're right, I'm sorry. I promise I won't take any unnecessary risks. Please don't be mad at me."

"I should put you over my knee! But I forgive you." He kisses me and I feel his length harden beneath me. We don't have time for that right now.

"Good."

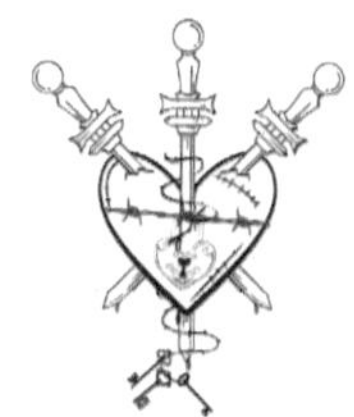

Chapter Twenty-Six

Pierson

She apologized to me and Austin leaning between the seats kissing us to make up. I wasn't mad at her, I mean I don't want her to die but I know she can take care of herself and I don't worry as much as Jackson. Of course I wasn't around when she was shot in her abdomen either.

"What did you learn going up there, Baby?" Austin asks after giving everyone a moment to calm down.

She describes the lobby, security system, procedures, and Odin. Most importantly she confirmed her beastly grandma is up there. I have a radical idea and I offer it to my partners.

"Hear me out. What if we ignore her for a while? Forget she exists, go about our lives? She'll feel like we gave up or something else made us move on and she'll come out of there. We can have someone watching and grab her when she sticks her toe outside."

"No, dumbass, what if she takes off to Europe or some shit while we're going about our lives and not at all ready to deal with her?" Austin shoots down my suggestion.

"He might have something, she's a strict schedule follower. Not going to her weekly lunches and dinners will make her nuts. Kristos will probably be sick of her complaining in no time, he'll assign her security and send her on her way. She's a huge pain in the ass." I smile in triumph at Austin, he can eat his *dumbass* remark, Violet likes my idea.

"You think?" Jackson questions.

"Yeah. Let's have a meeting with Dozer and Colby, we can work out a plan."

Once we have a strategy meeting scheduled, our conversation strays into game play. I had all but forgotten about the game. We each got a riddle with coordinates on it from the antique shop. Colby's annoyed that only one of us has been playing and he wants us to remember to play no matter what else is happening. I don't care that much, but he's extremely invested and I don't want to make him upset and thereby make Violet unhappy. I pull up a photo of the clue on my phone and ponder what it means, if I'm still a good shot, and who's been playing on their own.

I'm still thinking about the game when we head to the meeting with Colby and Dozer the next day. I know the entire clue by heart now after reading it so many times.

Greetings Player!

28.332411, -81.516022

Take yourself to these coordinates by car or by boot, you always miss the targets you don't shoot, but do not fear, because you'll shoot them here. From twenty-five yards see if you can hit the bullseye, shoot your best and you won't cry. You'll get the next part of your clue, when the middle of the target's hit by you. Ask for Artie Cupp, he'll get you all set up.

Good luck!

Your Game Master

Ugh, he's so cheesy, he really is like a game show host. This might actually be his most effective endeavor. I'm assuming this clue will take me to the range where I'll need a bullseye for the next clue based on the non-riddle we collected our last time playing. I've been using a three-fifty-seven from Violet's extensive armory, I don't have much practice time logged, I hope I can hit the target at all.

"Pierson?"

"Huh?"

"Are you coming?"

"Oh. Uh, yeah, sorry I was thinking about something."

"Yeah, I got that. Are you all right?"

"Yep. Just wondering if I can hit a target."

"You'll be fine, after one clip you'll be back in the saddle. Come on Dozer's already here so they're waiting on us."

"Was it you? Have you finished this task?" He looks down for a second and I have my answer.

"Yeah. You don't understand how close I've been in the last few games. I want to win one and plan a trip to Disney," Jackson states without a hint of embarrassment regarding his childhood fantasy.

"I can't believe you still want to go there, bro. You know you're over twenty-one, right?" I tease.

"Dude, don't even start. Austin's been bagging on me since we met Violet, besides Disney World is the happiest place on Earth for all ages!"

"What is it about that place that you're so obsessed with anyways?"

"It's magical, the whole place feels like a dream the minute you step foot on the property. It's paradise, from the perfectly clipped hedges to the sparkling towers on Cinderella's Castle. Don't you remember how amazing it was when we went there with mom and dad? The only thing missing was our very own princess and now we have her."

"You better not let her hear you call her that or your *princess* might slice off your nuts." I involuntarily shield my precious jewels from attack at the thought.

"Yeah, well, our princess might be a little dark, but she rules the underworld like a boss and she's hot as fuck." He smiles like he's remembering what we did with her last night. Motherfucker! Now my dick is getting hard thinking about our darkly beautiful Princess of Death. I love every twisted piece of her, but I don't want to make her mad so I haul ass inside Colby's clubhouse, I mean *pool* house.

"Glad you could make it, Pierson," Colby calls me out.

"Sorry, it won't happen again, *Game Master.*"

Violet stands and begins our planning session, "Come on guys, let's focus. We need to figure out surveillance, how we'll get her when she's back home, and what to do about... *him.*"

We go around and around until we've all expressed our thoughts and have a viable plan in place. It's risky but doable. We're going to join the surveillance team during the hours that won't affect work or school, though we're all prepared to take time off if necessary. Additionally, we needed to plan around the wedding in just a couple weeks. Violet wants to have them both in hand before we leave for Tallahassee, but we have contingencies in place if that's not possible. I'm confident in the steps we outlined and the details needed to succeed.

Once we're back home I tell them I want to go for a ride and clear my head of all this grandmother crap. Austin wants to clean out the refrigerator since it's his week for kitchen duty, Violet has a school project to complete, and Jackson gives me a knowing grin, asshole.

When I get to the *coordinates*, I'm at the better of the only two indoor ranges in our area, Mystic Range. Jackson told me it's one of the first places they went with Violet, when they were just friends. I approach the glass counter and look over the firearms inside the case.

"Hi, I'm Mitch, can I show you something?" The man up front seems friendly enough.

"Hey, I'm Pierson. I'm looking for Artie Cupp," Mitch starts laughing.

"What's so funny?"

"Sorry man. Jackson said you'd be coming. It's just, there's no Artie Cupp. Colby made him up just as a code so we'll give you the things you need for your task."

"Oh. Well, all right. What have you got?"

"Give me one second, I need to grab it from the back."

Mitch disappeared through a door marked, *Employees Only.* The swinging door barely has time to stop moving before he's back with a box. A large rolled up paper like a scroll sticks out but I can't see anything else.

"Okay, here you go. Did you bring eyes and ears?"

"Nope."

"Good. How about a firearm?"

"Yeah."

"Okay, hang on." He turns around and grabs something from a shelf. "I need your firearm, please."

Assuming this is a range that likes to examine whatever hunk of metal people are using on their property, I hand it over. He opens the cylinder, dumps out the rounds, and threads a gun lock in place through the barrel. I look at him perplexed.

"Sorry, the rules require each player to use the exact same equipment."

"Okay."

"Everything you need is in this box, you're on lane fourteen. If you need anything inside let our Range Master, Ashley, know."

"Thanks." I heft the box from the counter and go inside the range entry. Digging into the box I retrieve the provided eyes and ears. Once they're in place I enter the inner door to the shooting lanes. I find lane fourteen at the end and start sifting through the contents in the box. I lay everything neatly on the work surface and examine what I have to use.

The last thing I do is unroll the scroll, they're targets decorated with a small furry creature giving the finger. A caption at the top reads, *Who's the asshole now?* I don't get the joke, but it's cool. The bullseye is a black circle in the middle of his belly, I decide he looks like a badger. Then I load the target onto the track mechanism that sends it twenty-five yards to the back of the range and almost flat against the back reinforced bulletproof wall.

Damn that's far when you're looking through the small sight on the top of the barrel and trying to compensate for arc and distance. I don't know why but I cross myself before I get into my shooting stance, I have a burning desire to beat Jackson and Austin.

Taking aim I gently squeeze the trigger. My shot goes high and wide, I adjust and fire again. This time the hole left in the paper is too low, a classic overcorrection. I focus all of my energy on sighting in the bullseye and keeping my eyes on the target when I squeeze it again.

"Ha!" I exclaim to no one, this end of the range is empty.

I wait for the pissed off little badger to come back to me on its track and I'm able to confirm my shot is almost dead center of the bullseye. I place everything inside the box, remove the clip, and eject the round in the chamber before placing the firearm into the box. The target lies on top.

"That was fast. Let me check your target, please." Mitch pulls out a magnifying glass and carefully examines the bullet hole. He signs the target and asks me to do the same.

"To avoid any mix ups later," he explains.

"All right."

"Let me get your clue." I nod. He returns with a plain envelope.

I reach for it and he pulls it back a little, "Hang on, I have instructions. You can't open this envelope for at least twenty-four hours. When you open it, you'll only have twenty-four hours to complete your next task. If you fail to meet the deadline you must contact the *Game Master* for an additional task. Are these instructions clear?"

"Yep. Got it." He hands me the envelope.

"Please say hello to Austin and Violet for me."

"Will do, it was nice meeting you."

"Likewise. Good luck, I hope you beat Austin, he owes me a beer."

"I'll let him know. Thanks."

"My pleasure, see you."

"Yeah, see ya."

When I leave the range, I decide to take a drive, I don't want to lie to Violet and this way it's not a lie. There are some beautiful roads in this area you can be in town surrounded by tall buildings one minute or along the blue Gulf water the next and once you leave the immediate area you'll find endless country roads encircled by pasture land, cattle and horses dot the gentle hills and it looks like a photograph. Many of the winding miles of asphalt are lined with beautiful oak trees dressed in moss like an ethereal veil for a mystical bride.

I'm completely mesmerized by my soothing surroundings and I don't notice the asshole who's inching much too close for comfort to my rear tire, at first. What the fuck is this guy's problem? I'm going five over the speed limit. It's a double yellow line and he can't pass but I'm not an obstacle. At this speed he's dangerous, probably drunk or high. Rather than risk my life standing my ground I ease over to the breakdown lane and ride the line there offering him a way to get around me. When he keeps coming too close to my tire as if I haven't tried to move, I slow more and more while I simultaneously pull completely off the road. When I'm down below twenty miles per hour, I'm preparing to stop completely. He floors his gas pedal and slams into the back of my bike. It jolts my hands on the handlebars and they jerk the wheel along with his impact. The bike goes onto the soft shoulder before

I can correct it and the front tire sticks there sending me flying over the handlebars. I have two thoughts as I do a poor imitation of a bird, *oh shit my bike!* And, *I'll never see Violet again!*

I brace for an excessively painful landing, but I crash onto some sturdy bushes and oak saplings luckily the combination cushions my fall. When I'm finished rolling, I stand up and assess my body for damage. I'm surprisingly injury free save a few cuts and scrapes but I have no doubt I'll discover new injuries in the morning.

"Oh my God! Are you okay? I called nine-one-one!" A woman, likely in her mid-fifties, questions me.

"I'm okay, relax."

"Well I don't care, you're going to the hospital young man. My great uncle was in an accident at work, swore he was okay, walked around completely fine. The next morning they found him in his bed, dead from internal bleeding. I just couldn't live with myself if you died when I could've stayed with you and made sure you got help." While she talks, I notice my left middle finger is throbbing. My stomach flips over when I see the finger is bent at an odd angle, scraped, bruised and swelling.

"Thanks so much, but I promise I'm fine. Just this finger might need some attention," I raise the twisted appendage to show her.

"I can hear the sirens coming. Oh my goodness, you'd better lean on my car until they get here. You know why they call the hospital here MC2?"

"Okay, okay, I can lean, and I have no idea why they call it that."

"Well, it's Mystic Cross Medical Center, so it would be MCMC. But that's ridiculous, so they came up with MC twice or MC2. Clever, huh?" When the big truck with flashing lights arrives it occurs to me that she rambled on to distract me. It was kinda nice and extremely annoying, I thank her before she leaves and promise to let them check me out.

The paramedics aren't any better than the woman, they insist I take a ride to the hospital and since I have no other options available I consent. My bike is wrecked and I want to cry but my man card keeps the tears in check. They wanted to start an IV in the ambulance but I refused, I have a busted finger for fuck's sake. I called Violet but she doesn't answer. I try Austin next.

"Hey, what's up? I thought you were taking a ride."

"I did, then a fall, now I'm getting a ride to the hospital."

"What the fuck? Are you serious?"

"Yeah. I tried calling Violet, is she with you?"

"Hang on. Come here, Baby, I have Pierson on the phone. He needs to tell us something." I hear her question him in the background. "Here, it's on speaker, we'll find out. Go Piers."

"Some asshole hit the back of my bike and I flew over the handlebars, through pure luck and maybe the grace of God, I'm not hurt except for a broken finger, but they're making me get some tests in the ER to check for internal injuries. I promise I'm fine."

"Are they taking you to MC2?"

"Yeah."

"We'll meet you there."

"Okay, because I'll need a ride home, my bike is toast."

"I'll find out where it is and have it brought home. We'll fix it." Violet is calm and in charge, I like it. She's so different from other girls, I was expecting screams or tears but my girl is a badass and she doesn't have a meltdown over nothing.

"Thanks, I'll see you in the ER."

"Pierson?"

"Yeah?"

"I love you."

Austin calls out, "I love you too dude, we're leaving in two minutes."

"I love you too. Both of you. See ya."

When we pull up to the emergency entrance they wheel me in on the stretcher despite my vociferous protests. I feel ridiculous, it's one finger, I can walk. When they try to transfer me to the bed

I get annoyed and step off the stretcher and sit on the bed without assistance.

A large nurse comes in already speaking, "Hi Sweetie, I'm Maggie I'll be your nurse and Dr. Rosenfeld will be in to see you once we have you in a gown. Here you go, everything off but your briefs. Do you have any jewelry? Oh. Why didn't they start an IV?"

"Because I don't need one. I have one injury to my finger. I don't need an IV or a gown."

"Great. You're one of those. Listen sweetie I'm in charge in this room and you may not need an IV, but you *will* put on the gown. You have to go for X-Rays and maybe some other imaging so you will put on a gown and you will remove everything but your briefs without any further argument. Chop chop! We mustn't keep the doctor waiting." Her voice changes from firm school principal to sing-song *Glenda-the-Good-Witch* without a breath in between. Never one to want to make someone else's job difficult, I choose to comply with her request. I didn't want to argue because she looks like she might be able to kick my ass and that's more embarrassing than a hospital gown.

"Hello, I'm Dr. Rosenfeld. I'm ordering X-Rays, labs, and a CAT scan of your major organs just to be sure nothing is injured internally. Your vitals are good so it's just a precaution. Let's take a look at this finger."

I hold up my hand with my middle finger extended, it serves the usual purpose as well as facilitating the examination. A man from the lab comes in next and takes eight tubes of blood and I feel like I should get credit for a donation with that much removed. When he's done an orderly comes in to wheel me off for the tests.

The only discomfort during the testing comes from the X-Ray tech twisting my hand and finger for the images the doctor wants. It's all over quickly and I'm returned to my room where I find Violet, Austin, and Jackson waiting.

I extend my middle finger in greeting, specifically for Austin and he smiles his smart ass grin. "That's going to be fun. You can flip off everyone and blame your accident."

"I'm so glad you're alright." Violet kisses my cheek and hugs my neck. I return her embrace and give her a private smile to reassure her that I'm truly fine.

She continues speaking, "Please tell us what happened." I share the details with my family, and they listen with intent.

Jackson asks, "Did you get a look at the driver?"

"No. I was in my head and by the time I noticed them I was just trying to avoid being hit, but it was definitely a man. I could see a silhouette and he was fairly large."

Then Violet asks, "What type of vehicle was it? Make? Model?"

"It was a dark colored truck, dark tinted windows, and only two doors. I think it was a Ford, but I don't know the model and I didn't see the license plate, I was in a bush when he took off."

"Any witnesses?" Austin queries.

"I think so, there was a lady who called nine-one-one. She seemed like the type to notice details, her info should be on the police report, right?"

"It should be, I'll put Colby on it. Your bike was being towed to the police yard, but I was able to divert it to our house. We'll check it over and decide if we can fix it or if we need to hire someone," Violet explains.

"It looks awful. I would look worse if it wasn't for the bushes and saplings that broke my fall. I went flying off the bike and I didn't think I would get out of it in one piece."

"Well one piece, except for that," Austin points at my swollen and bent finger.

"Yeah," I agree.

"I don't think it was a random accident. I think we're being watched, and it was an attempt to end you. Jackson, you're right, we can't go out alone until this is resolved. I don't know who's watching us, whether it's her or *him, b*ut we can't take any chances, we'll need to be vigilant at all times."

I'm a little shell shocked and it didn't occur to me that it could've been on purpose. I look at my beautiful girlfriend and my brothers thanking all of the divine beings who intervened on my behalf. I could be dead right now or worse, paralyzed or something. I had a friend who got paralyzed on a mission, he killed himself eight weeks later. I don't want to know how difficult it is to cope with a life changing injury. I'm grateful all I got was a busted finger.

"What makes you think that, Babe?"

"Just the circumstances, it's highly suspicious, don't you think?"

"I agree with you. It's suspicious as fuck," Austin lets us have his opinion.

"Okay, Sweetie, the doctor says everything looks good except for that nasty finger. You can get dressed and the doctor will be in to splint it and give you instructions. Once he signs off, I'll print out your discharge paperwork and send you on your way. I'm sure your family will appreciate it." She smiles at Violet who smiles in return.

The doctor comes in two minutes later and it takes almost an hour to complete everything before I can walk out the door. Nurse Maggie tried to insist on pushing me in a wheelchair, but I'm done, that's not happening. When we get home, I'm starting to feel sore between the bruises, muscle strain, and the adrenaline wearing off. I'm really feeling it in my spine and of course my injured hand.

Chapter Twenty-Seven

Violet

I'm so relieved Pierson is okay, my heart almost fell out my chest when he first told us what happened. I can't lose him, not any of them. Colby and I need to get this figured out ASAP, we can't go everywhere together all the time and we can't spend all of our time looking over our shoulders. Dozer's guys will still shadow me at school, maybe the guys need a shadow too. They'd never go for it at work, maybe I can arrange some help without them knowing. I'll have to chat with Dozer and see what he recommends.

In the meantime I'm frustrated thinking this is going to send Jackson off the deep end. He's normally overprotective and for whatever reason he feels the need to be in charge of our safety, especially mine. Maybe if I tell him I'll agree to being chaperoned he'll accept that and stop giving me a hard time. When I check on Pierson, he's falling asleep.

"How are you feeling? Do you need anything?" I ask softly.

"Nah, I took the pain meds and it's making me sleepy. I'm just going to let it knock me out. Are you doing all right?"

"Yeah, I'm good. I'm working on a few things to keep us safe. We're doing your *ignore-my-wicked-grandmother* plan, but I guess she's not going to ignore us."

"Do you know for sure it was her?"

"Not yet. I have a gut feeling, I mean she was already trying to kill me, why not get rid of you guys too?"

"You might be right. I love you."

Kissing his lips and rubbing his chest I respond, "I love you too. I'm so glad you're okay. You go to sleep and I'll check on you in a little while. Sweet dreams."

"They'll be better than sweet, all about you." He has a ridiculous grin plastered on his face and his eyes are closed. I watch as he begins snoring, poor guy, he's had a rough day. I'm afraid to tell him about his bike, I'm pretty sure the frame is bent. At least I know a good mechanic. Dad and I used to get help from Reggie of Reggie's Motorcycle Repair, he's a good guy. Hopefully a miracle worker, to save Pierson's poor twisted baby.

Since Pierson is tucked in and Jackson and Austin went to the warehouse to work out, I'm on my own, except for Sawyer.

"Hey handsome boy, what are you up to? Want to play with a toy?" He has one of those sticks with feathers hanging off the end and he loves it. I tease him by dragging the feathers near him but just out of his reach. He pounces on it and rolls onto his back while I shake it at him. He swats at the brightly colored plumes.

Eventually, he decides he's finished and leaps onto his tree, perching on top watching me with his tail twitching. I think he can tell I'm on edge. This situation, with my fucking *father* has me tied up in knots. I need to take a ride but I promised them I wouldn't take off alone and I can't go out to stab anyone either.

The next best thing is online hunting. I focus on dear old dad and start ripping his life apart, searching for weak spots.

When I'm checking out his company website it says they're hiring IT personnel. I click on the application and I meet the requirements for a tech. Taking a shot I fill out the request for employment, I don't even need to lie except about my name. Conveniently, I picked up fake IDs for me and the guys after we made our first group unaliving trip. I got one for Pierson after he joined my crew of *Villains*. Using my fake identity I complete the application and submit it. Before I can find the next thing on my search list I receive an automated response from *Sunshine State Solutions, Your Future Shines Bright With Us!*

It's vague enough to keep you guessing, what do they do? Turns out they're a money laundering front for the mafia, but they claim to be your *financial advisor.* Investment manager? Wealth building firm? A stock broker? Who knows. Question one on my list for them is, what does *Sunshine State Solutions* do?

Question two will be do you know your CEO is a mob boss? They probably do. While continuing to search for more information about my father, I get another message regarding my employment application.

Emmy Quinn, we're happy you're interested in a future with Sunshine State Solutions! We have the following dates and times available to interview you in person, please choose your first and second choice and we'll confirm your appointment.

It goes on to describe what I need to bring with me and then it actually has a link to some articles about how to do well on an interview, how to write a winning resume, and how to land the job with the best pay rate. What the fuck is happening? Isn't a job interview supposed to tell the potential employer if you're capable of figuring out those exact things? Sometimes the world is too dumb and I want to slap it across the face so hard its orbit and rotations will spin.

After I make my choices I respond with a sappy note thanking them for this *wonderful opportunity.* A confirmation for my first choice comes back in sixty seconds. Perfect, I have an appointment at eight tomorrow, I want to get in there as fast as possible. I called up Dozer to share the change in my plans.

"Everything okay?" he answers.

"Pierson was riding his bike when a truck decided to rear-end him and take off. He's all right, just a broken finger but he should've been killed. You should see his bike, it bent the frame. I'm pretty sure my grandmother is responsible. We're going to pair up as much as possible but I still need someone for school and tomorrow, I have an appointment." I go on to describe the job situation and he agrees I need someone close, his computer person is going to apply for a position at *Triple S* too. They'll work right with me if we get hired.

We talk over my request to have the guys chaperoned without them knowing, and he says, "I won't lie to them. If they ask me, I'm telling them the truth."

"I didn't ask you to lie. You can tell them, if they ask. Otherwise this is a covert operation for their safety."

"Want to make a wager?"

"On what?"

"How long before they figure it out?"

"I know you're just trying to make a point, but I'm going to take that bet. I figure three days but I hope I'm wrong, or at least it's long enough to stop her."

"What are you betting?"

"If I win you take Danielle on a double or quintuple date with me and the guys."

"Okay. If I win, you have to mow my lawn for a month."

"Wait a minute, do you have a huge property?"

"What do you consider huge?"

"Anything over ten-thousand square feet."

"It's a little more than that, but I usually mow it, you can do it no problem."

"Okay. It doesn't matter because I'm going to win."

"We have a bet?"

"Yeah."

I'm laughing when we hang up and Sawyer gives me a weird look. "What? You never had a friend goad you into a bet?" He looks at me like he's trying his best to understand what I said. His head is tilted and his paws are crossed making him look like a scientist documenting all the characteristics of a new species.

He meows a quick sound under his breath. *Mew!*

His entire tail switches back and forth like a pendulum guillotine blade. It occurs to me he's never had a friend which makes me think it might be cruel to only have one cat. He must get lonely when we're not home. I'll have to ask my guys what they think about getting a friend for him. After Sawyer and I have some snuggles which cheer up both of us, I go through my closet looking for an interview outfit. I settled on a black leather skirt, pale purple blouse, and a leather trimmed jacket, paired with chunky heeled boots.

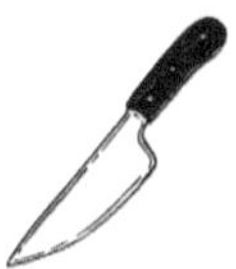

When my alarm goes off the next morning, I check on Pierson first, then get ready for my appointment. After breakfast Pierson says he's sore and his finger is swollen and throbbing. He kisses me for luck and heads back to bed. Austin and Jackson are going to work and I know they'll have someone watching their back.

"You can't leave until your shadow gets here, promise me, Babe."

"I promise. He's also sending someone to watch over Pierson."

"Good. Just, don't tell him. He'll feel useless or some shit," Austin advises.

With a low chuckle I responded, "Great idea." They each kiss and hug me before they leave. I hope they're not too mad when they figure out what I did.

When my shadow arrives I head towards town to the biggest flashiest building, I wave to the guy staying with Pierson on my way past. When I pull into the parking garage a red machine gives me a ticket and raises the metal bar. Instead of parking, probably for free in the building's garage, I opted for another garage on the corner. I don't want to be at their mercy in their garage. The lobby is manned by security guards who check off my assumed name on a list and send me to the elevators.

When the doors slide open the floors shine so bright I wonder if the expensive marble has something reflective in it. In a tasteful font next to the large double doors are huge letters in perfectly straight lines on a stone wall, displaying their name and motto. The polish on the door gives it a mirror like finish and I consider how many coats of gloss must be on the wood. It drips with money and I haven't even been inside yet.

The receptionist is tall and slender with dark hair and brown eyes. I smile at him and say hello before describing why I'm here. He asks me to take a seat after he checks me off on his list.

"Miss Quinn?" A small blonde woman calls me and I feel like I'm in a doctor's waiting room.

"Yes."

"We're ready for you. Did you bring a resume?" I reach into my leather satchel and retrieve the items they requested. Diploma, resume, certifications, ID, the usual.

"Thanks. I'm Molly, I'm a technical engineer in the department. Follow me." She hands off my documents to another woman as we pass.

"I was surprised to see your age with your experience and you look even younger in person. We're excited to have the opportunity to hire you. Do you need a glass of water or anything?"

"No. I'm fine, thank you." She pulls open a large door. Inside is a conference table with ten people seated around it. I'm not nervous, but this many people for an interview is intimidating.

"Everyone, this is Emmy Quinn, she's applying for a tech position. Emmy, please, have a seat."

The same woman who got my resume comes in and hands each person a stack of papers. Everyone shuffles through them, each reading different pages. I wait quietly for them to finish.

"Miss Quinn, I'm Bronson, I'm the head of IT. Thank you for coming today. This says you learned *JavaScript* and *C/C+* twelve years ago? Weren't you just a child then?"

"I was young but I'm a fast learner and programming just clicked with me."

"This says you have experience with *Julia* and *Crystal* as well?" A different person asks and then introduces themselves. It goes on and on around the table. Mostly they don't seem to be able to grasp my age. My Emmy ID says I'm twenty-four, to help throw off anyone's suspicions I wear glasses hoping they make me appear older and hide my lack of wrinkles, just like Clark Kent. I also worked on makeup to make me look more worldly, literally there was a video for younger girls trying to look older, I guess to get into bars. I sent the post to Colby to see if they need to be on our list.

When we're finished they ask, "Would you mind stepping outside for a moment? We'll call you back in when we're finished."

There are a few seats in the hallway but I've been sitting and being grilled for the last forty-five minutes, so I choose to stand. While I'm standing there, I can hear the woman who took my resume chatting with another woman.

"He's so dreamy don't you think?" resume woman asks.

"No. He's old."

"He's not that old, he's distinguished. Besides you can't tell me he's not good-looking for an older man."

"I guess, but he's our boss. You can't say shit like that here."

"They're all in the interviews. He spoke to me the other day, maybe I have a chance."

"Ick! What's wrong with you? Why would you want a chance? Besides I heard from Lacey that he's a dog. He sleeps with a different woman every night and he even sleeps with prostitutes. Trust me, you don't want whatever he's got."

"But he's so smart and funny, he was so kind when he spoke to me. He asked my name and when he left, he winked at me."

"Oh my God! Madeline, Kristos Chitto did not wink at you! I think you need to call HR and make an appointment for Employee Assistance, you're mentally ill."

"Ha, ha. I've always been attracted to older guys and he's so powerful, running this whole company, he must be so rich, too. I'm just saying I wouldn't mind a date with him. If it was just one night, I'd be okay with that, it would probably be a wonderful evening in some Michelin Star restaurant, then maybe a concert in VIP seats, if we ended up at his place after I wouldn't mind. I've always wanted to see that penthouse."

"Okay, forget HR, I'm calling nine-one-one and having you committed! Please don't say any of this to anyone else, you'll get fired. Speaking of, what do you think would happen to you if you had a one night stand with the boss? You think he would want to bump into you on the elevator? I think not! You'd be gone so he wouldn't have to deal with an uncomfortable elevator ride. Please, for your own good, just don't!"

"Yeah, yeah. Come on, we need to go get the deli order from downstairs, the suits will be out soon complaining..."

As their voices fade, "Miss Quinn? Please, rejoin us."

"Thank you."

The department head speaks once I sit down. "Miss Quinn, we'd like to offer you the position. Are you amenable to the salary and benefits you received by email?"

"Thank you, Mr. Bronson. I'm amenable to the salary and benefits package, but I didn't see in the description when the insurance benefits become active."

"In thirty days, but if you become ill during the training period, the company has a grant we offer to cover any medical expenses, technically you're covered from day one."

"Wow, that's a great benefit. Thank you."

"If you have no other questions for us, I'm ready to send you to HR for the on-boarding paperwork. They should be able to have you sign a few documents and then get you set up in the employee portal for everything else. Before you leave this room, we need you to sign the NDA in front of you."

"NDA? I wasn't aware that would be required. Please give me a moment to read it."

"It's the standard form, we have some proprietary software and we need you to sign the NDA before we can get you started, you'll be accessing the software almost immediately. Is there an issue?"

"No. Sorry, I was surprised, and delighted that you have proprietary software. I'm happy to sign, I believe in protecting patents and copyrights."

"Excellent, just sign and date the bottom." *Sign the correct name* is repeating over and over in my head. I smile as I sign Emerson Quinn, I chose the first name to honor my mother, my last name is for Harley Quinn of course. I kinda like it when people call me Miss Quinn.

He has Molly hand me off to Jessica in HR. I spent a half hour getting myself registered in their employee portal and signing my life away. I'm so relieved when I'm finished. As I'm leaving the office I spot one of Dozer's guys, he's being led to HR by Molly, I guess he got the job too. I've met him once before, and he's hard to miss with his shock of strawberry blonde hair. He looks like a total nerd and he knows computer programming inside and out but he's also a trained killer who's an excellent shot. I met him at the range when Dozer challenged me and the guys to a shooting competition. He chose his top two marksmen to bring with him and we still almost won. Maybe with Pierson here now we could beat him. I'll need to bring it up to Dozer and see if he's up for a rematch.

Since I've only missed one class this morning, I decided to head to school. I'm dying to check in on Pierson but I know he's safe and he's probably sleeping anyway. I'm so close to finishing the term and I want those credits just in case I ever decide to finish my degree. Plus, it would feel like I wasted my money if I quit before I got them. It's the least the school can do, though that's probably harsh. It's not their fault they're not teaching me anything, it just feels like it should be.

The rest of the day on campus went as expected. I didn't think about changing my clothes, so everyone made a comment about how I'm dressed. Most people asked if I went to a funeral, I said yes to limit the questions. My friends teased me that I look like an old lady which reminded me of my grandmother and my father.

By the time my classes were over and I made it home I was ready to rip off my clothes. Thankfully, I ran into Pierson and he said the right thing to give my clothes a chance to be worn again another day.

"Whoa! You look gorgeous, Killer! I bet they hired you dressed like that!"

"It was actually ten people who interviewed me and I'm pretty sure they didn't notice what I was wearing. They only cared about my brain, go figure. Should I be offended?"

"No. They're probably computer nerds who didn't even notice you're female."

"Aren't you a computer nerd?"

"Yeah, but I have a streak of cool jock, and with my military background, I'm a badass computer nerd. I would definitely notice what you're wearing because it looks sexy as fuck."

"I'm not sure you're stating your position in a way that shines a positive light on your badass computer nerd persona."

"I'm high on painkillers, I'm not a credible witness."

I bust out laughing. This may be the most ridiculous argument I've ever had. Damn he's cute.

"Okay, I won't hold it against you in a court of law if you cannot afford an attorney. I agree you're not competent to stand trial. How are you feeling? Have you been putting ice on your hand?"

"Yes ma'am, every hour. It's feeling less painful. I think the swelling has gone down."

"That's great."

"You never said, did you get the job?"

"I did. They wanted me to start next week but I offered to start tomorrow. They were impressed and said because they have two others who can start tomorrow, they'll do it. I'm calling in sick to school, they don't require proof from a doctor for the first three days. Of course I have a doctor if I need proof, but Uncle Randy hates doing it when it's not true. But I'm hoping to know before next week if working there is going to be helpful or not."

"You're sure Dozer's guy got hired?"

"Yeah, his name is Tyler. I saw them take him to HR plus I'm sure he was one of the people who wanted to start tomorrow."

"Okay."

"Austin and Jackson aren't home yet, huh?" I question.

"Nope." He looks at me with one side of his delicious mouth tilted up. His hazel eyes caress my face and my nipples harden. His good hand rests on my hip and he pulls me in for a kiss. I wrap my arms around his neck and deepen the kiss. He leads me to the bedroom and when he closes the door he presses me against it.

I can feel his interest pressed against my stomach, I swear my nipples get even harder. My hands trace his chest muscles and feel his strong arms. I whip my shirt over my head and he clumsily fights with my skirt. His finger splint keeps getting in the way. He gives up and pushes my skirt up my hips to my waist. I slide his sweats down his legs taking his boxer briefs with them, he tugs on my panties and the flimsy black lace rips. He tosses them to the floor and tries to lift me up to be impaled on his rock hard dick but his finger impedes his attempts and he struggles.

"Watch your hand," I growl like an angry badger.

I jump up and wrap my arms around his neck, almost resting my forearms on his shoulders. With my head start he's able to lift me with his good hand and presses his body against mine to hold me in place. I slid my slick pussy onto him and we both thrust hard and fast. He doesn't have his other hand free to grab my breasts or pinch my nipples but he improvised and bites my nipples through my black bra.

We're grunting and groaning as our bodies slap together and make wet sounds. I don't know if I've said anything coherent or if I'm just making animal noises. He feels amazing and I want to get him deeper, it's this aching need that sparks with pleasure each time he hits the perfect spot. I use my feet against the curve of his ass to gain leverage and thrust harder. My clit is rubbing against him and when he hits that target inside right when my clit rubs just the spot I need, it lights up my world.

"Oh, Pierson! Yes!"

"Fuck, yes!"

"I'm going to come!"

"Don't stop, Killer!"

In a flurry of forceful thrusts he raids my pussy with his steely cock, hitting all of my sensitive spots and making me bounce on him faster. I'm so fucking close!

"Oooooh! Yes! Yes! Oh God, yes! Pieeeerson!" My body breaks out in goosebumps, my pussy clenched down on him, and my climax explodes like fireworks in Times Square on New Years.

"Fuck! Yes!"

“Oh, yea, that was incredible“

“Mmmm, I don’t want to stop. You feel so fucking good, Killer.” He continues moving inside me slower and slower.

“You do too, but put me down before you hurt yourself, please.” He gently lowers my feet to the floor. Like a lady I press my thighs together and move to the restroom. He gives me a moment alone and joins me when I flush. I turn on the shower and remove my bra and skirt,.It’s going to need the dry cleaners after spending twenty minutes bunched up around my middle.

“Can I join you?”

“Of course, like I would say no after you fucked me so good!”

“Yeah I suppose that makes sense.” He smiles like a cat that ate a canary.

“Did you hear that? They must be home,” I said when I heard something like maybe a door slammed closed.

“I didn’t hear anything but I trust your ears.” Sure enough, the bathroom door opens and Austin opens the shower.

“What are you guys doing in here?”

“Just showering, I’m done, you can use it now.” I give him a devilish grin.

“As much as I'd love to join you and soap you up again, we have dinner. I just came in to get you.”

“Okay. We'll be right out.” We finish up and join everyone at the table.

They brought home Chinese food, and it smells delicious. They’re the best, Jackson has my favorite chicken dish opened in my place at the table. I’m starving, I guess we worked up an appetite because I might hurt someone if they prevent me from eating. After shoveling in a few chunks of honey chicken and a few globs of fried rice I feel less murdery and settle down to keep eating.

“How was your day?” Austin asks.

"I got the job. I start tomorrow, the rest went by quickly until I found Pierson and he was, *ahem,* feeling better. How was your day?"

"Same old, same old. You know, dig a hole, mark a hole, dig another hole."

We all chuckle at Austin's description. I picture an assembly line making holes, it's a weird image like a cartoon in an old factory.

"Tell us about the job," Jackson insists. I tell them about the interview, the people, Madeline and her friend's conversation. All three of them are fascinated by a job in an office. Pierson's previous work comes the closest but his was usually on a ship, although he did work in a building on a base a few times. For the most part none of them have had an office job, they ask me about where I'll be working, the other IT people, what type of things I'll be tasked with, we chat through dinner and afterwards we settle in front of the TV for a movie.

When the truck drives through the big arch that says, *Jurassic Park,* Austin asks, "Have any of you moved on to the next clue?"

Jackson looks down briefly before saying, "I thought we weren't doing the joint thing anymore because Colby said we can't. Plus he knew, and we shouldn't have done it."

"You did the next clue!" Austin accuses.

"I'm not confirming or denying if I have, but I think we need to get back to working on it alone."

"You did! Shit! How many clues ahead are you?" Austin exclaims.

"I said I wasn't admitting shit, but if I did get the next clue I'm not the only one," Jackson says throwing Pierson under a bus with a look.

Austin looks between me and Pierson and I shake my head subtly, he narrows in on Pierson at my movement, "It was you wasn't it?"

"I thought the same as Jackson, aren't we supposed to work alone now? Isn't that how it works?"

I answer, "It does. You shouldn't feel bad for working on it, that's how the game works. Austin and I just need to get our asses in gear and get some game tasks completed. Right Austin?"

"Yeah." He gives in and drops his annoyed tone. I'm sure he was just fooling around but he almost sounded angry and a little hurt they worked on it without us. I don't mind, it's the nature of the game. I know Jackson is desperate to get us to Disney. I'd love to let him win so he can have his trip, but I can't. First of all, if I didn't play my best, he would know and maybe Pierson too, Colby would be really mad, and I'm just not a cheater, you know, unless I'm saving the environment.

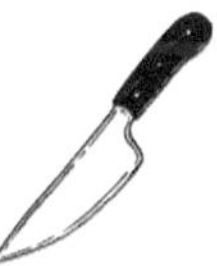

When I enter the lobby at my new job the security guard hands me a badge with a key card. He explains what I'll use it for and how I can use the express elevator on the end of the row with it. He's very friendly and welcomes me to the company like he's the designated greeter.

"Good luck, Emmy. Have a great first day."

"Thanks Mateo, it was nice meeting you."

Entering the last elevator car I try out my new card and I'm able to zip up to the tenth floor in less than thirty seconds. The force of it almost made me stumble when it first took off. I'm greeted by one of my fellow new employees, he's a pasty fellow who looks like he spends all of his time in front of a screen. His hair is pale brown and his glasses are thick.

I introduce myself and discover his name is Nathaniel, he goes by Nate. When I run out of things to say to him, Dozer's guy, Tyler joins us. Not to be obvious I introduce myself to him as well and we act like we just met.

Molly shows up and takes us to the main IT section of cubicles. I thought they stopped using cubicles in IT departments like a decade ago. When she has us move into a training room with terminals on tables instead, I'm much happier. Hopefully I won't be here long enough to make use of my claustrophobic nightmare desk.

"Ben will be here in a minute; he's going to train you on our proprietary system. Once he's finished with you, you'll be free for an hour to have lunch, then Shelly will finish up your afternoon training. Do you have any questions?" Nate raises his hand.

"You can just ask, Nate."

"Is there an employee lunchroom? I need to put my lunch in the refrigerator."

"Sure, why don't you all follow me, and I'll give you a quick tour, then Ben can skip it."

She takes us around the floor and shows us the small break room with a refrigerator, a few tables, chairs, and two sofas. Nate puts his labeled brown paper bag on the bottom shelf. There's also a coffee station and a water cooler. She points out the team leaders and supervisors offices, including Mr. Bronson, the department director. His office is in the back corner and takes up a nice chunk of real estate. I'm sure he has a beautiful view of the town as well. The floors above us house the rest of the executives and below us are all of the other departments, HR, sales, marketing, billing, and more.

When Ben meets us back at the training room we begin with standard HR instructions, they cover workplace safety, corporate espionage, workplace equality, inappropriate workplace behavior, and finally cover our proprietary system. The system is user friendly and a simple version of any office software. We'll be using the reporting portion to keep track of the IT service tickets we will be addressing. When someone has trouble with their terminal, a glitch in the software, or a hard wiring need, we'll be assigned the work on a service ticket. We'll document what we fix and the amount of time spent doing it, and our department will charge that department for our services. It's all very simplistic and after they show me how it works once, I'm up to speed. Ben gives us an assignment to make a repair, and when we're finished we can go to lunch. He leaves for his own lunch break claiming we can resolve any issues when we return from our breaks.

Once he's gone I ask my co-workers, "What are you doing for lunch?"

Nate responds immediately, "I brought a sandwich. I'm going to eat in the break room and come back here to practice."

"Great. How about you, Tyler?"

"I didn't bring a sandwich. I'm going out I guess, you can come if you want."

"Sure. Thanks. You don't want to join us, Nate?"

"No. Thanks, but if I don't eat my sandwich my mom will know." Tyler gives me an incredulous look, I shrug. When we leave the building and check our surroundings carefully, we relax once we're certain no other employees are around.

"What the fuck is up with that Nate guy, right?" Tyler asks.

"I don't want to know. Thanks for doing this."

"It's my job, plus I don't mind. It's fun to pretend to work while I'm at work." He gives me a cheesy grin and I chuckle.

"I guess. I don't know how much Dozer shared with you, but I have an agenda at this company."

"He didn't specify, just said to stick to you like glue and watch your back."

"Are you carrying a firearm?"

"Just my ankle piece. I've got some blades, you?"

"Just blades, it's harder for females to carry firearms undetected because of the cut of our clothing, but I'm covered."

"So, what's your agenda? Can I help?"

"You may regret that offer. The company is a laundering front for mafia enterprises like trafficking flesh, guns, and drugs. The top guy, Mr. CEO himself, is my biological father and he's a very bad guy. I've never met him, but I want to bring him in for a friendly reunion."

"I see. What can I do to help?"

"I'm going to hack the system and dig for proof. I want to disrupt and destroy the things he's doing. You can help by surveilling the staff, tracking any patterns, suspicious staff, and watch my back when I'm looking around his files."

"I can do that."

"Great. So, do you want to grab some food?"

"Sure. How about a slice at that place on the corner?"

After we eat and return to our training room we listen to more instructions for the uses of the system. I signal Tyler to alert me if Shelly comes this way and start exploring the system. They should have this terminal locked down so new employees can't mess with anything in the actual programs, but I'm in and I quickly gain access to files I shouldn't be able to open. When Shelly steps out of the room I connect a USB drive and download some suspicious files. I check out their firewalls and safeguards. There's nothing tracking what I'm doing and I decide to upload Colby's little gift to the monsters we encounter.

His modified *Comet* program will hide itself in a safe place and start sending him all of the information we could possibly want. While I'm wandering around the files I find one labeled *JM Holdings.* Joyce Morgan? I add its contents to my drive and finish up before our lovely instructor returns from her coffee run.

I quickly complete more tickets than I was assigned and wait for further instructions. Tyler shoots me a conspiratorial grin and I give him a thumbs up. She finishes our afternoon much like Ben at lunch, with an assignment, which once completed is the end of our day. I want to walk out with Tyler, so I finish and act like I'm still working. He's doing the same while we wait for Nate to finish. Finally, the odd guy closes up his terminal and wishes us good night. When we're sure he's gone, I speak softly, just in case someone can hear us.

"I want to try going to the top floor, do you want to join me or watch from here?"

"I'm going with you."

"Great, I'm going to act like I got us lost if we get caught just play along."

"As you wish."

"Oh no, don't tell me you like those sappy movies too."

"It's not sappy, it's action adventure. My girlfriend likes those movies, so I've seen a few."

"It's not action adventure, it's a love story. I had to watch it."

"You don't like love stories?"

"Not in a movie that's supposed to entertain me. I'm much more happy with a good slasher flick or even super heroes."

"So, who made you watch it?"

"Jackson. He was very upset when he discovered the breadth of movies I've missed out on. He keeps a list so I can get caught up. He keeps trying to make me watch Titanic, but it's three freaking hours!" He chuckles.

"Yeah, that one was brutal. Just drink while you watch it and you can use the restroom a lot to escape. Beer works great."

"I'm not a fan of alcohol, but lemonade works."

We step onto the last elevator and I insert my key card, press the top floor, and hold my breath. The elevator springs upwards and I'm surprised it took us with my lowly IT Tech key. When the doors open the reception area is dark and empty. I step out of the car and listen for any sign of life. Not hearing anyone we make our way past the front desk and down a hallway. The names on the doors are somewhat familiar from the digging I've done so far about the company. All of the doors I try are locked. When we round a corner there's another reception desk and behind it, the double doors of the CEO office. I step past the empty desk and rest my ear against the office door.

"I don't hear anything. I don't think anyone's here." I try the handle, and it's locked. An idea strikes and I check the receptionist's desk for a key. When I open the thin drawer below her keyboard, there's a set of keys. Before I can grab them we hear footsteps and voices coming this way. We both look around for a place to hide and he grabs my arm and tugs me into the ladies room. Right before the door closed I caught a glimpse of men's expensive black leather shoes and a similar set of brown men's shoes.

"She's going home today, I don't even care what happens to her, she's a huge pain in the ass. She sent home the girls who were staying with her without even asking me."

"I told you she would be a problem."

"I know, but I didn't think she was this bad. I don't think Milos died of natural causes, I think he killed himself to get away from her."

"Are you sending some guards with her?"

"I had to pay them three times the usual rate to deal with her. I'm sending Peter and Nick, they're the only ones who would even consider it. Niccos told me to just kill him if I was going to assign him to watch her." Both men laugh and enter the CEO office.

Tyler holds his finger to his lips in the universal *be quiet* gesture. We make our way from the restroom and down the stairs one flight. Then we enter the regular elevator from that floor and ride it to the lobby.

Once we're outside he says, "That was him, did you see his face?"

"No. Just their shoes. It doesn't matter, it's good to know he's on the floor with only one guy. It might be helpful. Where did you park?"

"In the garage on the corner."

"Me too. Let's go."

Chapter Twenty-Eight

Pierson

When Violet gets home, she's wound up and wants to work out. She also wants to talk things over with Dozer, so he meets us at the warehouse in his gym clothes. Colby joins via video, and we talk about what she learned at work and what we're going to do about it. She started off wanting to go after Grandma Grim tonight before the evil old woman has a chance to get settled, but we decide it makes more sense to give her a few days to let her guard down. We have to see Colby's tailors again this weekend for a final fitting, so we decide to go after her when we finish there, like last time. Only we won't leave her locked up alone this round, we're going to guard her until Violet is finished with her.

Violet is quiet on our way back home. No doubt plotting in her head.

"Are you doing okay?" I ask her.

"Yeah. Just going over details in my head. How's your finger?"

"Better. I was able to work out one arm. It's not throbbing anymore, so it's a big improvement. I'm probably going to work tomorrow. Ryder said I can do the paperwork and be a spotter for the guys working in the parking lot."

"That's good. I know you hate sitting around." Her beautiful smile encourages me to smile back.

"Yeah. Speaking of work, do you think you're safe there? No one's suspicious of you? Nobody caught you spying?"

"Nobody noticed anything. They're so busy trying to go home as early as possible I don't think they'd notice if I wore a shirt that said, 'H*ey, I'm a spy.*'"

"Well, just be careful. I don't feel comfortable with you in his territory."

"Tyler is right there watching my back."

"Yeah, but who's watching his back?"

Her lips smack closed. She glares at me then chews on the inside of her cheek. I rub her arm hoping to soothe the turmoil I just caused. I just want her to be safe. Luckily, the other guys weren't listening to our low conversation, so they didn't hop on and give her a hard time.

When we get home we're all tired from a long day and we eat leftovers then go to bed early. When we're lying in bed trying to fall asleep Austin is fidgeting more than usual.

"Dude, stop moving around. I was almost asleep," Jackson complains.

"Sorry. I'm worried about Violet going back there tomorrow."

"Why?" she asks.

"I don't know. I just have a bad feeling. I don't like you being inside his building without us. I know you've got Tyler, he's a good guy and a great shot, but what if Daddy Dearest has an army up there, one guy isn't going to be enough to keep you safe. I'm sorry, Baby, I can't help it."

"It's okay. I understand your point, but I promise I'll be safe. They're just a bunch of suits doing corporate stuff, the bad guys are only a few people at the top as far as I can tell. Colby should know more soon. Remember I can take care of myself."

"I know. It's just hard to know you're there in the lair of the beast while we're digging holes across town."

"Dig me a Daddy sized hole so we can drop him in it when I slice his throat."

"You got it, Babe. Auz and I will dig you two tomorrow. One for him and one for her."

"Yeah, we'll have them ready to plant those evil pieces of shit," Austin adds.

"I guess I'll watch everyone else dig," I laugh at my not helpful addition to the plan. Everyone laughs and Violet kisses my shoulder.

"Sorry you can't participate, Piers. I'll let you stab him with your good hand if you want."

I tickle her with my good hand and she squeals. It's a wonderful sound and it lifts all of us out of our funk. We fall asleep with smiles, at least I know Austin did and I think I fell asleep right after him.

When my eyes open again there's a slight glow at the windows and Sawyer is curled above my head. I pull him to my chest and scratch his ears. He purrs in response. We're past our previous differences, he accepted me as another person in his limited world and I accepted his annoying traits, which don't bother me anymore.

Austin and Violet are gone, Jackson is snoring softly on the far side of the bed. My finger only hurts when I move it wrong which keeps happening, otherwise I feel good.

When I hear Violet through the bathroom door I can tell she's with Austin. Jackson hasn't stirred, I climb from the bed and leave Sawyer snuggled on my pillow. Making my way to the kitchen I think about what we have on hand for breakfast versus what I'm capable of cooking.

Scrambled eggs and toast are the main staples of my kitchen skills. I also cut up some fruit for Violet. She loves strawberries and blueberries, since we have both I put them in a bowl with some sliced bananas. All three of them join me at the same time and everyone digs into my fancy spread.

"Thanks so much, Pierson. You must be feeling better." She kisses me before she pops a blueberry onto her tongue.

"I'm pretty good."

We all leave the house together when her shadow shows up to follow her to the office. It's not Tyler so I'm not sure if this shadow hangs out all day or only when she's not with Tyler. She looked beautiful as always, today she wore gray pants that were tight against her legs and a black shirt that had a ruffled front hiding her weapons at her waist.

When we get to the job site I check in with Dave and ask where he wants my lame ass.

"Why did you even show up if you can't dig?"

"Ryder said I could be a spotter for the guys in the parking lot or help with the paperwork. Where do you want me?"

"I want you home on your sofa, but I don't get to make that decision. Go spot the guys in the lot, I don't want you screwing up my paperwork," Dave grumbles, always such a pleasant fellow.

In my highly visible vest and hard hat I follow the workers in the parking lot with an orange reflective flag in my good hand making sure no stupid people go around our cones and taped off safety zones to run over my co-workers. It never ceases to amaze me how many people are oblivious to their surroundings and somehow miss all of our markers. They literally lift the tape and walk through our work zone like it somehow doesn't apply to them. Just last week an old guy almost fell into an open trench because he ignored our safety barriers. Jackson told me they had two guys run over by a soccer mom who was running late and couldn't go around our work space. She drove through the middle of it and almost killed one of them. She actually yelled at the workers, lying, bleeding on the ground, for keeping her even longer.

At lunch Austin takes us to a Mexican place close to the work site. The food is excellent and I think Violet would love the place.

"We need to bring her here. She'd love the food and all those sugar skulls, they're like works of art."

Austin and Jackson exchange a look. "We tried to bring her here once, we had an incident in the back parking lot and had to leave abruptly."

"Did she stab someone?" I ask jokingly.

"Almost. We ended up kicking the shit out of the dude. He attacked her," Jackson answers.

"What the fuck? Why?"

"It wasn't her fault, he was a sick fuck and she fought back. We finished for her."

"He met her before and you know how she is, she sees everything and remembers everything. She tried to freak him out by telling him how they met previously and he flipped and attacked her instead of backing off like she hoped," Austin fills in the details.

"Damn. Our girl is a magnet for trouble."

"She can't help being gorgeous and attracting attention."

"True, but I wish she was safer," I submit.

"Get used to it, man. She's not going to change; she's just one of those people who can stop traffic. It's why we love her." A faraway look shades Austin's eyes.

"Yeah, I guess. I definitely love her."

"We all do, it's why I was thinking, with her friend getting married, do you think she's going to want to get married? If not now, someday?" Jackson asks a question I've considered myself.

"Maybe. She's not a traditional type of girl. Why?" Austin questions.

"It's not legal to marry more than one person, would we want her to marry just one of us? Or maybe have some kind of relationship ceremony for all of us but it wouldn't be legal as far as the government is concerned," Jackson elaborates.

"I think we're good as is for now, but let's ask her and see what she wants after all this grandmother crap. Knowing her, she has some ideas we never even considered," I offer my opinion.

"You're probably right. She's one of a kind. We're so fucking lucky." We both nod agreeing with Austin.

I'm still thinking about our lunch conversation when we head home at the end of the day. I'm relieved seeing her SUV is in the garage when Austin opens the door with his remote. She's cooking something when we walk inside. It smells burnt and I see some blackened bread sticking out of the trash. She greets us without stopping stirring the pot of lumpy red stuff on the front burner and what looks like rice on the small burner in the back.

"What's cooking, Baby?"

"Chinese chili, my dad used to make it when we were camping."

"Never heard of it."

"It's good, you'll like it."

She wasn't wrong, when she piled rice on my plate, loaded it with shredded cheddar and then covered it with red stuff, which turned out to be chili, I was skeptical. But it's delicious. The only thing missing is some bread, but since it had a Viking funeral, and there's no coming back from that, so I enjoy it without.

"Tell us about your day, Babe."

"More training, all morning was boring. But when we came back from lunch, there was a man standing with his back to us at the far side of the room. It was him, my biological father."

"Holy fuck! What happened?" Austin exclaims.

"Nothing. He just wanted to meet the new recruits as he usually does, apparently. He met *Emmy,* and didn't flinch. I don't think he has a clue who I am, so it went fine. Tyler was on edge, I'm positive his hand was on his firearm, but he didn't need it. Tomorrow we get to do our real jobs with close supervision. They want us on our own next week."

"How are you feeling after seeing his face?"

"I'm all right. It wasn't as bad since I've seen his photo, you know the initial shock was difficult, but now I'm adjusted to him existing. I just want to end him and shut down his vile enterprise."

"We will. We're going to get him soon. He'll be gone and his businesses will close up shop."

Her hands touch her favorite blades in their hiding spots. Sometimes I swear she thinks of them like a safety blanket; she doesn't realize when she caresses them for comfort. We help her clean up the kitchen and get ready for bed. None of us are ready to sleep so we decide to watch a movie, it's Violet's turn to pick and she goes with *The Ref.* She says it's one of her holiday favorites from her years with her mom and dad.

It's funny and we laugh through it. The old lady reminds Jax and Auz of Violet's evil grandmother which makes us all laugh even more. It's especially enjoyable when they tie her up and silence her, we're looking forward to doing something similar but more permanent.

When the movie ends Violet climbs on my lap and kisses me. My dick instantly stiffened in response and I want her. Austin grabs her ass and kisses her arm while she moves on my thickening lap. Jackson lifts her top over her head and pulls it off. Her tiny panties disappear and I think both of them did something to remove them. Austin moves behind her and fondles her perfect breasts. She moans and kisses him over her shoulder. My good hand pulls her hips so she rubs against my ready cock.

Jackson and Austin move her so she's long ways on the couch and her curvy ass is my view as she leans across me. My non broken fingers find their way between her legs and I feel her arousal sliding my fingers through it before pushing one inside her. She moves to accommodate my hand. Austin is under her chest pinching her nipples and she moans with pleasure.

Jackson is naked, he's always the first one of us to be naked. He strokes himself and moves to her face. When he touches her cheek with his dick she immediately takes him into her mouth. I add another finger and move in and out of her rhythmically while I make sure to tickle the special place that makes her scream. I use my thumb to circle her little clit and she moves with me.

Austin slaps the cheek of her ass and she presses against me in response. His hand print glows red on her smooth skin and it looks perfect.

"Your ass is gorgeous, Babe. You should see how hot it looks with Auz's hand marked on it." Jackson is moving in and out of her mouth and she's making some slurping sounds. I want to fuck her so bad I'm rubbing my dick on her hip for some relief.

Jackson magically produces some lube and pours a little on her perfectly rounded ass. Next Austin uses the jeweled plug to smear the lube around her back entrance. She wiggles excitedly when he pushes the tip inside her rim. He slowly plays with her ass pushing the silver metallic plug in and out turning it around, stretching her open. When he has it fully inserted, she screams out and her pussy tightens on my fingers as her climax implodes. My fingers are extra slippery now, and the wet sounds of her mouth are competing with her wet pussy. Jackson starts fucking her face with gusto and calls out his own release while she swallows his cum.

When he pulls out of her mouth he helps her move so she's straddling me, but facing away from me. I pull down my bottoms and my hard cock springs free standing tall. I stroke the length and when she hovers over me I line up with her entrance. She slowly pushes down on me and her tight little pussy squeezes my dick so fucking good. Jackson sits next to me with his leg helping to support her and his hand moving the jeweled plug. I can feel it inside her pressing against my cock. Austin steps in front of her and scoots the coffee table closer to the sofa. He sits on it and he's at the perfect height for her to go down on him. She licks him all over before she takes him into her mouth.

"She's so fucking perfect. Look at that gorgeous ass."

"Mmmmm!"

"Yes, Baby, suck me. You're a fucking angel!"

"Fuck yes, Killer! I'm going to come so fucking hard!"

She makes a sound that's muffled by the dick in her mouth but I feel it down to my balls. She's moving like a porn star on my cock and my nerves are popping with energy. I could probably light up the house with the electricity zipping around in my body.

She begins to make a high pitched sound, "Mmm! Aaaaaah!" Her pussy tightens around my dick and the plug moves against me through her walls.

"Holy fuck!"

The feeling building in my nuts shoots up and down my spine, my balls pull up tight and the burst of light in my central nervous system detonates out of my cock with my cum.

Austin is saying something too but I can't hear him over the blood rushing through my veins. Jackson removes the plug and Violet comes hard, her pussy squeezes more cum from my body rebooting the flashes of sensation in my nether region. She's moaning as she swallows Austin's release and it reminds me of the way Sawyer eats, growling as he pigs out. I can only assume it's a pleasurable experience. It's definitely pleasant for Austin, he's humming with his head thrown back in rapture.

"Holy fuck!"

She giggles, "You already said that."

"I might need to say it a few more times. Holy fuck, Killer. That was so fucking good. Your pussy is heaven."

"Thank you? I'm not sure how to respond to that, but it's a compliment right?"

"Definitely. You're...you're fucking incredible."

Jackson offers her a towel and she pulls off of me. Fuuuck. She takes off with the towel and he hands me some wet wipes. I clean up enough to move and head for the shower.

After we're all clean we snuggle in bed. She fucked my brains out and I don't remember anything until I wake up in the morning. We eat and get ready together, then we say goodbye to her as she leaves with her shadow. Jackson checks his rearview several times but doesn't say anything and I assume he's being overly cautious. On our drive to work Jackson keeps checking his rearview mirrors.

"What's up dude?"

"I noticed this van yesterday and thought I was just paranoid, but the same van is behind us again, it's two rows over behind the red truck. Do you see it?"

Austin looks over his shoulder like he's talking to me in the back seat, "Yeah, I see it. Turn up here and let's see if they follow." Jackson turns right.

The van follows, now there's only one car between us.

"Turn again."

Jackson signals and turns left. The van follows, now there's nothing between us. We all act casual like we're just chatting. He takes a quick right and another quick right into a parking lot. The van misses the turn and enters the parking lot through the next entrance. Jackson parks and acts like he's going into a shop. Austin gets out and enters the store. I stay seated watching the van in the mirror, there are two guys inside. They're looking around at the shops trying to keep track of my brothers.

When I see Jackson double back and come up behind their van I exit and start walking right at them but looking away like I haven't noticed them. They look panicked when I steal a glance from the corner of my eye. Austin is coming at them from the side in their blind spot. When they start the van, I look at them like that's what got my attention, they're both watching me wide eyed. Jackson rips open the driver's door and Austin does the same with the passenger door. I rush at them from the front, and we rip them out of their van.

"We're with Dozer! Wait!"

"Stop, we work for Dozer!"

Jackson stops his fist in midair, "What?"

"Call him, we work with Dozer. We're just watching your back."

Austin dials, puts it on speaker, and Dozer answers, "You spotted them?"

"We're about to kill them."

"Please don't, I told her you'd notice them watching you. I also told her I wouldn't lie, she even made a wager."

"What's the bet?" Austin asks.

"She said you wouldn't notice for three days."

"When did you start watching us?"

"Wednesday morning."

"Today's Friday, it's day three, I think you have to give it to her," I proclaim.

"No way! It needs to be three days without you noticing, she didn't win."

"Maybe. We might need to let it ride; we'll think it over. Why did you agree?"

"I hate mowing the lawn, she bet she'd mow it for a month. I knew I'd win, but she loves you and she wanted your backs covered, she's a sucker."

"You have a mean streak, Dude," Austin calls him out.

"Are you surprised?" he chuckles.

"Nah, I just thought you had a soft spot for her."

"I do. Trust me, she gets away with much more than anyone else."

"She's got that effect on people. Well, they can go, we have to get to work," Jackson states.

"Can I speak to Smith?"

Austin aims the phone towards the passenger.

"Head back to the office."

"Ten-four, Boss. Talk to you later."

"Later."

"See ya."

"Bye."

"All right, you heard the man. Head to your office, thanks anyway. I'm Austin, that's Jackson, and Pierson." He points at each of us.

"I'm Smith, that's Jimmy. Thanks for not killing us."

"Sure. Nice to meet you. See you later," Austin says.

"Yeah. Okay, see you," Smith says for both of them.

"That was close. That girl of ours is something else."

"Yeah. It's kind of sweet that she was worried," Jackson muses.

"Come on, let's get going, we're gonna be late," I submit.

We pile into the truck and make it to work right on time which gains a dirty look from Dave. I'm still on spotter duty since my finger makes my hand useless. But the day goes by relatively quickly so it's not total torture. I'm glad it's Friday and I get two days without Dave's snide comments and bad attitude.

When we pull out of the lot Jackson is checking his rearview obsessively. He keeps switching between his side mirrors and the rear view. He's making me nervous, and I look behind us, there's a black van a few cars back.

"What's up?"

"Not sure. Hang on." He takes a quick turn and the van follows.

Austin dials his phone on speaker, *"You've reached Dozer's phone, please leave a message."*

"Hey man, we thought you were done following us, what the hell? We might have to scare the crap out of these guys to keep it interesting," he laughs and we join in.

"Are you going to lose them? Or catch them like the last guys?" I ask from the back.

"I think we should catch them and scare the piss out of 'em," Jackson says.

"Yeah. Park and we'll get them," Austin laughs.

Jackson pulls into a parking lot and parks around the corner from the shops under a tree. It's plausible because in Florida, shade is a premium.

He pretends to enter a shop and Austin does the same. When they're both moving in, I exit the truck and walk right at them like last time. When we're all close to the cab of the van, another van comes right at me and brakes in a screech with the side door right behind me. Before I can wrap my brain around this development, the door slides open, and a gun is aimed at my face.

When I reach for my waist he says, "Don't move, hands up."

My hands raise in the air, and I watch as both guys from the original van point guns at my brothers. They point their own weapons back at the occupants from the van but drop them when they threaten to shoot me. Before any of us can stop them, they have our firearms and phones. Our phones and guns go in the original van and they take us into the second van. They tie our hands and feet, we stay quiet and watch them carefully waiting for a chance to overpower them or escape, but none of us are willing to leave our brothers behind.

When we reach our destination which seems to be a parking garage just like every other parking structure, they put hoods over our heads. Now I can't see what they're doing to my brothers. They lift me onto a gurney of some sort, I can feel one of my brothers next to me. It's Austin, I can tell by his cologne, I think it smells like shit. They wheel us into a building and then we go up in an elevator, it must be a freight elevator to hold this cart with us on it. I don't recognize anything about this place. They wheel us somewhere and stop. I hold still and listen. A door closes but we're not alone. Austin's finger touches my hand, and I think he's signaling me when he taps me three times, I think he's telling me the three of us are here, Jackson must be on his other side.

When there's a knock on the door I hold my breath. The door opens and two men have a hushed conversation, I can't hear what they're saying and it's killing me.

"Okay, okay. I won't." There's an aggravated sound, like he smacked the roof of his mouth with his tongue. I have no idea what they were talking about but I feel like we just got screwed over somehow. Who would take us? It has to be Violet's fucking grandmother, I don't know anyone else who would grab us off the street. I keep working my hands trying to loosen the flex cuffs holding them too tight. There's a way to snap out of them but I've never tried it. With my finger in a splint, I don't think I could do it anyway, but if they loosened, maybe I'd be able to get them off more carefully. I know for a fact both of my brothers have blades hidden on them somewhere, mine's inside my boot, I can't reach it with my hands behind my back. When I feel Austin moving there's a loud click of a gun cocking to fire.

"Stop moving around! I have orders to shoot if you do anything, so I suggest you hold still." Austin freezes.

"What do you want with us?" he asks, a ballsy move.

"Not my job to worry about why you're here."

"Whose job is it?"

"Someone who makes more than me. Quit talking."

"Where are we?" I ask since he told Auz to shut up.

"The last place you'll be alive if you don't stop asking me questions."

"What are they paying you?" Jackson tries.

I hear the man approach and very close to us he says, "I'm going right outside the door so I don't have to listen to you, but if you make a sound, I'm coming back shooting. You better think hard about how you want to die because I promise it will be from my gun if you try anything or talk." His footsteps retreat and the door opens and closes.

"Asshole put his gun to my forehead," Jackson gripes softly. I feel Austin moving again next to me.

"What're you doing?" I ask him in a whisper.

"I'm trying to reach the blade in my belt. I can't get it. My hand won't bend the way I need with these stupid cuffs on. Can you move your hands?"

"I'm struggling with the cuffs because of my splint. How about you Jax?"

"Grrrr! Almost. Got. It." Jackson growls under his breath with effort. The door opens fast and hits the wall with a smack!

"Freeze! Stop whatever you're trying to do, the boss is coming. Hold still and shut up." The same voice from earlier whisper shouts at us. I hold still and focus on listening.

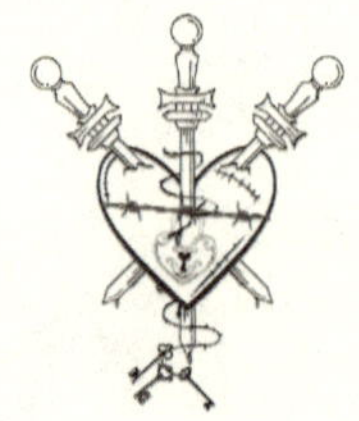

Chapter Twenty-Nine

Violet

When Molly comes into our training room I smile at her, she's been nice every time I've talked to her. Our training supervisor this afternoon is Liam something, she whispers to him and his eyebrows raise in surprise. Then she says something else and he nods and checks his smart watch. She returns my smile on her way out the door. I shrug, and continue to act like I'm busy working on our assignment, while he continues to act like he's watching what we're doing. I've been finished for an hour just poking around in the files, there are records of some of the crap they're doing. I found some bills of lading for crates on a ship, they supposedly contained Chinese weed-eaters, but what would a *financial services* company be doing with twelve-thousand weed-eaters? It's got to be something illegal, I sent it to Colby as a good file to drill into.

"Hey everyone, we're going to call it a day. They want you guys upstairs for some final paperwork before you leave. Check in with the reception desk on the top floor when you're ready to go." Tyler gives me a look with raised eyebrows and I lift my shoulders to let him know I'm just as clueless as him. I didn't bring much with me, so I'm ready to head upstairs the moment I toss out my empty coffee cup. It was filled with ice water since I don't drink coffee often. Tyler is ready almost as fast when he closes out of whatever he was doing. We watch as Nate continues to poke at his keyboard.

"So, uh, Nate, are you almost finished? I have plans tonight and I'd like to get a move on." Tyler tries to guilt him into moving faster.

"Almost finished. Were you able to complete the assignment?" Nate asks with a little surprise lacing his words.

"Yeah, I finished. How about you, Emmy? Did you finish?" Tyler asks with blatant sarcasm.

"Why yes, Tyler, I did complete the assignment. I too am ready to get going." My reply also drips with sarcasm.

"Okay, I'm done. Let me log out and we can go after I stop in the restroom." I can't keep from rolling my eyes. I feel kind of bad for him because he's like a lost puppy, but he's old enough to act like a grown man, so he just aggravates me.

By the time we finally enter the elevator I'm struggling to keep from stabbing Nate in the throat. He's on my last nerve and if he whines about one more thing Tyler is going to need to disarm me by force.

Lucky for Nate, the doors open on the top floor and we're faced with a receptionist before I draw a blade and kill him. The small dark-haired woman smiles as we approach.

"Hello. I'm Abby, you must be the new IT people. HR closed early today, so I have the paperwork you need to sign. I'm sorry they missed these forms, but they need to be notarized and I'm the only notary here right now."

"Hi Abby, this is Emmy and Nate, I'm Tyler, what do you need from us?"

"I just need your ID, and if you give me a minute, I'll get everything documented in my log and you can sign the forms. It's just for your insurance beneficiaries, I guess the forms didn't print out when HR had you sign everything. She noticed today but she had to leave, sorry to keep you from your weekend." Her smile is bright and consoling. We hand over our ID, and she marks our information in her log. She has each of us sign the form, then she signs and stamps them. We're finished quickly and I'm relieved to be heading home, I probably won't be back next week and neither will Tyler. If there's still a company once I shut down the illegal enterprises, I'll wish Nate luck.

When we're finished, I'm last to step into the elevator and as the door begins to close, an arm stops the doors. We all look to see who the arm belongs to and I'm surprised to see Kristos himself.

"Miss Quinn, may I have a moment?" I tense and swallow hard. Tyler's hand goes to the back of his waist reflexively.

"I was heading home. Is it something that can wait until Monday? I'm already late." I try.

"I just need a quick moment of your time. I want to get your opinion on something." His smile reminds me of a crocodile, too many teeth and overflowing with evil intent.

I move to step out of the elevator and Tyler moves with me but our *boss* moves to block his exit.

"Not you Mr. Aames, just Miss Quinn. Please go ahead to the lobby, you can wait for her there if you like."

Tyler looks at me panicked and I'm not sure what to do. I can't blow my cover when it's just me and Tyler here, we have no idea who's around to help him, plus there's Nate and I don't want to involve him. I decide to handle it myself, what choice do I have?

"Yeah, go ahead guys. I'll be down in a minute. If I'm not there in twenty minutes, send in the troops," I laugh like I'm joking and Kristos chuckles with me.

"That won't be necessary, I just want to show her what I want her to work on next week. I need her opinion about the method. She'll only be a few minutes, thank you. Come this way Miss Quinn, to my office."

"Sure. See you later, guys." I try to raise a smile on my face and make it subtle when I wiggle my eyes at Tyler for help if I'm not downstairs fast enough. He acknowledged my signal with a nod. Kristos is turned away so he didn't see our communication, I follow him with no other option. I'm pleasantly surprised when he walks me around his desk to see his computer screen. There's a spreadsheet pulled up and I recognize it. It's exactly what I do when I see the labels on the tabs.

"This is what I need your expertise for, I want you to head up this project, we're impressed with your work. You have an eye for details that we need to organize this swap out." He quickly explains what he wants done and asks for my input on the formatting and priorities. If I actually wanted this job, it would be a perfect undertaking for me. I explain my thoughts on the parameters and he thanks me profusely. I'm relieved when he wishes me a pleasant weekend and thanks me for my time.

Unfortunately, when I'm ready to step through the threshold of his office he says, "Oh, Violet, wait up..." I stop and hold my breath. It didn't escape my notice that he just used my real name.

"I have one more thing to show you. Won't you join me?" He's right behind me now, his hand falls firm on my shoulder. He's a large man, probably six foot four at least, and he's built solid despite his age and the gray at his temples, he's a threat in every way.

"Sure." I let him lead me by my shoulder to a door down the hall. There's an armed man standing outside the door. He opens the door when we approach, and Kristos pushes me into the room one step and holds me still in his firm grasp.

There, on a flatbed cart are three hooded men, they're tied at the wrist and ankle, with a gun pointed at them by yet another guard. I don't need to see their faces to know it's my boyfriends. I gasp and my mind spins with scenarios to kill my biological father, his guards, and save the loves of my life.

"I know what you're thinking, and I promise at least two of them won't survive anything you might try. You need to restrain yourself if you want them to live."

"What do you want from me?" I ask between gritted teeth.

"Come back to my office and we'll have a nice chat. Come along."

"Fine." I march angrily back to his overly luxurious office. When I step through the door another guard asks for my firearm and any other weapons I may be carrying. I hand over my Sig, then I remove blades from my waist and ankles making no move to take the one from my bra. He also takes my cell phone and leaves the room. I'm brooding trying to come up with a plan that will save all three of my guys.

"I realize it may be difficult for you to focus, but you need to or they won't be alive to distract you for long. Besides, you might actually like what I have to say."

"I doubt it."

"So negative. I'm offering you the chance of a lifetime and they can live, if you cooperate. You only recently found out about me, right? I can only assume since this is the first time you've sought me out. I was surprised to see you here, I didn't even know it was you until I saw your face in my training room. I wasn't lying when I said you're good at your job. I know how smart you are and I know about the rest of your skills. I've been keeping tabs on you since you were born."

His words stick in my gut like a knife. He watched while I was abused for years? What the fuck?

"You're angry, probably thinking about that asshole stepfather you had. But I assure you by the time I found out he was abusing you, he was dead, and I was so proud of you. When you sliced his throat, I knew you were going to be perfect. I almost came for you then but when the Henley's wanted you, I knew you were safe and they were obsessed with teaching you how to survive. Your grandmother hated when they adopted you, she thinks you're a worthless gold digger," he laughs.

"I don't like her either."

"Oh I know, but I can't have you killing her, she's an integral part of my operation. She knows all the rich scumbags who buy my products. It's a symbiotic relationship made in heaven, or maybe hell. Either way, I promised Milos I'd keep her safe and more importantly she does some very necessary tasks with a legitimacy I can't quite pull off."

"What do you want from me?"

"I want to teach you, my business. I want you to be my right hand until I'm ready to step down, then I want you to take over."

"Aren't you part of the mafia? I thought women weren't allowed to be in charge."

"Things are changing, plus, when they see how ruthless you are they'll be chomping at the bit to have you running things. Our enemies will be unhappy, but our partners will be thrilled."

"Do I have any choice?"

"No. It's time, I've left you to your own devices long enough, you're ready to start learning the ropes of what I do, now. Your men will be safe but kept under lock and key until I see evidence of your full commitment."

"And if I refuse?"

"Do you really want to know? Let's just say you'll be unhappy and regret it if you fight me on this. Won't it be nice having a real parent? I can offer up lots of evil souls for you to vanquish. You'll be feared in our world all around the globe. People will do what we want for fear of your wrath. You'll be wealthy beyond measure and have anything you want. You could have dozens of men if you like. Doesn't that sound like perfection?"

"Sure. It sounds great but why should I trust you? I've never even met you until this week and you let me go through hell. You left me with my mother to be abused."

"I told you I didn't know about that until it was too late, but you must be happy she's gone."

"What do you mean? Who's gone?"

"Your mother."

"Gone where?"

"You didn't know she died? She overdosed almost a year ago."

Another blow to my gut. I hated her and never wanted to see her again, but there's still an emotional reaction to learning your biological mother is dead. For me it's more of a fleeting feeling of lost opportunities for payback. She deserved punishment for what she did to me and I thought I had time to deliver it. I'm disappointed, that's the emotion I'm feeling.

"I suppose it's not a surprise considering her habits."

"Yeah, she never could escape her demons. All right, let's go over what we're going to do to bring you up to speed. I have a few clients coming into town this weekend and I'd like to have you by my side. You'll need to stay with me for a few weeks. Your men will be kept in my building and they'll remain alive as long as you do everything I ask. But if you fight me, or try anything, they'll be tortured until you fall in line. Do you understand?"

"I do."

"Are you going to cooperate?" His brows lower and his eyes narrow as he measures my response.

"I have some terms of my own." His face breaks into a broad smile. I think it's pride behind his sudden joy and it makes my skin crawl. The idea of him being proud of me makes me want to vomit.

"Of course, please tell me your conditions, my brilliant girl."

"First of all, I don't want you to refer to me as your daughter in any way. I'm an equal, a colleague, not a product of nepotism. Secondly, I will stay with my boyfriends, if it needs to be on your property that's fine, but I won't be separated from them. Lastly, my cat goes where I go."

"I think we can make those terms work, but if you try to break out your *guys*, they'll suffer for it."

"One more thing, I'll kill Joyce if I need to, and you too. I won't cut either of you any slack, mess with me or my men and you're both dead," he laughs out loud.

"You're perfect! I love it. I can't wait to show you off." That gleam of pride is back in his eyes and it's difficult for me to swallow without gagging.

"Yeah, I can't wait. You're going to need to untie my guys and let me handle them. They'll do what I want, we won't give you any reason to harm anyone."

"All right. I'll let you have your boyfriends, but if you can't control them, they'll be back in cuffs. I won't hesitate to end them all if you don't cooperate."

"I heard you the first time, there's no need to repeat anything with me. Let's go, I want them free."

"Okay. Come on." I follow my biological father back to my boyfriends, if they have a mark on them, he's going to be sorry. I slip my hand under my loose top and retrieve my last blade, keeping it hidden in my palm and ready to stash in my pocket if necessary. When we get to the room where they're being kept two guards are outside the door, the one from before and the one who took my property. They both straighten up when they see Kristos approaching and I notice the one who took my things has a black eye. No wonder dear old dad was impressed with my threats. It looks like this mafia kingpin rules with an iron fist.

"Open the door," Kristos demands and they quickly open it for us. He enters first and the guard sitting on a chair inside the room quickly stands and waits for instructions.

I don't hesitate to order him into action, "Remove their hoods and untie them, now." I feel like I'm watching a Discovery Channel special about meerkats. All three of my guys snap their heads towards my voice and sit up straight. All three guards shift their attention to my boss and it annoys me.

"Do as she says, now."

The three guards jump into action and immediately remove the hoods from my boyfriends and they pull the flatbed cart away from the wall so they can reach their cuffed hands and the third guard, the one with a black eye, begins removing the ropes binding their ankles. Austin smiles at me and Jackson scrutinizes my face carefully. I nod subtly at him and he acknowledges my signal with a narrowing of his eyes. In our special relationship silent language, he's telling me I'm in charge and he's ready for whatever I say, but I better be careful. Pierson looks worried, he rubs his wrists and his splinted finger must be throbbing from being restrained. He gently shakes it out by his side.

"Gentlemen, my *partner* has requested your release, I'm granting her request as long as you cooperate. If any of you tries anything you'll regret it. She could be injured and one or all of you would likely die. So, please act responsibly and do as she asks without making any sudden moves. Understand?"

They all nod to one degree or another, but none of them look happy or all that willing to cooperate. But I know they'll do whatever I ask.

I make an announcement, "I've agreed to work with Kristos. He's going to teach me his business and we're going to stay with him for a little while. Will we be able to pack some clothes? And I told you I need my cat." I directed the last part at Kristos.

The man who made my life possible puts his fist to his lips in thought before answering, "We can go to your house and pack some things. You'll go inside with my men and *your* men will stay with me, so I know you won't do anything you shouldn't. Jon, call for the cars, we'll meet them in the garage."

"Yes sir." Jon steps outside and I can hear him speaking over a device to someone about the cars. I slip my blade into my back pocket, now isn't the time. I look at Jackson who hasn't taken his eyes from me, he saw what I did. He tilts his head the tiniest degree towards Austin and that tells me Austin is also armed. I glance at Pierson and Jackson's shoulder lifts such a subtle amount if I didn't know him like I do I wouldn't have seen the movement. He doesn't know about Pierson and I'm going to assume that if Pierson's armed, he can't easily access the weapon with his bum hand.

When my lips purse slightly, Jackson shakes his head and coughs to cover the movement. Jackson doesn't have easy access to any weapons either, so only Austin is armed, and me. When Jackson opens his eyes wide in question, I assume he's asking where my shadow is right now, and even though I don't exactly know, I do know Dozer, and I can reasonably assume Tyler has alerted his leader and they've sounded the alarm for all hands-on deck. Which means Colby is in charge of the tech in the building and maybe the cars, Dozer is enroute with a rescue crew or he's already here. It's been more than twenty minutes since Tyler and I were separated. I'm going with a plan that includes lots of support in the parking garage and I hope nobody disappoints me by being late to the party.

The elevators are large, but we take the freight elevator which is twice as big as the others and easily fits the eight of us. It's also around the corner from the rest of the elevators and it goes to a basement level inside the parking garage. When it opens there's a loading dock area that's got one large black box truck parked and backed up to the deck. There's a long limo style SUV parked near the stairs and another behind it. There's an exit from the building's staircase past the freight elevator and I caught movement through the reinforced glass window in the door.

There's a driver for each vehicle here now bringing Kristos's staff present and visibly armed to five, plus him. His guards have weapons in their hands aimed at the ground and Kristos and his drivers are armed, but their firearms aren't drawn. When the door opens for the staircase everyone's attention is pulled to the pale, gangly man who exits. His face lights up with recognition when he spots me.

"Hey Emmy! I've been lost for at least ten minutes looking for a way out of the building, for some reason the elevator wouldn't work after I stopped in the break room. What are you doing down here?" Nate asks. Dread fills my stomach because I have no choice but to use him as a distraction. When I move, Austin moves and we both throw our blades at two of the armed guards. My blade lodges in the side of my target's neck and he drops his gun and falls to the ground as blood spurts across the guard next to him who simultaneously catches Austin's blade in the trachea, right below his Adam's apple. He also falls to the ground bleeding but his gun fires a shot before it leaves his hand. Jackson and Pierson tackle the third guard and disarm him easily, Jackson cracks him over the head with the gun he now holds.

The drivers both draw guns and before they can harm anyone some men dressed in black tactical clothing shoot and kill them as they approach us. All of this unfolds in the blink of an eye and the one person I momentarily lost sight of, grabs my arm and yanks me against his chest placing the barrel of his gun to my temple. Everyone freezes and watches us. I don't have a weapon anymore. I know some of these guys are excellent shots, but I don't know if they're willing to risk my life. My guys aren't willing and they immediately drop the weapons they confiscated and put their hands up in compliance with whatever my evil father wants from them.

"I'll kill her. Step away from my car, she's coming with me. If you let us out of here, she'll be safe, and I'll release her when I can get away clean. So, don't try anything and don't follow us."

Jackson speaks for our side, "No problem. Just don't hurt her and you can go. We won't follow. Everyone steps back and lets them through. Weapons down." Dozer's guys all follow orders and put their weapons on the ground and their hands up.

Kristos is holding my arm tight and it hurts, his nails are digging into my skin. He's tense and his finger rests on the trigger, a dangerous circumstance. When he pulls on me to keep me in front of him as a shield, I hear a small scuff of something against the concrete floor, a sound that wasn't me and wasn't my sperm donor. My instincts scream at me and I cover my ears and fall limp, causing Kristos to shift his attention to me and move his gun away from my head.

BANG! A shot goes off and for a moment I'm not sure if I've been hit. When I take a breath, I know it wasn't me. The gun fell from Kristos' hand and he collapsed to his knees. I kick the gun away from him and step back. Standing behind us is none other than pasty Nate, he's holding a smoking gun and looks me over.

"Are you okay?"

"Yeah. What the fuck, Nate? Where did you get a gun?" He pulls a chain from inside his collar, and on the end dangles a shiny badge.

"FBI, I was here investigating the illegal activities of this mafia organization." The breath puffs out of my lungs and I feel light headed. No need to worry because three sets of arms wrap around me and kisses cover my hair and face. Then they each look me over and hug me. I'm so relieved they're safe. But holy fuck, Nate...scrawny, *Nate*, is FBI?

Nate speaks into a radio and calls his team into the garage. My crew of *villains* is quiet as we watch the events unfold. Kristos Chitto is placed under arrest and taken to the hospital under armed guard. A slew of FBI agents with a variety of monikers on their jackets show up in droves with search warrants and EMTs check me over, then my guys. Dozer and his men are separated from us and taken away for questioning.

Nate introduced us to his supervisor and we're taken into a conference room for questions as well. The supervisor, Agent Castleman, sits across from us with Nate.

"Like I reported earlier, Mr. Pierson Nash, Mr. Austin Matthews, and Mr. Jackson Hunter, were abducted from a parking lot and brought here against their will. Miss Quinn was hired with me and I'm not sure what she knew and when she knew it, sir."

After scanning our faces, his gaze lands on me and SA Castleman clears his throat, "Ahem, Miss Quinn, I understand Mr. Chitto is your biological father, is that correct?"

"Yes sir. I recently discovered he existed, my mother always told me she didn't know who my father was, but when I found information that he existed I arranged for a DNA test to confirm he's my father. Then I got a job here to check him out, I was curious. I had no idea he was a criminal."

"I see. And the team of men who came here to rescue you, who are they?"

"Just some friends who work in security, when they became concerned for my whereabouts and the whereabouts of these men, they chose to come here and see if we needed help." I point at my guys while I answer.

"Uh huh. Do you know where you were being taken prior to Agent Winston's intervention?"

"Kristos was demanding that I come stay with him and I refused unless my boyfriends could join me, and my cat, Sawyer. He agreed to take me home to collect some clothing and my cat. He said he would harm my boyfriends if I didn't cooperate. I was trying to keep everyone safe."

"I see. Is there anything else you'd like to share?"

"No sir. I would like to go home, this has been a very upsetting day."

"No doubt. I'll try to get you out of here quickly. Give me a few minutes and I'll be right back. Agent Winston, please join me." They leave the room and a sigh escapes me. I want to admit my real name because I'm not certain my identity will hold up to FBI scrutiny, but then they'll want to know where I got my excellent false identification from, and it would open a whole new can of worms. In my everyday life I strive for zero contact with law enforcement. Pierson holds my hand, and it helps. Austin rubs my thigh under the table and that helps even more.

"How are you holding up, Babe?" Jackson asks.

"I'm okay. I just want to go before I say something I'll regret."

"You're doing great, don't worry, Baby. You've got this," Austin offers his support.

The door opens and Nate steps inside, he walks to the table and retakes his seat but his eyes are down. A knot twists in my stomach.

Nate lifts his head and his eyes narrow as he looks me over, he glances at each of my guys and comes back to me. He tilts his head and continues to examine my face. I try to look as innocent as possible. What a joke, I haven't been innocent since I was five.

"SA Castleman will be a few minutes, he had to do something that shouldn't take too long. I have some questions, off the record. Would you answer me honestly?"

"Depends on the question, Nate. Now that it turns out you work for the FBI, I feel like I might need to watch what I say, and hire an attorney."

"You don't need an attorney."

"Isn't that what cops say right before they entrap a witness?" I purposely fumble the terms and act like I learned my legal knowledge from a TV drama.

He chuckles and smiles at me, then asks, "I think you're extremely intelligent Emmy, I think you're much smarter than any of us can comprehend, but I want to know the story with your father. Why did you come here to work?"

"Well, co-worker Nate, I came to check into him. I wanted to find out if he was someone I'd like to know. I wanted to know if he knew I existed, and if he felt bad about missing out on my entire life. I came here to figure him out. Obviously, I didn't like what I found and I wasn't interested in working with him or anything else. Today was going to be my last day, before he kidnapped my boyfriends and threatened to kill me."

"Just so you know, in my reports you're the victim and you've done nothing wrong. We may need you to testify later if there's a trial, but in my eyes, and SA Castleman's, you're innocent in this mess. But your father is probably going to be indicted on multiple charges, depending what we dig up in his files he might be behind bars for the rest of his life."

"Good. It's what he deserves. Is your boss going to be hounding me after this?"

"Don't worry about SA Castleman, he's a good guy. He works with some groups that function outside the law, in a gray area, he's also extremely intelligent and he sees things other people don't, like you, I suspect. He works for the greater good which isn't always found through the Justice System."

"Do you share his appreciation for the gray area?" I question.

"I see the benefits of the gray area."

"All right, Nate. I'll accept that response. Can I ask you a question?"

"Sure."

"What made you jump in and shoot him?"

"I analyzed all of the circumstances and you seemed like you were trapped in a no-win situation. I saw the opportunity to take him down and I went for it."

"Can I ask another question?"

"Go."

"Do you really live with your mother?" He bursts out laughing. Austin smiles and looks at Nate with a new lens.

"No. I'm not as haphazard as I acted. I'm sorry I was annoying, I find acting like a bumbling idiot makes people underestimate me and it helps with my work."

"I can see that. You were definitely getting on my nerves today. You may want to tone it down a little in the future, someone might punch you." He laughs more and I smile.

"Were you going to punch me, Emmy?"

"I wouldn't, but I wanted to punch you in the elevator." He chuckles a little more, probably remembering what he was doing to be so annoying. He literally went into a detailed description of how he makes tuna salad. Each freaking ingredient, the brand name, the exact measurements, it was brutal and he's definitely lucky he was innocent or he would've met my blade the hard way.

The door opens and SA Castleman returns. Nate loses his grin and waits for his boss to speak.

"All right Miss Quinn, we have all of your information and your boyfriend's. I understand you live nearby, so I don't need to ask you to stay in town in case we have more questions. This might be a long case, there are extensive charges pending against Mr. Chitto. Do you have any questions for me?"

"No. I have your card, I'll contact you if I think of anything. Can we go now?"

"Yeah. Please follow up with your physician if needed."

"I will. Thank you, it was nice meeting you."

"Yes, you too. All of you, try to enjoy the rest of your weekend."

"Thank you."

"Thanks, man."

"Bye Nate."

"See you."

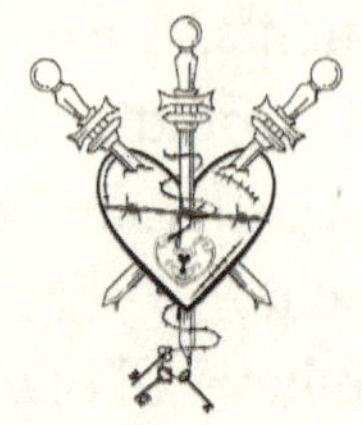

Chapter Thirty

Pierson

We walk silently to Violet's SUV. She hands the keys to Jackson and he climbs into the front seat, I sit behind him. Austin opens the front door for Violet and then sits behind her. Feeling a little shaky, I think some PTSD symptoms are creeping up on me as the adrenaline works its way out of my system. When that asshole had a gun to my girl's head, I felt an overwhelming panic and it took me right back to that mission which led to my discharge. I wanted to kill all of them and rescue her. With the way things played out I'm glad I didn't snap and charge Kristos, I might've been shot by Nate or even worse, Violet might've been shot. That's the thought that has my gut twisting in knots.

"Are you okay, bro?" Austin asks and pats my arm.

"I don't know. I'm having a little PTSD, I feel dizzy and shaky. I'm so sorry, Violet."

She turns and peeks at me between the seats, her brows squished in question, "Why are you apologizing to me? You didn't do anything wrong, Pierson."

"Yeah, but I almost did. I almost gave in to my inner need to rip that asshole's head off. You could've been hurt. I hate feeling out of control."

"Dude, you controlled yourself. No need to beat up on yourself now," Jackson states.

"He's right, Piers. You did a great job of controlling your actions and you handled everything just right. We're all safe, and that's thanks to all of us and our choices. You did good, no need to second guess thoughts you had during an extremely stressful situation. I trust you with my life, and I wouldn't do that if it wasn't warranted. You know me, I don't pull my punches to keep from hurting anyone's feelings. I love you. I love all of you and you all did great today." I see the sincerity in her beautiful dark eyes and my intestines untwist.

"I love you too."

"I love you too, Baby!" Austin adds.

"I love you too. But now what?" Jackson asks, always the practical one.

"Now we go get that evil bitch and strap her to my work table. I have so many new questions for her and she's going to answer every single one of them."

Violet doesn't waste any time, she calls Colby and shores up our plans for tomorrow night. We're not delaying anything, after we finish with Colby's tailors, we're going straight to evil grandmother central, tying her up, and dragging her psychotic ass back to Violet's BASIL for an interview with *David Bowie* himself. I'm excited, I still need to cut someone and that bitch will do just fine.

When we pull up at home, Dozer is there with Tyler and three other guys. They have our truck that was left behind in the parking lot. Tyler and Dozer approach us and hand back our weapons and cell phones. Violet was able to get hers from Nate of the FBI, back at her former place of employment.

"You guys doing all right?" Dozer asks.

Violet smiles, "Of course, why wouldn't we be?" He chuckles and Tyler and the other guy's smile. They've seen her in action a few times, they've seen her through some difficult situations, and nothing phases her. She's strong, resilient, and so fucking beautiful. I catch myself before she sees me staring at her with puppy love all over my face.

We usher everyone into the house and we take turns showering while Dozer and his guys go over plans with Violet and us if we're in the room. Tyler cooks some bacon and eggs and we make sandwiches for everyone. The other guys with them are Ray, Franco, and Barney, like the dinosaur. Tyler explains Barney has a purple muscle car the same shade of purple as the annoying fossil. It's a wickedly fast car according to Tyler, but they think the purple color is funny so they tease him. I personally think a car with so much horsepower it requires wheelie bars to keep from flipping over because of the torque, can be any color it wants. I'm not a car guy and I'm easily impressed by the speed and beauty some of them possess.

Since purple is Violet's favorite color, I may need to see this car and draw it for her, maybe with a nice set of wings. After we eat and have all of our plans confirmed with Colby by video, exhaustion hits me right between the eyes. I notice Violet is blinking more than usual and I hint to Jackson it's time to wrap up our planning session. He has no qualms about kicking everyone out so our girl can rest.

"Thanks for everything, Dozer. I'm grateful you were there today. We'll see you tomorrow." She hugs Dozer and I'm pretty sure she whispers that she loves him into his chest. He hugs her close and closes his eyes as he places a kiss on top of her head like an older brother who's thankful his little sister survived a harrowing event. She hugs Tyler too and surprises him, he awkwardly hugs her back while his cheeks turn pink. That's the thing about Violet, her circle is limited to only a few people, but she loves them fiercely. Once you're part of her family there's no escape, and you wouldn't want to go anywhere anyway, she's spectacular.

Tomorrow's crew will be composed of the men here today, plus another team of six. Our plan is solid and that Evil Witch is going down. When we fall into bed we snuggle together. Violet slings her leg over me like always, Austin is half under her, and Jackson is cuddled at her back. Sawyer is curled on Austin's pillow above his head, not one to be left out of a pile of sleeping loved ones. I'm not sure how fast anyone else fell asleep because I was out as soon as Violet's leg landed on me.

When the sun rises the glow from the window wakes me as the heat warms my face. I'm quickly too hot and when I open my eyes, I find Sawyer pressed against my chest. He's like a radiator, we could probably heat the whole house with the amount of warmth he generates. Violet is still next to me but the other guys are gone. I turn away from Sawyer and wrap myself around my girl.

"Geez! Why are you so hot?" Violet mumbles into my neck.

"You'll need to ask Sawyer. I think I have third degree burns from him."

"Yeah, he's like a nuclear reactor. Sorry."

"I don't mind. He and I have made our peace with each other."

"Good. I wouldn't want to have to dump you. I like having you around."

"I like you too. What time do we need to leave for Colby's?"

"Probably around eleven, what time is it?"

Looking at my phone I answer, "Crap, it's almost ten. Are you hungry?"

"Starving."

After dragging our feet for a few extra minutes we force ourselves to get up and get dressed. Jackson comes into the room and smiles.

"Good. You're up, we need to go soon. Austin wants to stop and eat brunch on the way to Colby's."

"Brunch?" I question.

"Yeah. The meal between breakfast and lunch, you've seen it in movies," he teases me.

Violet exits the bathroom in cut off shorts and a tank top with her hair slicked back from her face. She gives Jackson a stern look and leaves the room. He follows her, then Sawyer follows them, I'm ready so I follow too. When we get to the kitchen Austin's there and ready to leave. He and Jackson must've packed up everything we need for tonight because we're fully loaded.

We take both trucks and I ride with Austin. After brunch, which was delicious and filling, we aim right for Colby's pool house. His parents are out of town again and the guards recognize our vehicles now, so they let us pass with a wave. Colby is standing on a large ottoman in the middle of his great room, he has on a tuxedo and one of the small Italians is pinning the cuffs at the bottom of his pants. Colby is as tall as us, but he's substantially thinner than any of us, even Austin. He doesn't appear to have any discernible muscles, but his tuxedo fits him perfectly. It's a champagne color, or maybe gold? But it doesn't have glitter or anything sparkling to make it more like gold.

Violet admires him, "Wow! You look great! I can't wait to see the rest of you in your tux's."

The Italians swarm us and before long we're all wearing parts of our tuxedos and the talented men are pinning and sewing various hems. Violet is in a bedroom with her tailor... seamstress... I don't know the correct terms. When she enters our room, my tongue almost falls out of my mouth and onto the floor. She's in a different red dress from last time, but it's no less stunning, maybe more so.

The top sparkles and is tightly fitted to her body. Her breasts look amazing and she has a little more than a respectable amount of cleavage on display. The skirt hangs almost straight except where it curves to follow her hips. The bottom of the dress drags along the ground a little in the back and it gives her a regal appearance. I hope Harmony doesn't get mad if Violet outshines her, but in this dress, she looks like a glamorous movie star. It's like if I dreamt the perfect vision of the most beautiful woman in the world, and she magically appeared. Hell, and I'm lucky enough to have her love, how did that happen?

Jackson can't get his tongue to stay in his mouth and I check that my own mouth is closed. Austin whistles loud, and makes her laugh. She acts like a shy Victorian woman and bats her eyelashes, while the three of us drool.

"You're embarrassing me, gentlemen." She puts her hand over her mouth embracing her chaste role.

"Then don't show up looking like a sex goddess embodied! Damn, Violet my pants are going to need extra room in the crotch with you looking like that," Austin has no filter.

Colby covers his eyes, "TMI! TMI! No best friends sex talk!"

"Sorry Colby, I'll go change." Violet spins and the three of us lean to watch her walk down the hall.

"Holy fuck," Jackson is finally able to speak, I don't think I'm there yet. I may have swallowed my tongue. My Italian tailor, I think his name is Lorenzo, smiles and kisses his fingertips like when you appreciate a good meal.

"Bellissimo!" I have no clue what that means but I nod. He smiles and continues tugging on my sleeve. After a couple hours of trying on pants and jackets with custom shirts, we're finally finished with the last fitting. The wedding is coming up fast, we leave Thursday, and the tailors will have everything completed by the end of this weekend. Colby will ensure all of our formal clothes make it to Tallahassee in perfect condition.

Violet is focused on tonight and she's perfectly at ease leaving the wardrobe details to Colby. She's not that into clothing, and it's one of the things I like about her. She always looks great, but she doesn't try and she doesn't pay any attention to labels. She's perfectly happy with a second-hand pair of jeans at a garage sale if she likes them. She shops for comfort and I've never been with a woman whose appearance is so effortless.

When we're all finished with Colby, he fires up his command center and checks the surveillance at the *Wicked Witch's* estate. There's a few extra cars in the driveway, and he immediately begins tracing the license plates. He's able to cross reference the tags with the people on his shit list and he discovers the cars belong to some of the worst people Grandmother Grim knows. Violet decides we're going to deal with them too. I'm ready to crack some skulls, I've been eager to remove a threat since I left the Navy. After yesterday, I'm bouncing off the walls with the need to stop these assholes.

When we're dressed for the mission, we leave in two vehicles and meet up with Dozer at a park a few blocks from the target. They said all of their names but I didn't catch them all. I recognize the guys from yesterday and I'm proud of myself for remembering their names, forget a whole new crew. When we're ready to strike, Violet takes out her phone and makes a call.

"Morgan residence, this is Roman, how may I assist you?" She has the call on speaker so we can all hear the conversation. She smiles and it comes through in her voice.

"Hello, Roman. It's Violet Henley. How are you?"

"Oh, what a pleasure, good evening, Miss Henley. I'm well. How are you this evening?"

"I'm great. I want to surprise my grandmother and her guests. Would you be willing to help me out by not saying anything to her that I'm here?"

"Of course, Miss Henley. I'm always willing to do whatever you need. Would you like for me to quietly continue my work?"

"Actually Roman, I think it would be best if you head home and let us clean up when we're finished with our surprise. What do you say? Are you willing to keep quiet?"

"Yes, of course Miss Henley. I'm happy to cooperate. If you'll give me just a few minutes, I'll be on my way. Is there anything you need before I go?"

"No. We're all set. Thank you so much! You've been so helpful and I appreciate your kindness, Roman, I won't forget it."

"Thank you, Miss Henley. I'm leaving the main gate open so you're able to enter the property. Please, don't hesitate to contact me if there's ever anything I can do for you. Have a pleasant evening."

"Thanks so much, Roman. I wish you a pleasant evening as well. Good night."

"Good night, Miss."

Violet smiles, "He's a good guy and I'm fairly sure he hates my grandmother. He lives in a guest house at the back of the property. He's not to be disturbed, everyone got that?"

Everyone nods and makes affirmative sounds around the group. Next, she confirms that everyone is ready and knows where to go and what to do. Once everyone has confirmed the instructions one last time, we leave the park and descend upon the witch's evil castle. I hope her flying monkeys are out for the evening.

I'm in the truck with Austin, Tyler, and Franco. Jackson is in front with Violet, Barney, and Ray. Dozer is behind us with two guys and one more vehicle, a large box truck, follows them with the rest of the crew. We split off and park in separate locations, and we quickly disable their vehicles first. There's no security guards, the vile woman is so confident in her wicked guests being able to protect themselves she apparently didn't see the need to keep any additional personnel for safety. She's arrogant to the point of it being detrimental to her life, a big mistake.

Tyler tries the door to the house, it's a side entrance into the kitchen area, and the door is unlocked. He peaks inside and signals we're clear to move in. Violet goes in first, her group with Jackson watching her back. Dozer moves to flank them and watch both their backs, one step further. Austin leads us with Tyler next and me and Franco bringing up the rear. The group behind us spreads out and clears the rooms closest to the kitchen. We eventually pinpoint the group in a parlor room near the front entrance.

A woman leaves the room to use the restroom, we collect her and the retrieval team gags and binds her before loading her into the transport truck. When we're all in place surrounding the room where Violet's grandmother is telling her guests about the next venture she has arranged, Violet signals that she's going in. The room contains fifteen people, ten men, and five females now that one has been removed. We have to assume all fifteen people are armed and dangerous.

Violet enters the room with her gun in the holster at the back of her pants and she casually leans against the wall near the entrance. She waits quietly and motionless for someone to notice her. Her eyes are locked on the evil bitch who tried to hurt her so many times. From my angle, I can see Violet clearly and I get glimpses of Grandma Grim and two other guests. I'm going to venture a guess that nobody at this party is under sixty. With any luck maybe one or more of them will just have a heart attack and save us the trouble.

"Oh! What are *you* doing here?" Violet's nemesis asks when she finally notices the beautiful woman observing her activities.

"Hello, *Grandmother*. I just stopped by for a friendly visit, is now a good time?"

"No, it's not. Can't you see I have guests? I'd like for you to leave immediately."

"Or what? What will you do if I choose not to leave, *Joyce?*"

"Joyce, what's going on?" A woman who's had an alarming amount of plastic surgery questions.

"Relax, Jessica, I'll take care of this. Violet, please step into the kitchen with me, now." Joyce Morgan demands. Violet slowly shakes her head from side to side in defiance. Grandma Murder looks constipated as she purses her lips in annoyance.

"Now, Violet. I'm not playing with you!"

"Oh, but I'm playing with you, Grandmother Dearest. You and your *friends* are surrounded. They'll be going to jail, and you're coming with me. Unless you want to make this difficult, because I would love it if you tried to fight me. What's it going to be?"

"I most certainly don't need to take orders from the likes of you! You're nothing but a used-up whore who tricked her way from a white trash life into my daughter's world. You stole everything from her and it should've rightfully been mine. I won't hesitate to end you right here, so I can get my inheritance from *my* daughter!" Joyce has worked herself into a tizzy and she's making large exaggerated gestures to emphasize her words.

One of the men suddenly sprints to Violet and tries to grab her arm, she twists away from him breaking his hold easily and places the barrel of her gun to the side of his head. She laughs like this is the most fun she's had in a while and maybe it is.

"Anyone else have something to say?" Violet questions the rest of the guests. Nobody moves. "Good. Here's how it's going to go, the women, minus Joyce of course, are going to line up and hand this nice man their phones and bags." One of the women protests and Dozer steps in front of her immediately silencing her without a word. I can't help but chuckle as her eyes keep trailing up and up taking in his enormous size. He paints an intimidating portrait.

The women hand over their possessions without further complaints. Then one of Dozer's guys, whose name I don't remember, guides them towards the exit. I lose sight of them when they round a corner. Violet looks over the remaining men and her grandmother. Two of the men visibly squirm, I'm guessing they're the worst offenders. Violet uses her gun to point at the sofa, indicating the dumbass who charged her should take a seat. He complies.

"I have an idea, let's play a game," Violet announces.

"This is ridiculous! If you're robbing us, get it over with, we're not playing any games!"

"You'll do what I say, Grandmommy Dearest. Here's what we're going to do, does everyone have a drink? Tyler, can you give them some refills please?" Tyler takes a bottle from the bar and begins pouring clear liquid into the cups of guests who are empty or low. He acts like an overly dramatic server, and it makes me chuckle under my breath. Clearing my throat, I try to pull on my serious mask.

"Thanks Tyler. The game is called, *Never Have I Ever.* In case you're not familiar with it, I'll say something I've never done and if you've done it, you'll take a drink from your glass. If you haven't done it, you won't drink. Everyone got it?"

They nod half-heartedly. Violet walks to the bar and opens a lemon-lime soda, she pours it into a glass and adds ice, all with her back turned to the room insinuating she has no fear of the people seated there. Some of the men definitely felt her intended dig, and they shift uncomfortably.

"All right, let's play. *Never have I ever... stolen money.*" Two of the men drink from their glasses and a few others fidget with discomfort.

"I started us with an easy one so you can get a feel for how this works, but I can tell some of you weren't honest on that question. You have to be honest or you're out. Dozer shifts his firearm as she says that, implying they'll be shot if they lie, though neither of them say anything.

"Let's try another one, and remember, I might know if you're honest or not, because I might know some things about you all. Right, Mr. Benjamin?" She turns and steps in front of a bald man who's seated in an uncomfortable looking chair. He jolts at her use of his name and looks like he might be ill.

"Yes, m-ma'am," he stutters.

"Okay. *Never have I ever... killed a child.*" My gut clenched at her horrific question. One man takes a shot from his glass and another holds it in his shaking fist until he finally takes a sip.

"Good job. But there's two of you who weren't honest on that question. One more lie and you're out." Again she hints they'll be killed if they don't tell the truth. A tall sweaty man who seems like he's wearing a toupée looks ready to cry and he takes a sip of his drink. Joyce is showing the first crack in her façade, and it makes me think she's the other liar.

"All right, anyone else want to come clean? No? Okay, moving on. *Never have I ever... raped an adult.*"

Four of the men take a drink, the toupée dude is turning green and shaking like there's an earthquake, but he doesn't drink this time.

"Never have I ever... groomed a child." Toupée vomits in his lap and collapses to the floor. Violet ignores him like he doesn't exist. The remaining nine men seem to be having difficulty breathing. One is so pale he's almost transparent. All but the pale man take a drink.

"Never have I ever... molested a child." Violet looks each of them in the eye and they all give in and drink again. My skin crawls with disgust, only Joyce abstains, and I think maybe she didn't directly do anything, but she facilitated the despicable crimes and she's just as guilty in my eyes.

"Never have I ever... killed an adult." Violet very pointedly takes a drink from her glass and the nine conscious men are watching her with open fear. They should be afraid, because she won't hesitate to kill them too.

"Never have I ever... run a trafficking ring that harms innocent women and children." Violet stares at her grandmother with intense hatred plain on her face and the bitch trembles when she takes a sip of her drink, along with everyone else in the room.

"I don't see the point of this. If you're taking us to the police with some flimsy story of trafficking, let's get it over with!" the youngest offender in the room snaps. Violet points her gun at him and shoots him dead with one shot between the eyes. My ears ring from the sound of the report in this enclosed space with too many marble surfaces.

"Anyone else want to share their opinion about my methods?" she asks, perfectly calm and with her hand steady as a surgeon's, holding her glass of soda.

Chapter Thirty-One

Violet

All right, I'm done messing around, I want that witch on my table. She's still got a resting bitch face but she's gone silent and it's nice to have finally found a way to shut her up. The unconscious vomiter is still on the floor and I recognize him as a registered sex offender who has been arrested for harming his own children, a niece, and a neighbor. He's incredibly wealthy and because of his connections and probably a few campaign contributions, he's served a total of twenty-five hours behind bars. He got out of every charge, his only punishment was being required to register as a sex offender. He's not just an offender, that's a title that could be given to a guy caught chatting to a prostitute on a street corner. No, he's a registered *sexual predator*, which marks him as a sick asshole who is a repeat offender, used violence during the assault, and/or committed a sex crime against a child.

I don't want him getting off again, I call over Pierson, "This guy on the floor, he's a really bad one. I want to end him, are you interested?" His eyes light up like I promised him a blow-job. I can't help smiling with a little giggle, I love seeing him happy and I'm excited I was able to make him smile like that.

"Oh yeah! Right now?"

"Go for it." He doesn't hesitate pulling a nice sized Bowie knife from the sheath on his thigh. He looks over his prey and seems disappointed. He kicks the scumbag's foot until the evil man stirs.

"Hey asshole, did you hurt some kids?"

The man's eyes flick rapidly from Pierson, to me, to Dozer, and back again. He looks like he might puke again, but he nods.

"Why?" I wasn't expecting Pierson to ask that question, I don't know that I've ever thought to ask why any of these sick fucks do what they do. I've always believed they're just evil and twisted, for whatever reason they have sick desires they aren't able to contain. In the case of the people in this room, it's also about the money. They make millions off of their victim's torture and it's what motivates them to commit those horrific acts against the most innocent of souls.

The man shakes his head and gags trying to keep from vomiting on himself again, he's fighting an internal battle nobody will win.

"I don't know. I'm sick. I was abused when I was a kid, my uncle used to touch me. It's not my fault!" he pleads. But Pierson doesn't accept his excuses, he slashes the blade across the man's throat in a quick movement. For a brief moment, time stands still, the dead guy's eyes open wide in shock and his hands reach for the wound in his neck. But time catches up and blood spurts from the gash, it falls in a tidal wave down his front and he twitches a couple times before falling dead at Pierson's feet.

My boyfriend turns to look at me and his eyes are lit up like he's just won a jackpot. He smiles a huge grin that splits his face in joy.

I can't help smiling in return, it feels good to make him happy and remove a threat to the safety of innocent children everywhere.

"That was fun! Who else can I kill?" Pierson asks and looks around the room at our other captives.

Austin steps in and puts his arm around Pierson while carefully guiding his blade away from their bodies, "Why don't we go rinse off your knife and take a minute, *Mr. Ripper.*" Austin gives me a look like he's handling our wily toddler so I can get back to work. I blow him a kiss and mouth, ***thank you,*** to him. He winks and takes Pierson from the room.

One of the remaining men is crying silently except for an occasional sniffle. The rest just look defeated and tired. My Grandmother has her lips pinched together so hard I bet I could make some diamonds if I put coal in her mouth. I might need to try that out.

"All right, let's get these monsters loaded up for transport. Colby, are you ready for their delivery?" Colby answers me over the bud in my ear. He's been silent since we didn't need him for surveillance, or anything else until now.

"Yeah. The agents are ready to collect them from Dozer's team, all of the evidence is uploading to them now. They'll have more proof than they know what to do with to prosecute these assholes. It all corroborates the evidence regarding Kristos as well. None of them will be able to buy their way out of this. There's tax fraud and RICO law violations on top of all the trafficking, they're caught, dead to rights, and they're all a flight risk, so no bail. You've got them VioleNt One."

"Perfect. All right, let's cuff them and get them out of here. I'm sick of looking at them." The Wicked Witch of the West tries to stand up like she's going with them. I point my Sig at her face and it gives me great pleasure to inform her it's not the case.

"Not you. Sit back down."

"Must you aim that thing at me? You've made your point, you win."

"As much as I enjoy hearing you admit defeat, we're not finished. You're coming with me." Her neck almost snaps as she twists to look at my face.

"Coming with you? Where?"

"I'm bringing you to my place, I have a few more questions for you. I think we should discuss some family business in private." She looks confused and very concerned, but she doesn't say anything else. I'm loving how easy it is to silence her when I use a weapon to do it. I should've tried this years ago.

Jackson kisses the corner of my mouth and then helps the other guys cuff everyone and march them outside to the transport truck. When it's just me and Grandma, and two dead guys, Austin and Pierson return. They both look me over, and I smile at them to let them know I'm perfectly fine.

"Are you ready to go, Baby?"

"Yeah. Are you all set, Pierson?"

"I'm good. Sorry I got a little excited before, I've been dying to be more hands on. Oops, pun not intended." He flashes a goofy grin my way and I would swear he was high if I didn't know better. He's so freaking cute I want to cover him with kisses, but I won't let my evil grandmother see such a personal moment between us. Austin chuckles and guides him by the elbow towards the door.

"We'll meet you outside, Baby."

"Okay. Come on, Joyce. Let's go." She gingerly steps over the trail of blood running away from the vomit guy's ruined throat. Holding her head high, she walks towards the front door where the others have been exiting.

"No. We're riding in another truck, through the kitchen." I point the way with my trusted firearm and she gives me a dirty look before clicking her tongue and stomping to the door I indicated. This will be fun. I'm going to break her, I'm going to wring every bit of information I can out of her, and then I'm going to end her as painfully and slowly as possible. My own goofy grin breaks across my face, and I can relate to Pierson's excitement.

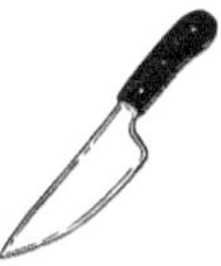

When we get to the warehouse she's subdued and watches me with wide eyes. Where's her bitchy attitude now? Jackson cuffed her hands behind her back before putting her in the back seat of the truck. Austin and I rode next to her with Pierson and Jackson up front. When I help her down from the seat she almost looks like a frail old woman, for just an instant, but I'm not fooled. She's Satan's right hand and she deserves everything she gets, she's evil to her core.

When I pull open the door to my BASIL, she stops and is frozen in place. She won't cross the threshold. You'd think I made a barrier of salt to keep out the wicked, but this room was made for them, for their demise. With some encouragement from Jackson, mainly a swift shove, she stumbles into the room.

"Please make our guest comfortable in her new quarters." Austin and Jackson lift her onto the table, she doesn't struggle and I almost respect that, almost. Pierson steps forward and straps her legs to the foot of the table by her ankles. Austin removes her flex cuffs and then he and Jackson attach her wrists to the metal cuffs at the top of the table. When she's secured, I look her over and she looks smaller somehow. But her resting bitch face has left permanent lines on her stretched too thin skin, she can't look kind or innocent when she's spent her entire life looking down on everyone else. The evidence of her evil soul is carved across her face in an angry frown and mean looking creases by her brows.

Still appearing defeated, she looks at me and asks, "All right, what is it you want from me?"

"I told you, I have questions. I want to know about your marriage to Milton Morgan, start with how you met him and when you knew he was a gangster."

She rolls her eyes and chuckles under her brimstone breath before she speaks, "You're a naïve child. I knew exactly who and what he was when I set out to land him. He was handsome, powerful, and loaded. My Emerson was already grown and off in the world, so I went after what I wanted. Milton was enamored with me the moment our paths crossed. He could have any woman he wanted, they threw themselves at his feet, but I wouldn't let him have me and it drove him mad. You young girls are so stupid, with your *body counts,* and kinky sex, letting them choke you and calling it love. Milton had to earn me, I refused to let him touch me until we were married. He couldn't stand not having me when he wanted. He flew me to Vegas and married me so he could collect his prize. But I held back, I only gave him small tastes until it pushed him over the edge. He married me without a prenuptial agreement, he bought me anything I wanted. When I asked to be included in his business, he let me join him and learn all of his skills until I no longer needed him. When I got bored with him, I killed him. Does that satisfy your curiosity?"

I have no doubt she could see surprise on my face, I wasn't expecting all that. I didn't expect her to be honest at all, but I think she was telling the truth. She must be a narcissist, she thinks she's smarter than everyone else, she believes she's in charge and she'll come out on top no matter what. She can't admit defeat, classic narcissistic traits.

"How did you meet Kristos? What's your relationship with him?"

"Your father? He was Milton's lackey even before I met him, when I became involved in all of the business dealings, Kristos thought I would eventually take over. He's a greedy, grasping, ladder climber, who rode Milton's coattails for far too long. He thought he could do the same to me and take over when I got rid of Milton. But I made him a figurehead and I ran everything from behind the scenes. Emerson always said you were smart, are you? Or are you a grubby handed kiss-ass like your father?"

"I'm not here to answer your questions, you'll answer mine. This isn't quid-pro-quo, I'm in charge in this room. When did you know Kristos was my biological father?"

"When I met him, he told me about the drug addict he was shacked up with, when she got pregnant, he left her. He told me when you were born and every once in a while, he would brag about you and show me a photo. All I saw was a beautiful girl that would bring me top dollar if I could get her into an auction. He wouldn't let me have you, imagine my surprise when you showed up at my daughter's house. I'm sure you can understand why I was disgusted to know a product of a drug addict and Kristos was sponging off of my child. Her hard-earned money was supporting a piece of trash that belonged in my barn, not in my family. Kristos told me he thought your mother was allowing you to be abused, Emerson filled in all the details of the *terrible abuse* her foster child had suffered. I tried to tell her not to adopt you, not to let you taint our family with your trashy blood. But as you know, she didn't listen."

"How many children have you trafficked?"

"One-thousand-two-hundred-seventy-four, give or take a dozen." Holy fuck! I wouldn't have ever guessed it would be so many, how does she know the exact amount? God, she's so fucking evil! I swallow and try to maintain my composure, it's one of the most difficult things I've ever done, because more than anything, I want to carve my initials right across her vile face.

"How many adults have you trafficked?"

"I currently have four-hundred and twenty-two workers over the age of fifteen working across the country. We transport them to a new location every few weeks, there's a pipeline of trucking routes and truckers who move them around for us."

"Do you have any remorse or feelings at all about the people you've hurt?"

"No. Why would I? They're a means to an end. I would've stopped human trafficking if it wasn't so profitable, it does better than the drugs and guns, and gets disrupted by authorities less often. Law enforcement is much more willing to take a payoff over a prostitute than an ounce of marijuana."

I'm actually speechless. I storm from the room and slam the door closed. I haven't even introduced her to *David Bowie* yet, she's been talking like we went out for coffee without any influence from me. She's so much more vile than I suspected. I've met some truly evil people, but none of them have been as detached, cold, and disturbing as this woman.

Needing some relief from the disgusting feeling curled in my intestines I pull my gloves from their locker, slip them on, and begin hitting the heavy bag while I alternate imagining it's Kristos or Joyce's face I'm hitting over and over. Every time I think about how many people she's hurt, just with the human trafficking alone, my anger is renewed and I hit the bag harder.

"Everything all right, Killer?" I stop punching and turn to look at Pierson.

"No! That fucking bitch has hurt so many people and she doesn't care, it doesn't bother her at all. What kind of person does that?"

"A very disturbed person. She's obviously very sick and abnormal, it's no excuse, but it's what must keep her from feeling anything about what she's done. Is she answering your questions?"

"Yeah. She's just chatting like we're girlfriends and this is normal friendly conversation. I got so frustrated I had to come out here and use the heavy bag."

Pierson wraps his arm around my shoulders and pulls me into a hug. I grab his waist and hug him back, then I lean up on my toes and kiss him. He smiles at me and kisses me again.

"Do you want some company in the BASIL?" I look into his gorgeous hazel eyes, they're more gold than green right now, and I see no hesitation, just an earnest wish to support me. I pop one more kiss on his lips and pull off my gloves. After I put them away, I take his hand and lead him back to the vilest room in the building.

When we enter, Grandma Murder opens her eyes as if she had just been resting.

"Those guests, who were they, and what were you doing?"

"They're some of my investors. Most of them also like to sample the products, thus the reason your little game was so effective."

"And..." I push.

"We were going over some plans to expand parts of the operation, I was asking them for more money."

With no further encouragement from me she lays out all the details of her operations, she even names high ranking officials, and celebrities over the next hour and a half. Thankfully this is all being recorded so I don't need to remember every name and amount she mentions. But I can't forget four-hundred and twenty-two people are currently being forced to do terrible things so this monster can make a buck.

After I calm down from all the new information, I return to the BASIL with all three of my guys. They're concerned about all the heavy bag punching going on. It's a frequent stress reliever for me and they've never seen me hit it so intensely.

When we open the door, she opens her eyes again. Her annoyed eyes roam along the faces of my three loves and it pisses me off. It feels like she's touching them and everything inside me wants to rip her arm off at the socket, she looks at me last.

"You're such a pretty girl, if you would've never met my daughter everything would be fine. You could've brought in a small fortune on the auction block, such a waste."

"I know you're trying to upset me and manipulate me, but I don't care what you think. And even though I know you won't really hear what I have to say, I'm going to tell you a few things."

"If you feel you must." She rests her head back on the table.

"My mom was the most wonderful person, she was smart and kind. She loved to help others and was willing to volunteer at the drop of a hat. She didn't make a donation for a photo op, she actually got her hands dirty and helped. I don't know how such an amazing person could be the product of someone like you. Despite your objections, she adopted me and made me her child. She loved me and wanted me to have a great life. Even though she tried to keep a relationship with you, she wasn't willing to let you harm her child the way you tried to harm her. She didn't want to be like you, she didn't want to be near you, and eventually even my sweet mother was driven away by your evil soul. I would fight you to the ends of the earth to make sure nothing of my parents ever falls into your hands. You don't deserve even an old sock she wore from the clothes hamper."

"You already have everything. I lost my case against you, why do you keep harping on the things that belonged to my daughter?"

"Because I want you to know that you'll never have anything of hers or my dad's, you're not worthy of one thing from either of them."

"Your whining is getting old. I'm done with this discussion, let's wrap it up and you can deliver me to the authorities." She closes her eyes as if she can make me leave if she ignores me. Maybe she thinks I won't do anything if she can't see me, or maybe she thinks this is a dream.

"Grandmother, I thought I told you, I'm not taking you to the authorities."

"Then what else do you want from me? I've answered your tedious questions." Her eyes remain closed and her hands are fisted at her sides. Now she purses her lips in annoyance. I pick up *David Bowie* and scrape his blade along the metal table, it makes a painful squeaking sound that reminds me of a wounded animal, maybe a wolf or coyote. She refuses to open her eyes, and holds them shut tight, her face scrunched up with the effort. When I get to her hand, I press *David Bowie's* pointed tip between her fingers, she tries to hold her fist closed against my blade but she doesn't have the strength. Since his edge is razor sharp, it cuts into her skin every time she touches it. I choose the finger that's at the best angle and press my body weight down on my hand holding my knife, with a crunch of bone the finger comes free and rolls away from her hand.

She began screaming and it took a beat before it penetrated into my thoughts past the adrenaline rush of hurting her. Before I say a word, Jackson gags her with a ball gag that's uncomfortably large. She can't scream, but some more guttural sounds escape from her throat. Her eyes are open wide now, too wide and full of fear, tears stream from the corners, she's shaking, and her head moves from side to side, a constant gesture of, '*No!*'

I feel nothing but hatred for her, a hate so hot and raw it burns at my insides. I walk to the other side of the table and stab in a downward arc into her wrist, there's a ringing sound as the metal-on-metal connection resonates like a bell when the blade strikes the table through her wrinkled wrist. She makes a higher pitched noise, but I ignore it. The shiny metal of my close friend is now coated with blood, the tainted blood of someone I'll never consider family.

I drag the very sharp instrument along her knee and down to her foot. She lost her shoes at some point during transport, she didn't need them, so I left them where they fell. I stand parallel to her legs and face towards her gagged visage. I watch her reaction while I force my weapon of choice into the arch of her foot. I'm rewarded with a scream, muffled as it is, and then she faints. I twist the blade until she stirs and screams again. I wanted to stab all the way through her foot, but it gets hung up in her bones. When I twist the handle that my dad once held, it pops free of her metatarsals. No matter, I stab again into her heel. She makes a strangled sound and faints once more.

It's no fun if she's not awake. Austin waves a smelling salts packet under her nose. She jolts awake and then her eyes grow wider than before, her head moves back and forth again, still pleading I'll stop. She watches me carefully and when I raise my knife, she flinched away from it and I crack up with laughter.

"Joyce, you're fun to play with. I was thinking earlier that you clench your teeth so hard at me I could probably make diamonds if I had some coal. I didn't have any, but I'm sure Santa will leave some in my stocking this year. But I found an alternative, let's try it, huh? If you make a diamond, I promise to bury it with you."

Her eyes pull so wide I can see the whites all the way around like a cartoon. Using *David Bowie,* I slice off her gag, cutting her cheek in the process. She screams incoherently. I pull a charcoal briquette from my pocket and drop it into her open mouth. She chokes and gags which leads to more choking. It broke into more than one piece and I think she probably swallowed some, and some is in her teeth, stuck to her tongue, while she continues to choke on another chunk.

She spits and coughs, black saliva runs from her lips down her chin to a puddle of coal on her chest. She keeps hacking and gagging and I watch with a satisfied smile. It makes me think about the times the Beast and his friends would try to make me swallow things, it's a terrible feeling, choking, not knowing if you'll get another breath of air. I'm happy to see her struggling with that fear, how many of her thousands of victims never got that next breath?

I had a plan to carve her up while she watched, I wanted to cut into all of her nerve endings to make sure she felt every one of them in the most painful ways. But something comes over me, an idea becomes focused in my mind and I can't banish it. Placing *David Bowie's* handle in my mouth like a Disney pirate, I hoist myself up onto the edge of the table. Jackson takes one step towards me but checks himself when I don't fall. I use my foot to press my weight upwards and stand up above her, then I step over her so her hips are between my feet and she's looking up at me, continuing to cough and drool. I take my knife from my mouth and hold it where she can see the bloody blade.

"I guess we aren't getting any diamonds. Oh well, it was fun to try. Joyce, I want you to know I won't miss you. I won't ever think of you. When I dismantle your trafficking ring, I will donate every penny you have to the victims of abuse. I'll sell everything you own and give that money to survivor's who need some help. All of your work to become the boss, make all the money, and grow your evil empire was for nothing, I'm shutting it all down. I'm going to kill every one of your employees who are involved in trafficking humans, but the others will go to jail. I'll make sure they all know you gave them up, that you cried and screamed while I cut you. They'll all know I won and you lost."

She screams out in frustration and fear, "Aaaaaaaaahhhhhhh!" It's the feral sound of a wounded animal. She yanks at her restraints trying to pull free from them. She struggles and tugs over and over, a trapped wild thing facing her demise.

I sit on her stomach and she stops, frozen with her mouth still open. Her eyes grow larger once again, and I can't stand to look at her any longer. I stab my knife into her shoulder aiming for that spot, the narrow passage where all the nerves are close together. She turns and looks at the handle protruding from her shoulder. I don't even hear the screams anymore, I'm not listening to anything but the song in my head. I love *Halestorm*.

I wrap my fingers around her neck and she tries to pull away from me, but there's nowhere to go when you're lying on a table. I lean on her throat, my fingers try to crush her trachea. The soft tissue gives, her skin is weirdly smooth like plastic. Her face begins to turn pale, her lips a bluish shade of gray. Her eyes bulge, but now I think it's more blood flow than fear. I keep applying more pressure and her eyes plead with me. I can still see the fear in there, I squeeze harder making her face and lips begin to turn a pale blue, her veins are bursting in her eyes causing them to bleed.

The nails of her remaining fingers fall from my arms, I didn't even notice she grabbed me. Her pupils dilate and the life leaves her body. I can't let go until I know she's really gone. My skin breaks out in goosebumps as I feel a light breeze blow past me. When I glance up at my guys, they're all smiling at me, proud of me. I swear I felt the evil leave the building, the air is lighter, my burdens are lighter, the world is free of her at last.

After I hop down from the table, I rinse *David Bowie* in the sink, and leave him on the counter to be sanitized, polished, sharpened, and returned to his special place in the weapons room. Next, I wash my hands all the way to my neck and remove my clothes.

Standing in my underwear I ask Austin, "Hey, will you please grab me some clothes, sweetie?"

"Why would I do that?"

"Because you want to take me home and fuck me."

"I'll be right back!" He takes off to the other room, I have some extra clothes in there.

"I know it doesn't happen often, but I'm on Austin's side. I think you look fine, mighty fine, Babe."

"Do we have any chance for a democracy?" Pierson asks.

"Why?" I tilt my head in question.

"I was thinking there's three of us, if we voted, you'd need to wear what you have on."

"Lucky for me it's not a democracy, this is a monarchy and I'm the Queen Bitch in charge. Nice try though. I would consider it if there wasn't a possibility of Dozer or his guys appearing to clean up. Plus, we have to go home for what I have in mind, what if we got pulled over and I was wearing this?" I point to my breasts which are barely encased in bright blue lace, it matches the streak in my hair.

"Oh. Yeah, I don't want anyone but us to see you like this." He smiles at me and I know he's picturing me with no lace at all. I smile back with the knowing grin of a devious feline.

Austin returns and shakes open the clothes and tries to help me get dressed faster, "Austin, I've got it. Thanks."

"Sorry, I just want to hurry home. I don't think you appreciate the sex appeal of watching you end that evil hag. You're glowing right now and I want you so much it hurts." When my hand comes through the sleeve of the shirt, he takes it and presses it against the hard rod in his pants.

"Mmmm." I can't keep the moan from coming out. I want them too. My nipples are hard and my pussy is aching for them to touch me. We need to hurry.

We rush past Dozer and his crew as they come down the hall, "Where are you going?"

"Home."

"Are you ready for us in there?"

"Yeah."

"Do you wanna talk about what happened with the prisoners?"

"Later!" Austin shouts.

"We gotta go!" Jackson says.

"See you!" Pierson calls.

"Bye!" I exclaim as I walk through the door.

Dozer chuckles and says, "Yeah. See ya!"

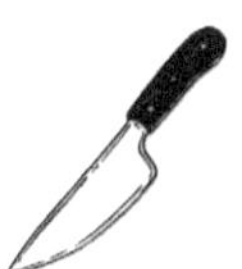

Showered and ready for fun, I climbed into the middle of our bed. My hair is still damp and my skin is cool, but there's a heat growing between my legs. We couldn't stop kissing in the shower, it was a little crowded with the four of us, but it was efficient with everyone working together. Though there was a little redundancy when my breasts and ass got washed three times. It was fine because it gave me time to wash three large swords, just this once that's a euphemism.

Austin climbs in on one side of me and Pierson the other, they both kiss my cheeks, ears, and neck while fondling my breasts and pinching my nipples. Jackson is at my feet and he gently pushes me to roll onto my stomach. A thrill of excitement travels from my toes to my clit and then continues until it spreads out enough to disperse. Both Austin and Pierson are rubbing and squeezing my ass cheeks. Jackson begins kissing my Achilles tendon and gently nibbling on it. Those excited sensations burst from their fingertips with each touch.

My pussy clenched in desire and my voice is rough with arousal, "Oh. Yes! Mmmm, right there, harder." I'm directing three sets of hands and mouths, it doesn't matter that they're doing what they want, I'm happy to be on this ride. I reach out for skin and smile, pleased when I find a hard cock with one hand and balls with the other. Both my hands cause vocal reactions in them and it makes my need throb.

"Fuck!"

"Yes, Baby. Stroke me."

Now Jackson is gently squeezing where my thighs meet my ass, and next I feel cool gel land directly on my rear entrance. Soon the bigger plug is working its way inside me and it still feels foreign, but it always reaches a point where it feels amazing and my pussy begs to be filled. Austin presses his way beneath me and his body raises my ass into the air. He plays with my nipples and rubs his dick against my pussy, every time he touches my clit my pussy throbs. When the head of his cock catches at my opening the moisture there allows him to slide inside. I want to cry. It feels so incredible, I press hard against him and he thrusts into me causing us to meet with a smack.

Jackson continues to play with the jeweled trainer and it's making me feel so full and the bursts of pleasure are so strong I'm hurtling towards a climax at rocket speed. When Austin's pelvic bone hits my clit on an especially perfect thrust, my pussy clenched down on him and I wiggle, so my clit keeps rubbing against him while I come.

When I settle back into a rhythm, Jackson pulls me towards him so I'm on my knees more than lying on Austin. He has more room to thrust up into me and he takes advantage of the new angle. Jackson is using the plug to stretch me and it feels so good. Pierson who's been twisting my nipples and kissing and licking me pulls up onto his knees and offers me his perfect cock. I lick some salty perfume from his head and then I lick around the edge, concentrating on the spots that make him moan.

Another orgasm is starting to build for me, I can feel Jackson rubbing against it. He removes the plug and gently squeezes my ass cheek. He slides his cock through the lube around my rim, then he softly presses the tip against it.

"Take a breath, Babe, and push back against me." I do what he says and with a small pop his dick is inside. I keep breathing while I adjust to the stretch. Pierson distracts me with his dick in my mouth and all three of them are able to work me into a pleasurable ride. Jackson and Austin are working in time with each other and it leaves me feeling filled and close to a climax.

"Can you feel me, bro?"

"Yeah, it's weird. Enjoy it while you can, cause this is the only way our swords will ever cross."

Austin laughs.

Pierson begins to fuck my mouth harder, and faster he's getting close too. When Austin thrusts up next he grabs my hips and presses as deep as he can and he moves in a way that makes me feel his cock rubbing against Jackson's through my walls. That just made my orgasm speed up and it's right there, I can feel it.

I suck harder on Pierson and he moans before, "Holy fucking hell! Yes!" He comes in the back of my throat and I swallow everything he gives me. Then my climax lands hard, my whole-body trembles, I'm writhing erratically chasing the next jolt of pleasure.

When Austin starts to come, I fall on him and he continues to thrust as much as he can. Jackson is about to come too and he thrusts hard, but it feels amazing with Austin and me coming too. I'm not sure who said what but there's cursing and moaning before we all collapse on the bed in bliss. My body is tingling all over, when any of them move it sends electrical charges across my skin. I'm panting softly and I feel so perfect in a sweaty and satisfied pile of the loves of my life.

When my eyes open, I'm tucked into bed with all three of them, Pierson is watching me.

"Hey, Killer, how are you doing?" I vaguely remember someone washing me off and making me take a few sips of water, but nothing after that, I guess I fell asleep.

My lips curl in a smile at his sweet concern, "I'm awesome. How are you?"

"I'm great, the most beautiful woman in the world is in my arms and I love her. What more could a guy want?"

"I love you too. Are you the only one awake?

"No. We're awake, Baby. How was it for you?"

"It was unbelievable. I love you too, both of you."

"I love you too, Babe. I didn't hurt you?"

"No, the exact opposite."

"Are you willing to do it again?"

"Yeah."

"Dibs!"

"What did I say about that, Austin?"

"Sorry. I know you're not an object for us to fight over, it's just, I want to try it next. I love you, Baby."

"Mmmhmm, nice save. You can be next, or we can see what happens. I might end up in a bathroom with one of you before we have a chance to do this again, you never know."

"Dibs!" I half-heartedly punched Pierson's upper arm. He laughs and the other guys join in.

"Sorry, Killer, I was just trying to be funny." He kisses me.

"Ha, ha, yep, very funny. I love you naughty boys." I clap my hand on Austin's cheek then rub Jackson's shoulder. The satisfaction is only outshined by the love I feel for these gorgeous guys, I'm so fucking lucky. Crap, doesn't thinking that cause a curse that brings your world crashing down? Hopefully whoever's in charge of curses stepped out for a smoke.

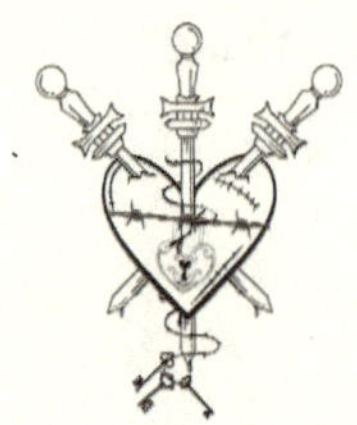

Chapter Thirty-Two

Pierson

I haven't flown since I got out of the Navy, and this is such a short flight it's barely flying at all. We should arrive at the hotel with just enough time to get ready for the themed pre-wedding party. Colby wanted us to get dressed before the plane ride but Violet pointed out the risk of airplane spills and wrinkles, so he caved.

She's currently laughing with Colby about something only they understand. They have tons of inside jokes between them, and she teases him about his sense of humor, but hers is just as out there as his. They're both looking forward to the party tonight and their excitement is filling the plane making everyone a little more animated than usual. It's hard to tell with Austin because he's generally too bouncy, but even Jackson has a little pep in his step.

I'm a little less excited. I've never met any of these people and they're some of Violet's best and oldest friends. I don't mind meeting her friends, I'm just not the biggest fan of parties, and I haven't been to a wedding before. But if I'm honest with myself, I'm a little worried about Violet seeing her ex, Max. Austin and Jackson are solid and secure in their relationship with our girl but I'm still new. What if he doesn't like me and she decides to dump me. I'm feeling very junior high right now, but I can't help feeling insecure about our relationship when she hated me at first. Actually, that's not fair. I hated her and she tried to get past my stupidity.

I know she loves me, I know nothing will come between us, it's just that niggling little fear that somehow, she'll remember she loves him and ditch me. When the pilot announces we're beginning our descent, I forget about my insecurities and focus on what I need to do as we land. I want to remind Violet to collect all of her bags and Colby brought more than she did. He says there will be some valets on the ground to collect our luggage along with a few cars to transport us, the crew, and the bags to our hotel.

He wasn't kidding, a troop of men and women in bellhop uniforms come onto the plane when the door opens and they immediately begin collecting our belongings without getting in our way. We load into a limo and drive the relatively short distance to Hotel Duval, the most exclusive hotel in Tallahassee. The hotel manager shows us to the penthouse suite on the top floor, personally pointing out the features of the four bedrooms, bar, lounging area, balcony, and four individual bathrooms. The room comes with two butlers who will be at our beck and call for our entire stay. Apparently, they will unpack our clothes, order and set up our meals, run errands, and kiss our asses. Austin thinks this is the height of living large and he immediately assigns Tremont to get him some candy and comic books. I'm not saying he acts like a child but... Tremont might be *thinking* it even though his face reveals nothing and he smiles before heading off to do Austin's bidding.

Evan is the other butler and Violet doesn't let Austin abuse him. She won't let him unpack her bags either, she implies she doesn't want him touching her panties, but I suspect it's her blades she doesn't want handled by a stranger.

Colby is perfectly at ease with the servants in our room and he looks like a royal prince posed on his throne, a plush recliner in the more casual section of the suite. His face is pointed towards his laptop screen as he rapidly pokes the keyboard.

"Quit fooling around and get ready! The ballroom will be prepared and waiting for us in an hour. Austin, don't do anything to mess up your tux before we get down there, okay?" Colby begs.

"I'm taking the smaller room for my dressing area!" Violet announces and drags her bags down the hall. I haven't even gotten far enough to see a bedroom. No better time than the present.

"Mr. Pierson, may I offer you any assistance?" Evan asks when I stand.

"Oh. I was going to check out the bedrooms, do you know where my bag is?"

"Yes sir. Please follow me." I follow and he leads me to a very large bedroom. It has the biggest bed I've ever seen with a huge ornate padded headboard and dozens of fancy pillows. There are doors on either side of the bed. He opens the one on the left first and it's an enormous walk-in closet with cushioned benches and drawers, plush satin hangers, and multiple full length mirrors. My things are hanging in their own space, my shoes are neatly lined up, and my baseball caps are arranged on a shelf above. It looks like a high-end boutique, even my old-school faded Lynyrd Skynyrd t-shirt seems fancy in this room.

Next, he shows me what's behind door number two, and I win the jackpot. There's a massive jetted tub in the center of the room. It looks like a black marble swimming pool, behind it, the entire back of the room is a black marble shower with openings on either side of the huge tub. From here I can see two shower heads, but I have a feeling there's more. This is going to be such fun with our girl, I wonder if the bride would forgive us if we blow off the wedding to stay here naked in the pool-tub.

There are long counters along each side of the room with two sinks in each, also a matching door to a smaller enclosed space with a toilet on each side of the room. This might've been made for us, we may need to stay an extra week or build a replica onto the back of Austin's house. I'm so impressed by all the details I completely forgot about Evan.

"Sir?"

"Huh?"

"Did you need anything before I go?"

"Oh, uh, no, no, I'm fine. Thank you. This is unbelievable."

"Yes sir. Just ring the bell if you desire anything."

"Yeah, uh, thanks." The luxurious bathroom has me stumbling to find words.

I decided to step under the shower for a quick rinse even though I showered before we left. I feel a little grimy, travel always leaves a layer of dirt on your skin, even in a private jet, and I hate that. When I walk into the gigantic shower, I'm stunned to find four shower heads and dozens of jets in the walls. I turn on a faucet and watch as the shower room becomes a car wash for people with hot water shooting in every direction. I take my entire shower walking through each spray of water. It's very Austin-like and I'm glad he's not in here to see me behaving like a tourist who's never seen a shower before. The top half of the exterior wall is tinted glass and I'm certain it's the type I can see out of but no one can see in. The view from the shower is incredible, the city sprawls before me and I feel like a king.

When I'm finished playing with the water and dried off, I get dressed in my tuxedo putting on all the pieces except my jacket. It fits me like a glove and it's the most comfortable suit I've ever worn. Lorenzo and his brothers out did themselves. I guess I need to sing Colby's praises as well since he chose the fabric and the design.

"Hey. Oh, dude you look great. I came in to get dressed, did you see that fucking bathroom?" Jackson asks with a touch of awe.

"I took a shower in there. It's awesome."

"I wonder how Violet's doing."

"I can't wait to show her the bathroom."

"Yeah. Man, that's going to be fun," he says with a twinkle in his eye, probably imagining the same things I did when I pictured our beautiful girl in that amazing tub.

I leave him to it and go looking for Violet. When I find her, she's dressed and applying makeup with her eye close to a mirror. She's making a face with her tongue poked out in concentration as she applies liner to her lid.

"Hi, how's it going in here?"

"Great. I'm almost finished. There!" She smiles and focuses on me with a suggestive intensity.

"What?" I question.

"You look so handsome. That tux is perfect on you. Is Austin dressed yet?"

"I'm not sure where he is, Jackson's getting dressed in our room. I didn't see Austin before I found you."

"We better go find him and make sure he's getting dressed, so Colby doesn't kill him."

"Okay, I'll follow you." She listens for a breath when she steps out of her dressing room. She turns to go further down the hall, another double doored bedroom is in front of us. She knocks loudly on the door.

I can hear muffled voices in the room and when the door opens, we're greeted with a half-dressed Colby. Thankfully his bottom half is covered.

"Is Austin in here?" Violet asks.

He points to the door on the far side of the bed. I think this room is an exact mirror to our giant bedroom. I expect to see a large walk-in closet when the door opens and I'm not disappointed. Tremont is on his knees tying Austin's shoe and it looks wrong.

"What are you doing?" Violet questions.

"Getting ready. Whoa! Baby, you look gorgeous!"

"Thank you. I mean why is Tremont on his knees, couldn't you tie your own shoes?"

"Oh, don't worry Miss Violet, it's my job. I offered for Mr. Austin to let me tie his shoes, that way he can keep his pants from wrinkling while he bends down."

"I see. Carry on." Violet rolls her eyes at me and shakes her head. Austin is always up for anything, offering him a butler might not be ideal, but he's going to make full use of the service. He's not a pretentious jerk or anything, he just gets joy from stuff like this, stuff he would never experience in his daily life. When we're all dressed Evan offers to take some pictures of us. We pose around Violet and Colby steps out of the last few so we have some pictures of just us. When Colby sends me all the images, I'm happy to see how good we look. We clean up nice. Of course Violet is the jewel at the center of our relationship and she's a stunning gem in red.

The ballroom is massive and it looks like a fantasy of twinkle lights and white surfaces. Our tuxedos are a vibrant contrast to the neutral surroundings. Violet is a beacon in her red dress, she looks like the star of the show and I hope her friends aren't the jealous type because not even the bride will outshine her.

There are four long tables set beautifully with glimmering China and sparkling glasses, the rest of the room is taken up by a buffet and an enormous dance floor. The staff immediately come to life with more appearing as if by magic. They circulate with trays of hors d'oeuvres, I take something on a stick and it's delicious but I have no clue what it was. Several other guests arrive and the servers continue to move amongst them. I'm searching for someone who could be Max. So far, no one is meeting the description I got, nor do they look like someone Violet would date.

"Don't forget you need to introduce me to people, I don't know any of them," I remind her and take hold of her hand. She smiles at me.

"Don't worry, I couldn't possibly forget about you, handsome."

As if a wave passes through the room, the guests turn almost in sync and my attention is drawn to a tall man with dark hair. He has visible tattoos on his hands and neck, a piercing in his brow, and multiple earrings hang from the ear I can see. His hair is long on top and hangs to one side while the sides are shaved close. I think there's a tattoo on his scalp beneath the thin layer of hair. He scans the room and when his eyes are drawn to the beauty in red held in my grasp, he smiles and his eyes sparkle. My gut clenched uncomfortably at his reaction to his ex, who's my current.

Austin steps close and encloses Violet between us. Then I notice Jackson is right behind her with his hand on her waist. She squeezes my hand and I accept it as affectionate reassurance. She tenses when Max approaches us, it's subtle but with her hand in mine I feel the shift.

"Violet. You look stunning, I love your hair."

"Thanks. It was getting in my way and I needed a change. You look great."

"Thanks. Do you want to introduce me?" he asks looking between the three of us, I'm not going to lie, we're standing tall and our chests are puffed out. We've never dealt with a threat like this before and we're being overly cautious until we know it's safe to relax.

"Sure. Guys, this is Max. Max, this is Pierson, Austin, and Jackson, my boyfriends." Max reaches to shake my free hand and I shake his hand with a friendly but firm grip. Austin has to release Violet's hand to shake with Max and Jackson comes from behind us to shake his hand.

"Nice to meet you."

"Yes, nice to meet you." We exchange the expected pleasantries.

Max looks at us then at Violet before he asks, “Would it be all right if we spoke in private?”

Violet answers, “Sure.” She kisses each of us, then looks to Max, “Lead the way.” He puts his hand through her elbow and leads her from the room. We watch them leave and then look at each other unsure of what to do now.

“Let’s get a drink.” Austin suggests and we follow him to the bar. The servers are setting up the buffet items and they’re covered but I caught a glimpse of some lobster tails. My stomach grumbles in response to the food and I realize it’s been a long time since I ate a meal. I had some snacks on the plane but I haven’t eaten since breakfast. Jackson and I get bottles of beer and Austin has a caramel-colored liquid in a short glass.

“What do you think they’re talking about?” I ask my brothers.

Jackson answers, “They’re probably apologizing for how they left things last time they saw each other. I know Violet wants to apologize to him, she feels bad about breaking up with him when she was so distraught about her parents. She says she doesn’t feel bad about killing his scumbag father, but I know she’s worried it somehow made his life more difficult. They’re probably catching up, filling in the months they’ve been apart.”

“I’m sure he’s got questions about us. She dumped him and met us not that long after she said she didn’t want to be in a relationship, that’s gotta burn at least a little, right?” Austin asks and takes a sip from his glass.

“Yeah. I’d probably be pissed if I was him. But his whole life blew up and he took off so who knows how things have been for him. Maybe he’s just happy she’s happy,” I add, hoping what I’m saying is true.

A huge guy with a tiny pixie on his arm heads our way and I think this must be the bride and groom. She’s bubbling over with excitement and she rushes in to hug Austin and then Jackson.

“Hi! You guys look fantastic! Oh! You must be Pierson, hi. I’m Harmony and this is Mike, it’s so nice to meet you, finally.” I hold out my hand to shake hers and she pushes past it and hugs me. Mike gives me a resigned smile.

"Just go with it, she hugs everyone. It's nice to meet you at last. I've been hearing about you for weeks, thanks for your service." Ugh, I never know what to say to that.

"Yeah. Sure. Nice to meet you both."

"Where's my maid of honor? I thought for sure I'd find her attached to you guys."

Austin responds, "She stepped out for a minute, with Max."

"Oh. Sorry. How was that... meeting him?"

Jackson answers this time, "He seems decent. We only met him for a moment."

Mike speaks next, "He's a great guy and he's in a good place now. I think they'll be able to work out their friendship. He was nervous to meet you guys."

"Why?" I blurt.

"She didn't love him like she loves you. Plus, there's three of you, duh! That's got to be intimidating for her ex," Harmony explains.

"Yeah. That's probably harder than us meeting one ex. I hope they can be friends, she felt really bad about the way things ended between them," Austin adds.

"I know. But it was the right thing to do, it was just unfortunate it happened when she lost her parents and she wasn't in an emotional space to deal with it in the best way." Harmony expands on her thoughts with sadness filling her voice.

"Well, it's between them and it's not up to us so we'll just support their choices, right?" Mike asks Harmony.

"Of course. It's totally up to them." She pulls on him and he leans down to kiss her. He's big enough to be a linebacker for the Bucs. He reminds me of Dozer, if I remember right Violet said he doesn't play sports, except golf. He's a suit in a law office somewhere.

"Didn't Violet say you're moving to Texas after the wedding?" I ask hoping to change the subject.

"Yeah, Mike got a job offer we couldn't refuse. It's why we moved up the wedding. We still get a honeymoon but it's going to be shorter than we planned originally."

"Where are you going for your honeymoon?" Austin asks.

"A few Caribbean islands. It's ten days by sailboat to the different ports."

Jackson says, "That sounds amazing. I always wanted to sail off to an island. There's a lot of pirate wrecks down there, do you dive?"

"Yeah, we both got certified before college and we keep up with it. It's almost a sin if you live in Florida and you don't make the most of the water, right?" Mike asks.

"Yeah, I got certified in the Navy. It's a whole other world below the surface."

Harmony looks at me, "Have you dived in the Caribbean?"

"No. I've been around Africa, Australia, and close to Japan." I don't specify locations; some of my diving experiences are classified.

Colby comes over and hugs Harmony then shakes Mike's hand, "How do you like the party?"

"It's beautiful Colby! You did a great job, I love the opulence of the art deco style, thanks for arranging this. When do we eat? I'm starving." Harmony bounces while she talks. She's like a little kid unable to keep still and she reminds me of Isabel.

Colby checks his watch, "It should be ready in a few minutes. Have some hors d'oeuvres while we wait." He waves over a server with a full tray of three choices. I take something on a piece of crisp bread. Harmony takes a napkin and then loads it with one of each type of the small treats. Mike smiles at her while she eats and it makes me remember Violet said Harmony used to have an eating disorder. She's very small but she looks healthy and she wolfs down her appetizers.

Colby looks around and then he wanders off towards one of the uniformed workers who appear to be in charge. There is a DJ setting up a few pieces of equipment and plugging things into large speakers on poles. When he plays some soft music, I see Colby heading for him next.

A side door opens and Violet enters followed by Max, she joins us and takes my hand. She looks good, happy, and Max seems okay too. Before any of us can say anything, the DJ asks us to find our seats. Violet pulls me towards the main table surrounded by the others. Jackson and I sit next to Violet and Austin sits across from her. Colby sits next to him then Harmony, Mike and Max round out our table. I hoped Max would bring a date, then I'd be more relaxed about him but he seems to be here alone.

"Everything go okay with Max?" I whisper to Violet.

She whispers back, "Yeah. We're good. He forgave me, he told me about what he's been up to and he asked me more about you guys. He's happy in Europe and plans to stay there for now. He has the board running the family business and he's taking some classes. He's studying marine life near Norway."

"That sounds interesting."

"I think so too. I'm happy for him and I think we'll be friends, but probably never as close as we used to be."

"Are you okay with that?"

"I'm good. Mostly I wanted to apologize, he made it easy and forgave me instantly. He said some nice things about me and I think he's actually doing well, not just saying it to make me feel better."

"Good. I'm glad you were able to put it behind you. Do you feel better now?"

"Much. My anxiety was really high worrying about how things would go with him, but he's a really good person and he doesn't hold grudges. I've changed so much I expected him to be different, but he's still kind and sweet. He's dating someone, she might make it for the wedding but she was having trouble getting here in time for the party. We'll see." I feel a huge weight lift from my chest.

Knowing Max is dating someone helps me accept that he's not going to take Violet away from me.

Feeling much lighter, I'm excited to eat some dinner. My stomach's been waiting with an attitude. Once we're able to get some food my appetite settles and I'm having a good time, out with our girl and my brothers, dressed up, it's a nice change. When Violet's finished eating, she pulls me onto the dance floor and I hold her close while we sway to the music. When the song changes Austin comes to take over, I take a break and head out to the restroom. I bump into Max in the hallway.

"Hey. How's it going? Are you having fun?"

"Yeah. The food was great, now we're dancing."

"I'm probably going to head out soon, jet lag is kicking my ass."

"Where did you fly in from?"

"I had to go to London for something at work, then to New York and from there I was able to fly here today. But I'm still on Norwegian time and it feels much later than it is in this time zone."

"Well, I know Violet is really glad you were able to make it. She wanted a chance to talk to you before the wedding."

"Me too. She's the reason I worked so hard to get here today." My stomach tightens.

He continues, "I'm very happy with what I'm doing and with my father gone, the only negative thing in my life was my relationship with Violet and being at odds with how it should be. Talking things out with her is a huge relief. She was a great friend and I felt terrible. I left with her grieving both parents and I wasn't there for her at all. The guilt was weighing on me, but she forgave me and we can be friends again, it's lifted a huge burden."

"For her too. I'm really glad you were able to work things out."

"You and your brothers are very lucky. Violet's a special girl and I'll always love her, like a sister. I'm happy for her that she found the loves of her life, nobody deserves love as much as she does."

"Yeah, we think she's very special and we're very much in love with her. We're thinking about making it more permanent." I don't know why I just told him that. We haven't even asked Violet about it yet. It must be my insecurity trying to make him aware how strong our relationship is so he won't get any ideas. I want to kick myself, I hope he's not as gossipy as I seem to be.

"Wow. That's cool. I hope you guys can work it out, I've never seen her so happy. She's obviously very much in love with the three of you." Max smiles a kind grin and my testosterone calms down. He's a nice guy who's happy for his friend.

"Thanks, man. Well, I'm gonna hit the head. If you stick around for a few minutes, I'm sure Violet will want to dance with you."

"Yeah. I'll check it out. See you in there."

"Okay." I smile and take off to the men's room. Geez, I'm such a blabbermouth I hope my brothers don't kill me and Max doesn't blab.

When I step back into the ballroom, Violet is dancing with Max, they're laughing and chatting, she looks happy and I feel like an idiot for being jealous. Jackson watches me approach from across the room.

"How you doing?" Austin asks when I join them at the edge of the dance floor.

"I'm good. I feel kind of stupid for worrying about her seeing him."

Jackson offers his opinion, "Don't beat yourself up, you're not used to being in love and Violet's different from most girls. Now you know how she rolls and you can be relaxed in the future."

"I guess. I did something really dumb." They both examine my face and I can feel the heat of embarrassment for what I told Max. They wait for me to elaborate.

"I was talking to Max in the hallway and I may have blurted that we want to make things more permanent with Violet." They both roll their eyes.

"Bro, what the fuck? We haven't even asked Violet about it yet, why would you tell him?"

"I wasn't handling his presence all that well as you mentioned, it just came out. I think I was trying to warn him off, maybe?"

"Dude, not cool. We're going to need to talk to her before he says anything. Hopefully he's not saying it right now," Jackson admonishes.

"Yeah, we need to talk to her about it."

"Talk to who about what?" Violet asks.

"You. Will you come with us?" I ask her in return.

"Sure. Where are we going?"

"Let's step out on the balcony." We file out through the door and the patio looks like another fantasy wonderland. It's decked out with fairy lights and the pergolas have wispy drapes that move in the gentle breeze. There are palm trees and other greenery keeping this space private from the patio and pool beyond. It makes me feel like we're on our own private island.

"What's up?" Violet looks between us.

Since I was the jackass who blabbed our personal business, I speak up, "We've been talking and we wondered how you feel about our relationship, what do you see in the future for us?"

"How far in the future?"

"I don't know, like a few years?"

Austin tries to clarify, "How do you see our relationship over time?" She looks confused but I give her a minute.

"Are you asking if I want to get married someday?"

"Yes," Jackson answers.

"I haven't thought much about the legal aspects of our relationship. Marriage is just a contract saying we agree to share our finances, property, and responsibilities. I think we can agree to all of that without involving the government, and we could have some sort of ceremony just for us. You know like they used to do for gay couples in the dark ages. I'm not opposed to making our relationship official between us with our friends and family to celebrate. Is that what you meant?"

"Yes. We love you and we want to spend our lives with you, forever." Jackson takes her hand and looks into her eyes.

"Yeah. That's what we want." Austin takes her other hand.

"I want that too. I'm so in love with you and I want you to be mine, ours, for the rest of our lives." I stand in front of her between my brothers and rest my hands on her hips. I place a soft kiss on her lips and then search her dark eyes for her response.

She carefully looks into each of our eyes and takes her hands to place on each of our cheeks when she kisses us.

"I love you. I only want to be with you, forever. If you want us to have a ceremony of some sort, I want that too. You have me, now and always, I'll never want anyone else. You're the ones for me, you understand me, you support me, you take care of me, you love me and my cat, you accept all of my baggage. You're perfect for me. Plus, I'm pretty sure nobody else would be willing to box with me, practice parkour, go to target practice, and hunt down and kill the bad guys like you three. There's nobody else for me."

I fall to my knees and my hands squeeze her waist, "Violet, will you marry me?"

"Yes." She leans down and pushes her tongue into my mouth kissing me passionately.

Austin gets on one knee and still holding her hand he looks into her eyes and asks, "I love you Violet Henley, will you marry me?"

"Yes." He stands and wraps his arms around her pushing me out of his way, they kiss. I keep one hand on her.

Jackson clears his throat gaining her attention, then bends on one knee, "Violet, will you marry me?"

"Yes."

"Fuck yeah!" He lifts her up and she wraps her legs around him while he kisses her, not an easy feat in her dress and she'd probably be flashing everyone if we weren't alone.

Austin points out, "We don't have a ring."

"I have an idea for that." The three of them look at me, "We can figure out the details when we get home. Okay?"

"Okay."

"Yep."

"Cool."

I made a couple drawings after we talked about marrying her the other day. I came up with a design that has three stones to represent the three of us. If they like it, we can have it made for her. I'm feeling much better after coming clean about my big mouth and even better she agreed to marry us. This might be the best day of my life!

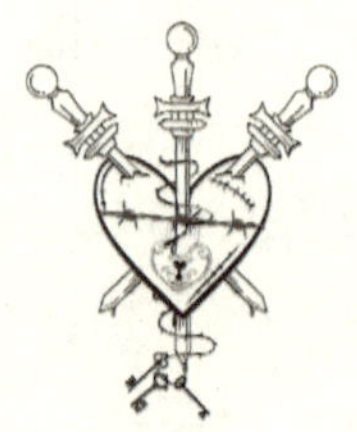

Chapter Thirty-Three

Violet

It's good to be back home. The wedding was great, Harmony made a beautiful bride. It was fun seeing all of my friends and I enjoyed having some time with her before she takes off for the lone star state. I'm also really grateful I was able to work things out with Max. We're friends once again, but we'll never be close like we were. He's living across the ocean in Norway for now and he's probably going to stay in Europe because his girlfriend is Swedish. She's also a student and they met on a boat, it's a sweet story. I'm okay with things being this way with Max, I just couldn't stand to be enemies, I would've hated that.

The thing that made my head spin was when my boyfriends asked me to marry them. I didn't fully understand what prompted them to ask right then, but Pierson explained in more detail later and I get it. Poor guy was worried about Max, I never loved Max the way I love Pierson and his brothers. We're all good now and our relationship is more solid than ever.

I'm going to miss that beautiful enormous bathroom. We may need to build a bathroom addition like the one we had in that hotel, it was spectacular. We had hours of fun in that tub and shower. I'm pretty sure Jackson has been measuring the back of the house trying to lay out the boundaries to build it. He really liked the tub, he was able to fuck me so long and deep in there it was amazing. We tried out so many new positions and they're only possible in that tub. I came so hard, I can still feel the tingles now. At one point, we all came so much we had to request Gatorade from Tremont to get our electrolytes back on track. Overall, it was a great trip.

I'm excited about today, I'm getting the first part of my new tattoo done. It's a big piece so it has to be done over a few sessions. I wanted to start with the hardest part and get it over with, so Nemo's getting the section under my arm completed first. All three of them are coming with me to see Nemo, the tattoo artist who put the hideous tattoo under my arm in the first place. He made stencils from Pierson's drawing and he's lining it up perfectly to make the ugly rectangle into the side mirror on the handlebars of my black beauty. The forks and front tire will wrap around the front of my ribs. Then the majority of the bike will be on my back with the wings arching up towards my shoulder blades. Pierson's drawing is wicked and sexy.

My phone rings with an unknown number, I usually wouldn't answer but my mood is too good and I'm up for a chat with a salesperson, probably about my car warranty.

"Hello?"

"Is this Violet Henley?"

"Yes. Who's this?"

"Hi. I'm Patricia Bear, I believe you know my cousin, Kristos Chitto. I was hoping you would be willing to meet with me."

"Why?"

"I want to meet you because we're related and if you're willing, I'd like to introduce you to some of your other family members. What do you think?"

"I have other family members?"

"Yes, you have some blood relatives, but you also have the family clan of our tribe. You're a quarter Ishkohatchee, we want you to get to know us and our ways. We want you to visit whenever you like and we hope to build a relationship with you. Your father wouldn't do anything for the tribe, he wanted nothing to do with us. His only interest was in the money he could get from the tribal income. We removed him from our tribe and his ability to earn any income, but it doesn't keep you from interacting with us, if you like."

"I have very few family members who are still alive and Kristos is my only living blood relative, it would be wonderful to meet some others since I refuse to have anything to do with him. When are you available?"

We arranged to meet on Saturday, at a coffee shop. I can't wait to tell the guys.

My under arm is mostly numb at this point. Nemo has the outlines finished and he's working on shading now. My shoulder is cramped, but I can suck it up for a while longer.

"Baby, what's hurting?" Austin asks as he stares at my face from only inches away.

"Are you watching for me to be in pain?"

"Yeah. I came to help you. If something hurts, let's move you until you're more comfortable,"

"It's no big deal, I just have a cramp."

"Nemo, will you stop for a second and let her stretch?"

He stops and leans away from me, "Okay, Violent, you can move. Go ahead and stretch or shift until you're more comfortable. You've got about thirty more minutes in this area."

"You don't have to call me that anymore. You can just call me Violet," I say, stretching my arm out above my head. I twist my waist and then bring my knees to my chest and pull on them. My back cracks and the cramp in my shoulder releases.

"I know. It's just what I've been calling you since we met, plus I think it's cool." If he knew precisely how true that name is he may not be so enamored with it. But his suspicions have not been confirmed, so it's just a fantasy for him. Like if we all pretend we're wizards attending Hogwarts, but in my case, I know Dumbledore personally and nobody outside of a few people would ever believe it.

"Thanks. All right, let's get back to it."

"Your wish is my command, Violent One." I barely keep my eyes from rolling, I think some of his excitement with code names comes from playing video games with Colby, he sounds just like him sometimes.

"I forgot to tell you guys about the call I got." I explain about Patricia Bear and the possibility of more relatives. They're happy for me but skeptical.

"All I'm saying is, we don't know these people and after how your father turned out you just need to be cautious."

"She doesn't want anything from me, she just wants to meet me. She said my father didn't want anything to do with them beyond any money they could give him, but they knew about me. They're family oriented and they want to offer me a chance to know my heritage."

"Jackson's right, you just need to be careful. Hopefully they don't want anything but a friendly relationship, but until you find out for sure, watch your back," Austin adds.

"Will they let us go with you?" Pierson questions.

"We're just meeting for coffee. I want to go alone, but if she invites me to her home, I'll bring you."

"We might just hang out near the coffee shop for safety."

"Jackson, come on. A coffee shop is safe, people meet blind dates from the internet at coffee shops because they're safe. It will be daylight, a bunch of people will be around, I'm going alone."

When Jackson opens his mouth to argue Austin cuts in, "That sounds very safe. We trust your judgement and you can call us if you need us. So, Nemo, how long will the rest of her tattoo take?"

Nemo looks between me and Jackson, probably to make sure we're done, "I think I can get it finished with three more sessions like this and then after it heals you can come back for some fine details and touch ups."

"I'm looking forward to having it completed." The time passes slowly when you're being stabbed by tiny needles in a nerve center, but it does pass eventually. I broke down and took the pain reliever Pierson offered. I feel a little like I got run over by a train that backed up and ran me over again.

We skipped our plans to eat dinner out because I wasn't up for it, thankfully my guys are sweet and understanding. They took me home and pampered me with foot rubs, snacks, and horror movies. I fell asleep during the last one and somebody carefully carried me to bed. When I woke up in the middle of the night Pierson was there with a glass of water and more pain relievers. I need to ask if they took turns watching me all night or if it was just him.

I've caught them whispering a few times and I'm not sure what they're up to. We put the game on hold when everything went down with my relatives, and then the wedding was right after that, but it's back on now. They're probably sneaking around getting all their tasks done so they can win and plan a trip. We gave up on the chores as a prize. It just wasn't enough incentive. We always work together to do the chores and it's almost like a family bonding ritual. It would be weird if we had one person sitting around not working while the rest of us were cleaning. Austin was a little disappointed, he hates dishes and laundry.

My plan is to meet my relative, Patricia Bear, today at the coffee shop near town and then I'm going to the range to complete the next task. By going alone I'm hopeful they won't know I got the task done and they'll be a little behind. Although, I'm fairly certain Jackson has already completed the task. When we were talking about restarting the game he kept using past tense for the clue I'm on.

Once I'm showered and have tattoo cream smeared all over my armpit and side, I dress in long pants, boots, and long sleeves. I struggle to get my jacket on without pain, and it pulls on my raw skin a little when I move wrong, but it's tolerable. I left on my bike and I tool around a little before going to the coffee shop. I was only looking for nosey boyfriends following me for the first five minutes of the ride, I swear.

When I enter the shop, I spot a dark-haired woman who looks to be in her mid-fifties. She smiles when she sees me and waves. I texted her a description so she'd recognize me assuming my father never shared any photos. I order a chocolatey coffee and approach her table.

"Hi, you must be Violet, nobody else in here has your hairstyle, I like it by the way, it suits you. Please, have a seat. I'm Patricia, you can call me Patty if you like."

"Hi, Patty. It's nice to meet you. I ordered a coffee, can I get you anything?"

"No. One is enough for me." She holds up her half empty cup. Her hair is long and straight with some gray near her temples. She has pretty dark eyes and very few wrinkles. Her cheekbones are high and her lips are full, like mine. She's a nice-looking woman and there's kindness in her eyes. She has some features in common with Kristos, but there isn't a kind bone in his body.

"When did you last hear from Kristos?"

"Me personally, it's been maybe fifteen years. The tribe elders spoke with him not too long ago, he was threatening to sue the tribe for his earnings again, but we have a judgement from the Federal Court banning him from the tribe and the right to earn any income from us. It doesn't matter, tribal law supersedes anything in the courts, but he had an attorney file a suit against the tribe, so we had to fight back in the courts. The tribe banished him and to us that's all that matters. But like I explained on the phone, none of that applies to you. I have to confess I looked you up online and I read about your parents. I thought it might be good for you to meet some relatives that are nothing like Kristos."

"It would be nice to meet a relative that isn't trying to kill me."

"Kristos tried to kill you?" She looks alarmed.

"Yeah. He held a gun to my head. My adoptive grandmother also tried to kill me and my boyfriends, so I haven't had the best luck with relatives lately."

"Wow. I'm sorry to hear this. I knew Kristos was bad news but I had no idea he would harm his own child."

"He wanted me to work with him doing mafia stuff, but when it looked like he wasn't going to get away with that, he tried to use me as a hostage to escape. Thankfully the FBI was right there and they were able to take him into custody."

"I wondered if you knew about his crimes. He's a bad man without any morals. The tribe doesn't put up with any criminal activity, we refuse to engage with the mafia or any other criminals. They don't like it because of the casinos. They try to get us to work with them but it's not our way. We make money and we support the tribe, we don't need to steal or do anything else illegal to make a profit."

"Good. I wouldn't work with him. He and my grandmother were involved in multiple illegal enterprises and I'm helping the FBI shut it down."

"Yes. Good. If you'd like to meet some relatives, you have my parents who are Aunt and Uncle to your father. You have more cousins like me, and your grandfather."

"My grandfather? I didn't think Kristos's parents were alive."

"His mother isn't. She left with him when he was a child, and his father tried to care for him and see him but she made it difficult. There was a time when we were in our teens that he came and stayed on our land with us, but he left after he got into some trouble. After that we only saw him when he wanted money. Unfortunately, there is one cousin who still communicates with him. He's not of good moral character himself, he has trouble with addiction. He's always been willing to follow Kristos around and do his bidding. We're hoping now that Kristos is in jail, Henreid, or Henri as we call him, will be free of that monster."

"After meeting Kristos I can see how he can be persuasive, he had some people in his office following him around and wanting to do anything to get in his favor."

"But not you."

"No. I'm against trafficking, especially of humans. I would never work with someone who's capable of such terrible crimes."

"Good. I think you should meet your grandfather and the rest of the tribe."

"I'm willing to meet any relatives and members of the tribe, but I don't want anything from them. I don't need any money, will it be a problem?"

"No, it's no problem. If you like you can set up your earnings to be donated back to the tribe, you can even designate it to specific purposes." She grins at me and her teeth are wide and straight, she has a small dimple on one side of her kind smile.

I smile in return, "That sounds perfect. Please tell me about my grandfather."

"He's a strong man with many skills, very intelligent. He's part of the tribal elders now and his guidance has benefited the tribe, he's respected. Kristos's sins do not taint any of his family. Your grandfather's name is Bartholomew Chitto, he is the leader of the snake family clan. We are joined with the Bear and Turtle family clans and we work with two other clans. My father is of the Bear family clan, my mother is from the snake clan."

She goes on to explain some of the significance of the clans and the representative animals. She tells me a story of how the Snake came to be a clan, the Snake is smart, strong, and efficient. The Snake outsmarted the Fox and was able to feed his family for many days with his kill. The Turtle questioned if the Snake was evil, but the Turtle and the Bear determined the Snake was smart and not evil. It's all very interesting. I wonder if they would think I'm evil for my kills, or if I'm just smart, strong, and efficient. Are those virtues worth having?

We make a plan for me to visit the tribe and when we say goodbye, she hugs me. Though I'm usually not a fan of hugging, especially people I just met, her hug is kind and warm, I'm okay with it. After I walk her to her car, I take off on my bike for the gun range.

Mitch is at the counter, "Hey Violet!" He looks around behind me, after a moment he seems to come to some conclusion, "You're here for the clue, aren't you?"

"I am. Can I assume my partners have already been here?"

"You know I can't tell you that. Let me grab what you need, be right back."

I look around and I don't recognize anyone else in the shop right now. I look over the smaller handguns in the glass display case in front of me. There's a pink twenty-two, I mean Pepto pink, who would want that?

"Okay, here's your supplies. You have to use everything in the box, you can't use anything of yours. Did you bring a firearm?"

"Yeah. Here, you can hang onto it." I pull my Sig from the holster in the back of my waist and eject the chambered round and the clip then clear it for safety. I hand the butt to him and he threads a lock through the barrel and places it into a locker behind the counter.

"All right, you're on lane fourteen, talk to Ashley if you need anything. Any questions?"

"Nope. I'm all set, thanks." I take the box and enter the outer chamber, I put on my eyes and ears and look over the rest of the items in the box.

After I load the badger target and send it to the far wall. I sight the gun and squeeze the trigger. I hit the center of the bull's eye only slightly off to the left, I make a minute adjustment and fire again. This time it's a little to the right. I fire again and hit a little lower and between those two shots. I continue to adjust and fire. When I've emptied all of the rounds, I pack up and head back to the counter. I set the box next to my used target and wait for Mitch to finish what he's doing.

He has a confused look on his face when he asks, "Are you okay? You need something?"

"No, I'm done."

"Oh. That was really fast."

"Yeah? Compared to who?" I smile, giving him my most innocent look.

"Not going to tell you that. Let me just check your target." He lifts the page and from the back. I can see the smiley face made of bullet holes clearly.

"Holy fuck! Who shot that?" Some large sweaty guy dressed in camo from head-to-toe leans over me to look at the target. "Look at this Gabe!"

Another large man presses in on my other side and I'm about to shoot them both. Haven't people heard of personal space by now?

"Whoa! Mitch, who's the sharpshooter? You gotta tell us! We could use him on our team." I shake my head at Mitch and step away from the cavemen.

Mitch chuckles, "Aww come on guys, you know I can't talk about other clients. Gun range client privilege and all that."

"Dude, seriously, I'll buy another gun, I'll give you the twin hundred bucks in my wallet, what will it take? We gotta talk to this guy and see if he'll join our team. We could wipe up the floor with Reggie's team if we had a guy like this. Come on man, spill!"

"Sorry guys, no can do, but when I see this client again, I'll mention your team and let them decide if they want to call you."

"You suck!"

"Hey, do you want me to tell them or not?"

"Fine, you don't suck, but you gotta talk to him for us."

"He said he would, come on, let's go practice."

"Yeah, all right, see ya later."

"See ya."

When they enter the range, I go back to the counter.

"I'm assuming I don't actually need to ask you if you're interested in their team?"

"No. Please don't. What do I need to do for the next clue?"

"You passed. Give me just one minute and I'll get it for you." He takes the box into the back room and leaves my target on the counter. I push it away from me.

"All right, here you go. I have instructions. You have to wait a minimum of twenty-four hours to open the clue. Then you have twenty-four hours to complete the task. If you're unable to complete the task in the allotted time you must contact the *Game Master* for a new task. Do you understand these instructions?"

"I do." He hands me the clue. "What did Colby give you to do this for him?"

"Ha! He didn't give me anything, I was excited to participate. I told him next time I want to be a contestant, but not if it's a shooting competition. I would lose." He offers me a goofy grin.

"All right. Thanks, Mitch. Give the baby a kiss for me."

"Oh, I will, but I have news."

"Yeah?" I pause.

"We're expecting. She's due in June."

"Congratulations! That's great! You made my day."

“Thanks, we’re pretty excited.”

When I leave the range, I consider what might be inside the envelope secured in my saddle bag. If the guys already have their clues I wonder if they opened them yet, maybe they haven’t since they haven’t rushed off anywhere to complete a task, that I know of anyways.

I decided to make a stop and check in with my favorite librarian on the way home. When I was at her house, she mentioned there’s a special collection in the reference section at this branch about the local tribes, and the Ishkohatchee are included.

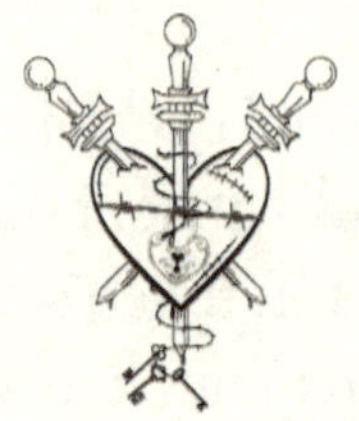

Chapter Thirty-Four

Pierson

I haven't opened my clue yet. I've held onto it for far too long now, since wrecking my bike and everything that went down with Violet's father. I haven't been focused on it but I just need to do it. I'm worried it'll be something really difficult and I won't have time to finish it. I'm pretty sure Jackson and Austin have already completed theirs. For all I know maybe Violet has too and pacing around the envelope isn't helping. Violet's out meeting her relatives, Jackson and Austin went to work out, it's the perfect time to open it.

Sawyer's been watching me from his perch on his cat tree, his eyes are closed now but his tail continues to twitch. He doesn't think I'll do it.

"Okay, I'm doing it, quit judging me." His eyes open a crack and he closes them again indifferent to my accusation.

I tear open the end of the sealed envelope. I press on the edges forcing open the torn end and shake it until the paper inside falls onto the table. Eyeing the folded page as if it may attack me, I swoop in and unfold it to find a message:

Congratulations!

Welcome to your next task. Remember you have only twenty-four hours from now to complete this activity. Mark down the time, better yet, set the timer on your phone so you don't go over. If your task isn't completed within the time, you MUST contact the Game Master before time runs out. You will be given a substitute task. Yes, it will be much more difficult to complete but it won't be timed. Trust me, you want to finish this task on time.

Go to: Ponce de Leon Springs Park

Ask for: Maryanne, she works in the North snack bar

Once you have the items you must not go home until the task is complete. You must deliver $1,000 to the Sisters of the Sacred Heart Church before time runs out. You cannot use any of your own money. All of the money, every cent, must be given to you by strangers. You can beg and plead, even perform, but you cannot steal. Good luck!

"Holy fuck! Thanks a lot Sawyer! Why'd you make me open it? Fuck!" Sawyer takes off when I yell, "Eh, who needs him anyway." I need to think about this. I'm seeking gifted funds to donate to a church. I can beg for it or I can *perform.* Maybe I can do something else to bring in that kind of money. I collect my supplies and dress for the weather. I even apply sunscreen which I usually forget.

I work on a note for my brothers and Violet, I'm borrowing her SUV and hope she doesn't mind. I crumple the note and start over.

Dear Violet, Jax, and Auz-

I needed to run some errands and since my bike's still in the shop I borrowed the SUV. I don't know how late I'll be or if I'll have a signal. Don't worry about me for dinner.

See you later.

Love, Pierson

It'll have to do. I wonder if they've already done their task. I don't recall any of them being MIA for any significant amount of time, how would they hide it from us? I didn't do a good job, they're going to know what I'm doing.

When I pull up at the park, I've added a cooler filled with ice, water, and three sandwiches to my supplies. I find the North snack bar easy enough, there are signs. The line for snacks is long but they move quickly, there's only five items on the menu.

"May I help you?" A girl in a ponytail with braces asks.

"Yes, may I speak to Maryanne?"

"Maryanne! There's a guy for you!" she yells.

"Thanks."

"Next!" I step aside and wait for Maryanne.

She's older than the teeny-bopper with braces, but not by much, maybe a sophomore in college. The girl is tall and extremely thin with blonde hair, also pulled into a ponytail. She walks around the counter and curls her finger at me.

"Follow me." I follow her outside and she unlocks a storage cabinet. She hands me a bag that seems to contain a camp chair, a huge rectangular bag with a handle which is as heavy as it looks, a lock box, and a gold legal envelope. I stand like an idiot waiting for her to tell me what to do.

"That's everything. The rules and signs are in the envelope. Make sure you only go to the marked area or Franklin will kick you out. Oh, and good luck." She rushes back inside the shop and I drop the heavy stuff to open the envelope.

The first page is a map of the park with red circles drawn on four areas. The next page is a sign that says: *Please make a donation for abused children.*

The last page has what could be considered instructions.

Rules

1. *Don't set up outside of a red circle on the map.*

2. *You're only allowed the one sign.*

3. *You must set up the chair and tent.*

4. *Collect the donations in the lock box, keep it safe.*

5. *When you believe there's $1,000 in the box, take it to the place named in your clue.*

Good luck, the kids are counting on you!

I'm flabbergasted, this is going to be one hell of a long twenty-four hours. The park closes at sunset, but it opens at sunrise, so I can finish in the morning if I have to. Not wanting to waste any more time, I throw the tent and chair handles over my shoulder and trek to the car. According to the circles on the map I can set up in the parking lot by the playground, the parking lot by the south snack bar, the parking lot by the pier, or the area in front or the dog park.

I drive to each location and look over the crowds. It's a sunny day but there's a coolish breeze warm enough to be on the beach but not heat stroke weather. Because it's a nice day the dog park is packed. I can do this.

I pull into the grass to unload and set up and attach the tent to the SUV so it doesn't blow away. Opening the chair I place it next to the cooler and set out the table. Once I have everything arranged, I open my easel on the table and lay out my charcoal crayons, watercolor pencils, and erasers. The sign gets taped to the edge of the tent so people walking into the fenced dog area can see it.

I sit down and start drawing Sawyer. I have his details in my head so it's quick and easy. I draw him in a cartoonish, comic book style. He has an expression of superiority and I draw a little thought bubble above his head. Inside it says, *Really, a dog park?*

I'm hoping it will be received as funny, not offensive to these dog people. I love dogs and if any of them speak to me I'll make it clear. I hang the picture next to the sign. I immediately begin drawing a German Shepherd, there's one inside the park right now. This one almost looks more like a caricature and the dog has a very human expression. His thought bubble says, *Yo! Did you bring a bag?* I hang it next to Sawyer and start on another one.

This time I drew a Border Collie, they're such cute dogs. I have it lying down on a dog bed and it looks annoyed. The thought bubble for it says, *I hate counting sheep!* I add a few outlines of sheep like they're imaginary jumping over the dog's stomach. When I stand up to tape it next to the other dog picture a couple is looking at the pictures, they have two Yorkies on leashes.

"Can you do Yorkies?" the woman asks.

"Sure." I smile.

Her husband looks at me skeptically, "How much will it cost?"

I point to the sign, "I'm accepting donations for abused children in exchange for the pictures."

"How much do we have to donate?" he asks like he caught me doing something wrong.

"I suppose that's up to you. How much do you want to donate to help abused children?"

"How do I know you're really giving the money to the charity?"

"I'm going straight to Sisters of the Sacred Heart Church the minute I'm finished here and handing them that box and whatever's in it. You're welcome to escort me or call them and check afterwards."

"Come on honey, the pictures are so cute and I believe him. Give him fifty dollars."

"Are you crazy? Fifty dollars?"

"Yes. It's for charity. I really want the picture, it'll be so cute, we can hang it in the study. Pleeease?" She bats her eyelashes at the guy and he caves.

"Fine. Here, it better be good." He pushes a fifty through the slot in the lock box.

"Yes sir!" I get to work drawing the two Yorkies, I draw the one jumping up at the other one. The first thought bubble says, *Yay!*

It's mom and dad, they're home! The second bubble says, *Yeah, but what did they bring us?*

The woman is delighted, "Oh my goodness! I *love* it! Thank you so much. You're so talented."

The man calmed down, "Thank you. Good job." He pushes another twenty into the box.

"The children thank you."

"I'm calling Amanda, she has to come over here with *Binky* and *Bubbles*, she'll just die if she misses out." The woman wanders off with her phone pressed to her ear. The man drags the Yorkies to the gate and brings them inside where they can go without their leashes. Another couple is waiting for a turn, and a family stands beside them watching what I'm doing.

I spent the next four hours drawing pets and a couple people. I'm not as good with the people, so they're very much caricatures, but everyone loves them. My hand is killing me and I need to use the restroom. I write a sign and tape it to my chair.

Back in ten minutes! Then I lock the money in the car and walk to the men's room shaking out my hand the entire way. I've been trying to keep track of how much money people are donating but it's not easy because some of them try to hide it from me. I should be right on the cusp of a thousand dollars, I've been averaging five drawings an hour so that makes twenty drawings, at fifty dollars a pop I should be there. But a few people gave more and a few gave less so I really have no idea. When I'm on my way back to the tent I decide to put in at least one more hour just in case.

The line of people watching and waiting never seems to dwindle, the beautiful weather has brought out every dog owner within a hundred miles, and they all want a drawing. After two more hours I've had more than enough. My hand is ready to fall off and it keeps getting pins and needles so I think I drew myself into carpal tunnel syndrome. I made an announcement that this is my last drawing and a few people made a disappointed sound but nobody harassed me. After I finish the drawing of some type of hound mix with long droopy ears, I take down the sign and quickly load up my supplies. When I'm breaking down the tent a little kid asks me what I'm doing.

"Where are you going?" he asks.

"I'm all done so I'm going to take the donations to the church then I'm going home. Are you here alone? Did you drive yourself?"

He giggles and says, "No! I can't drive yet. I drived a go cart when I went to the castle place with my dad. But I can't tell mom cuz I'm not supposed to. Daddy takes me to do fun stuff now that him and mommy are deevorced."

"Yeah? Is your mom here with you?"

"Uh huh. She told Auntie Mawissa my daddy is a badsterd because he didn't get me today. But I think that's a bad word so I'm not supposed to say it. I wish I had a dog."

"Maybe you can get one when you're a little older. Or maybe you can get a cat."

"I like cats. The man next door has a cat and he lets me pet it."

"That's nice. I have a cat at home. Here's a picture of it." I handed him the first picture I drew, the one of Sawyer.

"That's a pretty cat, what does he say?"

I tell him what it says and he laughs hysterically like I told him the funniest thing he's ever heard.

"You can have that drawing if you want."

"Really? Wow! Thanks, mister."

"I'm Pierson, and you're very welcome. What's your name?"

"Bennett. I'm four. I go to school but I can't read yet."

"Don't worry you'll learn in no time. All right buddy, I need to get going. Do you want me to help you find your mom?"

"No. She's right there. She said I could look at the dogs." He points to a woman with very long braids and a lot of gold jewelry, talking on her phone she holds with too long, blue nails. I'm disappointed she's not paying any attention to the adorable but very young boy. If I was one of Violet's victims, I could drive off with him right now and she'd never know. I sigh.

"Okay. Will you do me a favor?"

"Sure, what?" He's so eager.

"Will you please go inside the dog area and not come out until your mom gets you?" It's not the best scenario but it makes me feel a little better. I mean the kid is wandering the parking lot talking to strangers.

"Okay Peer son. Thank you for the picture."

"You're welcome, Bennett, it was nice meeting you."

I watch the kid make it to the gated area and reach up to lift the latch, he pushes it up to open the gate by standing on his toes. He makes it inside and an older woman who got a drawing of her corgi from me, helps him latch the gate. She was a nice lady, so I feel like she'll keep an eye on the kid. I take one last glance at the mother who's still chatting away oblivious where her child might be. Why do people have kids if they're not interested in being parents?

After I drop off the supplies with Maryanne, I get back in the SUV and my phone rings.

"Well hello stranger, how are you?"

Tori answers, "I'm great. Mom asked me to call and see if you guys will come over for dinner tomorrow."

"I'm free but I'm not at home. You'll need to wait a while for me to get home or call one of the others. What's going on with you?"

"Kody and I are dating, well we've been on two dates with a group of friends. He's so sweet, I really like him."

"That's great. Wait until I tell Violet."

"She knows, we talk on Insta almost every day." Huh?

"I didn't know that. Why didn't you ask her about dinner?"

"I haven't talked to you in a while, so I decided to ask you."

"Thank you, I feel honored, but it's going to be at least an hour until I get home. I'll call you after I check with them."

"Where are you going? Can you chat and drive?" Who has taken my sister? This new Tori is something else. It's like the situation with Violet was a catalyst for a personality transplant. That might be too harsh, she was just a bratty teen and now she's more mature, she's grown up fast but it's very becoming.

I didn't hang up with Tori until I arrived at the church. In the darkness I could tell the neighborhood is sketchy, but I didn't realize it was this neglected. The church is old, it's not in good repair, and I feel bad they don't have more support if they're helping abused children.

Carrying the lock box which hopefully contains more than a thousand dollars, I try the chapel door. It's locked so I walk around the church and try two other doors, they're also locked. Worried I won't complete my task on time if I can't hand over this money, I take a minute to look around. At the back of the church, connected by a crumbling asphalt parking lot, is a small equally poorly maintained house with the glow of lights coming from inside.

When I knock on the door, there's immediate movement inside. The door opens with a groan of rusty hinges and a small, old, woman looks at me through thick lenses.

"May I help you?" she asks in an age roughened voice.

"I hope so. Are you associated with the church?" I gesture towards the sad building.

"Yes, I'm the pastor's wife, everyone calls me Ms. Maybel. He's not here, he's at the hospital visiting the sick children. Is there something I can help you with?"

"Yes ma'am, my name is Pierson, and I was in a competition of sorts, the task I had to complete includes bringing you this lock box. You might have a clue of some kind to give me in exchange for the box?" She looks at the box and back at me with confusion.

"No, I don't know anything about any clues. Earl would've told me if he knew about any clues. What am I supposed to do with the box?"

"There's money in it, a donation for the abused children. Does that sound right?"

"You have a donation for the children? Well come in, let's see about this box."

She leads me into the small kitchen, and she takes a tea kettle from the stove and fills it with water, then with a twist of a knob flame ignites on the burner beneath the kettle, she turns, and looks at me. I feel awkward and uncomfortable under her scrutiny.

I set the box on the table and we both looked at it.

"Do you have a key?" she asks.

"No. They only gave me the box and asked me to bring it here."

"Wait here." She leaves the room and I hear some things being moved around down a hall. The kitchen is modest and in desperate need of some updates, but it's clean and quaint despite the worn parts of the floor in front of the sink and stove.

She returns with a hammer, a screwdriver, and a small pry bar, "One of these should work."

She puts them on the table and looks at me expectantly.

"Oh, uh, sure I can probably open it with these." The tea kettle begins to whistle and she busies herself with making two cups of tea. I use the screwdriver to push against the lock mechanism, it loosens but won't budge. Next, I try the pry bar and I'm able to get it into the gap I made with the screwdriver. Turning the box onto its side, I lean on the bar to pry at the lock, with a scrape and a pop, it opens.

I'm afraid to touch it, "It's for the church, so I'd feel more comfortable if you look inside."

She purses her lips and looks in my eyes before she nods and turns over the box so it's upright. She lifts the lid and cash falls out onto the table. She looks at me again and gasps.

"It's so much money. I thought it would be a few singles. Pierson, son, this looks like hundreds of dollars."

"Yes ma'am, my task required me to collect at least a thousand dollars." She holds her chest and gasps again.

"Oh my goodness, that's amazing. I don't know if I should thank you or whoever included us in your competition. This will help so many children, we've been having a hard time keeping them all clothed and sheltered. This money will go a long way."

"I'm glad to hear that, ma'am. May I trouble you to count it? I need to make sure it's over a thousand dollars so I can collect the next clue."

"Hmmm, that sounds like quite the competition. I would be happy to count it, but with these hands the finer movements needed to count thin pieces of paper aren't possible. If you'll do the counting, I'll supervise. Please, call me Ms. Maybel, we're friends now." She holds up her chunky swollen and gnarled fingers, she can barely bend them and I'm much more impressed she made the tea.

"Okay, Ms. Maybel, I'm going to take it all out and stack the like bills together to make it easier."

"You're smart and polite, I like you, Pierson."

"Thank you."

I begin separating the bills, there's more fifties than I realized, two hundreds, and lots of twenties. There are a couple smaller bills including fourteen singles. I only saw a kid put in a couple, people must've been putting money in the box when I wasn't looking. After they're separated into piles, I count out each pile and she adds the numbers to make sure we agree. When I'm finished counting, we both stare at the stacks of bills, thoroughly stunned.

"That can't be right, let's count it again."

We count it a second time and again sit stunned when I finish. She regains her wits before me and even with an elderly body, she jumps out of her chair and wraps her arms around my neck jumping up and down. It's a bit awkward because despite her stature, her bosom is plentiful. She steps back suddenly and I think she realized she was crushing me with her large chest.

"I'm sorry, please forgive my unchurch-like behavior, I'm just so excited! I can't believe a strange white man has brought us a gift like this for the children! Bless you son! Bless your contest!

Oh my, Earl is going to be beside himself! Bless you! Thank the Lord! What a blessing this is for the kids!" She's practically yelling in her excitement. I'm pretty excited too, I can't believe my art raised almost eighteen hundred dollars!

"I'm excited too, Ms. Maybel, this is amazing. I had no idea it was this much, I'm so glad it'll help." Tears are streaming down her cheeks and she pulls a lace edged handkerchief from her ample bosom and dabs at her eyes.

"Son, do you have a minute to finish your tea?"

"Yes, I'd like that."

"Earl has been a pastor for forty-two years, we've been married for fifty-eight. We came here after our daughter and granddaughter passed. I used to have a real job back then. I was a legal secretary and he was a car salesman for upscale German cars. We did very well and we lived in a good neighborhood even though it was close to the city. Our daughter got married right out of college to a man in the military, he was a Marine. They got married and he had to leave, after a few years he was able to get military housing and she was able to stay with him. They were living in Maryland after our granddaughter was born. Then they moved to South Carolina, Mekeale was gone for months at a time and Christine and Tiffany spent a lot of time alone, but they were safe on the base, Tiffany was able to attend daycare on base so Chris could work. She was a manager at a hair salon but the owner was into some illegal businesses and one of the criminals got interested in Chris. He kept hanging around and he started off really nice and helpful but when she refused to be involved with him, you know because she was married, he wouldn't take no for an answer. He started stalking her and even though it was base housing they didn't keep civilians from the housing on base, just the military installation."

She takes a sip of tea before continuing, "One day, he decided to attack her. He broke into the house and assaulted her, our granddaughter was home sick and she saw what the man did to her mother. The man killed our daughter and stole our granddaughter. We searched for her for years and the FBI found her picture online, she was being molested and the bastards were selling videos of what they were doing, but they couldn't find her. They never caught any of the men who did this, even the man who killed our daughter was never caught and they knew exactly who he was, it was like he disappeared."

"I'm so sorry, what a terrible thing to happen to your family."

"Her husband killed himself, he couldn't stand the grief, the guilt, and he blamed himself. We lost our three kids in one horrible crime. It almost broke us, Earl and me, but the Lord saved us and helped us find a purpose again. Amen."

"Amen. Is that why you help children now?"

"Yes, we came here twenty-one years ago. The neighborhood was a little better back then, but the folks around here are still plenty nice. Even the drug dealers and the hookers stop by for a blessing, a meal, or to make donations sometimes. But it's not much, nobody in this neighborhood has much. We vowed to help abused children with our ministry. We've been working with DCF and the authorities, the only women's shelter, and the homeless family shelter for twenty-one years."

"Wow, Ms. Maybel, that's very admirable. I'm really glad I was able to make a donation, I've also enjoyed meeting you very much."

"Pierson, you come back any time, Earl will want to meet you. Let's put the money back in the box. I'm going to have to get Earl to the bank first thing."

"Definitely. Please be safe. Here, I'll put it in there for you." When I open the lid and reach to set in the first stack of money, I notice an envelope still in the box.

"Oh, my, I wonder what that could be. Another surprise? Or maybe it's your clue!" She grabs for the envelope and tears it open, sore fingers my foot! She's quick and nimble when she wants to be.

She takes out a piece of paper and smiles, “It’s your clue. I’m going to read it, I’m nosey.”

She clears her throat, “Ahem, Dear Contestant, Congratulations on completing your task. If you haven’t collected at least one thousand dollars, stop now and contact the *Game Master.* If you’ve met the requirement, you may continue reading. Good job! We knew you could do it. You may have noticed the recipient does not have any knowledge of this game. Please have them sign this note, or take a selfie with them, something to prove they got the donation. The next task is your final task but it involves three steps. You have no rules or deadlines, but remember the first person to complete all the tasks wins. Here’s your first step. It tells you what you need to do, I'll let you handle that part. Sounds like an interesting game, what do you win?”

“Oh. Uh, the winner gets to choose a vacation for all of us. It’s a huge prize for us because we each want to choose our trip.”

“I see. Might there be a young lady on this trip with you?” I swear I’m blushing. This is worse than confession with a priest.

“I, uh, there might be.”

“I’m old, but I’m not dead. I’m okay with love of any kind. God wants love to rule the world, he would never be unhappy with love. It’s alright if you tell me, but you don’t have to tell me.”

“You’re quite persuasive Ms. Maybel, but it’s still difficult. I’m in love with a wonderful woman. She’s also in love with me, and my two brothers. The three of us are more brothers because we grew up together. I'm not related to them, but the other two, they're cousins. We dreamed of a woman we could share when we were kids, a product of our troubled youth, so to speak. Anyway, we found her and we’re very happy.”

“Pierson, that’s just wonderful. Not everyone can find the perfect person for them. I was lucky to find Earl, that man is one of a kind. Thank you for sharing with me, I think I’d like to meet this special young woman.”

"Violet, that's her name and my brothers are Austin and Jackson. Violet *is* really special, she also likes to help abused children and she advocates for survivors of trafficking. I think she would like you very much, and so would my brothers."

"A lovely name. Here, you write down your name and your number and we'll set up a meeting. Now, it's getting late and she's probably worried about you, but you'll hear from me soon." I stand and go to take my tea cup to the sink. She touches my hand and shakes her head then she stands and gives me another hug.

"Thanks, Ms. Maybel, I'll look forward to seeing you again and bringing my partners to meet you."

"Thank you, young man. You drive home safe and you win that game for your girl."

"I will. Have a good night, Ms. Maybel."

"I will, thanks to you, and God bless you, Pierson."

When I get to my vehicle I send Colby a picture of Ms. Maybel, the money, and the clue with her signature. Then I take off for home hoping Violet will be there so I can tell her about Ms. Maybel. Oh, wait, I'm not allowed to talk about the game. Dammit, it's going to be so difficult to keep the details of my day quiet.

Chapter Thirty-Five

Violet

I had such an amazing day. After Jackson finally agreed to let me go to the village alone, it was great. Patricia, Kristos's cousin, who I met a couple weeks ago has been visiting with me and we've been getting to know one another, today she finally brought me to the village to meet my grandfather and a few other relatives. I was most excited about my grandfather, he's a tribal elder and I figured he must have some wonderful things to teach me.

When I entered his home, it was clean and quiet. He was seated in an old wooden rocking chair reading a book. He's a large guy like Kristos, his hair is white and his skin is wrinkled and tan. His hands look worn and rough from years of hard labor. He shook my hand and held it for a moment before releasing it. It was weird but he's a little mysterious, so I just brushed it off. After everyone else came and went he wanted to talk with me, alone.

While I'm standing in the living room giving Sawyer a scratch, Pierson comes in from the garage. He jolts when he sees me like I was hiding and surprised him, or maybe like he's sneaking around and I caught him.

"Hi Pierson. Are you just getting home?"

"Uh, yeah. I was out running errands most of the day, I just finished up. I'm exhausted and a little hungry. I'm gonna grab a quick shower, eat something, and go to bed. Did you have a good day?"

"I had a great day, but I can tell you about it later. Go get your shower and I'll see what we have to eat. I could have a snack." He looks relieved and rushes off.

"All right Sawyer, he's up to something. Since he looked guilty, he was definitely working on the game. It's so hard for him and Austin not to talk about it. I wonder if he did the task at the park today. It's pretty late, he probably worked for hours to fill the box and then the drive to the Urban Children's Ministry Building to drop it off is pretty far. Yep, he's on the final task."

Meow!

"Yeah, I know, I've gotta hurry up."

Meeeow!

With that, I searched the refrigerator for some edible leftovers. I spot the beef stroganoff, rolls, and broccoli from last night. I heat everything up and make two plates. I set up our places at the table and pour us each something cold to drink. Then I check for other brothers in the house. I don't think they're here but I didn't make it as far as the bedroom. Nope, nobody's around, just Pierson in the shower. While I'm standing there, he turns off the water, I go back to the table to wait for him.

"That looks great, thanks, Killer. Tell me about your visit to meet the family." He takes a fork full of meat and noodles then shoves the whole thing into his mouth. I take a bite too before starting my story. I tell him about the cousins, the aunt, and my grandfather. He asks follow up questions about the squirrelly cousin who was still in cahoots with Kristos, Patty's words not mine. Then I told him about what my grandfather wanted when I was alone with him.

"So, were you scared when he wanted to talk to you alone? I'd be freaked out like I was called to the principal's office."

"He was a little scary but more in an *I respect you so much* way, not a spooky ghost way. He asked me to sit across from him and he stopped rocking, leaned forward and told me, *Kristos is an evil man. He's turned his back on all of his heritage and family. If he gets out of jail, you must kill him. He has dishonored our family and our tribe, he has hurt so many innocents. The Elders have decided his punishment is death.*"

"Holy, fuck! What did you say?"

"I froze, my mind was spinning, does he know? Does he think I'm innocent and it's a family sacrifice? Why does he want me to kill him?"

"I can imagine."

"Then he says, *I see what you are, like the wing of the crow, you are dark but also so complex with many shades of swirling colors. You wield the axe to save the innocent, you are chosen and it will be by your hand his sentence is carried out.*"

"Whoa!"

"I know, I was totally mesmerized by him. I asked him why he wants me to do it, you know, trying to see if he actually knows what I do. He told me he was shown a vision of his offspring, that I'm chosen to reap the evil ones who walk among us. He said I couldn't tell anyone in the tribe anything about this, and I must continue on my path. He said the tribe would support my work and help me if they could. Isn't that wild? He spoke about it like it's perfectly normal to go around killing bad guys and he had no doubt it's what I'm meant to do. He was proud of me."

"That's cool. He sounds like an interesting guy. Will we be able to meet him?"

"Actually, he insisted on meeting you. I think he wants to vet you and see if you're worthy of the *chosen one*." Wiggling my fingers in the air like I'm casting a spell I burst out laughing, he laughs with me but he also looks a little nervous.

Before we're finished eating Austin and Jackson make it home. They already ate but they brought some dessert and we all have a few bites of the apple pie. I tell them about my day and they share about theirs. They ran errands, had lunch with their friends, and worked out. This time of year, *ran errands* might mean shopping for gifts. The big day is a week from Tuesday and I'm almost done. I need three more small things and that's it.

I got another section of my tattoo finished and even though it was a couple days ago it's still a little sore. It's been a long and interesting day, Austin and Jackson shower with me but Pierson goes to bed. Poor guy, I'm pretty sure he fell asleep the second his head hit the pillow. He was talking to me one minute and snoring the next. We found a way to enjoy our shower despite his absence.

Once we're all snuggled in bed, I'm not far behind him. *I wake when I hear a sound and I follow it until I find the cause. It's the door to the garage blowing in the wind banging on the frame. I wonder why I'm the only one who heard it as I pull it closed. But I step in something damp and I look down to find red footprints leading back to my room. When I look inside, a large man is looming over my bed and my three loves are dead and bleeding. I scream and charge the man but he vanishes in a puff of smoke. I rush to my guys and no matter what I do I can't wake them. But they aren't dead, they're just sleeping. Finally Austin wakes up and looks at me, his eyes are glowing bright blue, so much so that it lights up the room. His voice sounds deep and booming; it reverberates around the room.*

"Kristos is free! You must kill him or we won't wake up. Find him and kill him to save us." I try to get to Austin since he's talking to me, but I can't reach him. There's thick fog close to the floor and

no matter how far I walk across the bed, he's further away. I walk miles and I still can't get any closer.

Then I see Jackson is awake and his eyes are glowing gold, they're like beacons in the dark fog. He looks at me and says, "Find him Babe, don't let him get away!" But I can't get closer to him either.

Next, I see Pierson in the fog, he's seated and hunched over, when I get a little closer, I can see he's playing chess with my grandfather. Both of them have glowing green eyes.

Pierson says, "He's going to try to run, catch him first, Killer."

And my grandfather tells me, "I will be waiting for you." I try to ask him what he'll be waiting for and I start to lose sight of all of them, I scream in frustration.

"Violet!" my eyes open and Austin is leaning over me with a worried look on his face. I reach out and pull him on top of me hugging him tight. I can touch him, he's real and his eyes aren't glowing. It was only a dream, thank God.

"What?"

"You were crying out in your sleep," Jackson answers.

Austin asks, "Are you okay?"

"Sorry. Yeah, I'm fine. It was just a weird dream." I describe it to them and they look equally thoughtful. Pierson is having a hard time staying awake, I kiss him and then climb over him to get a drink. I decline company but Sawyer ignores my preference. The little fur ball follows so close he taps his nose against my leg with every step. I must've scared him, he's usually not this clingy.

While I chug some cranberry juice from the bottle I can't shake the feeling from the dream. It's like this urgency that's pressing against me, I need to act before it's too late, but it was just a dream, there's no action to take. I can feel the pressure of the need to accomplish something, in my gut. Kind of like when you feel like you forgot to turn off the oven before you left the house and it just keeps needling the back of your neck until you can get home to check, only to find out it wasn't on.

There's no way I can just go back to bed when I'm this keyed up, I bring the bottle of juice, my fluffy chaperone, and go to the office to fire up my laptop. Maybe I can find some information that will ease this unpleasant feeling. First I check local headlines, then police reports, nothing catches my eye so I check my email.

There's a message from Krewe, my Attorney Extraordinaire. He's so good at his job and such a nice guy I'm lucky to have him on my team. He's grown with me and my needs and he's hired paralegals solely to work on some of my business. My parents left me a lot of assets and money, including very large life insurance policies. It was hard to let him tell me about everything they left for me, knowing it meant they'd never return, but eventually it became a necessity and I had to let him show me everything. I have managers running things at the properties and businesses, and more managers managing them, with Krewe's people overseeing the whole thing. When I see an email from him, I can't ignore it no matter how much I want to bury my head in the sand.

Hey Violet, when you have a chance, please call my office and schedule an in person appointment. We need to talk about your evil grandmother, it's somewhat urgent so please call back when you see this message.

Later,

K

Below his personal note is another hundred lines of legal disclosures and warnings, it must be exhausting trying to live every minute in such extremely tight legal parameters. Even law abiding citizens who consider themselves incapable of breaking the law are likely breaking laws every day. There are laws still on the books from when our country was founded and it's such a big effort to change or remove those laws, they remain. Nobody uses them anymore, but because they're there, they could be used, it's part of what keeps lawyers in business. For example you could be charged for sodomy if you ever went down on your partner in most states, I'm in big trouble if someone enforces that.

It's four in the morning, too early to call his office. I mark the email unread and I'll call later once they're open. The unread email will serve as a reminder. I finish the last of the juice and toss the bottle into the trash before I go back to my room and snuggle between my guys. I carefully make sure I'm touching all three of them, I need to feel them after that weird dream and the residual discomfort.

When I next open my eyes there's nobody staring at me concerned, and I feel a warm twinge in my chest. Relieved I didn't scream in my sleep again I feel the bed looking for my partners, they're all gone from our sheets. I have class, it's just the last few sessions this week to finalize any projects and get them turned in before the school closes Wednesday. That's it, all of my finals will be completed. The new semester starts after everyone comes back from the holiday break, but I'm not going back. It's bitter sweet, but I'll keep my friends and I can go back if I want a degree. When I make my way into the kitchen I find a note:

Babe, we had to leave early and didn't want to wake you. Don't forget to eat.

Love you-

Jax

Baby there's English muffins in the drawer in the fridge. Have a great day!

I love you! Auz

Killer, I felt left out, my words of wisdom are to drive safe. Even though your grandmother may not be a threat anymore, please watch your back.

With all my love,

Pierson

I can't help laughing at them, they compete over stupid little stuff and then they can share me with total happiness. They're enigmatic and I guess it's part of why I love them. My chaperone stares at me from his position seated on the other end of the island. When I turn to the refrigerator to seek out the English muffins, he lies down.

"You think you're getting some of my muffin don't you?"

Meow!

"It's a small muffin, I don't think I can spare any, but I might let you lick some of the cream cheese, if you behave."

When I'm ready to leave for school he watches from the top of his cat tree where he's licking the cream cheese from his face using his paw to swipe it then cleaning it with his pink tongue. He barely acknowledged my exit.

I take the bike and spend my time at school enjoying one of the last days with my friends. My projects are complete and submitted, they have been for more than a week. I just wanted to share a few more minutes with my friends as a fellow student. I think we'll remain in contact but let's face it, without school as our common ground, we won't have many reasons to interact. Although, we'll probably still meet online for games, which I enjoy.

As I leave the building and head for the parking lot my phone rings, "Hey Krewe, I thought I was going to see you tomorrow. What's up?"

"I had a cancellation, can you make it this afternoon at four?" checking the time, it's only two-forty-five but I was hoping at least one of the guys would be able to join me.

"Yeah, I'll be there. See you soon, thanks." I immediately dial Jackson, he's the one most likely to be away from loud equipment at work, he's been handling more of the supervisory tasks on the job.

"Hey, Babe! What's up?"

"Krewe switched my appointment to today at four. Can any of you make it?"

"Piers should be able to leave early enough to meet you. Austin had to go pick up material and he won't be back in time. I can give Piers my truck and ride home with Auz. I'll call you back if he can't make it, otherwise he'll be there. How was your day?"

"It was good. I'm going to miss those ridiculous boys, but I'm fine. How's your day going?"

"Busy, but it's going well. We're on schedule and that's a good thing. Ryder just came in, I'll see you tonight."

"Okay, I love you."

"Love you, Babe."

Even though I'll be early I take off for Krewe's office, and decide to take a ride past Grandmother's house, or what used to be her home. Curious, I slow at the gate and try to see if it looks like anyone is home. I can't tell, but eying the intercom I impulsively press the button.

"Morgan Residence, how may I help you?"

"Roman! Hi, it's Violet."

"Oh! Hello! Come up to the house!" He sounds awfully excited, he must be bored.

"Okay, but just for a minute, I'm on the way to an appointment."

The gate swings open and as I drive the path to the front door a weird darkness falls, like when the sun disappears behind a cloud. Things associated with Grandmother are always filled with dread and foreboding. The front door opens and Roman stands there in his uniform, his smile is a light in the darkness of the Morgan house.

"Violet! It's a pleasure to see you. Please come inside and I'll fix you some tea. I also have cookies."

Not one to turn down sweets I follow him inside. The kitchen is warm and inviting despite the fact my grandmother used to haunt these halls. There's a plate of freshly baked chocolate chip cookies on the counter, they smell delicious.

Seeing me eyeing the plate he offers, "Have a cookie, I'll get the tea. Tell me how you've been."

I choose a cookie and take a big bite, "I'm good. My grandmother hasn't been around so things have been much better. One less person trying to kill me."

"About that, they've declared her dead. There was some evidence along the river at the back of the property that she may have fallen in or been *pulled* into the water. The authorities searched for a few days but they didn't find her body. I told them she often walked along the river."

"I see. Any news about what will happen to you? Your job?"

"For now her attorney is paying me from her trust but I've been warned a new owner may very well fire me immediately. Which is fine, I need to go visit my sister in Columbia anyway. After that, who knows, but I'll find something, there's always a job."

"That's good. I'm here if you find yourself without a job, it would be my pleasure to help you find a new one if nothing works out."

"You're so much like your mom, she was always so kind and concerned about others. She would volunteer to help me with the most horrible tasks without a second thought. Of course I didn't allow it, but she offered, which meant a lot to me. You remind me of her, your kindness runs deep."

"I appreciate the compliment and I would love to be anything like my mom, but I don't think I have her level of consideration for others."

"Well, people aren't always what they're cracked up to be." He smiles, and I finish off my cookie and take another. The tea is mild and sweet, like Roman, and I have a thought.

"Do you have any clerical experience?"

"Not exactly, just what's been needed to run a household, budgeting, and staff. But I can use a computer and the full suite of office programs if that's what you mean. Why?"

"I'm thinking about making my foundation more concrete. Instead of just a few transactions behind the scenes I want to turn it into brick and mortar, have some physical places to help the victims of trafficking and abuse. If I'm able to do it, I'll need some managerial help to run the day-to-day stuff. What do you think? Would you be interested in something like that?"

"Not only would it be an honor to work with you, but I'd love to work for such a noble cause. If you need me, I'll leave any job for you."

"You're too kind, Roman. I need to get to an appointment, but I'll give you a call as soon as I work out some details. Thank you for these cookies and your time." I take one more for the road. He walks me to the door and takes my hand.

"Your parents would be very proud of you, Violet. Drive safe."

"Thanks, I will. Bye." I kiss his cheek and he chuckles. He reminds me of a sweet uncle and in my life, that's a place of honor. My last uncle became my dad after all.

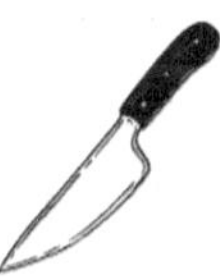

Krewe's receptionist shows us into a small conference room. There are some papers spread on the table but my eyes are focused on Pierson. He's so handsome and he's being very quiet.

"Is something wrong?" I whisper.

"No. I'm just not comfortable in a lawyer's office, it feels like I'm in trouble for some reason. I know it's silly, but I can't relax."

"You must have gotten in more trouble than I've heard about as a kid, you said something similar last night, like you were called to the principal's office." He offers me a sheepish smile.

I put my hand on his knee and squeeze, he leans in for a kiss. With my lips on his I press my tongue into his mouth and deepen our exchange. I'd love to have one of those movie moments and shove all the papers off the table and climb on top of him to have my way, but Krewe enters and I have to rein in my fantasy.

"Ahem, break it up! No fornicating in my office," he chuckles.

"We were only kissing, old man Krewe," I sass.

"Only because I interrupted. I remember what it was like to be your age, I'm not that old."

"Sorry," Pierson's cheeks are pink. I don't get embarrassed about stuff like kissing or sex anymore, but he looks cuter than ever.

"What's up, why am I here?" I question diverting us back to the topic at hand.

"I had an interesting meeting with your grandmother's attorney, for all her talk of hating you and not wanting you to get any family assets she didn't make sure of that in her will. The police declared her dead, there was enough evidence at the scene of her disappearance to suggest she went into the river. They believe an alligator either helped her into the river or got ahold of her when she fell in. They think she was consumed and it's why they haven't found her remains. Sorry, I know it's gruesome, but after how she's treated you, I didn't think you'd be upset by the facts."

"I'm not upset. She was an evil person and she probably gave the poor gator indigestion."

"Harsh, but true," Pierson adds.

"Anyway, her will didn't change from naming your mother as the sole beneficiary, since she's no longer with us, everything goes to her beneficiary, which is you. The attorney was annoyed with your grandmother, he told her multiple times when she disparaged you that if she passed away without changes you would get everything. Apparently, she thought she was invincible, or for some strange reason she thought you, a perfectly healthy and significantly younger person, would pass away before her. Regardless of her twisted reasons, she didn't take his advice and you'll be getting everything in her estate."

"Holy crap! I wasn't expecting this. She hated me so much I figured she'd have it burned before she'd let me have anything. If she had a grave, she'd be turning over in it right now."

"No doubt. I have paperwork here for you to sign for her attorney, there are some transfers of ownership for her property, and the bank accounts will be changed to your name by next week. After he collects his fees, everything left will be yours."

"Whoa, how much is that, Violet?" Pierson asks.

"I don't want to know specifics. What I want is for you to set up The Henley Foundation to take over those accounts. Donate all the cash and property to the foundation. I'm going to use all the assets for the victims of abuse and trafficking. Also, draw up a job offer for her butler, Roman, he's going to manage it. Colby has specifics about the foundation as it is so far. We have some money already, I also want my parent's house donated to the foundation. I'm going to make both houses into transitional housing for trafficking survivors. If I think of anything else I'll let you know. Show me where to sign."

"I don't know why I'm surprised, of course you have a plan. I think you were born thirty-five, and you just started talking the minute you arrived. I'll take care of everything, I'll get with Colby and Roman, and I'll call you with questions. Sign here." It went like that for half an hour, and when I finished signing, Pierson and I picked up some Mexican food from the place by Krewe's office. He took it home in the truck and I followed on my bike.

Jackson and Austin were both home when we pulled up. My insides were still happy from the ride home, nothing settles me like my beautiful bike. But I'm happy to be home with all of my guys. Pierson and I fill them in on the news.

"If she was alive when they ate her, she probably would've been a hard fight for the gators. But since you made sure she wasn't, they probably had a peaceful meal," Austin speculates. He's so into the story of the alligators eating her, like a kid mesmerized by dinosaurs.

"It was brilliant of Dozer to feed her to the gators in the river behind her place and to leave evidence on the shore. He's a murder clean up savant," Jackson chuckles with his observation, he's not wrong.

"Yeah, Colby's a good judge of character, he's found the perfect people to join our team."

"Violet's Villains?" Austin asks.

"No, that's just you three. We'll have to call the rest of our team something else."

"Let's think of a name later, I'm ready for dessert and it involves you, naked on our bed," Jackson gives me a devilish grin and it makes him irresistible.

"You'll have to catch me!" I squeal and take off running. Pierson moves fast and he's right behind me. Before I can make it into the bedroom, he scoops me up by my waist and I pretend to struggle but when Austin joins us pressing himself to my front I can't fight it anymore. He kisses me and they lay me on the bed. Jackson starts removing my pants and I wriggle to help him while Pierson and Austin kiss and fondle me.

Bang, bang, bang! Ring! Ring!

"Holy fuck! Somebody better be dead!" Jackson leaves to answer the door before they beat it down. Pierson follows him and Austin hangs back to help me get dressed. Nobody bringing good news knocks on your door like that.

When Austin and I arrive in the living room we find two men in suits standing there with Pierson and Jackson, all four of them looking grim.

"What is it?"

"Are you Violet Henley?"

"Yes."

"I'm sorry to disrupt your evening, I'm Detective Bond and this is Detective Muñoz, we're with the FDLE. We need to inform you that Kristos Chitto has been released from jail and the majority of the charges against him have been dropped. He's only charged with one misdemeanor now and they can't hold him without bail on that charge."

I can feel the blood drain from my face and Austin must see it because he supports my elbow. I feel the room shift and I want to sit. He guides me to the chair and looks at me with concern.

"Why did they drop the charges?" Pierson asks.

"The state attorney decided there wasn't enough evidence to prosecute. I'm sorry."

Jackson is trying his best to keep his anger in check, "That doesn't make sense, we were kidnapped by him, he tried to kill us, the FBI watched him hold a gun to Violet's head. How is it not enough fucking evidence?"

"I'm sorry Mr. Hunter, we don't have any say on the legal side of the argument, we just arrest them, it's up to the state attorneys to prosecute them. We came to let you know so you can take precautions. As his victims, we're required to notify you of his release. The judge has put a restraining order in place for all of you. If you see any signs of Mr. Chitto, please call us immediately."

"Well thank God! A piece of paper will certainly keep Violet safe. Why even bother?" Austin's anger rivals Jackson's.

"Thank you for telling us. We'll call if we see him. Good night." Pierson takes my hint and shows the officers out the door.

When he comes back, he asks, "What do you need, Killer? What can we do?"

"You can get dressed, we're going after him, right now. I'm not giving him a chance to run."

Austin claps his hands together, "Yes! Let's do this."

"Are you sure you want to do it tonight?" Jackson asks.

"I'm sure. I can't let him escape. I'm going to call Colby, we need to go by the warehouse for supplies. Let's meet Dozer there and then we'll storm his penthouse before he can escape." My dream comes back to me and I decide to call my grandfather and let him know too. I want to warn him though it's no protection just like the Florida Department of Law Enforcement left us to figure it out, he'll need to do his best for self-preservation.

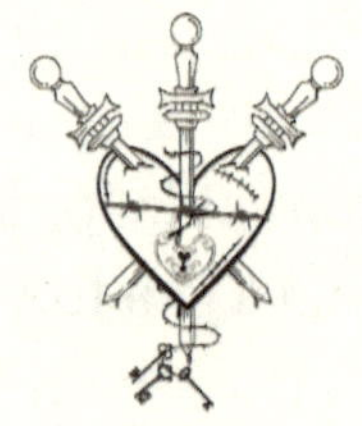

Chapter Thirty-Six

Pierson

When we arrive at the warehouse Dozer and his guys are waiting outside, I don't know how they manage to be on call all the time. Do they never sleep? We pull into the warehouse and Dozer pulls his truck in next to ours to load up. The van and another truck remain outside. Barney stays outside to guard the entrance, we don't tell Dozer how to run his guys and he always errs on the side of caution.

Violet is on edge, she's all business though she's usually more relaxed especially when she has the opportunity to hunt down a bad guy. She's choosing what she wants to bring and the rest of us are loading up everything she selects. She's also strapping on her holsters and blades, she's such a badass and when she's in all her gear you can see it, I'm not sure if it's her confidence or some other inherent trait. She's the best marksman of all of us except for two of Dozer's guys. But she's always improving, she works hard to be the best she can be. I wouldn't be surprised if she's ruling the world in ten years or less.

"Pierson, will you grab that trunk? The one with the charges in it, please?"

"You got it, Killer."

I heft the case and it's heavier than I expected, but it's not unwieldy so I manage to get it to the truck. As I'm heading back to the weapons room our lights go out. I stop and listen while my eyes adjust.

Bang! A gunshot outside, fuck!

"Here, put these on and stay down!" Austin whisper shouts at me. I take the night vision goggles and pull them over my head, I can instantly see like the lights are on.

"Where's Violet?"

"I'm up here," she calls from above me and I look up, she's perched on a beam.

"Is the roof access locked?" Dozer asks.

"Yeah, from the inside. The key is on the hook in the weapons room," Violet replies to him while she makes her way across the beam like it's nothing.

"Ray, head up to the roof and see if you can get eyes on anyone. We're going to COMMS three."

I don't have any communication devices on me yet and I have no idea what code three is, Dozer has his own way of doing things. I don't know if he was in the military but he's very methodical and organized, it reminds me of a military operation when we work with him.

Trying to keep a low profile I make my way to the exit door past the BASIL. It's the door we never use and it looks like it's boarded up from the street, but it's camouflage. Violet thought it would make a good secret entrance or exit if we ever needed one after those guys took her grandmother out of here. When I look up in search of my beautiful girl, I spot her lying in wait with a rifle aimed at the door next to the overhead door.

Jackson locked the overhead door with the hurricane bars so nobody could open them from outside. Then he set up on the landing for the stairs right outside the apartment. He has a rifle propped against the railing. Austin was in the workout space but I can't see him from my spot. I'm pressed into the doorway for the BASIL, I can watch the hallway and guard the secret exit from here.

I have no idea where Tyler, Dozer, and Franco set up or maybe they're going outside. With Ray on the roof, they might have a clue where they are and if we can move against them. I catch a movement at the end of the hall and see Tyler heading towards me. He presses into the doorway across from me, it's just a closet.

"Dozer assigned us to stick with each of you. He's up top with Violet, Franco is with Austin and Jackson. Ray can see three guys and Barney is down."

"Fuck. I'm sorry man, he's a good guy, we need to help him."

"It was a headshot, I don't think we can help him."

"Damn, I'm sorry."

He holds his ear and then updates me, "There's a van with four more guys crawling down the alley. Franco and Austin are guarding the door. Dozer can see everyone inside except me and you, but he knows we're here."

"Okay."

"The guys are out of the van, Ray can get two of them but he wants to wait for us so we can get them all."

He pauses then says, "Two are approaching the door, they're going to blow it. Auz and Franco are clear."

BOOM!

Even when you know it's coming an explosion of any size still jolts you with surprise. I jump a little at the sound and it echoes through the mostly metal building.

"They're coming in, be ready."

Bang! Bang! Pop! Pop! Pop! The bullets fly and I have no idea who's shooting who. I just have to trust my brothers are safe and our girl is protected. I keep my barrel aimed down the hall and my eyes focused so I can fire if a bad guy comes this way.

A guy I don't know comes towards the hallway low, I'm about to shoot him when he gets hit and falls. I'm pretty sure my hot girlfriend just shot that dude. When there's a break in the fire, I hear movement above me and Violet falls from the sky right in front of me. I reach out for her and pull her behind me.

"I'm good, don't worry. Tyler, have you heard if the rest of our guys are alright?"

"They're good. We neutralized theirs, Kristos wasn't with them."

A few more bangs sound off outside and I look at Tyler for an update. Violet watches him too as he holds his hand over his earpiece.

"Don't worry, that's Ray, he's setting off fireworks to cover for the gunshots." That's pretty smart, in this part of town nobody will think twice. There's already firework tents set up all over town in preparation for New Year's Eve.

"I gotta go help Dozer. You're gonna want to take off the goggles, Jackson's turning the power back on." The lights come on as he finishes his sentence and it's like a nuclear bomb went off in my face. Thankfully, I was already grasping them to get them off and now I rip them away from my face and close my eyes trying to stop seeing brilliant purple circles.

"Are you okay, Pierson?"

"Yeah, I can't see your face though, it's just a purple circle."

"Well, I promise it looks the same as always. Come on, I'll guide you to where everyone else is dragging in bodies."

Dozer wanted to get the bodies off the street as quickly as possible. We don't need any nosey people or cops looking into what's going on here. When I can see again, all the bodies are inside and it turns out one is still very much alive. He's tied up and bleeding but doesn't have any fatal wounds.

"Will you bring him to my office? *David Bowie* would like to have a chat with him." The guy looks at Violet with confusion. I can't help smiling because he's about to be unpleasantly surprised when he discovers it's not a dead rock legend waiting for him, but just a well-loved and incredibly sharp knife.

Our guest doesn't like the idea of being strapped to a metal table and he tries to fight, but Jackson and Austin don't give in. Once he's settled, Violet makes a show of handling *David Bowie* so he can see the glint of light along the sharp edge of the blade. The guy squirms.

"Hi, I'm Violet. This is my place and I'd like to know why you and your friends decided to shoot it up." He watches her silently.

"You're not much of a talker, huh? That's okay, *David Bowie* here has a way of making people speak up. Isn't he beautiful? His blade is honed to such a sharp edge it's almost like a scalpel. What's your name?" His eyes wearily watch the blade but he remains mute.

"Maybe, you should encourage him a little, Baby," Austin suggests.

She poises the blade over his arm and he tries to move out of the way, she pokes him with the tip and it goes in deep, like a hot blade through butter. Blood pools in the cut and then flows down his arm and onto the stainless-steel table.

"Have anything to say yet?" she asks. He cringes but holds strong, until she moves the blade over his crotch.

"I'm Luis. Our boss told us to come here and kill everyone then burn it down."

"Good job Luis, you just saved yourself some excruciating pain in your man parts. Who's your boss?"

"Nicholas."

"What company does Nicholas work for, Luis?"

"He uh, he works for um, Kristos."

"I see. And where is this boss of yours?"

"He sent us to do this while he takes Kristos someplace else."

"Where?" She skillfully plays with the large knife and his eyes never stop following the blade. I have no doubt he's calculating what type of damage *David Bowie* can inflict upon his tiny dick.

"I wasn't supposed to hear, but they talked near me. They said they were going to stay with Henri and they're leaving in the morning for the West Coast, Oregon I think."

"Thanks Luis. You can relax for a while."

Violet leads us out of the room and in the hallway, she looks thoughtful as she leans on the wall with her back.

"Do you need anything, Baby? A drink?"

"That actually sounds amazing. I didn't realize how thirsty I am until you said it. We need to go to the Ishkohatchee village, Henri lives there. If Kristos and Nicholas are with him, we may be able to catch them off guard. We need to go now."

She springs into action and wipes *David Bowie* on her pants below her knee, then she puts him back in his sheath. She goes into the weapons room and starts reloading and tells us to do the same. We quickly get everything we need and since we were already loaded up, we're ready to go fast.

"I want you to take Tyler, he can keep us posted and if you need us, he can let us know. Plus, he's a great asset."

"All right, come on Tyler. Thanks Dozer, we'll see you soon." She hugs him with her head in his chest. She's not a short woman, but next to Dozer everyone looks like a kid. Tyler doesn't hesitate, he joins us and climbs into the front seat of the truck. Usually Violet sits up front, but she needs to sit in back since she's the smallest of all of us, she can sit in the middle. Jackson drives and Austin and I sit beside her.

I can't keep from touching her, my hand holds onto her thigh and Austin holds her hand. She's calmed now and lost in thought.

"Tell us about this Henri's house, how big is his yard? Is there foliage? A porch? What are we looking at here?"

"It's a small, single story, ranch style nineteen-fifties era house. There's a small front porch, a single-entry door, low roof, some bushes and two trees in the yard. There's no fence, and the driveway is dirt. There's a big window in the front room, so he may have a good view of anyone approaching. I would also guess it's the common floor plan of the time period, bedrooms and bathrooms at one end with kitchen and living room at the other."

Tyler asks, "Did you go to his house before?"

"No, but I drove by once."

"You know all that from driving by once? I knew you were seriously smart, but dude, you're like freakishly smart. You're like that guy on that show...I can't think of it."

Jackson asks, "Big Bang?"

"Nah."

"Criminal Minds?" Austin asks.

"Nope."

"Numbers?" I ask.

"No."

"House?" Austin tries again.

"Nah huh."

"Elementary?" Violet suggests.

"Yeah! That's it."

"You know any of the shows we said would've worked right?" Austin complains.

"Well, yeah, I guess, but I was thinking of that guy specifically. Actually, maybe you're more like the guy from Criminal Minds. He's sort of a smart nerd but still kinda cool, some of those others are too quirky. You seem almost normal."

"Wow. Thanks?"

"Oops, my bad. Sorry, I didn't mean it like that, it's not that you're abnormal in a bad way, you're *extraordinary.*"

"Well that's something I suppose," Violet says with a hint of sarcasm. When we get close to the village Violet's phone rings.

"Hello? Okay. I will. Yes, I have plenty and four guys. Okay. I promise, you too."

When she hangs up she relays, "My grandfather says Kristos is definitely with Henri and the tribal elders are gathered at the hall in the center of the village, but he's home. He said to be extra careful because Henri is mentally unstable and Nicholas worships Kristos. They could be especially dangerous because Henri knows the tribe ruled against Kristos. He doesn't know they sentenced him to death, but all three of them are likely to fight like their lives depend on it. So, we need to be extra cautious, and nobody goes off alone. We split up into two groups, Jackson with Tyler and Austin and Pierson with me. Everyone good with that?"

"Maybe Tyler should be with you Violet, since he has the comms and he can reach Dozer?" Jackson asks.

"No, I wanted him with you so you guys can watch the outside while we go in, that way you can report to Dozer if we need more help. Does that make sense?" she explains.

"Yeah. Okay, you're with me Tyler," Jackson agrees.

"Before we get to the house there's a small wooded area, we're going to need to turn off the headlights before we even turn on his road, then we'll park by the woods. It won't draw attention because people hunt in those woods so you can find trucks there any time."

"Deer season is finished, what do they hunt?" I question.

"It's tribal land so they can hunt whatever they want, but they sell hunting permits for their land to hog hunters. There's no season for them since they're such a nuisance."

"Yeah, they're the worst, they can destroy a whole field of crops in a couple nights," Austin adds.

"My parents took me hog hunting a few times when we camped. I helped butcher it, I just never learned how to cook it."

"I'll teach you, Baby. I'm the grill master, I can smoke hog like a pro."

"You guy's suck, now I want barbecue!" Tyler complains.

"I'll host a barbecue this weekend if you want, everyone can come, we'll have a memorial for Barney," Austin offers.

"I love that," Violet states.

"I'm down," I add my opinion. If there's food involved, I'm usually up for whatever.

"Okay, here's where you need to cut the lights, then turn right at that post."

Jackson blacks out the truck and slowly proceeds along the poorly maintained road. Some of the asphalt is more potholes and gravel, if we go too fast the sound could carry if they have the windows open. It's a nice night, they might be open or maybe just to keep an eye out.

When we reach the woods, Jackson is able to pull off the road where it has a wide section, it's obviously regularly used for that purpose. We quietly move along the edge of the trees, when we get a visual on the house, we switch to hand signals. We're just learning them so I'm not sure how successful we'll be. But with my military experience and Tyler's more in-depth training on it we might get by.

Jackson and Tyler stop at a tree with bushes surrounding it. Violet leads me and Austin to the house and we squat below a window. Violet signals and I think she wants to cross the door and get beneath the large window on the other side of it. I nod and follow her to this side of the door. Then watch as she dives below the window successfully. She freezes and tilts her ear towards the window. They're crappy ancient jalousie windows and she can likely hear whatever is happening inside pretty well.

Austin signals that he's going to try to listen at the window behind us while I stay by the door to help Violet. Our girl signals she's hearing something. I freeze and try to listen as well. I can hear voices through the door but I can't make out most of the words. It sounds like the grownups on a Charlie Brown special with the occasional curse word sprinkled in.

Austin rejoins me and signals he heard nothing at the windows he checked. Violet signals to us that she hears at least three voices or she has three foul balls. I'm leaning towards the first option. She comes back and whispers to me and Austin by putting her lips next to our cheeks.

"They're in the front room, they sound like they're drinking, I think they have no idea we could find them here. I have my lock picks, let's signal Jackson and go to the back door to break in." We both nod. I signal to Tyler and he confirms they understand.

Violet leads the way, we stay below the windows and go the long way around to the back door so we can avoid the big window. The back of the house only has two bathroom windows and two doors. One door is a utility room and laundry room. The other door is the back door to the inside of the house and through the glass window in the door, it looks like the kitchen. Violet checks inside carefully when she decides it's clear, she picks the lock. She hesitates to open the door, so I ask what's wrong with signals.

She points to the hinge and I think she's worried it might squeak. I decide to try the utility room, people use them as a storage area like a tiny garage. The door is unlocked and I carefully twist the knob and pull it open slowly. It makes a sound but nothing loud. I can tell Violet and Austin both let out a relieved breath. I search inside for WD-40 or any other lubricant. I'm about to give up when I spot an old school oil can, just like from the Wizard of Oz, the one the Tin Man uses to oil his joints. I try it out on the hinge for the utility room door, it works great.

I take it to where Violet waits, I quickly oil all three hinges and the doorknob just in case it's squeaky too. I set down the can and stand next to where Violet crouches, I'm covered by the wall. She takes a deep breath and turns the knob. I'm holding my breath, I'm sure Austin is too. I follow her inside and she stays low while we move as one, clearing the places a person could hide. Austin follows a few beats behind, he's semi guarding the door we came through and partially guarding our backs.

Tyler and Jackson are posted out front and they can either chase someone who runs or storm the front door, depending on our needs. When we get to a corner we can hear three distinct male voices, I think they're drinking and playing cards. She's right, they didn't expect us to find them here. She signals and while I'm trying to decipher what she's saying she charges into the room.

Holy fuck! I charge after her.

"Everyone freeze! Hands up!"

"You heard her, hands up!" I add.

"Ah, Violet. I wasn't expecting you, can I assume you've come to join me?" Kristos asks like we're not here with guns pointed at him.

"Definitely not, I'm going to need you to keep your hands up and stand, now slowly backup towards me."

"Nobody else moves, if you flinch, I'll shoot," I try my best to be clear.

Kristos listens and keeps his hands in the air while he backs up towards her, she tugs a set of flex-cuffs from her pocket.

"Okay, hold out your hands and keep them together."

She carefully puts his hands through the loops and pulls them tight. I'm ready to cuff the other two as soon as she gets him seated where she wants.

Pop! Pop! Pop! Pop!

"Get DOWN! Down! Now!" I dive on top of Violet and hold her beneath me trying to protect her head and body underneath mine the best I can. Everyone scattered. I can't see where anyone went, and I don't know where Austin is. We turned the corner and he was behind it. I can see flashes outside through the big window and the shots continue to pop off. I pray my brothers are okay while I make sure Violet stays safe.

The front window takes a couple hits then shatters onto the floor around us. I pull her away from the glass but keep her beneath my body. Amid the gunshots outside I hear yelling and some sort of vehicle, maybe a dirt bike or four-wheeler. When the shots die off, I check her over and when she looks at me, I kiss her and thank God she's all right.

I direct her to the back door so we can find Austin, when we turn the corner, I see a very still body on the floor in a puddle of blood and my heart sinks. Violet tries to rush forward but I grab her and keep her from being exposed to possible gunfire. We slowly approach the body and when we're close enough, we can see its Nicholas, Kristos's right-hand man. I almost feel bad for the guy, but it doesn't stick. He's just as guilty as Kristos for every innocent person their activities have harmed. We make our way to the door and I peek out in search of Austin. There's no sign of him and I'm freaking out inside but I hold strong for Violet.

I crouch down and pull the back door closed. Then we keep low and start working to clear the house. We work from room to room checking every space where a person could possibly hide. There's no-one here but us and the dead Nicholas by the back door. No shots have been fired for a long time, more than five minutes and I consider if that means it's safe, like when the popcorn quits popping in the microwave, is it finished?

"Violet? Pierson? You can come out, the coast is clear!" Jackson's voice sounds like music to my ears. Violet takes off running and she jumps up into his arms and wraps her legs around him while he kisses her whole face. Tyler comes in and walks to the body at the back door. He looks outside and then turns to look at us.

"Where's Austin?"

"We don't know. He was guarding the back door. I assumed he killed Nicholas but we don't know where he went."

"We need to look for him. Come on!" Violet heads out the back door and we follow her.

When we get to the woods, I can hear voices and I try to get ahead of Violet but she won't let me. She charges towards the sounds and I try to keep up with her. When we reach the people making noise I stop, at first, I don't know what I'm looking at, but then I bust out laughing.

"Holy hell bro! What the fuck happened?" Jackson asks between laughing fits.

"This fuckhead thought he was going to escape, I did what I had to do to stop him," Austin explains quite proudly.

"I love you so much, but you've got to explain in specific details, because what I'm picturing is killing me," Violet spits out between giggles.

"Well, he ran past me when I was busy with the other guy, his body is by the back door."

"That was Nicholas."

"Okay. I chased after him, well you know, I wasn't going to let anyone escape on my watch. He probably knows these woods because he was starting to gain ground and I didn't want him to get away but I couldn't catch him, so I threw the branch at him and it tripped him up. I was able to jump on him and I got him on the ground but I didn't have any cuffs or anything, and I didn't want him to escape."

"So, of course this was your only option."

"It probably wasn't my *only* option, but it's what came to mind and seemed to work at the moment."

"Well, I've got to hand it to you, I think you win the most creative restraints award by a mile."

"Does anyone have cuffs so I can get dressed?" Austin pleads.

Henri looks embarrassed and wild eyed. He's pinned to the ground with a pair of tactical pants tying him down. There's a big stick poked through one part of the pants, it's probably the branch Austin tripped him with, and a knife is stabbed through another spot and it's sticking into a big root. Another knife is through a loop on the pocket of the pants and again stabbed into a tree. He looks like he sprung a booby trap built by MacGyver or maybe Spider-Man shot him with sticky pants that stuck him to the ground like a glob of web.

Jackson and Tyler try to cuff him with flex cuffs and they struggle to get the knives out of the tree roots. All of us are laughing hysterically. It's a good stress reliever in the middle of this fucked up situation.

"Do I even want to know why Austin has no pants?" Dozer asks when he steps into the clearing.

Tyler tries to tell him but he can't stop laughing long enough to get full words out, Jackson tries but he can't get past how he used his pants. Dozer is confused and amused.

Violet finally gets through the story and Dozer laughs, he offers to buy Austin a beer as the winner of the B*est Capture Ever* award. Once he's wearing his pants again Austin looks around thoughtfully.

"Who started shooting?" he asks the group.

Tyler answers, "Some of Kristos's guys showed up, they were behind us and when they started shooting at us they were hitting the house. Then Dozer showed up with more guys and helped us stop them."

"Where's Kristos?" Violet asks.

"He's not inside?" Jackson questions.

"No. Everyone scattered when the bullets started flying and I dove on top of Violet. I didn't see where anyone went, but we searched the house, he's not in there. Auz, you didn't see him with those other guys?"

"Nah, just those two came my way."

"We better find him."

"Oh no! My grandfather lives close to here, just over that little hill on the other side of those trees. What if Kristos went to his house?" Violet sounds panicked.

"Let's go, I'll drive, Tyler you and Jackson see if you can find any trace of him in the woods between here and there. I'll send Brandon and Rick to help you. Violet, Austin, and Pierson come with me. All right?" Everyone agrees with Dozer and we all take off for our assignments.

Violet climbs into the bed of Dozer's truck so I join her, Austin gets in the cab with him. When the truck starts to move Violet stands and holds onto the roll bar at the back of the cab, I stand next to her but I watch behind us while she watches ahead. She's focused and silent, she's worried for her grandfather and it makes me worry what it would do to her if she lost yet another family member.

When we crest the hill, I spot a small house tucked into some trees. Despite the income they make here, none of the houses in this village are elaborate or even out of the ordinary. I continue to look behind us but I can't help trying to see what's happening in that house. When we pull off the road and make our approach to the house Violet wants to rush ahead but Austin and I keep her from making the dangerous move.

We can't see any movement in the house and only one low light is on in the front room. Violet is vibrating with energy, a nervous expression of her fear for her grandfather's safety no doubt.

"Violet, why don't you try calling your grandfather?" Austin suggests.

She dials and we wait, his voicemail picks up and there's no movement inside the house in response to her call.

"Why don't we cover her and approach the front door and then you cover the back?" I ask pointing to Dozer and Austin.

"Yeah, all right. Baby, you stay between me and Pierson, stay away from the windows and the door. I'll knock and you talk if he answers. Try to get him outside without alerting him that we're looking for Kristos."

"Okay, but if you see Kristos, you shoot him. I don't care about the kill, I just want everyone safe."

"Deal." I nod my agreement and take my place as her guard. We move to the front porch of the house keeping low and not getting in front of the windows. In all reality the guy could be looking at us through one of those dark windows, he could have us in his sights.

When we reach the door, I put my back to the wall and keep my eyes searching for any movement. Austin knocks.

When there's no response Violet calls out, "Grandfather? It's Violet, please come to the door!" There's a movement from inside and I tense in preparation to fight or shoot. Austin is ready to fire at whoever is coming to the door.

"Step away from the door!" A male voice calls from inside. I look to her to see if she knows who's giving the command. She shrugs.

"Grandfather, it's Violet. Can you please come outside?"

The door opens inward, and standing there is an older man with white hair. He's tall and looks to be in his late sixties. Holding a gun to his head is a younger and taller version of the man who must be Violet's grandfather.

"All of you, back up or the old man gets it. Now!" We move back off the porch.

"Why are you doing this Kristos?" Violet questions.

"I need to get out of here, my ride won't be here until the sun comes up. I just need you to cooperate for a little while."

"Let him go and we'll leave you alone. You can escape and disappear."

"Nice try, he's my only bargaining chip, I'm not giving him up."

"Are you all right?" Violet asks her newly discovered grandfather.

He tries to nod and Kristos yanks on him, "Don't move!"

"I'm okay." His voice is soft and rough, his eye looks bruised and his lip has a spot of blood like it's split.

"Please let him go, he's hurt," she pleads.

"He's fine. You're a tough old guy, right pops?"

The older man doesn't answer, but his injuries appear superficial.

"Why did you send men to shoot up my warehouse? Were you trying to kill me?"

"No. I was hoping to collect you and have you join me. Imagine my surprise when you showed up of your own free will. I wanted to grab you and take you with me when the shooting started but your performing monkey dove on top of you and I had to get out before anyone could catch me. But here you are again, seeking me out. I think you're drawn to me, we'll make an unstoppable team. Why don't you put down your gun and come inside?"

"Why would I do that? So you can shoot him? Or both of us?"

"I wouldn't shoot you, you're my daughter, and you're amazing. I haven't been able to think of anything else but you and me working together, we could rule the state or maybe even the entire southeast if you join me. Don't you want to have that kind of power? You could do anything you want, have anything you want. Nothing would stop us. You saw for yourself, I was let out of jail and the charges dropped, you could have that kind of sway over the courts if you join me."

"How did you manage that?"

"I have connections in high places. You might be surprised by the people who partake of my services, some of them might be in law enforcement, local government, in the courts, you never know who you might find at my club or one of your grandmother's parties. Speaking of Joyce, she seems to be missing, you wouldn't know anything about that would you?"

"I heard she went missing from the riverbank behind her property and they called off the search. It's so dangerous to walk alone near the water. I read an article just the other day that not only do we have pythons invading our state, but anacondas too, and now Nile crocodiles have been found in the waterways around the everglades and the farmlands further North. Can you imagine what a Nile crocodile could do to a brittle old woman?"

"Well, I hope you're wrong and she's just lying low like we planned. She handles some important details of the *business*. But you could certainly learn her part of the game. Your adoptive parents were well-to-do, you must've attended fancy parties with them. They probably knew a lot of the same people too."

"Hardly. Look Kristos, I don't feel like standing here all night. Why don't you put the gun down, let him go, and we can chat about what we're going to do. You said yourself you're a free man, the charges against you were dropped, you can just walk out of here and nobody can stop you."

"I'm not sure your group of followers agree with that statement. Why don't you put down your gun and come inside, then I'll put mine down, and the three of us can have a seat and chat about anything you want."

"It seems like we're at an impasse. I find it hard to trust you when you held a gun to my head so recently."

"I was just bluffing to get us out of there. I wouldn't ever shoot you."

"I wish I could trust you, but your actions speak louder than words."

"I---" He collapsed to the floor before he could finish his sentence. Dozer is standing behind him holding up Violet's grandfather who almost went down with Kristos. She rushes in and hugs her grandfather, then holds him at arms-length to look him over. Austin and I step in and help Dozer collect Kristos's gun and cuff him.

"Hey, good job, you found him," Jackson states the obvious from behind us with a smirk.

"What do you want to do now, Killer?"

"Do you want me to take him away? Or should I administer his sentence here?" Violet asks her grandfather.

He's holding onto her shoulder, he looks into her eyes, and very softly, so only the five of us can hear, "His punishment must be completed as quickly as possible. He is like a snake, very difficult to keep caged, please do what needs to be done, now."

"I will. These are my boyfriends, the ones we talked about." He looks up at Dozer and back at Violet with wide eyes.

"Oh, not Dozer, he's a trusted friend. This is Austin, Jackson, and Pierson, they're my boyfriends. I'm sorry you have to meet them under these circumstances."

"I'm not. It was good to see how hard they protect you. Please, bring him to the back." He indicates Kristos who's beginning to move as he wakes up from the blow to his head Dozer gave him. Austin and I help Kristos to his feet and drag him through the house to the back patio. We drop him on the ground and he smacks his face on the concrete, unable to catch himself with his cuffed hands.

"What the fuck?" he complains through bloody lips.

"So, I thought about everything you said and I don't think I can trust you. I'm going to pass on the family business idea. But, if you wanted to tell me about who you know in the courthouse, I might be persuaded to change my mind."

"I'm not sure I can trust you. As much as I want to work with you, I still need proof you're really on my team."

"I'm not doing anything unless you give me a name. If you do, I'll have them remove your cuffs and get you some first aid. Then we can make some plans for what happens next." She's trying to get him to admit something, to give up one of his partners in crime, but I don't think he'll crack he's been around a long time.

"I need you to remove the cuffs and then I'll share one name to show my loyalty to you. Then you can help me get to my ride and I'll know I can trust you."

"I'll make a deal with you, give me one name, and I promise I'll remove them." She holds up *David Bowie,* and he thinks she's ready to cut him free. She smiles at him like she's conspiring with him, his head tilts as he analyzes her face.

"All right, it's a deal. The judge, Suchinski, is a long-term customer of the younger products in my barn. He's a seriously fucked up individual, he's got a habit of damaging the goods to a point where we can't even resell them. He's spent a lot of money with me and he handles whatever hits the courts, he keeps things flowing. It would be hard to work if my people were behind bars every time they got arrested. All right, let me out of these." He turns a little so she can get to his hands easier.

She approaches him and he smiles at her, relief has him relaxed. She steps behind him and bends down holding her favorite blade out towards him, he closes his eyes trusting her completely.

That's the thing about Violet, she can act extremely well, she's had experience while trying to stay safe and alive her entire life. She's had to act every emotion in the rainbow, when your survival depends on it you become skilled at whatever's necessary. So when she makes her move, Kristos doesn't see it coming.

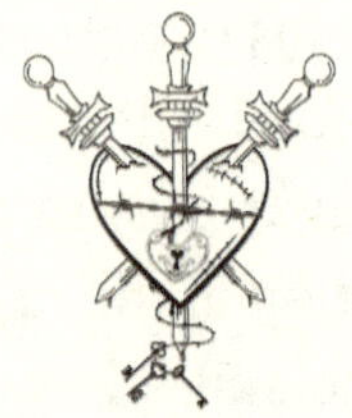

Chapter Thirty-Seven

Violet

My so-called *father* is on the ground in front of me, his hands cuffed behind his back, and he honestly believes I would work with him, he thinks by giving me one measly name I'm going to trust him and cut him free. He's such a narcissist he can't fathom that he can't out smart me, he can't control me, he can't charm me into doing what he wants. What an idiot.

I plunge my most prized weapon into his back. I'm careful to avoid his spine, I aim for just left of his vertebrae and make sure to puncture his evil heart. After the numbers my grandmother told me, I can only imagine how many innocent people this monster is responsible for hurting, for killing. With my finely honed and trusted companion, I take revenge for his crimes against those who couldn't fight back. I put an end to his reign of terror with one swift move. He chokes and tries to speak but his lungs are filling with the viscous fluid leaking from the four chambers of the failing muscle in his chest. It's pumped his blood for forty something years and it doesn't want to stop now, it's what it was built for, it's all it knows. The muscle memory of that particular organ makes it continue to contract even though it's just pumping death into his lungs with each contraction. It knows nothing else until it knows nothing at all. With a few jerky last spasms it comes to a stop and the silence rushes in to greet me. Slowly, the crickets, cicadas, and frogs begin to fill in the sounds of the night.

A sense of euphoria flows over me and I feel the pleasure of relief, the evil that was the man responsible for my life-in more ways than one, lifts from us, into the night, and away from this place. The air smells sweeter, the colors appear brighter, my own heart, though it may be dark, swirls with the colors of the people I love. They light up my soul and keep me from being as dark as the man who just died at my hand. I won't stop until I kill them all, my mission will continue as long as evil walks the Earth.

"Violet? May I speak with you?"

"Yes, of course, Grandfather." I follow him inside and he gestures for me to sit on the sofa next to his rocker. He sits, but he doesn't rock. He leans forward and studies my face, what does he see? Am I a disappointment? Do I repulse him now that he's seen what I do with his own eyes?

"You did well. I know it's a burden to hunt down the evil ones, to taint yourself with their blood, but you're very strong, you are an excellent hunter. This is what you're meant to do. Your strength and your partners will keep you safe, keep you on the right path. Trust your instincts, when you need to hunt and when it's time to stop, you'll know. I'm very proud of you. There's something very special about you, and I'm so glad I was able to meet you, finally. I hope that you'll visit me often and you're welcome in our village any time. I want you to spend time with all of your family whenever you like. They will keep you grounded and remind you why you do what you must."

"I'd love for you to meet my partners under better circumstances and my Uncle, my little sister, everyone. Would you like to come to a Christmas celebration?"

"I would be honored to attend, and I look forward to meeting all of the people who are important to you."

"Thank you. I'm so glad I met you, too." He stands and I stand, his arms lift open, and I move into his embrace without a thought, for a hug he delivers with affection. Even though I've been through too many terrible things, I'm pretty damn lucky to have people like him in my life.

We decided to spend Christmas Eve alone in our house. We're going to see everyone tomorrow since we were able to work out a huge celebration at Uncle Randy's house. My grandfather will be there, Dozer and Tyler are coming, the guy's parents and sisters, even Colby. I'm excited, but I'm also happy for this time alone with just us. We decided to exchange our gifts tonight so we can focus on everyone else tomorrow. Isabel requested that we arrive bright and early so she can open her presents at first light, none of us can say no to that girl. Colby said he has a huge surprise planned and I reminded him of his hundred-dollar spending limit, he swears he didn't go over but he's so excited I have to wonder.

But enough of all that, we're here now and I'm going to take the time to revel in the love between me and my guys. I can't stop smiling.

"All right, who wants to go first?" Austin asks.

"You go first."

"Well, our gift is from all of us. Ready guys?" Jackson looks at his brothers who nod enthusiastically.

Pierson hands me a box, it's wrapped in beautiful silver paper with glittering white snowflakes. It's not particularly big, like a deep shirt box, but it's not small either. It hardly weighs anything and I'm dying to shake it, but I hold back.

They're all staring at me with anticipation, and I hope I react the way they want. I slide the blue and silver ribbon off the box and Austin takes it from me. Then I pry my fingers beneath the corner of the folded paper pulling it free. The seam on the bottom pulls apart when I run my finger along the taped edge, and Jackson takes the paper from me. I lift the lid and there's a collective inhale from them, the anticipation growing.

When I move the silver and white snowflake tissue paper, I find a silver envelope with my name drawn in beautiful calligraphy, and a small box. I smile at them, my nerves are ramped all the way up to high. Pierson takes the small box and sets it next to me, then Austin takes the bigger box away leaving me with the envelope. I turn it over and it has a wax seal.

"Wow, it's fancy. It's like a wedding invitation, so pretty."

"Pierson did that, he drew your name too, his talents are useful for something."

"Ha, ha. What talents do you have?" Pierson asks with mock agitation.

"I've got plenty of talent right here, ask Violet!" He grabs his crotch and I can't help laughing. It's so junior high, but their ridiculous argument is funny regardless, my *boys* certainly keep me entertained.

"Bro! Chill! We've all seen your talent, remember we're usually there too. Come on, let Violet open her gift."

"Yeah, let Violet open her gift!" I say between giggles. They make me so happy no matter how childish they act, they're fun and I love them.

I snap the wax seal and open the flap of the envelope, then remove the card and papers inside. The card has a beautiful drawing of me, I'm holding *David Bowie,* and in the blade is a reflection of the three of them. It's an ethereal drawing and my eyes get watery as it makes my heart fill with warmth.

"This is beautiful! I love it, thank you."

"Babe, that's just the card, you need to see what's inside," Jackson teases.

"All right, don't rush me." Inside the card is a certificate, and a folded paper, along with the message written in more beautiful calligraphy.

Our Beautiful VioleNt One,

We love you so much and we're so thankful you were willing to give us a chance, because we can't imagine life without you. As you know, Jackson won the contest, and we all agreed to let him choose our next trip. You guessed it, we're going to Disney World. You'll see the surprise when you read the enclosed page.

We love you with all our hearts,

Austin, Pierson, and Jackson

I look at the folded page, when I open it, there's another beautiful drawing, this time it's of Cinderella's Castle. When I look closer, there's an arrow pointing to one of the towers and it says, **You're Here** um, what?

"I don't understand what I'm looking at, why does it say that by the tower?"

Jackson can hardly contain his smile, "It says that because you're going to be staying in a room in the tower of Cinderella's Castle! We're all staying there!"

"Seriously? Oh my God, you guys! That's amazing! I'm SO excited!" I jump up and hug Jackson, he kisses me and I fling myself at Pierson who catches me despite his injured finger and gives me a kiss, then I attack Austin with a tight hug and a kiss.

"I'm so glad you're excited about it. We weren't sure, but Tori and Isabel both said you like Cinderella and her castle, so we took a chance."

"It's incredible! I can't believe it! Isabel's going to be jealous."

"She promised she'll be fine if we bring her a *Cinderella blue gown*, she said you'd know what she means."

"I do. I'm a girl, regardless of how I throw a knife."

"There's more for you to see. Keep going," Austin prods.

The certificate says we're spending a week in Disney, starting the day after Christmas and through New Year's. We're visiting all four parks, and we have a VIP tour at Animal Kingdom that involves up close and personal interactions with animals. We can feed them, we can help in the infirmary, we can hold and feed the babies in the nursery, and they have a new baby giraffe!

"Oh my God! I love it! This is the best gift ever! Thank you so much! I give them all kisses again. Pierson hands me the small box, I forgot all about it. He looks nervous and I wonder if he picked this one out. I open the outer box, inside is a velvet box, it feels like a puzzle or Russian nesting dolls. But when I open the black velvet lid, inside is a stunning ring nestled in beautiful blue velvet. The ring is platinum, with a purple heart shaped stone in the middle, then a piece of the metal curves out around the purple stone, along the curve are three diamonds, it's so pretty I'm shaking.

When I look at them, they're all three in front of me on one knee and they have puppy dog eyes with the sweetest smiles. My eyes fill with tears, and I'm smiling so hard my cheeks hurt.

"Will you marry us?" They say it together and it's adorable. I put my finger to my chin and raise my eyes in thought.

"Hmmm...I think, uhhh..." they all start tickling me.

"Okay! Okay! Yes! Yes! I'll marry you!"

"Damn right!"

"You better!"

"I love you, Killer." He puts the ring on my finger, I've never seen anything so beautiful.

"I love you, too."

I love you's go around between all of us and then we start kissing, their hands roam my body and I instantly feel my nipples harden.

"Mmmm, yes. Touch me here." I push Austin's hand under my top. Jackson puts his hands in my sleep shorts and touches me in all the best spots. Pierson kisses me and I'm so blissfully happy. I love these men so much, and I feel loved by them. I must be the luckiest girl alive. Before long, their kisses turn urgent and my body responds with zings of electricity raising goosebumps across my skin and my pussy grows wet with arousal. Jackson pulls my bottoms off and Pierson lifts my top over my head. Austin never leaves my breasts alone, his tongue circles my nipple and his teeth tug on its hard peak. Pierson kisses my lips and squeezes my other breast while Jackson kisses along my pelvic bone teasing me. I want him to touch my clit so bad I can't stop wiggling hoping he'll get the hint. My hands lift Pierson's shirt until he has to break our kiss to remove it. I scratch my nails down his chest and he groans into my ear and then traces my lobe with his tongue.

With a growl I take over, wanting to be in charge, I throw my leg over Pierson skillfully avoiding kicking Jackson. I press Pierson down on the bed and straddle him, his boxer briefs disappear with ease and I take full advantage rubbing my soaking pussy along his shaft.

"Jackson, switch places with Austin," I demand. Austin smiles a devious grin and Jackson joins me with a passionate kiss. Austin takes my hint and he uses his finger, covered in lube to play with my ass. He presses against the rim until it stretches enough to let him in and he takes his work seriously, making room for his hard dick. Jackson kisses my ear and my neck, his tongue teases the lobe before he nibbles it and along my jaw to my neck. He sucks the sensitive spot where my throat meets my shoulder and I moan with pleasure. I'm grinding on Pierson's erection and I'm ready for him to fuck me.

I stroke Jackson's hard cock and he growls into my neck sending chills down my spine. Unable to wait a moment longer I push myself down onto Pierson and he feels so good filling me, stretching me. I suck Jackson's nipple into my mouth and swirl my tongue around it. Pierson thrusts into me while I push down on him. Austin has three fingers in my ass and he moves them just right while he pulls on his hard dick, when I look over my shoulder, he's a perfect picture of abs, tattoos, and man meat. An orgasm starts in my stomach and then follows every neuro pathway to my pussy where it blooms and makes me cry out.

Austin presses his cock to my back entrance and when Pierson's rhythm allows, Austin pushes into me and I'm instantly full to the point of breaking, Austin can't take his eyes from his dick in my ass.

"Baby, this is fucking amazing. Your body's heaven, the way your muscles are crushing me is unbelievable. Oh, fuck, yes!" I move my hips in a circular motion and both Austin and Pierson murmur with pleasure. Jackson brings his erect shaft to my lips and I'm so turned on I slurp his head into my mouth sucking so hard as he pushes in further that my cheeks are hollowed. This is my heaven, all three of my guys fucking me, loving me, there's nothing as hot as three tattooed bodies thrusting into me. My entire body is on fire, every nerve is alight with sensation. It's overwhelming and almost painful while also being as close to paradise as I've ever been.

"Mmmm, oh my fucking hell! I'm going to come so fucking hard!"

"Babe, I'm going to fill you up with my cum. Lick my balls, yes!"

We're all chasing the orgasms that are so close we can feel them building, and building. My body is experiencing wave after wave of sensations, the nerves in my scalp are tingling all the way to my curled toes. Zaps and sparks flash up and down my spine and keep bursting in my clit and then it gets stronger in the next wave. My eyes are rolling back in my head, I'm gasping for breath as Jackson fucks my throat so fast I can't quite get enough oxygen. My vision is a fog of flashing lights, sweat drips from my chest onto Pierson beneath me. Austin holds my hips as he ruts into me and the thin wall between him and Pierson makes it feel like both of their dicks are fucking my pussy together, the stretch is so fucking good.

"Mmmmm! Ooooommmggaaaa!" I can't form words with my mouth full of delicious Jackson. His thrusts stutter and he holds my face while he pushes into my throat and fills me with cum. I swallow to avoid choking and try to breathe through my nose, but I'm screaming with my climax. Pierson grabs my breasts and squeezes as I fall on him to grind through my orgasm, he joins me and the pulsing of my inner walls sends Austin over too. I have no idea what any of us are saying as we twitch and rub against one another teasing out every last sensation of our finish.

"Fucking hell that was amazing!" I can't talk, I'm still trying to catch my breath as I bask in the afterglow. Jackson is the least entwined so he gets a few towels to help us clean up. Once I'm able to stand I clean up much better and when I return to our bed, they have a cold drink and snacks ready for us to share. I choose some orange slices and they're cold and refreshing.

"Thank you. This is perfect."

"I love you, Baby."

"I love you too."

Pierson holds my hand looking at my ring, it's a perfect fit and every time I spot it on my hand I'm surprised again by its beauty.

"I love it, thank you."

"I love you so much, Killer. I'm so glad you like it."

"I love you too."

When I look toward Jackson, he's staring at me. I smile at him, "What?"

"I can't wait to take you to Disney, it's going to be so much fun. What's your favorite ride?" he asks.

"I've loved the Haunted House since my first visit, so for nostalgia's sake I'll go with that. My dad rode it over and over with me."

"I can't wait to ride it with you. I love you, I've never been this happy."

"I love you too. I think it's so sweet how much you want to share it with me. I've never done any special VIP tours, I'm really excited about Animal Kingdom."

"See, I told you she'd love it," Austin says. I love how they worked together to make my presents special and our trip is going to be epic. I hope they like my gift, I wonder if they can wait for it until tomorrow.

"I'm giving you my gift first thing in the morning, we have to go somewhere to get it. Is that okay?"

"I'll never sleep now, I'm too excited, Austin laughs, he's teasing me.

"I think you'll make it." I slap his face gently teasing him back. He kisses my palm and then, holding my hand so I can't get away, he tickles me with his other hand.

"No! Stop!" My laughter is hysterical and I try to tickle him back so Pierson tickles me, then when I try to escape him, Jackson grabs me and holds me to him with my arms wrapped up so Austin can tickle me again. We all laugh and joke until one by one we drift off to sleep. I realize I'm fading when Sawyer curls up on the top of my pillow.

When my eyes open again it's still dark, but I feel rested and I know I slept. I climb over Pierson and check my phone, it's the perfect time to go check out their gift. I quickly get ready and start some coffee. When I go into the room to wake them, Jackson is watching me.

I speak softly, "Hi. Are you ready to go see your gift?"

"Sure. You look beautiful, come kiss me." He pulls me into a sweet hug and kisses my lips.

"Can I have a turn, Baby?" Austin rolls into me and hugs me before planting kisses on my face.

"You need to get dressed. We're going to see your present."

"I'll get dressed after you kiss me," Pierson offers.

"I would never leave you out." I give him a kiss and he wraps me up in his arms, then rolls on top of me and kisses me back.

"Okay. I'll get ready now." His mischievous grin lights up his eyes which are more greenish today.

Sawyer follows me to the kitchen for his breakfast. While he eats, I put his gifts next to him.

"Look what Santa brought for you. Were you good or is it going to be coal in there?"

Meow!

"Yeah, I'm pretty sure you're on the nice list."

"Hey buddy, look at those presents! You better open them up." Austin sits on the floor and wiggles a gift at Sawyer who immediately pounces on it. Austin takes it away and then tosses it for him. He runs after it and rolls over it using his claws to push it around. Austin rips it a little and Sawyer realizes something fun is inside, so he rips into the package. When he pulls the little fish filled with catnip free, he dances around with his prize. Austin helps him get the other toys open, but he's obsessed with the catnip and ignores the other toys. He carries that little fish to the top of his tree and lays on it, I guess he doesn't want anyone to take it.

"All right sweetie, we'll see you later, don't party too hard."

Since Pierson doesn't have his bike back yet, he rides with me. We were smart and dropped off the gifts a couple days ago at Uncle Randy's, so we could ride our bikes today. Pierson rides bitch but he takes it like a champ. I lead us through town and just on the outskirts, where the farms and wilderness begin, we turn onto a gently curving road with beautiful oak trees lining our path. When I pull to a stop at an old metal gate, they look at me like I'm nuts. But I hop off my bike and using a key, remove the lock and chain to push open the bars of the barrier. Once I have it open and without a word, I drive into the property on the dirt track that's mostly grass and weeds. When I stop again, it's on a slope giving us a view of the pond and river beyond.

"Okay. I'm looking, but I don't see any Christmas presents," Austin observes.

"Are you sure?" I ask with a hint of mischief.

Pierson, with his artist's eyes, notes, "It's a beautiful view, I could draw some amazing pictures with this background."

Jackson watches me as I climb off my bike and take a 10 x 13 Christmas envelope from my saddle bag. I walk toward him and hold out the gift in my hand.

"What's this?" he asks as he takes it from me.

"It's for you three, from me." Austin and Pierson join us.

"Open it!" Austin cajoles.

"All right, relax." Jackson tears the end and the three of them peek inside. Pierson looks at me with questions in his eyes. I smile and nod, encouraging them to take out the contents.

A large, folded paper is pulled out by Austin, then he unfolds it. It's the size of a blueprint once it's unfurled. The three of them look at what's on the paper, they look at me, then back at the page. Pierson turns the page, so it's oriented the opposite way.

"Is this what I think it is?" Jackson asks.

"Depends, what do you think it is?" I ask with a grin.

Austin looks at me in shock, "Is this a blueprint for a house?"

"What's this over on the side?" Jackson questions.

Pierson is carefully studying the plan.

I decide to fill them in and explain what they're looking at.

"This is a dirt bike track, over here is a shooting range, and yes, this is a house, *our* house." Their eyes snap to me.

"What do you mean *our house?*"

"I inherited this eighty-acre plot of land, I came and looked at it, and I thought it would make a great place for our forever home. We'll have space to build anything we want, like the dirt bike track and the shooting range. What do you think?"

"Does this house have the amazing giant bathroom?" Austin asks with a huge smile.

"Yeah, the architect is working on the house plans, I want your input, but I already told him about the requirements for the bathroom. I also wanted to build a pool house for Colby to visit, if you're okay with it."

"It's fucking awesome! I'm in!" Austin hugs me and swings me around before he kisses me.

"Yeah, Babe, this is amazing! I love it," Jackson agrees.

"You know I'm in; this place is perfect. It feels special, like home," Pierson explains. I hug him, then kiss him and Jackson. I felt the same way when I visited our new place alone a few weeks ago.

While we stand with our arms around each other enjoying the view, a deer walks down between the pond and the river. She's beautiful and her tail wags rapidly as she sniffs the foliage. Then from the trees, three bucks with huge racks of majestic horns step out following her. She ignores them and eats some leaves. When they approach her, one rubs his cheek against hers. The other two stand guard, watching the surrounding area for danger. Then the four of them graze on the grass together, the bucks rub against her affectionately. They simultaneously raise their heads and look at us, then she playfully bounces off into another stand of trees. The bucks wait for her to be hidden by the woods before they follow. I take their presence as a good omen for this land, it's not lost on me the doe was leading her three bucks.

Epilogue

Pierson

Christmas has never been my favorite holiday. It's hard to enjoy it when your mother never remembered to get you any gifts, or a tree. Once I moved in with my brothers, it was always a nice celebration with Mom, Dad, and my siblings, my found family. But it also highlighted the disaster of my birth family. So, I prepared myself for a somewhat disappointing holiday like it's always been for me. But this year is different, Violet made it special, and I love her gift for us. Going to her Uncle Randy's and having all of our family there too is really special, these are my favorite people all in one place. Isabel is beyond excited, she got a little wired on candy from her stocking, but when she opened the box with her new puppy, you couldn't buy that much joy.

There's good news all around. Tori is a changed person; she's matured and is being agreeable and helpful at home much to my parent's delight. Kristin got a scholarship to her first-choice college. Even more exciting, Stephanie and Randy are expecting a baby. Violet and Isabel are thrilled by the prospect of a new sibling. But the showstopper is when Colby's surprise arrives. Apparently, in the midst of all his sleuthing and vigilante justice, he's made a new friend. When his friend arrives, we're all stunned to see our sister, Megan, at the door. We all cried, even Austin and our dad.

She's planning to stay for now, if things go well, she'll be getting her own place. When she holds Colby's hand, I imagine she might be staying for good. We're all happy to see her doing so well and Colby has been a constant support, our dad hugged him. She's forever changed, but despite her quiet and thoughtful demeanor, she looks happy and that's all that matters. She and Violet became instant friends, of course Violet makes friends easily, she just doesn't realize it.

Dozer stopped by with Tyler, they didn't stay long, but long enough to impress upon us that they're our true friends and make sure we know how lucky we are to have them on our team. They're both great people who care about Violet and her cause. I like them both and I know Violet loves them, our circle keeps expanding in the very best ways. When Tyler hugged Violet she smiled with joy, people are attracted to her like magnets. There's something so special about her, you can't name it, but you feel it when she's around and when she's not, you feel a need to seek her out. I fought it so hard at first because I desperately wanted to hate her, but once you're in her clutches there's no escape. It's true for her prey as well as her friends, and us, her partners. She's a born leader, a born hunter, and I can't wait to see what happens next. I'm grateful for my front row seat. I wouldn't want to be anywhere else.

At one point we found ourselves alone with Colby and we had a discussion about what Kristos shared before his demise. We now have the beginnings of a plan for the next name on Violet's list. A certain judge and maybe a few others in the local courthouse will be getting a visit from the most beautiful badass I know in the new year. They should be scared, they should run, but nobody ever thinks Violet is a threat until they look into her eyes while she's dancing with *David Bowie* and by then, it's too late.

Violet's grandfather and cousin Patty came for a couple of hours. He's an interesting man, and he's very proud of his granddaughter. He said he would be happy to perform a ceremony for us since we can't get legally married. I saw him joking around with Austin, I think he approves of us and that means a lot to me.

We got to talking about our future together and the ceremony and we decided we're going to get matching tattoos on our ring fingers instead of wedding bands. Violet's grandfather suggested a tribal symbol that means *love.* We liked his idea and he's going to get one of the tribe members to draw it for us, I'll tweak it to make it ours and then we'll get them tattooed for the ceremony. We don't know when it will be, we've got a busy year coming. A new house to build, a foundation to grow, more monsters to kill, we might not have time for another year or two for a faux wedding, but that's okay because none of us are going anywhere.

Before our celebration was over Kody showed up to pick up Tori, he wanted to bring her to his family's celebration. He's a nice kid. Jackson implied we'd kill him if he hurt Tori, but he laughed it off. He said Violet already scared the crap out of him, and we aren't as terrifying as our girlfriend. I should probably be a little offended, but I'm proud. Afterall, Violet's a very unique and violent girl, but she's ours and we love her.

THE END

Afterword

Thank you to my family, friends, editor Tylee Ertel, cover designer Monika M, from Ampersand Book Covers, all of the ARC readers, and Gypsy. I appreciate all of your support, pep talks, and the times you listened when I needed to vent. It's been a hell of a year for my health and my community with two hurricanes in two weeks. I'm thankful Helene and Milton didn't cause more damage.

I'm attending a lot of live events this year and next, if you're in the central Florida area come check them out. You can find details at

About the Author

About the author

E.N. Chanting writes spicy romantic suspense and horror. She lives in a haunted house with her high school sweetheart and three goofy Australian Shepherds.

Find more here: www.enchantingauthor.com

BOOKS BY E.N. CHANTING

Find them at available on Kindle Unlimited and other fine retailers.

Forces of Nature Series- Interconnected world standalones

Force of Corruption

Force Majeure

Force of Attraction- Coming 2025

Violet's Tales

.5 Origin of Violet (novella)

1 VioleNt

2 Vile

Short Stories

Haunted Hunting Camp

The Devil's Affair

Deadly-Go-Round- Coming 2025

www.ingramcontent.com/pod-product-compliance
Lightning Source LLC
LaVergne TN
LVHW090544110826
845146LV00001B/13

* 9 7 9 8 9 9 0 9 5 5 6 1 5 *